TIFFANY LYNN IS MISSING

DAN ALATORRE

TIFFANY LYNN IS MISSING
a psychological thriller
A JETT THACKER MYSTERY, book 1
© 2021 DAN ALATORRE

© This book is licensed for your personal use only. This book may not be re-sold or given away to other people. Thank you for respecting the hard work of this author. © No part of this book may be reproduced, stored in a retrieval system or transmitted by any means without the written permission of the author. Copyright © 2021 Dan Alatorre. All rights reserved.

This is a work of fiction. Names, characters, places, and incidents either are the product of the author's imagination or are used fictitiously, and any resemblance to actual persons, living or dead, businesses, companies, events or locales, is entirely coincidental.

OTHER THRILLERS BY DAN ALATORRE

Killer In The Dark, *Jett Thacker book 2*

The Gamma Sequence, *a medical thriller*
Rogue Elements, *The Gamma Sequence Book 2*
Terminal Sequence, *The Gamma Sequence Book 3*
The Keepers, *The Gamma Sequence Book 4*
Dark Hour, *The Gamma Sequence Book 5*

Double Blind, *an intense murder mystery*
Primary Target, *Double Blind Book 2*
Third Degree, *Double Blind Book 3*

A Place Of Shadows, *a paranormal thriller*
The Navigators, *a time travel thriller*

CONTENTS

ACKNOWLEDGEMENTS

TIFFANY LYNN IS MISSING

ABOUT DAN ALATORRE
OTHER THRILLERS BY DAN ALATORRE

ACKNOWLEDGMENTS

I work with so many amazing people, it's always difficult
to mention them without leaving some out,
but I owe a debt of gratitude to all the team members
who help me do what I do.
You guys ROCK!

Note to Readers
If you have the time, I would deeply appreciate a review on Amazon or Goodreads. I learn a great deal from them, and I'm always grateful for any encouragement. Reviews are a very big deal and help authors like me to sell a few more books. Every review matters, even if it's only a few words.

Thanks,
Dan Alatorre

CHAPTER 1

Emily Becker kneaded her fingers together, the knot in her stomach growing larger as she craned her neck to sneak another glance toward the studio doors. "When will she come out?"

Phones in the outer studio rang in a nonstop barrage, answered as quickly as the four receptionists could get to them. A dozen administrative staffers rushed about, carrying advertising folders or checking show production schedules.

Pulling her gaze away from her computer, Olivia Cantando peered over her reading glasses at her young trainee. "It is now nine fifty-eight." Olivia pointed to a large clock on the wall. "Unless a hole in the Earth has opened and swallowed everyone on the production soundstage, our boss will be coming through those doors in about ten seconds."

"Really?" Beaming, Emily sat up straight and smoothed out her skirt, eyes fixed on the studio doors. The red light had turned off almost a full minute ago.

"Mm-hmm." The elder production assistant sighed, turning her attention back to her spreadsheet. "But be careful what you wish for, Emily. Around here, we know—"

The studio doors burst open and the shapely Ashley Wells strutted out, followed by her most recent husband, Jake Prescott—and her army of well-dressed lackeys. Ashley stopped in the center of the room and slapped her well-toned thigh, glaring at the red leather skirt stretched across her slender hips. "Beverly! This ridiculous outfit is too hot for Orlando. If I'm sweating, I'm not concentrating on the show."

She unzipped the leather skirt as her assistant rushed forward with a white robe, barely getting it around the star before the skirt hit the floor. Most of the staff managed to look away.

Emily sat still, her jaw hanging open. Close to twenty-five people were in full view of the host's display of near undress.

Kicking the red skirt across the room, Ashley glared at her assistant. "Last time I expect to see that." She looked out over the production staff, frowning. "Where's Cassidy? Where's my mid-morning report?"

"Here!" A young woman sped around the corner, carrying a tablet computer. She held the device up to Ms. Wells.

"Are the overnight numbers in here?" Ashley peered at the screen as she knotted the sash of her robe.

TIFFANY LYNN IS MISSING

"No, ma'am. Not yet." Cassidy cringed. "I—"

"What! What am I paying you for?" The blonde TV host threw her hands out, glaring at her young staffer. "Those numbers are posted promptly at nine fifty-five each day! Can you read a clock? It's almost ten! Now, if you can't do your job properly, I'll find someone who can—is that understood?"

Cassidy stared at the floor, her cheeks turning red. "Yes, ma'am."

"And that goes for all of you!" Her hands on her hips, Ashley narrowed her eyes, peering at her employees.

The room fell silent. Receptionists held phones to their ears without speaking. One of the lackeys behind the star tugged at his collar.

Somewhere down the hall, a lone phone rang.

Ashley clenched her jaw. "I have busted my rear nonstop for twenty years to keep 'Wake Up With Ashley Wells' the number-one program in our time slot. I work hard every day to keep it number one, including trying out a sweaty, roaster-hot, red leather mini-skirt because they're trending." She rolled her eyes. "Everybody *wants* to be number one at nine A.M., but I *am* number one—and all of your paychecks depend on me continuing to find new ways to stay there. So, act like it!"

The ticking of the large wall clock was the only sound in the room.

Cassidy swallowed hard, clutching the tablet. "Do… you want me to update the numbers and bring the report to you in your office, ma'am?"

Putting a hand to her forehead, Ashley closed her eyes. "Well, it's not very useful without the updated numbers, is it? Go!"

As Cassidy retreated to her cubicle, the receptionist on the far side of the room hunched her shoulders and raised her hand. "Uh... Ms. Wells?"

"Yes, what is it? I'm right here."

"Ma'am, you have a call."

"Sandy will take it." Ashley glanced at her watch. "I've got a board meeting in twenty—"

"Yes, ma'am, but..." The receptionist slunk lower in her chair. "He says he's Sheriff Dalton from Brimstone County, Colorado. Should I transfer it to your office?"

Ashley huffed. "Colorado! Great—another complaint about the zoning variance we got for the Wildfire Resort. Can't any of those yokels out there read a plat map? I'll take the call right here. Put it through to..." She turned to an empty desk. "Why isn't Cheryl at her desk? I haven't seen her all morning."

Jake stepped forward. "Uh, she's sick, dear."

"Of course she is. That's the second time this month. She's probably off interviewing for another job." Ashley looked at a tall brunette in the well-dressed army of suits. "Sandy, call her cell. If she isn't dead, tell her to get her butt in here and do her job or I'll find someone else to do it." She looked at the receptionist. "Transfer the call to extension 121. Jake, check the parking lot and see if Tom Masterson's limo has arrived yet. I don't want him waiting in the lobby."

Jake nodded. "You got it, Ashley."

TIFFANY LYNN IS MISSING

The phone rang at Cheryl's desk. Ashley jerked the receiver from its cradle and put the phone to her ear. Taking a deep breath, a wide grin spread over her lips. "Sheriff Dalton, was it?" Her tone had shifted to pure sweetness and southern charm—the kind viewers tuned in for each weekday morning. "How nice of you to call. How can I help you, sugar?"

She could have been a sweet, elderly grandmother receiving a bouquet of hand-picked daisies from a three-year-old.

Emily's eyes never left the beautiful TV star. "That's..." She shook her head, turning to her trainer. "What a transformation. She's intense."

"Isn't she, though?" Olivia Cantando nodded. "She goes from zero to sixty and then calms right back down again—allegedly. But don't be fooled. Her engine's still at sixty."

Emily sat back in her chair. "That's why she's a star. I could never do that. She's... it's almost like she's an actress."

"She *is* an actress," Olivia said. "And she's very good. Every word, every gesture... With Ashley Wells, what you see isn't always what you—"

"Oh!" Ashley's face turned white. The slender TV host put a hand on her abdomen, bending over the desk like she'd been punched. "Oh, no."

Jake rushed to her side. She gagged, her mouth hanging open. A slight groan escaped her lips, and she lowered the phone to her side. Ashley put her hand out, her shoulders sagging as she leaned on the desk.

She buckled over again, groaning as she lowered her head to the desk. "No, no, no…"

Several employees got up from their chairs.

"Should we call an ambulance?"

"Ms. Wells, are you okay?"

Jake leaned close to his wife, putting his arm around her and whispering in her ear.

Squeezing her eyes shut, Ashley shook her head and stood up. "Not here." She hung up the phone and waved her staff off, clutching her stomach like she was about to vomit. With Jake holding her elbow, she managed a step toward her office, then another. Each placement of her polished Gucci stilettos met the production room floor like it was a slick, icy sidewalk.

She straightened up and lifted her chin, her face firm and rigid as she and Jake navigated the twenty paces to her office. As she crossed the threshold, he hooked his foot behind the massive oak panel door and kicked it shut.

But not before every member of the *Wake Up With Ashley Wells* production team saw their boss double over one more time and sag to the floor of her office.

CHAPTER 2

Jessica Eve Tims-Thacker squirmed as she sat in Hair and Makeup at Miami's TV 5, poring over the Nielsen ratings on her laptop—and cringing. She glanced at the time readout in the lower right-hand corner of the screen, then went straight back to the never-ending rows of colored numbers on the spreadsheet.

The Jett Set was at the bottom of almost every chart.

In personality and likability of the host, the show scored well. In content, however, it did not. Audiences liked her, apparently; just not her new show.

Jett shook her head as she reviewed the ratings.

But I am the show!

The TV station's twentysomething makeup and hair stylist lifted a long, golden strand of her co-worker's locks, teasing it out as she peered at the laptop screen. "*Dios mio*, Ms. Thacker." Patti's Miami-Latin accent was thicker when she was excited. "Do you know what all those numbers mean?"

"Pretty much," the new host said. "And please don't call me Ms. Thacker. I'm still Jett, the same person whose hair you were doing two weeks ago when I was just an investigative reporter."

"*Ah, si.* Well…" Patti grabbed a bottle of hairspray. "Better safe than sorry. A lot of people get their own show and a nice company car, and next comes a case of *cabeza grande* when they sit down in my chair. You got millions of people watching you through that camera. How do you not get nervous? I get jittery just thinking about it."

"The camera doesn't bother me."

"You got used to it, eh *chica*? From being in front of juries when you were a lawyer?"

Getting in front of juries was definitely not Jett's thing. It might only be twelve people and a handful of observers in the seats, but talking to a group made her clench up.

TV interviews, on the other hand, were usually done on a set. One-on-one, with a videographer and producer along, or in the field with even fewer people, but usually all but one was a known work associate. A friend. Research for interviews was *none*-on-one, just her and a computer or a stack of books.

When it came time for the camera, it was just a lens, but maybe it was more.

"Smile Jessie!"

TIFFANY LYNN IS MISSING

Her grandmother leaned close with her Kodak camera, an "ice cube" flashbulb on top.

Pop!

"Nana, I can't see!" Jett laughed. "It's all dots now!"

"You can't see me, but I can see you. Hold up your Easter basket."

Easter, Christmas, birthdays, pool parties... Nana loved to take pictures. It seemed like the lens was always in front of her face whenever her grandchildren were around. And of course, holiday or not, if Nana was around, lots of candy was around, too...

"Smile, Jessie! Give James a hug and blow out the candles! Can you get all ten?"

James. She didn't think of her older brother every day, but just about.

The big camera lens reminded Jett of her grandmother. It didn't matter if anybody else understood, Jett just knew the camera lens was her ally. She could relax and open up, reaching millions by reaching one person. Nana.

Patti gave Jett's hair a spritz and stepped away, holding her hands out. "Enough of those numbers, *chica*. If you keep putting your head down, I can't do my job."

"Sorry." Jett sighed, shutting the laptop and sliding it onto the counter. "If my Q rating doesn't improve, you won't have to worry about my hair. Nobody will be seeing it because I won't have a show."

"Then you will need to look your best for your interview reel, eh?" Patti winked, picking up a finer comb and resuming her work on the station's newest star. "So—you keep your head up. A new show needs time."

"I know it's only been a week," Jett said. "We need to let the audience find me, but…"

"It hasn't even been a week." Rico Torres swept into the room, flashing a smile as he tucked the morning print edition of *The Miami Herald* under his arm. "You'll be hosting for as long as you want. Even Oprah took more than five days to get up and running."

Jett's shoulder's slumped. "Oprah didn't work for Martin Brennan."

Slipping between the two women, Rico grabbed the arm of the chair and spun Jett around to face the mirror. Framed with big, white bulbs all around its perimeter, the oversized vanity highlighted every one of Jett's beautiful, girl-next-door features—and to her eye, every flaw.

She saw the blonde hair and blue eyes, the high cheekbones and the full, pouty lips. She also saw the overweight, pimply eighth-grader whose best friend turned on her and ridiculed her in front of everyone at school and the awkward, uncoordinated teen who wished to be popular in high school.

Grinning at their reflections, Rico beamed. "Look at you. Smart, beautiful… The camera loves you, and audiences can't take their eyes off you. Now…" He swung the chair back to face him. "Who's the sharpest morning show TV host in Miami?"

"Stop." Jett looked away, holding back a laugh.

TIFFANY LYNN IS MISSING

"Come on." He rocked the chair back and forth. "Ten-thirty in the morning is a tough time slot for a half-hour panel show. But when you bring the numbers up—and you will—Martin will expand you to a full hour and move you to midday. From there, it's a short step to prime time. So, say it. Who is the best news personality in south Florida?"

"What am I, four years old?" Heat rose to her cheeks.

"You need a pre-show ritual," Rico said. "All hosts have them. Since you're not a raging alcoholic and you don't smoke, this will have to be yours. Unless you want to throw temper tantrums."

"Ugh." Jett grimaced. "Pass."

"Good. Psych yourself up with me. Who's Miami's hottest rising star on morning TV?"

She smiled. "I am."

"Yeah, but you don't sound convincing." Rico spun the chair toward the mirror, stepping away and folding his arms. "Put on your game face, counselor."

A graduate of Florida State University Law School, Jessica Eve Tims-Thacker had landed a position at the high-powered Greenman Trotter law firm in Miami and worked her way up. By age twenty-nine, she had amassed an impressive string of legal victories and was offered a partnership at the firm. She accepted, requested a two-week sabbatical—and never went back. An afternoon session of binge-watching *Oprah* convinced her to follow her real passion and not settle for less than her true goals in life. A week later, the youngest partner at Greenman Trotter had resigned to become the oldest intern at Miami's Channel 9 News.

She wasn't starting over. She was starting anew.

Within a year, she had migrated to Miami 5, after Rico took notice of her field work as a reporter, and promised her an interview with the station manager.

Jett thought about his salvo—*"Who's Miami's hottest rising star on morning TV?"*—and put on her best court room lawyer face. She sat up straight and squared her shoulders.

"I am."

This time, she meant it.

And, prior to the sluggish first week of *The Jett Set*, the Nielsen ratings had shown it to be true.

"Okay." Rico stepped aside. "It's game time. Jackson will be waiting for you."

Jett stood up and looked in the mirror, sweeping her hands over her suit to smooth any wrinkles from her immaculate attire. "If the show's content is holding me back after this morning's episode, then we'll make another change—and keep adjusting it until we have it right."

"Exactly." Rico leaned in, looking her in the eye. "And you just worry about being yourself. That's what got you here."

Nodding, Jett took a deep breath and headed for the door.

"Go get 'em, tiger. You are a rising star, Jessica Eve." He plopped into the makeup chair she'd vacated, turning to view the live feed monitor on the wall.

TIFFANY LYNN IS MISSING

In the hallway, Jackson Campbell clutched his sound equipment and put a hand to his headset mic. "Ms. Thacker is out of makeup and we are heading to the set." He smiled at Jett. "Good morning. How did you sleep?"

"Great!" she lied.

She walked with him down the long corridor. Up ahead, the stage announcer gave the audience some final instructions. "So when this sign flashes, we'd like you to applaud. If you want to cheer or express emotion at things the guests say, feel free. Ready?"

The sign lit up. The crowd of two hundred applauded.

"Terrific!" the announcer said. "And in just a moment, we'll start the show. But right now... are you ready to meet Jett?"

The crowd erupted again.

Jackson stopped at the end of the corridor and turned to Jett. "Mic check, please, ma'am?"

She turned around so he could access the little black box clipped to the small of her back.

"And... go," Jackson said.

Jett cleared her throat. "Hi, everyone, I'm Jett Thacker, and this is The Jett Set—live, from Miami."

"Good." Jackson nodded, looking at his VU meters. "I'll remotely switch you over to broadcast mode when you step out from behind the curtain. Is there anything you need?"

"Yes," Jett said. "One thing."

"Sure, ma'am. What is it?"

She folded her hands in front of her and pursed her lips. "Please don't call me 'ma'am.' Just call me 'Jett,' like you used to."

Jackson grinned. "You got it." He glanced out at the audience. "Good crowd this morning. And an interesting combination of guests for the panel. Mr. Brennan is in attendance, but don't let that bother you. Just be the star you are."

She smirked, shaking her head. "Did Rico tell you to say that?"

"Yeah," Jackson said. "But it's still true." He stepped back, taking hold of the curtain. "On with the show."

Jett checked her outfit from shoes to shoulders one last time. Many TV hosts suffered from pre-show jitters or "butterflies," but Jett was a bit of an exception. She never got nervous during her early investigative reporter pieces and drop-ins, and wasn't jittery when she accepted the Florida Association of Broadcast Journalists award three months ago for her in-depth report on a nursing home scandal. She didn't even get butterflies when she occasionally sat in for a vacationing news anchor during the six or eleven PM broadcasts.

It was just a camera. Cameras didn't bother her.

Cameras allowed Jett to make a name for herself at the station through tough, no-nonsense investigative reporting. Cameras made the FABJ award possible and had spread her reputation state-wide—and possibly further, if the rumors were to be believed.

TIFFANY LYNN IS MISSING

The Jett Set, however, utilized a live studio audience—a rarity in local TV—and she couldn't shake the feeling that being in front of a crowd was messing with her game—and as a result, the lackluster ratings her new show was getting.

She took a deep breath and flung her hands like they had water on them, shifting her weight from one foot to the other.

Today's panel will change that.

The stage lights brightened as the announcer moved to his offstage podium. "And now, ladies and gentlemen, let's have a big round of applause for the host of *The Jett Set*… Ms. Jett Thacker!"

The audience applauded.

"An interesting combination of guests," Jackson had noted.

It certainly was.

* * * * *

Ashley Wells remained on the floor of her Orlando office, leaning against the wall as Jake dabbed a damp handkerchief across her cheeks and forehead for a second time.

Scowling, she pushed his hand away. "What's the matter with you? Get me off the floor."

He helped her to her feet. Ashley took a few hesitant steps and then righted herself, walking behind a large desk cluttered with stacks of show notes and production schedules, and sitting down in the leather high back chair. Sunlight streamed in through the row of windows, the glistening waters of downtown Orlando's Lake Eola just beyond.

The office walls were decorated with numerous framed, 8x10 glossy pictures. The oldest ones were of a young Ashley Wells, appearing on Reverend Hadley Hemmins' weekly TV show. Darling Ashley Wells, as he dubbed her, had been an instant star—gathering enough popularity after a few years to leave the Hemmins broadcast and launch her own show—and five years later, a small TV network.

Other frames contained images of various local celebrities, commemorating their appearances on *Wake Up With Ashley Wells*, her *Sunshine Hour Music Special,* or one of the other weekly TV shows her network produced. Shelves displayed various awards.

The wall closest to her desk held framed pictures of the appearances her daughter had made on the network. Tiffany Lynn was as beautiful as her mother—and practically the mirror image of Ashley at that age.

Shoving the handkerchief into his suitcoat pocket, Jake picked up his bottle of water and pointed to the door. "Do you want to tell me what happened out there? What was that phone call?"

Ashley grabbed her mouse and shook it, waking up her computer. "Nothing."

"Nothing?" He leaned toward her over the desk. "You turned white and collapsed. That's not nothing. What did that Colorado sheriff tell you?"

Several banking windows and business reports appeared on her computer screen. Ashley plucked a pair of designer reading glasses off the desk and put them on.

"Was it about…" Jake's hand went to his mouth.

TIFFANY LYNN IS MISSING

"They think they found her." Ashley stared at her computer. "In Brimstone County, Colorado, near our Copper Mountain development."

"Tiffany Lynn?" He broke into a smile. "Why, that's great! It's—" Then, his face fell and the wind went out of him. "Oh. Oh, I see."

The cursor on the screen was still. Ashley's fingers trembled on the mouse. She slipped her hand to her lap, her voice falling to a whisper. "The... the sheriff said they found... that there was a..." She closed her eyes and swallowed hard. "They have a young woman's body at the Brimstone County morgue. The driver's license says it's her, and the description matches."

"Oh no." He lowered himself into the chair in front of her desk. "I'm... this has to be very hard for you, dear. I'm so sorry." Jake kneaded his hands together. "Do they know what happened?"

Ashley sat back in her chair, her gaze going to the wall of framed pictures nearest her desk. "Twenty-two years old. That's practically still a child."

"Maybe—maybe there's a different possibility. Maybe Tiffany Lynn's purse was stolen and it's the thief in the morgue. Maybe that's what happened."

She shook her head. "My daughter is gone, Jake. The description, the tattoo..."

"Lots of kids get tattoos these days."

"The fingerprints from the body will match the Florida real estate agent records, and that will be the end of it." Her hands dropped to her sides, her voice breaking as she spoke. "After three long weeks, this..."

She shrugged, her mouth opening but no words escaping.

The room was still. Silent. Ashley stared at the pictures on the wall by her desk; her husband of two years stared at the floor.

The young woman who had taken what police had proclaimed was probably a defiant, impromptu, extended spring break was now apparently laying on a cold slab in Colorado, awaiting positive identification.

Such things happened on TV shows, not to real people with real lives.

Certainly not to Ashley Wells. *Orlando Style* called her the woman who had everything. *Forbes* said she was one of the top fifty influencers in Central Florida. Now, she was just a mother who had lost a child.

Outside the oak panel door, work would go on more or less as usual.

Inside, nothing would ever be the same.

"The way she left..." Ashley's gaze moved to the span of large windows at the far end of the room. "She just ran off. And she was so... so *angry*. So completely filled with hatred for me."

"No, that's not true," Jake said. "It was an argument. The two of you just hit that patch—it's natural. Every kid goes through it. She loved you. She just wanted to spread her wings, and you—"

"Spring break." She looked at him. "Millions of college kids go on spring break without a hitch."

He nodded.

TIFFANY LYNN IS MISSING

Opening her desk drawer, Ashley pulled out three envelopes. "And I have these. That's how she ended things with me. That's what I'm left with."

"No. You have your good memories, too. Your years watching her grow up and become an amazing young lady, and watching her—"

"I have *these*." She threw the envelopes on the desk. "Sour, bitter reminders of the argument, and telling me unequivocally to leave her alone."

"The words of a letter don't always tell the whole message."

Closing her eyes, Ashley put her elbows on the desk and lowered her head to her hands. "The sheriff asked if I would identify the body." She looked up, her face pale. "Can you imagine? They want me to travel to Colorado and…" She shook her head. "And of course she went to Colorado. That's where *he* is. If I hadn't been getting letters postmarked from Florida every week from her, I'd have… But I should have known she'd go to Colorado eventually—to *him*. It's so obvious. He…" She groaned, shaking her head. "I—I can't think about all that right now. Can you…"

"Whatever you need." Jake stood.

"The staff. Tell them I've received bad news and will be taking a few days off. They don't need to know anything else. I need to get to Denver on the next available flight. And…" She glanced around the room. "I'll need a rental car when I get there. I don't want to use one of the company vehicles."

"I'll book us a flight."

"No, just me." She sniffled, wiping her nose. "You need to maintain my presence here or there may not be a business to return to. I'll call you with instructions. I need to go home and pack a bag. Have Emily come in and make my reservations."

"Emily? The new girl?"

"Cheryl is out sick, remember? Emily should be able to book an airline flight and rental car. She can text the boarding pass to me."

"What do you want to do about the board meeting?"

"Most of them are already here. It's too late to ask them not to come. Have the meeting without me, but don't discuss any actual business. Stonewall them on everything. Tell them I received urgent news about a family member and had to leave town—and don't say anything else. They'll assume my mother had another stroke and won't inquire further."

"Wait. Don't you think you should slow down? This is a serious situation and you're acting like—"

"My entire business..." She swept her hands over the cluttered desk. "The network, the real estate development, the college—it all carries my name and it's hanging by a thread. If my competitors think for one second that I'm weak or can be tripped up in any way, they'll swoop in and devour us. There can be no cracks in the walls."

"Our competitors," Jake said.

Ashley cocked her head, wincing. "Excuse me?"

"You said they were your competitors." He shifted his weight from one foot to the other and straightened his tie. "They're *our* competitors. I'm in this thing, too."

TIFFANY LYNN IS MISSING

She smirked. "It's annoying when you pretend to be bold and powerful. That may work on naïve, young starlets when you want to have one of your affairs, but I don't have time for such fantasies. Right now, just handle the board. Or shall I have Marcie do it?"

He lowered his head, nodding. "I'm on it."

"And Jake…"

"Yes?"

Ashley narrowed her eyes. "How I react to the death of my only child is nobody's business but mine. You need to understand that." She stood, sliding her purse over her arm. "Make sure everyone out there understands it, too."

"I'll call your brother. He can meet you at the Denver airport and—"

"No!" She wheeled around, glaring at him. "You will do no such thing." Gathering the envelopes from the top of her desk, she jammed them into her purse and stormed toward the door. "Aaron doesn't hear a word of this. Not from us."

© DAN ALATORRE

CHAPTER 3

Patti maneuvered herself around Rico and the makeup chair as the TV monitor in the corner beamed a live feed of *The Jett Set* into the room. Jett introduced the second panel guest, a young man in khaki pants and a white polo shirt.

"A *paper* newspaper, Rico?" Patti picked up a men's comb and a pair of scissors. "You're old school, *guapo*."

"Hmm." Rico took his eyes off the monitor and opened his newspaper. "What do you need, Patti?"

"Ay coño!" She threw her hands out. "What, can't I chat with a friend?"

"Sure. But... historically, you don't talk to *me* unless you want something."

Pouting, Patti stuck her hip out and rested a hand on it. "Well, since you mentioned it..."

"Uh-huh. Why did I think I could read the paper in here for a few minutes?" He put his hands on the armrests and went to stand up.

"Ay, cálmese." Patti laid her petit hands gently on his broad shoulders. "Sit. Let me give you a quick trim."

Rico took a deep breath and let it out slowly. It would be better—and faster—to just let the station gossip get to whatever she was trying to get to. He relaxed into the chair.

"Look at this nice hair. I wish I had so little gray." Patti eased a comb through the soft curls on the back of his head, snipping at an occasional pesky stray hair. "You and Jett are close, eh? You helped with her career."

"I met her in the field and introduced her to Martin and Mr. Nesmith." He shrugged. "She did the rest."

"That's all?"

Rico eyed Patti in the mirror. "I told them that Jett was talented—because she is. She has a nose for the truth of a story, and she's practically fearless about getting to it."

"Ay, she's very talented. But…" Patti dropped her hands to her sides. "I didn't join the news station to do makeup for the rest of my life. I'm a journalist, too. I only took this position until something opened in the field. Maybe you could help me like you helped her. She's rising fast. Already, she has her own show…"

On the show monitor, a tall black man in a gray suit crossed the stage to shake hands with Jett.

TIFFANY LYNN IS MISSING

The chyron at the bottom of the screen read: Florida State Senator Kendall Marks.

Putting his elbow on the armrest, Rico shifted in the seat and faced Patti. "Here's why Jett already has her own show. I'd see her in the field doing live shots for Channel 9 when she was starting out. She's pretty, so she's hard to miss, but there are a ton of pretty faces that can't do a decent news report. One time, I was shooting B-reel coverage with Derek for a piece on a drug bust in Biscayne Bay, and it was raining big time. Miami PD asked all the news crews to move near the sea wall because they were going to bring in the drug runner's boat. I helped Derek lug his equipment through the downpour so we don't miss the shot, and there was Jett, hauling her videographer's gear and getting set up. She was drenched—soggy shoes, waterlogged hair... Right then, a few gunshots go off. Some idiot from the gangster's posse was trying to scare everyone off or something. Derek and I hit the pavement. When I look up, Jett is running in the direction of the gunshots, yelling at her videographer, 'Come on, the story is this way!' Nobody else was doing that. I knew if we didn't get Jett over here, Channel 9 would beat us in the ratings every night." He glanced at the monitor, nodding. "That's what I told Martin and Mr. Nesmith."

"Beauty and bravery. That's some combination." Patti turned the chair away from the monitor, perusing Rico's hair in the light.

"It's more than that," Rico said. "Jett is... tenacious. Most new reporters aren't so driven."

"And then you two lived together for a year. Why did you break up?"

"We got to be close friends, and when her marriage ended, we sort of fell into dating. But she was living all the way up in Miami Gardens. She wanted to be closer to the station, so I suggested she move in with me. But…"

"Don't try to tell me it was all innocent. I know about you."

"… but we found out pretty fast that we were better as friends than as lovers. She was able to set that aside and so was I, so it all worked out—and now, look at her, with her own show. She loves investigative reporting, and she's the best at it. Anybody who watches her for five minutes can see that. She didn't need any help with her career. I may have opened the door, but after it was open, she did the rest."

Patti stroked his cheek. "Maybe you could help me like that."

He moved his head away, frowning. "I'm trying to tell you—Jett earned her promotions at the station. If anything, sleeping with me slowed down her progress. Mr. Brennan sure didn't care for it."

He turned to view the monitor. On screen, the senator balled up his fists, stomping toward the other seated guests and grabbing the man in the khakis by the collar.

"What is that?" Rico jumped up. "What is going on?"

The camera zoomed in. The two men shoved each other, gesturing wildly. Another guest threw a punch, and in seconds, the set had descended into

TIFFANY LYNN IS MISSING

chaos. People from the audience stormed the stage. Fists flew everywhere.

Rico burst out of the room and ran down the corridor toward the studio, his pulse racing.

At the far end, Jackson's voice blasted through the hallway. "Hey! We need help on set! There's a fight breaking out!"

Rico raced into the studio. The entire set was awash in a sea of madness. People were running in all directions, some screaming, some fighting. A folding chair hurled into a TV camera.

"Somebody call security!" Rico shouted. "Where's Jett?"

Three men grappled in front of him—two audience members and the stage director. Rico yanked them apart. "Break it up!"

He waded into the mob, forcing his way through the chaos. A stray fist grazed his ear. Grabbing his assailant, Rico wrenched the man's arm behind his back and threw him to the floor. "Jackson, call security!"

His gaze fell upon Jett. She had managed to separate the senator from the other guest. She stood between them, red-faced and disheveled, holding her arms out to keep the two men apart.

As Rico pushed his way through the rabble, a folding chair sailed over his head. It crossed the small stage, catching Jett in the face.

She fell backwards, disappearing behind the brawling mob.

DAN ALATORRE

CHAPTER 4

Crossing the bedroom of her palatial estate, Ashley Wells adjusted the Bluetooth earbud in her ear and tossed an empty Louis Vuitton suitcase onto her bed. "I'll be gone a day, maybe two. Make sure we get final signatures for the pledge drive today so we can feature them during Friday's show, and confirm with the mayor for Tuesday of next week." She slipped her phone into her pocket and entered the massive walk-in closet. Crystal chandeliers illuminated the racks of shoes lining the long walls from floor to ceiling; hand-woven berber carpet cushioned every footstep. She opened the top drawer of the first dresser. "No, I'll take a cab home if Jake isn't available," Ashley said. "He'll be late with the board tonight, but tomorrow he should be able to…"

She exited the closet, a car on the quiet street catching her eye.

The mail delivery truck.

Her breath caught in her throat.

"I'll call you back." Ashley ended the call. As the postal vehicle pulled out of her driveway and headed down the road, a knot gripped her stomach. She rushed across the tile of her spacious living room, the click-clack of her heels echoing off the thirty-foot-high carved wood ceiling. As she reached the front foyer, she stretched her hand out, letting her trembling fingers hover over the doorknob.

Swallowing hard, she grabbed the knob and cracked the door open half an inch.

Her long, tiled driveway was empty, as was the private drive beyond. Palm trees waved back and forth against a pale blue sky. A seagull squawked somewhere nearby.

Ashley clutched her abdomen with one hand; with the other, she opened the decorative white metal mailbox mounted near her front door.

The day's postal delivery was almost an inch thick, a standard mix of brochures, junk fliers, and bills.

Heart racing, she thumbed through the stack.

Halfway through, there it was.

She recognized the size and shape of the envelope.

An empty cavern of pain welled up inside Ashley as she pulled the letter from the stack, dropping the rest of the mail to the floor.

The fourth letter in the series had arrived.

Weeks ago, the size and shape of the first envelope had suggested it might contain a birthday card or Easter greeting, but the contents were far from a happy message. It contained a postmark from nearby Christmas, Florida, a small town thirty

TIFFANY LYNN IS MISSING

minutes east of Orlando. Tourists liked to mail postcards from there to receive its unique postmark during the holidays. The subsequent letters would carry the Christmas postmark, too.

The stamp on today's envelope had been cancelled two days ago. Putting her hand to her lip, Ashley choked back a gasp.

Two days.

Forty-eight hours ago, my baby was alive and in Florida, barely sixty minutes' drive from here.

Ashley had demanded the police scour the area around the small town of Christmas when the first letter arrived, but since her daughter was over the age of eighteen, the authorities had no real grounds to do so. And while a formal missing persons report might have gotten a few officers to make some rudimentary inquiries, it also would have created a public record—and the possibility of an embarrassing headline. That would never do. More than once, her staff at the TV station had been instructed: "There will be no scandals associated with this network, of any sort, ever."

Ashley inspected the newest envelope, turning it over in her trembling hands. It was plain white in color, as were the other three. The ink was the same shade of blue, with the name and address written in the same graceful, cursive handwriting that Ashley had taught her daughter as a child, and which she had admired so much as the little girl became a young woman.

The letter was identical to the others in every respect except one.

The first three letters had seemed to come from an angry child throwing a temper tantrum—a child who would come to her senses and return home in a few days or weeks.

This one was very different.

The writer of this letter would not be returning. At least, not the beautiful, vibrant, blonde dynamo that used to live at the address on the front of the envelope.

A bleak feeling swelled through Ashley.

The prior letters angered her. This one made her heart ache.

She stood in her marble foyer, staring at the outside of the envelope. She didn't want to open it. She already knew what the letter inside said. Its painful message would be the same as the others:

"Don't worry, and don't look for me."

It had been the only words her daughter cared to communicate to her since she left, the same message all three prior times; no more and no less.

And now, a fourth—but its arrival had come after the call from the Brimstone County Sheriff in Colorado. That changed everything.

Blinking hard to keep her eyes from filling with tears, Ashley carried the letter to the kitchen. Sitting down at the table, she slid her finger under the flap and opened the envelope, pulling out the single, folded sheet of white paper that it contained.

Unfolding the letter, she stared at Tiffany Lynn's elegant cursive writing on the page.

"Don't worry, and don't look for me."

A tear rolled down Ashley's cheek. There would be no need to look now.

TIFFANY LYNN IS MISSING

She slipped the letter back into the envelope and reached for her purse, removing the other letters and placing them all in a short stack. Outside her kitchen window, bright sunlight bounced off the crystalline blue water of her pool. Past that, the blue-green waters of Lake Butler shimmered in a gentle April breeze, lifting and rocking her boat against the dock as a neighbor's passing jet ski sent tiny waves toward the shore. Over the distant treetops on the other shore stood the tall buildings of downtown Orlando.

The woman who had everything.

Orlando was paradise for millions of residents and tourists alike, but not for Ashley Wells. Not today. Possibly, not ever again.

She stared across the house to the bedroom and the suitcase lying on the bed.

They found her in Colorado.
In Brimstone County.
Near the Wildfire Resort.
Near Aaron.
She closed her eyes and balled up her fists.
Of course that's where they found her.

DAN ALATORRE

CHAPTER 5

Aaron Wells leaned his athletic frame on his elbows, folding his hands on the large conference room table. The mirror finish of its polished mahogany surface reflected his square jaw and 24-carat gold cufflinks nicely. "So, your best offer is $153 million at prime plus one-eighth of a percent. Is that correct?"

Across the table, the three representatives from Goldmar Investments nodded. Tia Zinn, the lead negotiator, maintained a rigid posture as she glanced at her laptop. "And I am prepared to sign a commitment letter for another $500 million—if the sales of phase one are good."

"Oh, they're good." Aaron leaned back in his chair, smiling. "Sales in phase one are off the charts. You know the rapper Quantico? He just bought a unit for each member of his extended family *and* six additional units for the boys in his posse. And Ryan Gorelle, from last year's blockbuster movie

Hollywoodland bought a unit, too. In fact, sales are so good at our little ski resort that we seem to have attracted the interest of California Finance Group and Banque Internationale of Paris." Brushing a stray lock of brown hair from his temple, he put his hands behind his head and focused his big, brown eyes on those of Tia Zinn. "Of course, we'd rather do business with your firm, Tia."

"You played us." Zinn frowned. "You used our offer to negotiate a better deal with our competitors."

Aaron shook his head, leaning forward again. "I don't need to play you. I'm not sitting here with them, am I? I'm not interested in doing business with those firms. I just want your best deal—which I think is prime *less* an eighth of a point. So, if Goldmar can do that on the first 150 *and* the follow-up 500, then... I'm ready to sign with you right now."

"That's a quarter of a percent swing," Zinn said.

"Yeah." Aaron looked her in the eye. "So..."

Zinn took a long, slow breath and glanced at her associate. "So, run the numbers."

The young man typed on his laptop. When he finished, he turned his screen to her.

Staring at the spreadsheet, she rubbed her chin and looked at her client. "I'd have to get approval from Miami."

Aaron beamed. "There's a phone in my private office."

Pursing her lips, she nodded.

TIFFANY LYNN IS MISSING

Aaron punched the intercom button on the conference table phone. "Giselle, Tia needs to make a call. Would you please show her to my office?"

"Of course, Aaron."

He stood, buttoning his suitcoat and looking at the other members of her team. "May I offer you gentlemen a refreshment while we wait?"

As their boss rose from her chair, she closed her laptop and turned to her colleagues. "Go have some coffee. This won't take long."

An attractive middle-aged woman in a red suit stepped into the conference room. "This way, Ms. Zinn."

Peering at the two remaining reps, Aaron headed to the lobby exit. "Davis, Tanner—this morning we are serving an amazing blended-roast coffee from Hawaii. I'm told it's only grown on one side of an inactive volcano, and in blind taste tests it beat out the stuff they serve at the Vatican. Join me?"

He opened the doors and led the men out to the expansive lobby of DAW Holdings, where a silver coffee service and a uniformed server waited beneath the company's gold logo. Next to the coffee, a cedar humidor held an array of cigars.

"Now, Davis..." Aaron picked up one of the antique Tiffany & Company coffee cups. "I understand you have a weakness for café con leche and a fine cigar. Mr. Landy here can bring you a cup of whatever coffee you'd like, but try this first. It'll knock your socks off."

The young associate took the cup. "It's that good, huh?"

"Not if you don't like it. And don't be shy about having a cigar. They're Cuban—a Canadian business associate sends them to me, and I somehow never remember to tell him I don't smoke."

The men laughed.

"Tell me, gentlemen." Aaron placed one of the antique cups on a saucer. "When we close this deal, I assume you two will be making regular visits to the resort to check on the bank's investment. Is that right?"

"I don't know," Tanner said. "Maybe."

"I hope you will." Aaron handed Tanner a coffee cup. "I'll arrange for one of our 'Presidente' models to be available for you whenever you come—that's the one Quantico bought."

As Mr. Landy poured the aromatic java from a Revere silver and ivory urn, a man in a black sweater opened a door and stuck his head into the lobby. "Aaron. I... thought you were in a meeting."

"I am. We're just taking a short break. What's up?"

"Well, I'm sorry to interrupt." The man pointed into the room. "Your daughters' school called. No emergency, the girls are fine—but I put them on hold because I thought I heard your voice out here. Should I have them call back?"

"Uh... I guess I have a minute." Aaron patted Tia's two junior associates on the shoulder. "Guys, if you'll excuse me, I'll be right back." He walked backwards across the lobby, pointing to a small stack of glossy pamphlets on a nearby Chippendale's end table. "Davis, check out the Presidente model in the brochure. When you fly out, I'll get you into Ryan

TIFFANY LYNN IS MISSING

Gorelle's golfing foursome." He stopped at the door and smiled at them. "He's a terrible golfer, but he's got such hilarious stories that nobody seems to mind."

"If he comes out here with Gina Vershanne," Davis said, "I might have to take you up on that."

"Or you might not." Aaron chuckled. "Gina's not a golfer. She prefers to sun herself by the pool."

The associates laughed, and Aaron shut the door behind him. He faced the four spies occupying the small conference room. "Did I tell you? They went for it."

Matt Philson peeled off his black sweater, pointing to a purple-haired young woman sitting at a computer and wearing a headset. "Daria?"

"I think it's a done deal, Aaron." She looked up from her screen and put a hand to her earpiece. "Michaelson just told Zinn she can go to prime rate *less* one-eighth of a point to get the deal."

"Ha." Aaron rubbed his hands together. "I told you they'd go for prime less an eighth. From the look on Tia's face, Michaelson will fly out here if he has to. He needs this. Their quarterly earnings were dismal."

"But..." The young woman held up a finger. "He's saying if you'll sign the deal today, she can go to prime less a *quarter*. Zinn's... pushing back a little, but Michaelson's pretty insistent."

Aaron smiled at his tech guru. "See?"

"You always know." Philson tossed his pen onto the desk. "Why do you even have us in here with all this equipment? You certainly don't need us."

"You know why." He turned his attention back to Daria. "But we don't need to fleece them. Prime less an eighth will do it. We need them in business next year, too." He glanced at the other men in the room—Collier Bristol, the corporate attorney for DAW Holdings, and a man in his mid-forties that Philson had recently hired. "That will take three hundred thousand off our current operating expenses in the next twelve months, Collie. What do you think?"

Brisol folded his arms and put a finger to his chin. "Does it have the backing of her board of directors?"

"Yep." Philson nodded. "I saw that in Tia's email. Michaelson got Board approval earlier in the week."

"It's perfectly logical. He doesn't want to lose out to California Finance group." Aaron clapped his hands together. "That's nice work, people. Is there anything else? I need to get back before things start to look suspicious."

"Not unless you want in on Ryan Gorselle's next golf outing." The attorney stepped forward, his hands in his pockets. "He's just called. He's coming out again tomorrow with that comedian, Josh Louis."

"Ugh." Aaron winced. "Ryan finally found someone worse at golf than he is. I'll pass. But let's have a complimentary bottle of Cristal champagne waiting for each of them when they arrive—and yellow roses for Gina Vershanne."

"Done," Bristol said.

Aaron headed for the door. "Oh, and if Gorselle's planning on being longer than the day, let

TIFFANY LYNN IS MISSING

him know I'll buy his group a late dinner at Kensington's—and have a camera ready for some promo pics."

Daria looked up from her screen. "Zinn is hanging up, guys."

"Okay," Aaron said. "Thanks a ton, everybody." He strolled through the doors and into the lobby. The two junior Goldmar reps were still sipping coffee.

Davis set his cup down. "Everything okay?"

"Yeah, yeah. My daughters' school wants a donation, as always." Aaron waved a hand. "Hey, I heard Ryan Gorselle's coming out to hit the links tomorrow. But I have meetings planned all day."

Tia Zinn stepped into the lobby. "Not with California Finance Group, I hope."

Aaron shook his head. "Never. Tia, I'm a Florida boy. I don't like California banks any more than you do. Now, shall we go back into the conference room and sign a deal?"

Tia stared at him, then at her two associates.

"Come on." Aaron grinned. "Let's sign the paperwork and get you home to that beautiful three-year-old daughter of yours."

Pursing her lips, Zinn exhaled sharply. "Okay. Let's do it."

"Great. This means a lot to me." Aaron glanced at his assistant. "Giselle?"

She stepped forward with a large, pink teddy bear that was dressed in a t-shirt with the Wildfire Resort logo on it. "The t-shirt came from the gift shop, but the bear is a limited-edition adoption from the Boulder County Wildlife Fund."

"And it's pink!" Zinn broke into a grin. "My daughter's favorite color. It's adorable, Aaron. Thank you."

"Check this out." He leaned toward the bear, sniffing. "It smells like chocolate."

"Oh, she'll love that!" Zinn shook her head. "You are something else. You squeeze a deal so hard my eyes bleed, and then you turn around and do something like this, which makes it so darned hard to hate you."

"I know," Aaron said. "And I feel terrible about it."

"No you don't."

"No, I don't. Which is why I want you and Ron to bring your daughter out to play in the snow for a week. Whenever you can swing a vacation. It'll be my treat."

"That's really nice." Tia held the bear, putting her nose close to its pink fur. "But I can't."

"You can." Aaron wagged a finger at her. "I didn't offer it until after we had agreed to the deal, so it's a gift, not a bribe." He faced her associates. "And that offer goes to you guys, too. And old man Michaelson. You have my number. Call me and I'll have Giselle set it up—and remember what I said about golfing with Ryan Gorselle."

"Or taking a day by the pool," Davis said.

"Or that. It's heated with mineral water from a natural hot spring, so you can sip a cocktail outside in the pool while it's snowing all around you. There's nothing like it. And at night, you can hear elks bugling from the hills. Just amazing." He gestured to the conference room. "Now, shall we?"

TIFFANY LYNN IS MISSING

Half an hour later, the papers had all been signed. Aaron walked the representatives from Goldmar to the elevator, shaking hands and wishing them well. As the gold-plated elevator doors slid closed, he gave a final wave and breathed a hearty sigh.

Matt Philson opened the small conference room door. "Nicely done, Aaron."

"Thank you." Aaron shoved his hands into his pockets as he walked back across the lobby. "Giselle, would you please make a check out to Philson and Associates for fifty thousand dollars? From the Wildfire petty cash account."

"It's my pleasure, Aaron." She sat behind her desk, opened the middle drawer, and pulled out a check register.

"Petty cash?" Daria said. "Nothing petty about that much cash."

Giselle cleared her throat, looking at Aaron. She tapped the check register. "Uh... the Wildfire petty cash, correct, sir?"

"Yep!" He looked at her, then back to Philson. "A big commission for a big favor."

"Okay." Giselle wrote on a notepad, clearing her throat again. "If you could just endorse it, Mr. Wells."

Aaron cocked his head.

What's with her?

Giselle never called him "sir" or "Mr. Wells." It was Aaron for her and every employee on the staff. And she was authorized to sign checks for twice that amount.

He walked to her desk and peered over her shoulder. The check register indicated that the payment to Philson would substantially overdraw the Wildfire account. Giselle pointed to a recent withdrawal entry for thirty thousand dollars.

"I checked this last week when it happened," Giselle whispered. "Thirty thousand dollars was transferred out electronically using your passcode, so I assumed it was a special entry."

Aaron nodded, pursing his lips. "Special entry" was code for an off-the-books bribe to a local official.

"Everything okay?" Matt smiled. "Am I bankrupting you?"

"No, no. Just a..." Aaron broke into a wide grin. "Well, you know how things go around here. Had to encourage a politician to give us a zoning variance, and I did it from the wrong account." He faced Giselle, taking her notepad and pen. "No problem. Transfer some funds from my personal account at City Savings to cover the amount."

On the notepad, he wrote, "Call the bank and find out what happened with the $30k."

Giselle nodded and slipped the notepad under the check register. Aaron walked around to the front of the desk.

Taking the check from Giselle, Philson turned and faced Aaron. "What's on for this afternoon, boss man?"

"I'm heading out to check construction at Wildfire." Aaron strolled to his desk, opening a drawer and taking out his wallet and a set of keys. He slipped them into his pocket. "Then the landscape

TIFFANY LYNN IS MISSING

architect at our new Passionfire resort site wants to take the chopper to do some aerial scouting for ski slopes, and..." He shrugged. "The girls have a volleyball match. That's it. Wanna come?"

"No, thanks," Philson said. "I get airsick."

"Not to that. To the volleyball match. It's the semi-finals."

Philson folded his check in half and put it in his billfold. "I'd better go see my wife before she forgets what I look like."

"She's downstairs at Kensington's." Aaron walked back out of his office. "At my table. She's sipping a mimosa and waiting for you."

"Really?" Philson grinned. "You are a sly dog. No wonder Zinn can't hate you."

"I make Tia's company too much money for her to hate me." He clapped Philson on the shoulder. "Now, go to your lovely wife and order anything on the menu. My treat, as a way of saying thanks for all your hard work."

"Thanks, Aaron." Philson shook Aaron's hand.

"Matt?" Daria peeked out from the conference room. "Got a sec?"

Philson walked to his employee. They whispered for a moment.

"Okay." Philson nodded at Daria. "I'll take care of it." He faced Aaron, pursing his lips. "Boss man... I need to talk to you about one more thing."

Aaron wagged a finger. "Go see your beautiful bride. I'm sure any other business can wait until—"

"No..." Philson's face grew grim. He glanced over his shoulder. "We, uh... we should talk now. In your office."

"Okay, then." He waved to Matt's associates. "Good to see you two. Drive safely. It's supposed to snow."

"Thanks, Aaron," Daria said, keeping her eyes down. Philson's other employee waved quickly as he left.

Philson walked with Aaron to his private office, shutting the doors behind them. Lowering his head, Philson gazed toward the floor. "Daria intercepted a message a moment ago." He looked Aaron in the eye, his expression pained. "Have you... heard from your sister?"

"No," Aaron said. "But she has a board meeting today, so that's not unusual. Why?"

Philson grimaced, looking away.

"Matt, whatever it is, just tell me."

"Okay." Philson took a deep breath. "I'm sorry to be the one to break the news to you, but... according to an email Ashley just sent... they found her. Your niece."

A jolt of fear shot through Aaron's abdomen. "Oh, no." He dropped into his chair, his arms falling to his sides. "You, uh... you mean they found her *body*. Otherwise, you'd be happy."

"Yeah, that... that's right." Philson's shoulders slumped. "She was found right here at Brimstone Lake. I'm... very sorry. Can I do anything?"

The politically connected, financially powerful executive slouched in the seat, closing his

TIFFANY LYNN IS MISSING

eyes and putting a hand to his forehead. "Not..." Aaron's voice wavered. He cleared his throat and forced himself to speak. "Not right now, but please keep a phone handy." He looked up at his friend. "I'm sure my sister will be arriving soon, and she'll be needing me."

"She's already on a flight," Philson said. "Scheduled to touch down in a few minutes. That's why I was surprised to see you kept the meeting with Goldmar. Odd that she didn't call."

"Her daughter is dead. She's obviously not thinking clearly. Everyone... grieves in their own way."

"She wouldn't have called either way, you know that." Philson folded his arms. "It's not the iron maiden's style."

Aaron cleared his throat again. "Matt, you're my friend and you are very valuable to this firm." He looked up. "But if you ever speak about my sister that way again, your relationship with DAW Holdings is over."

Philson nodded. "I'm sorry. Your niece, she was... a great kid. I met her last summer. Smart, beautiful—an exceptional young woman in every way, and just starting her life. It's a shame your sister... well, it's a shame Tiffany Lynn was driven to all this." He stared at the floor. "If only you had known... maybe you could have done something."

Aaron lifted his gaze to the window. "If I had known."

Beyond the office glass, the mountaintops rose up through a smattering of puffy white clouds. As picturesque and bright as the scene had looked a few minutes ago, it might as well have been cloudy, gray and raining now. An unbearable sadness made Aaron's insides feel empty and cold.

"The last time I saw her," Aaron said, "she was walking across the street in downtown Orlando. It was about a week before spring break, and it was raining. She was carrying a big red umbrella. I remember... it was so strange. She was going off to meet some friends, and I was heading back here... she said goodbye and gave me a long hug like she knew I'd never see her again."

Philson watched his friend. "I'm really sorry to be the one to tell you."

"No, you've, uh..." Aaron stood, adjusting the lapels of his suit. He wiped away a tear, his voice breaking. "You've done me a great kindness by not letting me find out from the news. Do you know where my sister will be staying?"

"Her computer says she's booked at the resort," Philson said. "Presidente, suite three. She registered under the name of Jane Doe. She also reserved a rental car."

"Jane Doe." Aaron shook his head. "So many games." Squaring his shoulders, the chief executive officer of DAW Holdings walked to his office door. "Okay. If you need to contact me tonight, you'll be able to reach me there."

CHAPTER 6

Jett leaned back in a Miami 5 break room chair, holding a bag of ice wrapped in a dish towel to her nose. A dagger of pain ripped through her sinuses.

"Hold still." Rico carefully wiped her cheek and chin with some paper towels. "Let's clean you up a little so I can assess the damage."

The absorbent wad came away with blood all over it.

"I'm fine." Jett lowered her head, tossing the bag of ice into the sink. "It's not broken, it's just a bloody nose."

"Okay, Doctor." Rico continued dabbing. "Thank you for that update."

"Really... this is irritating me more than it's helping."

"Fine." He dropped the red-stained clump into a nearby trash can. "Let's have a look."

Jett blinked a few times to clear her eyes and peered at her friend.

"I guess it's not too bad." Rico smiled. "I have to say, I'm impressed with how you handled yourself out there."

Grabbing a fresh paper towel from the break room table, Jett wiped her nose. "Yeah, I can take a punch from the studio furniture. That's a talent."

"No, I meant how you managed to not get blood on your blouse."

She stuck her tongue out at him. Taking her phone from her pocket, she reversed the camera view and held it close to her face. A tiny red line about a quarter of an inch long crossed the bridge of her nose. Her eyes were more or less bloodshot, and her mascara was streaked. Other than that, she didn't look too bad—except for bruises forming under each eye.

"Great." She turned her head back and forth, inspecting the swelling. "I'm going to have two big, black shiners."

"Think concealer will cover it?"

"In a few days, sure. But they could put ten layers on me for tomorrow's show and I'll look like a racoon. Even if Patti can hide the black eyes, my cheeks will still be swollen up like a chipmunk."

"The viewers saw what happened." Rico got up and went to the sink, turning on the faucet. He ran his hands under the water. "They won't care about some bruising. They'll be impressed you came back the very next day and didn't beg off. Maybe we can—"

TIFFANY LYNN IS MISSING

"Jett?" One of the station pages appeared at the break room entrance. "Ma'am, Mr. Brennan would like to see you in his office."

Rico frowned, wiping his hands on a towel and opening his mouth to speak, but Jett placed her finger to his lips. "No, you don't. My show got his brand-new set trashed. He has a right to be upset."

"Yeah, that's fair." Rico put his hands on his hips. "Okay, let him vent—and be sure to ask to apologize to Mr. Nesmith personally. Then pivot to the new ideas you have for the show. Martin will forget all about the cost of the set if his morning ratings improve."

"Okay." Jett slipped her phone back into her pocket and picked up her purse. "I'll call you later to discuss my strategies."

The walk to Martin's office took her past the stage again. Several maintenance workers swept up papers and broken pieces of glass. One of the station carpenters stood in front of the broken *The Jett Set* logo, shaking his head as the sign dangled sideways from its perch.

Jett winced. She recalled one of the production assistants mentioning that the new set had cost over fifty thousand dollars.

Martin's upset and embarrassed right now.

Just let him vent. Then, apologize—and explain the other ideas you have for improving the show. That's what he wants, a successful morning schedule.

The elevator carried Jett to Miami 5's second floor. Martin's office was to the right of the receptionist; Mr. Nesmith, the owner of the station, maintained an office on the receptionist's left.

"Go right in, Ms. Thacker." The receptionist walked to Martin's office and opened the door. "He's expecting you."

Martin paced back and forth across his Miami 5-emblem carpet, his hands clasped behind his back. On the wall, a large TV monitor was replaying the fight from Jett's show.

As Jett stepped inside the executive's suite, the receptionist closed the door behind her.

Putting his hands to his forehead, Martin glared at Jett. "Would you mind telling me what I just witnessed happening on our network's live TV broadcast?"

"I'm so sorry, Martin." Jett wrung her hands. "Things obviously got… a little out of control."

"I'd say they got a lot out of control." Martin's face reddened. He picked up a remote from his desk and paused the monitor mid-fight. "A fifty thousand dollar set, ruined. Camera lenses smashed, chairs thrown through walls…"

She pointed to her swollen eyes. "Not just through walls."

He ran his hands over his face, taking a deep breath. "Yes. I'm sorry, Jessica—are you okay? Do we need a doctor to look at you?"

She thought about Rico's advice.

Apologize and pivot.

"No, sir, I'm fine. It's just a couple of bruises. I got worse from my older brother growing up. But I would like to say, we will definitely make some

TIFFANY LYNN IS MISSING

changes to our format so nothing like that ever happens again."

Martin folded his arms over his chest and leaned back on the edge of his desk. "What possessed you to put a known white supremacist Nazi like Bryan Keller on with a state senator who's black? It's a Christian network for Pete's sake. We can't have Nazis punching senators."

"It's a *former* Christian network."

"Oh, and Mr. Nesmith forgot he was a Christian, is that it?" Martin scowled. "That's not helpful, Jessica. You were able to get Marks because Mr. Nesmith gives money to the senator's campaign. He wants Marks to run for governor, and now the senator looks like an idiot."

"Sir, he doesn't."

"Senator Marks touts himself as a man of good judgement, and he just got into a fight with a twenty-two-year-old Nazi on a live television broadcast. *Our* broadcast." He set the remote down and held up his phone. "It's trending. Over ten thousand views already. By tonight, that mob action of yours will be the top item on the internet, and our network created it! I can't believe this. What were you thinking?"

"I was thinking they'd have a conversation and our audience would learn something." She looked down. "But every time I put a question to Keller, he would look at Senator Marks and begin his reply with a string of racial epithets. At first, Marks would ignore it or diplomatically call Keller on it, and I'd redirect things. But Keller kept at it. After three or four more ugly racial slurs, I guess the senator had put up with enough. He walked over to Keller, and Keller jumped up and started throwing punches. Then..." She shrugged. "It all went sideways."

Rubbing his chin, Martin backed up the video and played the fight again. "Think the Nazi brought some of his supporters?"

"He might have." Jett viewed the monitor over her boss's shoulder. The fight had looked bad in person, but it looked much worse onscreen—especially in slow motion.

Her heart sank.

People who saw this unfolding live will have already phoned the station to voice their outrage. The receptionists are probably getting slammed with irate calls, and the front office manager will have informed Martin.

"Maybe Senator Marks brought people, too," she said. "But I'm not sure how we'd have known that. I... I'm really very sorry, Martin. We thought spirited debate would educate the public and help the show's ratings. But clearly, in this case, we made a poor choice."

Martin bristled. "What do you mean *we*?"

"Me, Rico, the producers, you..." Jett nodded. "We all discussed the upcoming guest pairings in a group memo last weekend. Now, what we need going forward is—"

"Hold on." Martin put a hand up. "Are you implying I agreed to *you* placing an esteemed member of the Florida Senate on air with a Nazi?"

"Well, sir... you did." Jett's cheeks warmed. She struggled to keep her voice calm and even. "You

TIFFANY LYNN IS MISSING

signed off on it Saturday afternoon so we could get Keller here in time to appear with the senator."

"No, no, no. That's not how I recall it going down. I wasn't part of any conversation to that effect."

Her jaw dropped. "Sir, you absolutely signed off. I have the—your approval email is still sitting in my inbox. You agreed it would give the show the necessary boost to—"

"No. I never said that." Martin tugged at his collar. "There's no email from me approving anything of the sort. You're mistaken, Ms. Thacker—and I don't appreciate your attempt to drag me into this."

"Drag?" Jett took a step back, then regained her composure. "Martin, I don't understand. I can show you the emails right now. Let me use your computer."

"No." He looked away. "I don't think so."

"Well, I can show you on my phone. Look…" She took out her phone and tapped her screen. The Miami 5 email app brought up an error message. "Okay, it won't open, for some reason. But like I said, moving forward, we'll make the necessary changes to—"

"Let's slow down. I think it may have been a mistake to have given you so much responsibility so quickly." Martin cleared his throat. "Having your own show means finding topics, doing research, managing the talent coordinators that schedule the guests—that's a lot of work. Too much, possibly. And we should not have let Rico—ah, Mr. Torres—push for you to have so much authority. In hindsight, it was a fairly clear conflict of interest on his part, given the relationship between you two."

"What?" She folded her arms. "That's been over for months. And we disclosed it to HR long before you and I ever discussed me getting my own show."

"That's... not how I recall it."

Jett frowned. "Well, with all due respect, sir—one of us is suffering from a severe case of selective memory. There are company emails that document everything I've said."

Martin walked to his window, gazing toward the Miami skyline. "Because you are obviously upset, I'll ignore your insubordinate tone. But clearly, things cannot continue as they are. Our late morning ratings are a disaster."

"Yes. I agree." *Apologize and pivot.* "We'll improve that. I have a whole list of changes that—"

"Changes? Yes, change is definitely needed." Martin clasped his hands behind his back. "Your show is ranked at the bottom of just about every chart the Nielsen company makes. That won't do."

She winced. "I agree, but we can fix that. We just need some time for the audience to find us."

"In the meantime, you've caused a great deal of embarrassment to the station and to Mr. Nesmith personally."

"We have a plan to improve," Jett said. "Let me talk to him. I can explain."

Martin stepped away from the window, studying the floor and tapping his chin with one finger. "I think the best way for all of us to move forward—considering the numerous issues with the

TIFFANY LYNN IS MISSING

show and your obvious poor judgement, as evidenced by forcing Senator Marks to appear with a Nazi, which culminated in this morning's disastrous barroom brawl..." He raised his gaze to peer at Jett. "Is to terminate your employment with the station."

A jolt went through Jett's insides. "What? You're—you're firing me?"

"Effective immediately." Martin nodded. "For breach of contract and gross negligence. Security will escort you to your desk."

"But you approved of everything I did!" Her cheeks grew hot. "I have the emails!"

"As I said..." Martin tugged his collar again. "That's... not how I remember it."

Her heart in her throat, Jett put a hand to her forehead.

How you remember it? There are emails!

But you need a scapegoat, so you're trying to lay all the blame at my feet.

She took a deep breath and glared at Martin. "Fine. I have a contract. You can pay me to sit at home and watch cat videos on YouTube for all I care."

"You *had* a contract—which you breached. Now you need to go clear out your desk."

"You're being ridiculous, Martin. This is all a contorted pack of lies and you know it."

"A cab will be waiting for you downstairs in five minutes."

"I got a black eye, not a concussion." She turned to leave. "I'll drive myself home."

"No, the Mercedes was a bonus, contingent upon your continued employment with Miami 5—as was the company phone." He held his hand out.

Sighing, Jett walked back toward Martin's desk, pulled out her phone and her car keys, and dropped them into his palm.

"And," he said, "because we are terminating you for gross negligence and breach of contract, the station feels you are not entitled to the monetary payout of your remaining contract—nor are you due any severance pay." Martin set her phone and keys on the desk. "Quite the contrary, we'll be holding your last paycheck as partial compensation toward the damages you caused to our studio. You can expect a bill for the balance."

Jett's jaw dropped. "A bill!"

"I know right now you probably want to hire an attorney and sue the pants off of me and Miami 5, but remember…" Martin sneered. "TV stations talk. Filing a lawsuit against your prior employer is not the best way to make the next employer want to hire you." He looked at his office door. "Mr. Carter?"

The office door opened and a uniformed security guard stepped inside. "Ma'am, will you come with me, please?"

"Who are you?" She turned to Martin. "Who is that? Since when do we have uniformed security guards?"

"Since a few minutes after that Nazi took a swing at the future governor—on your show." Martin turned his back to her and faced the window again. "Goodbye, Ms. Thacker."

* * * * *

TIFFANY LYNN IS MISSING

Once Jett left and the doors were shut, Martin returned to his desk and looked at the speakerphone. "Was that okay, sir?"

"That was fine, Martin," Mr. Nesmith said. "Unpleasant business, firing someone, but it had to be done. The station is for sale. If it looks like management played any role in today's debacle, the price will plummet. We need to douse this fire with some headlines that say Thacker was already on her way to being kicked to the curb, and then get a follow-up campaign going to stomp out any lingering embers. We can weather some negative press, we just can't have it directed at us."

"Of course, sir."

"And Martin—what was that talk about the emails? You knew about that insane guest list prior to today?"

"No, of course not, sir." Still standing, Martin took his wallet out and removed a business card. "That was just some wild ramblings from a disgruntled employee, nothing more."

"Okay, then," Nesmith said. "I'll see you at the club later. Make sure this nastiness goes away quickly."

"It's already being handled, sir." Martin ended the call and punched a button to access an open line. Reading the number on the business card, he dialed quickly.

After one ring, a man answered. "Hello?"

"It's me." Martin sat down at his desk. "What's the status?"

"We're all good," the man said. "We put up an error message that showed the station's email system was undergoing routine scheduled maintenance this morning, and we altered every email about guest lists from Jett to you. They don't exist anymore. You were never in the loop. Not that she'd have access to her company email as a terminated employee anyway."

"Okay." Martin bit his lip. "She was pretty angry. What about the… other things we discussed? I need Jett to lack all credibility. As insurance."

"My contacts at Channel 10 are happy to run a breaking news story during their midday broadcast, describing the fight that aired live and saying Jett was let go because of a severe drinking problem—which my contacts at Channel 6 will also be told, so they can verify each other's stories. Viewers will conclude Jett was intoxicated and that's why she allowed things to get out of control. Then, my friends at *The Miami Source* will be going with stories about how difficult she was to work with—prima donna, temper tantrums, all that. How she's only concerned about her own glory and is a real jerk to work with, a crappy human being in general. The bots will make sure it all gets picked up by the news outlets."

"Very nice." Martin snickered. "Anything else?"

"My favorite is the meme we made. It shows Jett taking that chair to her face, with the caption 'Ego Queen And Her New Throne.' The bots will have that trending soon. And for good measure, we can leak it that she only got the job in the first place because she was sleeping with a producer at the station."

TIFFANY LYNN IS MISSING

"Let's hold off on that last one," Martin said. "We may be a former Christian network, but the big boss is still a Christian. As am I."

"It's your money."

Sitting back in his chair, Martin rubbed his chin. "How soon will I be able to start seeing results?"

"Why don't you go ahead and do a quick internet search of your former employee's name right now?" The man laughed. "I think you'll be pleasantly surprised."

"Really?" Typing on his keyboard, Martin opened a search engine and typed 'Jett Thacker.' The internet was abuzz with her. The on-air fistfight was matched by blaring headlines alleging alcoholism and subordinates discussing how they hated working with her. Martin smiled. "Oh, this is even better than I thought."

"Martin, in twenty-four hours, Jett Thacker won't be able to get a job as a blogger in Miami."

DAN ALATORRE

CHAPTER 7

The cab dropped Jett and her cardboard box at 100 SE 2nd Street, possibly the most prestigious address in South Florida. Miami Tower was known as the "wedding cake building," because of its unique, semi-circular, three-tier stacked profile that overlooked Biscayne Bay and Miami's many international cruise ship terminals. The building's white exterior could be lit at night in any color—pink for breast cancer awareness month, red and green for Christmas, gold for Easter—making it a prominent fixture of the Miami skyline as it repeatedly made cameo appearances in popular TV shows and movies. It was pricey real estate, filled with the offices of high-powered businesses on the lower twenty-five floors and Miami's aspiring rich and famous on the upper twenty floors.

Jett's residence was located on the twenty-sixth level, just one elevator stop higher than an international shipping magnate's offices.

She adjusted her sunglasses and lifted the box, maintaining a stoic face as she entered the building and marched across the grandiose marble lobby to the residential elevators. Jett's mind raced with the events of the day. Being in the middle of an on-air melee had been gut-wrenching. The meeting afterward with Martin was embarrassing, at best. Making her carry a box of personal possessions out of the building—while everyone watched—was borderline humiliating.

Even the cab ride went lousy. The car was hot, and halfway home she'd received a text from her agent, stating that his firm would no longer be representing her. Jett's plan of spending the afternoon scheduling interviews with her agent would become a search for a new agent.

Her heart sank as she considered the repercussions, but she tried to rally herself.

I'll find a new agent, and then I'll be right back in the game.

Screw you, Martin.

But inside, she wasn't convinced. Martin was right—television is a small world. It might be very hard to find work after this morning's on-air debacle and subsequent embarrassing termination from Miami 5.

As the elevator doors opened, she propped her box under her arm, struggling to dig her keys out of her purse. Halfway down the hall, a young girl with straight brown hair popped her head out a doorway. "Hi, Jett."

TIFFANY LYNN IS MISSING

"Hey, Leah." Jett shifted the box higher on her hip, her purse swinging back and forth. "What are you doing home in the middle of a school day?"

"I needed a day off." The child emerged from the doorway, dressed in a t-shirt, shorts, and flip-flops. She reached inside Jett's purse and removed her keys, walking to Jett's unit.

"Thank you." The box slipped down on Jett's hip. Sweat forming on her upper lip, she hefted the box higher.

A moment later, the door swung open and the alarm's warning tone filled the air. Leah stepped inside and entered the passcode on the keypad.

Jett walked past the girl, placing the cardboard box on the dining room table and removing her sunglasses. Even the slight pressure from the frames irritated her swollen cheeks.

Her spacious unit was an "open" floorplan, filled with expensive glass tables and white leather furniture, but only had actual walls for the bedrooms and bathrooms. The living room area spilled into the dining room and then the kitchen, creating one big room. Jett's cluttered desk sat next to a long row of panel windows that ran along the curved south side of the unit and let in the spectacular view.

Plopping down on Jett's curved, white couch, Leah sprawled flat on her back, her arms and legs going out in all directions. She lifted her head and scrunched up her face. "You have a black eye and you're all sweaty. What happened?"

Jett took a deep breath and wiped her brow with the back of her wrist. "I kinda bumped my head at work, and the air conditioning in the cab wasn't working."

"Oh. Why'd you take a cab? Is your Mercedes in the shop?"

Strolling to the refrigerator, Jett took out two bottles of water and handed one to her inquisitive neighbor. "Let's not skip over that first piece of information so quickly, young lady. You needed a day off from school? Where's your dad?"

Leah sat up. "Dad's in Puerto Vallarta with Janelle."

"Oh." Jett took a swig of water to hide her reaction.

Janelle? What happened to Christine?

"Technically, it's Mom's week." Leah set her water on the wide, round coffee table. "But she flew to Palm Springs, so I decided to take the day off. I've been looking out the window and watching the cruise boats leave the port."

"You're home alone?" Through her open door, Jett peered across the hall to Leah's unit. "Mrs. Dearmont isn't with you?"

"It's okay."

"It's not okay. I didn't help you learn to multiply fractions just so you could flunk out. You need to know that stuff for your quiz."

"Do you use fractions for news stories?"

"Kind of. I pay an agent ten percent. That's one-tenth, so yeah, I use fractions at work." Jett put her hand on her hip. "Doesn't your school call or something when you skip?"

"Yeah." Leah shrugged, going to the window. One pane of glass was smattered with

TIFFANY LYNN IS MISSING

fingerprints and smudges at the height of Leah's forehead. "But my dad's kinda into sticking it to my mom when she forgets the custody schedule, so he makes a point of not caring, you know?"

Jett sighed. "Well, I care. A ten-year-old should not be home alone, kiddo."

"I'm almost eleven."

"Oh, that makes it okay, then." She shook her head and walked to the desk, leafing through the scattered papers on its surface.

"Why are *you* home in the middle of the day?" Leah turned and peered at Jett. "You investigating something?"

"Sort of. I'm investigating a new job." She moved her mouse back and forth to wake up her computer.

"Wanna watch the Starlight with me?" Turning back to the window, Leah held up a finger and pressed it to the glass—along with her nose and forehead. "It's getting ready to set sail. It takes about eleven minutes for it to pull away from the dock and get too small to see without binoculars. The cruise website says it's heading to Martinique tonight and then to the Virgin Islands tomorrow."

"Sounds fun, but..." Jett gave a half frown. "I should probably start my job search. Wanna help?"

"I'm FaceTiming with Taylor, so I should get back. Mrs. Dearmont says it's rude to leave people on hold for too long." Leah pulled away from the window and walked toward the exit, leaving a fresh set of smudges behind. As she passed the curved couch, she stopped and turned to Jett. "I thought the on-air talent had agents to look for jobs for them."

"My agent apparently reconsidered representing me when he saw today's show, so now I'm kinda on my own."

Leah looked down, picking at her fingernails. "Being on your own isn't so bad sometimes. You can eat all the Oreos in the pantry and nobody fusses. You can FaceTime all day and nobody complains that you're hogging all the bandwidth. And you can order pizza, too. They even bring soda if you ask. You just put it on the credit card."

Jett looked up from her desk and smiled at her young friend. "I'm going to be fine and so are you, sweetie. Because what are we?"

"We're tough."

"That's right. We run toward the bullets. We might get knocked down, but we get back up again. Now, when you're finished playing with Taylor, we'll have dinner, okay? But tomorrow, go to school. You should be able to get an A on your math quiz, but you kinda have to be there for it, you know?"

"Okay…" Leah walked across the foyer area. "Mrs. Dearmont is coming to spend the night, so I'll probably have to go anyway."

"Good. Now, hold on." Jett picked up her phone and tapped on the screen. "I'm calling you from my new phone, so be sure to save this number."

"Did you drop your old one in the pool again?"

"It was a company cell phone, so I had to switch." Jett finished tapping and set the phone

TIFFANY LYNN IS MISSING

down. "Now, I need to get busy. Promise me you'll go to school tomorrow!"

"Okay, I will." She smiled. "Bye, Jett."

Leah shut the door on her way out. Walking to her couch, Jett sat down, put her elbows on her knees, her chin on her hands, and stared at the wall.

I need to find a new agent, update my resume, update my video highlight reel...

She slouched back on the couch. It had been an emotionally draining day.

Maybe go work out first, to wake up and vent the stress...

The impulse to yawn seized her. She fought back, but it won. Stretching, Jett rolled her shoulders and relaxed into her cushions.

Or maybe I should just take a nap and try to sleep through my depression...

Her eyelids grew heavy. The bright sunlight illuminated her Florida Association of Broadcast Journalists award; it caught her eye from its place on the shelf by her desk. On the wall behind the award was a framed picture of her receiving it. The presenter was Martin Brennan.

Jett got up from the couch, pulled the picture off the wall, and dropped it into the trash.

Firing up her laptop, she decided to check in on Instagram.

Martin Brennan and Miami 5 don't own that.

Among half a dozen social media accounts she maintained, Jett kept two Instagram accounts. One was her public profile as Jett Thacker, investigative reporter and news person with about 10,000 followers. It had Jett's professional head shot as its icon, and a lot of dramatic images from her various award-winning news stories.

The other account was for private use, under the simple name of Jessica Eve. It had no public image icon, and only a few hundred followers. Most were friends from Jett's high school in Coral Gables, trusted co-workers from TV stations, and a few other people she'd become close with over the years.

She avoided looking at the "public" account, assuming it was under siege with negative comments from this morning's exploits, and opened her private account to see if anyone had tried to message her.

Several friends had.

A few co-workers from Miami 5 had left messages for her to join them at a club that evening. Specifically, Carmen wanted to talk and commiserate, strategize, and generally get drunk as a way of showing solidarity.

Jett pursed her lips, brushing a strand of hair back and forth across her chin as she stared at the screen.

A night of drinking at a club might not be a good idea...

It might not be a bad idea, either. Carmen's trustworthy, though, and venting to friends might help my mood.

She updated the profile with her new phone number, double checked the security settings to make sure only actual friends could access it, and then went to a few other social media sites and updated things there, too. She had always maintained a private email account, so that didn't need changing,

TIFFANY LYNN IS MISSING

but when Miami 5 gave her a company phone, Jett found it cumbersome to carry two.

That won't be a problem for a little while...

She leaned back in the chair, drumming her fingers on the armrests.

What next?

Her resume was more or less current, minus the last few months of video footage. She'd kept it pretty up-to-date as she prepared to start showing it to network executives.

Her stomach jolted.

Networks.

They wouldn't be looking at her for a while. Not after this morning's on-air fight—and Jett getting fired.

She cringed.

What will they see if they do a search on me now?

She typed her name into a browser, recoiling as the images and headlines assaulted her screen.

The fight was there, of course, and the chair hitting her in the face. She touched a finger to her cheek. The skin was super sensitive, and the swelling was getting worse. Picking up her phone, Jett viewed herself through the camera again.

Both eyes were almost completely circled in black.

Groaning, she lowered her head to the desk.

I can't go out looking like this. If anyone takes a picture, I'll be a laughingstock—a bigger one than I am right now.

She forced herself to return to her online search—and regretted it immediately. The headlines screamed about her being a drunk and a witch at work.

Jett slouched down in her chair.

I'm ruined. All my hard work...

Channel 10 and Channel 6 were leading the charge, but the online gossip columns were right behind them. A few clicks showed that the stories were anonymously sourced, but it was still a shock to see so many quotes all creating the same narrative.

A drunk.

An egomaniacal prima donna.

A witch who was impossible to work with and who had it coming.

Jett clutched her stomach, a feeling of nausea sweeping over her. Each headline was like a gut punch; every quote, a painful knife to the heart.

She read through them for the better part of an hour, unable to stop herself, and feeling worse and worse with each story she consumed. And there were so many! She sunk lower and lower in her chair. Anonymous sources, alleging to be people close to her, were savaging her in the press.

So... my friends at work are saying these things?

What kind of person am I if my friends would say such lies?

Paranoia set in as she mentally scrolled through the roster of people she trusted and cared about, and who she thought trusted and cared about her. She questioned whether she had been so delusional as to totally misconstrue months and even years' worth of conversations. The tiniest of possible incidents came roaring back into her thoughts for scrutiny.

It was too much. On the verge of tears, she reached for the button on the side of her computer to power it down. As she did, her eye caught some peculiar phrasing in a quote from one of the anonymous sources. It contained the same few lines she'd seen in another article. Scrolling back through the sites, she saw the same phrases being repeated over and over in every article. She jumped from tab to tab, finding the quotes and lining them up.

They were almost all identical. Not just close, but exact—and purportedly from different "anonymous" people. They had allegedly worked at Miami 5... but it now seemed more likely that the quotes had been created by one person with an agenda.

Being in the business, she recognized an orchestrated smear campaign when she saw one.

Jett bolted upright, switching modes from punching bag to prize fighter.

Who would want to attack and embarrass me?

That was easy: lots of people. Her investigative journalism exposés had left a pile of corrupt politicians and negligent business people in its wake. Some lost their jobs; others went to prison.

But they wouldn't be just sitting around, waiting to launch an attack today. Not like this.

She had been asking herself those questions, but they were the wrong ones. She didn't need to answer why someone was trying to specifically hurt her; that was a by-product of the smear campaign.

The actual things she'd done wrong—the live, on-air fight and ensuing in-studio riot—were bad enough. There was no reason to pile on after she'd been terminated, so the smear was for something else.

She returned to her investigative reporter mindset.

Someone is pushing this false information. Why?

Because they benefit from it being out there.

She stood up, grabbing a pencil and notepad. Pacing around her living room, she tapped the pencil against her chin, talking out loud like she was interrogating an invisible witness.

"Who benefits from incorrect information being out there about me?" She shook her head. That wasn't precise enough. "Who benefits from smearing *me*?"

Better.

Drill down further.

"Who benefits from smearing me *today*?"

That was it.

That was the real question.

And there were only a handful of choices.

Few people had power and connections for this kind of campaign. One was Kendall Marks, the state senator—and that was an unlikely choice, because if the hit job was tracked back to him, his political career would be over.

That left Martin Brennan and Mr. Nesmith.

In hindsight, it wasn't even a hard puzzle to solve, but the personal nature of the attacks had kept her unfocused and looking at the wrong things. According to Martin, Mr. Nesmith was embarrassed

TIFFANY LYNN IS MISSING

about the fight; firing Jett removed the source of the embarrassment. It would also serve as a little payback for embarrassing Nesmith's friend, the senator. Putting out stories that were backfilled with a source "close to Jett" and having anonymous "co-workers" coming forward to say Jett had been a problem for a while, that made it appear like Nesmith and Brennan were dealing with a negative situation and let them say today's on-air fight was the last straw. Brennan simply did the dirty work of terminating her and arranging the smear. Throw in rumors about alcoholism, and "co-workers" dishing about how they hated working with her, and the general public would quickly become sated. The phony, salacious story would distract audiences from the truth. They'd shrug their shoulders and decide they were wrong about liking and trusting Jett.

What a simple—and effective—plan.

As soon as people learned about the fight, they'd see the firing and get the subsequent stories about the "ongoing problems." Nesmith and Brennan would end up looking like victims of an out-of-control TV show host.

I'd agree, if any of that were true.

She stared out at the city of Miami, balling her hands into fists.

I should hire an attorney and sue them! The anonymous sources will be easy enough to discredit, and the smear campaign is obviously coordinated.

It would be easy...

...if I could afford an attorney.

Her gut clenched again. Money would be tight until she got another job, and another job might be hard to arrange while she was in the headlines as a power-crazy diva.

Maybe impossible.

It could be months, maybe years. TV could be very unforgiving, and fighting back the wrong way would make her look petty and weak, doing further damage.

Jett put her hand to her eyes to prevent herself from crying—and launched a bolt of pain through her aching sinuses. She flung the notepad across the room and sat down on the couch, leaning her head back and closing her eyes.

Think.

Be tough. Distance yourself from the emotion of the situation and think about a strategy.

And do it quickly, because your reputation is going up in flames with each passing minute.

Or was it?

Maybe the public was smart enough to know she was being set up.

But nobody made me put that Nazi on the set with a black senator. I came up with that one.

"Ugh!" She pounded the sofa cushion.

Her phone pinged with an Instagram private message alert.

Oh, no. The media is starting to track me down!

She jumped up from the couch and ran to her desk, grabbing the phone. There were two direct message alerts on the screen, one from Carmen and one from Gloria.

They're friends... right?

TIFFANY LYNN IS MISSING

Pursing her lip, she opened the app and read them.

Carmen's first direct message made Jett smile: *Screw what that station said, we know it's all lies. Come on, we'll pick you up at eight and drink away your misery. Don't sit home and sulk. That's how the terrorists win.*

Jett typed a reply. *Have you already been drinking?*

Her friend's response was quick: *I can neither confirm nor denay that allegation, coneselor, see you at eight. Bahama Breeze in Coconut Grove.*

Jett chuckled at the typos and took a breath of relief. Maybe the whole world didn't believe everything they read.

Gloria's message was a lot like Carmen's. Friends were reaching out—real friends—and it helped. Updating her social media information had worked. But she didn't agree to go out with them, at least not yet. Appearing at a bar, in public, was a risk—especially after Jett had been accused of being an alcoholic. On the other hand, if any local paparazzi showed up in an attempt to embarrass her, she'd be able to show she *wasn't* a drunk. And she'd be able to show she didn't emerge unscathed from the fight drama on her show; her two black eyes might actually garner some sympathy.

Even if she didn't go out tonight, she'd have to go out *somewhere* eventually. Maybe sooner was better than later.

There were pros and cons to doing either. But what gnawed at her insides was the thought that the smear campaign might not be over. There were personal things she wasn't ready to have known publicly.

Her phone rang with the sound of an incoming FaceTime call. Rico Torres' name appeared on the screen.

Jett wiped her nose and sat down, laying the phone face-up on top of the desk so its camera viewed only the ceiling, then pressed the green button.

"Hey." Jett's voice was thick from emotion.

"Hey," Rico said. "I heard about what happened and I saw the internet. Guess I don't have to ask how your day's going."

"Please don't. I cried my way through a whole box of tissues. Now I'm starting on toilet paper."

Rico exhaled slowly. "Yeah... I know it doesn't feel like it right now, but trust me, this is going to pass."

"You know what sucks the most?" Jett threw her hands out. "My name and reputation being publicly trashed by people who were supposed to be my friends!"

"No, no. Your friends would never say that stuff about you."

"But the people reading this stuff don't know that. They're going to believe the lies they're being fed!"

On the phone screen, Rico rubbed his chin. "Some will believe different parts of it, but... most people won't want to believe it. They'll want to hear your side, and you need to get a statement out there so they can. Fast forward six months or a year,

TIFFANY LYNN IS MISSING

everyone will have forgotten all about it and they'll welcome you back."

"Six months!" Jett squeezed her eyes shut and lowered her head to the table. "What am I supposed to do for six months? Everyone hates me because I'm such a... a crazed prima donna!"

"First," Rico said, "stay off the internet. Second, you're a lawyer. Get a statement together. And then hire a high-profile PR person to do some counter-programming."

"I... can't. Martin held my paycheck and wants me to reimburse the station for damages to the set." Jett glanced around her residence. "I used my entire savings to move into this overpriced apartment because my agent said I had an iron clad contract! I can't even make next month's payment."

"Oh, for... Jett, you've got a spine of steel—for everybody but yourself. You're a recovering lawyer, for Pete's sake. Fight Brennan and his ridiculous allegations!"

She nodded. "I will, I will. I just... I need a little time to get my head straight."

"And don't worry about any social media crap right now. Distract yourself with something else."

"That's easy for you to say. You don't..." She folded her arms, raising a trembling finger to her mouth and biting the nail. "I'm sorry. You called to help me and I'm unleashing on you. I guess I am a crazy diva prima donna."

Rico chuckled. "Try this. Once upon a time, you were a pretty amazing lawyer. If the tables were reversed and I was in your situation, what advice would you give me?"

"Stay off the internet, that's for sure." Jett sighed. "Put a statement together, take some time off and think up a strategy for coming back stronger than ever."

"That sounds like a good plan. Wish I'd have thought of it."

Sitting back, she stared at the phone. "I've been getting messages from Carmen and some of the people at the station. They want to take me out to get drunk tonight."

"That sounds like a good plan, too," Rico said. "Why don't you do that, and I'll come by tomorrow before you go to the gym and help you update your video clips?"

She frowned. "Don't you have to work tomorrow?"

"Uh…" Rico scrunched up his nose. "Martin met with me after he went scorched-earth on you. I got a two-day holiday from Miami 5."

Jett gasped. "You got suspended?"

"Only for two days—so I can 'cool down.' It's his passive-aggressive way of sending a message to everyone at the station." Rico waved a hand. "Don't worry, it won't stick—but it will give me a little time to sit down and update your reel with all your latest stuff. It's probably been six months since you've updated your videos, and you've done a lot of great stuff since then."

"Okay." Jett tapped her chin with a finger. "I usually go to the gym at nine."

TIFFANY LYNN IS MISSING

"How about I come over at seven, then? Does that work?"

"Come at eight. I may skip the gym. Especially if I go out with Carmen."

"Okay," Rico said. "And listen, when it comes to investigative reporting, you're the real deal. You'll be on the air again in no time."

"Yeah, well, when that happens, then we'll talk." She lowered her voice and picked up the phone. "Martin might not have released all his bombs yet, and other stations can be pretty cautious when it comes to bringing on new people, especially hosts. If he hires a private investigator, it won't be very difficult to embarrass me with... you know."

"Don't worry about that stuff." Rico shook his head. "Nobody cares."

"You can afford to say that." She looked away. "I can't."

"Where's he going to find it? That didn't come up in your divorce, and once you get to the network level, your personal life won't matter."

Jett sighed. "But it's out there. One day it might not matter, but right now I'm not at a network. I'm not even on local TV. So, it matters."

"Wow, Martin really got to you," Rico said. "I've never seen you this way before."

"I'm just saying, there could be a phase two coming if he wants to hurt me more." Jett rubbed her abdomen, wincing. "It wouldn't take that much digging."

Rico shook his head. "He won't do that. You're just being paranoid. You need a break to let off some steam. Go out with Carmen and the gang and have some drinks. They're safe." He smiled. "I'll see you in the morning. Tomorrow will be better, I promise."

CHAPTER 8

The setting sun glowed a dim yellow behind the peaks of the Rocky Mountains and cast a gray pallor onto objects below. Ashley Wells adjusted her phone's earpiece as she drove her rental car into a small public parking lot. Across a small span of wide sidewalks, a one-story, beige-gray structure stood. Her GPS interrupted her conversation to announce the vehicle's arrival at her destination.

She parked the car and switched off the engine, staring out at the bleak, overcast sky as she wrapped up the call. "I just arrived. I'd like you to get here as soon as possible."

Ashley removed her ear bud and plucked her phone from the cup holder, dropping them into her purse on the passenger seat. The high desert wind carried a few snowflakes across the windshield.

It could have passed for a small school or an office. It had the look of government construction—bland, utilitarian and permanent, with no more windows than was absolutely necessary, and formed out of beige concrete blocks and dull, red bricks. Small plant beds held little, round evergreen bushes, surrounded by light gray rocks, neatly framed by a raised concrete border. Patches of snow huddled next to the edges of the building and under a tree here and there where the light couldn't reach them. The grassy areas around the building had been cut short at some point and were mostly brown, not yet having reawakened from winter dormancy by the coming spring thaw.

The entire place looked new and clean and cold and sterile.

Unfriendly. Unwelcoming.

A grim sense of dread filled her. She'd mostly managed to avoid it until now. There had been flights to catch and programming changes to make, cars to rent and highways to drive. But with all that done, only one final task remained undone.

The one awaiting her inside.

Taking a deep breath, she slipped her hand over the door latch and opened the rental car door.

The Colorado wind was dry and sharp, slicing through her Florida clothing as if it wasn't there. Sweaters and jeans that worked well during the sunshine state's winters did little against the jarring cold of the mountains' gusts. With the sunset, the temperature dropped precipitously, and the chill cut straight through everything. The warmth of the rental car was sucked out into the fading light.

Her breath formed white clouds that streaked past her shoulder in the unceasing breeze. Ashley hunched her shoulders and pulled her jacket tight as

TIFFANY LYNN IS MISSING

she exited the vehicle. The dry air and low humidity immediately assaulted her nose and eyes. She walked quickly, her fingertips turning pale in the twenty or so seconds it took to get from the parking lot to the front doors of the facility. There, on the grass, under the young maple trees and sapling oaks, a plain blue sign greeted her and anyone else unfortunate enough to have to make the journey to this cold, quiet location.

Brimstone County Coroner's Office.

She pulled open the door, a blast of warm air *whooshing* over her from an air exchanger mounted on the ceiling. The entrance rug was damp from people tracking in snow.

Across the lobby's linoleum floor was a stark, gray counter and several unmanned desk chairs. The clock on the wall said 5:13, but the sheriff had assured her that someone would be there to meet her—and someone was. The sheriff.

He lumbered around the corner, tall, broad-shouldered, and clean-shaven, his uniform still almost completely unwrinkled at the end of this long day. "Ma'am." He extended his hand, his voice solid and deep. "Clint Dalton, Brimstone County Sheriff. I'm very sorry for your loss."

Ashley nodded, shaking his large, firm hand. "I appreciate you seeing me on such short notice. I spoke with James Turley from Alcott funeral home. He said he would be able to come by tonight if... if we were to…"

"Yes, ma'am." Dalton hooked his thumbs into his wide utility belt. "Jim's a good man."

"He said he could come to help arrange the transportation release. I'd... like my daughter to return to Florida with me as soon as possible."

"I understand."

A small man in a white lab coat entered the lobby from the hallway. The sheriff gestured to him. "This is Dr. Bennet, our county coroner."

Ashley shook the doctor's hand.

"If you'd follow me," he said, "I'll take you and the sheriff to a private room where you can view the deceased."

Pressing her hands together, Ashley massaged one thumb and then the other. "Of course."

"We'd also like a DNA sample from you, ma'am, for matching purposes. It's done with a simple mouth swab."

The hallway was impeccably clean and bright. Its white walls and tile floors were a stark contrast to the foreboding Ashley carried inside her.

Halfway down the corridor, the doctor stopped and opened a door to a small room with half a dozen seats and a TV monitor. A small table in the corner held a box of tissues.

"What's this?" Ashley said.

Dr. Bennet held the door open for her from the hallway. "We typically seat the family members here, and when they are sufficiently prepared, we can bring the face of the deceased up on this monitor." He pointed to a TV mounted high on the wall. "Many people find this method to be... less impactful."

"No." Ashley frowned. "I'm not viewing my daughter on a TV screen." She turned to the sheriff. "I will see her face."

TIFFANY LYNN IS MISSING

"Doc..." Dalton rested a hand on his hip and stroked his chin. "The deceased was found in pristine condition. I think Mrs. Wells is okay to come into the examining room."

"Okay, Clint." He looked at Ashley. "This way, please, ma'am."

She followed him through a set of double doors with a wide, vertical gasket between them. The examining room was large and cool, with small windows at the top of the walls and rows of long fluorescent lights hanging from the ceiling. The pungent smell of cleaning alcohol filled the room, along with the acrid stench of formaldehyde and embalming fluids. Ashley's initial reaction was to not try to breathe too deeply and keep the foul odors out of her lungs. It brought back a rush of awkward memories of grade school dissections of worms, frogs, and a fetal pig—and the inability to eat meat for weeks after.

Thirteen-year-old Ashley flinched as her mother berated her, slamming a wooden spoon down onto the girl's arm. Ashley jumped back, staring at the cold pork chop on her plate. Tears streamed down her quivering cheeks as each of her mother's stinging blows turned her arm redder and redder.

But she would not pick up her fork. She couldn't. All she could envision was the dissected guts of the fetal pig at school. The formaldehyde permeated her nose, even at dinner, like it had somehow seeped into her clothing and hair, the way her mother's cigarette smoke did.

Ashley squirmed on the wobbly wooden chair, lowering her hands to the hem of her threadbare uniform skirt. She hated wearing the other girls' discarded uniforms, the ones that had been donated by the older girls that attended the school. She was embarrassed to attend Catholic school at all; her family wasn't Catholic. It was a good school, and it was close by, but all the other kids knew she was only there as a charity case. Kitchen workers at St. Margaret's, like all school employees, were granted free tuition.

If they knew her mother stole food from the kitchen, like tonight's pork chops, the nightmare might all come to an end. But then what?

She imagined her mother looking away for a moment and giving Ashley a chance to slip the cold piece of meat through the hole in the trailer's floor.

"We don't have money to waste on picky eaters," her mother screamed. "That's for spoiled, rich brats. Now, eat!"

The spoon hit Ashley on the side of the head. Her ear exploded in pain, swelling and growing hot.

She jumped up and raced away from the table. Covering her throbbing ear, Ashley flung open the flimsy screen door and leaped down the crumbling wooden steps as her mother shouted after her.

It didn't matter where she ran—to the treehouse on the vacant lot at the end of the road, or the covered slide at the park, or maybe Mrs. Carlin's... Her mother would be normal again in the morning when it was time to go to school. With the right shirt, the welts and bruises wouldn't show, and Sister Alexia wouldn't file a report.

Reports only caused things to get worse.

TIFFANY LYNN IS MISSING

Ashley had learned. She could keep quiet, and she could keep away for as long as it took.

She learned a lot of things.

"Mrs. Wells?" The doctor leaned into Ashley's line of sight.

She shook her head, blinking several times. "Yes?"

He stepped back. A sheet on a slab covered a petite human body. "Whenever you're ready, ma'am. Take your time."

"I'm ready." Ashley stood up straight and took a deep breath of the formaldehyde-laden air. Her pulse throbbed in her ears. "Do it now."

The coroner eased back the white sheet, revealing the face of the beautiful young woman underneath.

The long, blonde hair had been cleaned and dried, but not styled in the manner her daughter wore it—although lately that seemed to change from month to month. The big, brown eyes that Ashley had known were now closed and unmoving, like the paint on a statue; there was none of the sparkle and energy the beautiful face once possessed. The high cheek bones and youthful, unblemished skin were still there, and the dainty nose, but without the color and fullness they should contain.

Ashley held rigid, forcing herself to take short, shallow breaths, her fingers digging into the leather of the purse she clutched at her abdomen. Other than that, she displayed no outward emotion.

The young woman before them on the slab was dead, and she looked like it. No amount of tears would change that.

"That is my daughter," Ashley uttered.

Then she burst into tears.

Sheriff Dalton put his hand to her shoulder, and she leaned into him, a grief-stricken mother overwhelmed by the realization of death upon her child, wailing and sobbing in unbridled agony like she hadn't understood the truth until that very minute.

CHAPTER 9

The music at Club Vogue blasted across the crowded dance floor. Gloria and a few of Jett's other former co-workers swayed in rhythm to the beat with several well-tailored young gentlemen in expensive suits. Jett and Carmen sat at the bar.

Carmen's outfit consisted of four-inch heels, a tight, gold sequin skirt, and a low-cut white silk blouse. Her long, dark mane was teased out enough for a strut on the catwalks of Milan. Jett looked sexy and stylish in her black dress, but gave the appearance she might have taken a wrong turn on the way to a black tie fundraiser. She glanced in the mirror behind the bar. Several coats of concealer and the club's low lights helped obscure her two black eyes.

"You should get out on the dance floor," Carmen shouted, barely audible over the music. "Go move around a little. You'll feel better."

Shrugging, Jett stared at her untouched drink. "I don't know."

"You're the hottest girl in this whole club—everybody can see that." Carmen put her hand on Jett's, getting up from her stool. "I'm sure one of these rich lawyers or stockbrokers would like to show you his moves. They've sure been staring at you all night. I'm like the invisible woman next to you." She tugged Jett's arm and took a step toward the dance floor.

Jett gave her friend a half frown, gently pulling her hand away. "Maybe later."

"Okay." Carmen took some cash from her tiny, gold sequin purse. "Order a fresh drink. That one has turned to water." She picked up Jett's cocktail and moved it away. Waving to the bartender, Carmen dropped a few bills next to the glass and turned to face Jett. "Do you mind if I go dance? Just for one song?"

"No, it's fine." Jett clasped her hands in her lap. "Go."

Smiling, Carmen danced her way through the crowd to join her friends. Jett stared at them as they bumped and swayed, picking up partners as colored lights beamed across the room in time to the music.

Carmen's one song turned to a second, and then a third.

Sighing, Jett turned back around and put an elbow on the bar, resting her chin on her hand.

TIFFANY LYNN IS MISSING

The bartender picked up Jett's discarded drink and emptied it into the bar sink. She was slender and toned, with long black hair. A black ribbon choker necklace graced her neck, and she wore lavender colored contact lenses.

She glanced at Jett as she dropped ice cubes into a clean cocktail glass. "No offense, but you are too pretty to be sulking in here by yourself."

"Well, I had quite a day," Jett said. "Which you already probably know."

"Nope. I'm not psychic." The bartender took a towel and wiped the area in front of Jett, then placed another cocktail napkin down. "What happened?"

Jett cocked her head, her mouth dropping open.

Shrugging, the bartender set a fresh drink in front of Jett. "Not everybody watches TV."

"But then how would you even know I'm *on* TV?"

"I know you're on the news," she said. "There's a billboard with your picture on it over on Seventh Avenue. I just don't watch TV."

Nodding, Jett took her drink in her hand. "I like your eyes—your contacts. They're pretty."

The bartender tossed her bar towel into the little sink, lingering in front of Jett. "My shift is ending. Wanna take a walk and tell me your problems?"

Jett looked away, toying with the edge of her purse. "I wouldn't want to bore you."

"I'm Maria. And you won't bore me. I'm a good listener. It kinda comes with the territory."

Maria picked up Jett's purse. "They sell cigarettes at the store on the corner. We can share one."

"I don't smoke," Jett said, rising.

Maria nodded. "Neither do I."

CHAPTER 10

Aaron checked his watch for the third time in five minutes. On the volleyball court, the game was tied. The next point would decide which group of high school seniors advanced to the finals.

And I have somewhere I need to get to.

A long-legged teenager in a blue-on-blue uniform wiped her brow, her blonde ponytail hanging down to her butt. She spun the ball in her hands, backing up ten feet past the blue line on the hardwood surface. Bouncing the ball twice, she scanned the opponents' positions.

On the other side of the net, the girls in red shirts eyed the opposing team's server, crouching or raising hands as their position required. Coach Vellmer called out a last-minute adjustment; Aaron's daughter Mattsie shifted to her left. Her twin sister Monie stepped forward a few inches.

The auditorium fell silent.

The ponytailed server raced forward, tossing the ball high and leaping up to meet it. With a sharp grunt, she blasted the volleyball over the net on a fast, low arc, the backspin carrying it downward at a sharp angle.

Mattsie dived forward, barely getting a forearm under the white streak and keeping it from hitting the floor. The ball popped straight up, going eight or ten feet into the air as Mattsie's momentum carried her to the sidelines. Monie jumped high over her sister, chopping the ball as it started its descent and smashing it back across the net. As several blue uniforms careened toward the missile, it shot past their outstretched hands and landed in the far corner of the court before sailing out of bounds.

Aaron and the crowd on his side of the auditorium leaped to their feet, erupting in cheers and applause.

"Falcons win!" the PA announcer shouted. "And the home team advances to the finals."

On the court, Mattsie and her teammates jumped up and down, high-fiving each other as they pulled Mattsie to her feet. The opposing coach jogged forward to shake hands with Coach Vellmer as the two teams lined up in rows to congratulate each other.

Standing, Aaron glanced at his watch again. He stepped over the row of seats in front of him and walked to the edge of the volleyball court, a wide grin etched onto his face.

Mattsie spotted him first, rushing forward and throwing her arms around him. "Dad, we won! We're going to the championships!"

TIFFANY LYNN IS MISSING

Monie was on them a second later, plunging into her sister and father and practically knocking them over. "Did you see Mattsie's save?"

"I did," Aaron said. "Just barely. You're pretty fast."

Mattsie looked up at her father. "We're going to Pizza Dan's to celebrate. Can you come?"

"Uh, I don't think so." He checked his watch. "I have a late meeting."

"Please?" Monie squeezed him harder. "It might be our last victory of the season. We may not win next week."

The blonde girl with the long ponytail walked up to Mattsie. "Nice job, Wells. I didn't think you could stretch that far."

"I can't." Mattsie smiled. "I'll be sore for a week."

Aaron stepped back, looking at his daughter. "Did you get hurt?"

"Dad, stop."

"Ladies!" Coach Vellmer called to his players from center court. "Team picture by the net." As the girls ran onto the hardwood, the coach peered at the proud father. "Aaron—will you be joining us for the victory celebration?"

Aaron shook his head. "I can't, Jason. Late meeting."

"Ooh, do you have a date?" Mattsie winked.

Monie raised her eyebrows. "You think?"

"No." Mattsie cupped a hand to her mouth, pretending to whisper. "Dad never goes on any dates."

Aaron winced. "Please, let's focus on something else besides my social life. It's a business meeting."

Coach Vellmer smiled. "Aaron, if you don't come to the victory party, who's going to pick up the tab?"

His sixteen-year-olds clasped their hands together, leaning shoulder to shoulder at center court. "Pleeeease daddy?"

Looking down, Aaron put his hand to his forehead and swiped down over his face. When he looked up, he broke into a grin. "Ohhh, okay."

Monie and Mattsie cheered, rushing forward to hug him again.

He patted their heads and sent them back to the team. "But only for a few minutes."

* * * * *

At the restaurant, Aaron sipped ice water as a second pitcher of soda was delivered to the table. The six teammates seemed to all thrust their red plastic glasses under the pouring spout at the same time.

Leaning forward, Aaron placed his elbows on the red and white checkered tablecloth and folded his arms, speaking loud enough to be heard in the crowded dining room. "What do you think, Coach? How does the team look for next week?"

Vellmer took a sip of his beer. "I like our chances, but… Andalusia High is very good. They play a mixed pattern with a lot of odd rotations."

The door to Pizza Dan's opened and a stream of girls in blue jerseys entered, milling about near the hostess podium. As their coach and some parents came in behind them, the girls made eye contact with

TIFFANY LYNN IS MISSING

the Falcons team and turned back around, walking past the adults to the exit.

"Hold on, Jason." Aaron got to his feet, waving to the opposing volleyball team. "Coach, ladies—please, join us."

"Dad!" Mattsie whispered.

The crowded restaurant grew quiet.

Aaron looked at her. "Hey, be a good winner." He walked toward the door, smiling. "We would love for you to be our guests tonight."

"Thanks, Mr. Wells..." The coach put his hands up. "But I don't think..."

"Call me Aaron." He shook the coach's hand and looked at the players. "Getting beaten in a hard-fought match never feels good, but I always feel like if it has to happen, it helps to know it was to a tough opponent, and not some crappy team that had a lucky night." He glanced at the Falcons' table. "When I win, I want my opponents to have pushed me to give my absolute best, forcing me to exceed myself. You did that." Eyeing the girls of the losing team, he nodded. "This was a tied match until the very last point, so it could just as easily have been you advancing and not us. That's what I call a very worthy opponent—and one worth celebrating with. If we played you again tomorrow, I doubt we'd be victorious. Please be our guests."

He looked over at Mattsie. She stood, peering at the blonde girl with the long ponytail. "Dottie, you can sit here, next to me."

The other Falcons moved their plates and made room for the girls from the other team.

"Aaron," Coach Vellmer said, "you might have a future in politics."

"Oh, I hope not." Aaron made an exaggerated grimace. "Besides, they played Andalusia during the regular season. Their input could help you win next week."

* * * * *

The drive from Pizza Dan's to Wildfire Resort took about twenty minutes. Light, puffy snowflakes fell on Aaron's car the entire way, accumulating on the grass but melting as soon as they hit the road. Parking in his reserved spot, he checked the time and went in through the rear entrance.

His master key card opened the door lock on Presidente three. The door eased open, revealing the luxurious suite inside.

The model suites at Wildfire Resort were ornate and overdone for a reason. Displaying such conspicuous consumption—gold-plated bathroom sinks, Tiffany crystal chandeliers, carved wood living room ceilings—was a gaudy but necessary way of demonstrating to rich buyers that they were not going to keep up with the Joneses by simply moving in. Wildfire would be a party ground of Hollywood stars and New York moguls, and each one had to decorate their suite better than the next. Overdoing the models was merely a way of making that point in a subtle yet obvious way.

The Presidente suites were also used to impress important clients or to shower largesse on a friend, and sometimes to sway a reporter into seeing a story in a light that was more preferential to the

TIFFANY LYNN IS MISSING

company. Occasionally, a board member might stay in one.

Sometimes, the suites served other business purposes.

Tonight, the by-appointment-only Presidente three was quiet and almost completely dark, but the blue Louis Vuitton suitcase in the middle of the living room—with its Delta Airlines baggage claim tags still attached—meant that his sister was not far away. A purse lay on the granite kitchen counter next to a set of rental car keys; a sole light streamed outward from the master bedroom.

Aaron stood in the foyer, the polished marble floor reflecting the soft light as it bounced off the hall ceiling.

A shadow darkened the reflection. Aaron looked up to see a slim, hourglass-shaped silhouette standing in the master bedroom doorway.

"Hello, little brother." Ashley held a short, crystal tumbler in her hand. The ice clinked as his twin sister pointed the glass at him. "How did you know I was here?"

Slipping his hands into his pockets, Aaron stepped into the living room. "I'm in charge of the resort, so I know what goes on in it." He glanced at her, shaking his head. "Jane Doe? Really? It's like you were announcing your arrival with a bullhorn."

Ashley sauntered toward him, wearing a black silk robe pulled tight at the waist. Her hair was wet, as if she had just gotten out of the shower. "So sly, aren't you? Always knowing everything about everyone."

"Let's not play these games. Not tonight."

She smirked. "Why would tonight be any different?"

"Oh, so you're just in Colorado on a whim, then? Not because you got a phone call?"

Ashley narrowed her eyes. "How would you know about any calls I received, Aaron?"

He pursed his lips, assessing the situation. His sister was allowed to be drunk. The news she'd received would be hard for any parent to take, and numbing the pain with a few drinks wasn't off limits. But things happened when people drank.

She doesn't seem drunk. Not yet, anyway. But she's on her way.

Aaron adjusted a vase on the coffee table. "You can't be a TV star and run a small network with over a hundred employees and then collapse on the floor and think no one would call me about it. I worked at the station for too many years."

"Loyalty. Of course." She shook her head. "And of course they called you." Raising her glass, she took a sip of her drink. "So, you don't know why I'm here?"

Aaron sighed. "I can listen to gossip from Orlando, or what my employees out here think happened—or I can ask the source."

He knew what Philson had told him, but he needed to act like he didn't—at least for now.

Ashley walked to the kitchen, setting her empty glass on the counter. "Everybody always says the same thing about me when something happens. 'She's so cold. Why doesn't she react with more emotion?' When something good happens, I don't smile enough for them. When something bad

TIFFANY LYNN IS MISSING

happens, I'm not sad enough. My viewers love me, but to my employees and members of the press—to the people who *know* me—I'm a witch with a cast-iron heart." She opened a cabinet and pulled out a bottle of scotch. "Why is that?"

"You know why."

Ashley wagged a finger at her brother. "But they don't say that about you. Everybody loves you."

"Not everybody." He turned to face her.

Ashley splashed scotch into her glass and picked it up, cradling it with both hands. "You love me, don't you, little brother?"

"Of course I do."

"And I love you—like a brother." She burst out laughing, then took another drink. Staring at the window, her face fell. "I'm here because she's here. They found her."

"Tiffany Lynn?" Aaron looked at his sister. "Is she all right?"

She glared at him. "You know she's not. Your spies already told you." Closing her eyes, she tilted her head back and let her wet locks cascade over her shoulders. "My beautiful daughter is... with the angels, Aaron. She's in Heaven, at twenty-two." She sniffled, looking at him with tear-filled eyes. "And you knew that, but you made me say it anyway—so who's playing games?"

"I'm sorry." He went to his sister and put his arms around her. The muscles in her back and shoulders softened, and she put her head on his shoulder. As she wrapped her arms around him, she squeezed him tight, holding on like she was afraid to let go. He put his cheek to the back of her head, her wet hair cold against his skin. "I heard things, but I couldn't be sure. I guess I didn't want to be sure. Not about something like that."

She let out a whimper, burying her face in his chest. "It hurts so much." Her words were muffled through the fabric of his suit. "My heart is breaking, Aaron. I can feel it ripping right in half, it hurts so much."

He held her, patting her back and, letting her cry. The powerful woman the world knew was just a simple, grieving mother.

When the tears had finally stopped, he took her hand and eased her onto the sofa, taking a seat in the adjoining chair. She looked twenty years older than when he saw her a week ago, and she'd aged twenty more years before that, with the news of her daughter going missing. It was strain from the weeks of worry and uncertainty and anger, culminating in such terrible, final news—and the immeasurable pain it brought with it.

Many times during those weeks, he'd climbed into bed and stared at the ceiling, wondering what more he could do; wondering what he *would* do if it were one of his daughters that had disappeared. The very thought hurt him to his core. He'd helped as best he could, visiting Florida and trying to be supportive, almost as a hedge against karma.

"How did it happen?" Aaron whispered. "Do they know?"

Ashley sagged back into the couch, her eyes staring off toward the window. "She was walking with two friends on a high, snowy trail by Lake Brimstone, and she slipped. She slid a hundred feet

TIFFANY LYNN IS MISSING

down the cliff and went through the ice at the bottom. By the time anyone got to her, she had drowned."

"What, were they drinking?" Aaron's voice was soft, his tone genuinely curious. Tiffany Lynn was an athlete—graceful, and not prone to clumsiness. "And who were these friends? How did she manage to... to just *fall* like that?"

Ashley sniffled, wiping a finger under her nose. Her eyes were big and beautiful, as always, but rimmed in red from the crying. "She was with her boyfriend Remy Delphine and a local girl they knew, Brandy Bergeron, from out here. The sheriff played me the body cam footage from when he interviewed them at the lake." Ashley shrugged. "They both said she was goofing off too close to the edge, and just went over. Even then, they said it didn't seem like a bad fall. They were expecting her to stop sliding and stand up, and climb back up to them. But... she just kept sliding. When she hit the ice, she went right through, and... that was it. She never came up. The coroner said the water was so cold, her muscles locked up from the sudden shock. Everything just stops. The lungs, the heart... She just stopped breathing and died."

She lifted her gaze to Aaron.

"Her friends said she didn't even act very scared when she fell. She didn't scream or shout, she just... went with it. Like she was almost having fun."

"And that's it?" Aaron frowned. "The police talked to these friends and just took their word for it?"

"No." Ashley waved her hand back and forth, sinking lower into the couch. The alcohol was hitting her. "They talked to the two friends, a hunter who was nearby, and a group of teenagers who were trying to do some ice fishing. The teenagers were the ones who got to her first. The one boy said her jacket was so waterlogged, it was like she was wearing weights. He couldn't pull her out by himself. But they got to her fast, staying on the solid part of the ice, and when they were close enough, he jumped in. He was wearing waders up to his chest, and said the water was only waist deep, but he struggled to get her out because of how heavy her coat made her." Ashley sighed, lowering her voice. "He got really scared when he saw her face. She was unresponsive, but her face was white as a sheet. When they finally got her out, there were leaves and twigs stuck in her hair, and little pieces of ice stuck to her cheeks." Ashley's voice wavered. "Can you imagine? Being so cold that ice is frozen to your face?"

She let out an involuntary sob, her words catching in her throat.

"You don't have to say any more." Aaron patted her hand. "Not if you don't want to. I get the picture."

"The kids did CPR, the paramedics tried... no one could revive her. They pronounced her dead on the scene. She laid there on the cold, hard gravel and rocks, all wet and..." She swallowed hard. "One minute she was alive and joking around, and the next, she was gone." She lifted her eyes to meet his. "Why is our family meant to suffer so much? It never ends."

Aaron wrapped his hand around Ashley's. "Come on, come with me to the house. Don't stay here, all alone."

TIFFANY LYNN IS MISSING

Ashley dropped her head onto her brother's hand. Her tears were warm on his skin. "Aaron, the great protector." She sighed. "I had to identify my baby's body, little brother. Out here, in Colorado." Ashley's grip grew tighter. "She ran to you, Aaron. Out here. Why? For protection?"

She sat upright, shoving his hand away and scowling. "Was I such a lousy mother? Why didn't you tell me my daughter was here?"

He shrugged, shaking his head. "I didn't know where she was."

"No!" Ashley pulled away, jumping off the sofa and walking backwards as she held her glass out. She pointed at Aaron. "Don't lie. You knew she'd turn up here eventually, running to Uncle Aaron. How much money did you give her to escape from me, her evil mother?"

"Stop that." Aaron stood. "I didn't give her any money. She—"

"Don't lie!" Ashley threw her glass across the room, smashing it into the marble tile of the kitchen. Ice and shattered glass skittered away in all directions. She breathed hard, glaring at him. "I can always tell when someone lies to me, little brother—just like you can. We're well-versed in it, from necessity. Experts in secrets and cruelty in the dark, but we excel at telling lies and detecting them, and you're lying right now."

Aaron maintained his composure. His sister was prone to theatrical outbursts, but sometimes they weren't theatrical. Some went straight to the heart; some dredged up the horrible memories he wanted kept in the past.

"I didn't know she was here," he said. "I wouldn't have flown to Florida three times to help look for her if I knew she was here. But... we did discover something. Tiffany Lynn took thirty thousand dollars from a company account." He peered at his sister. "She *stole* it, from petty cash, using the passwords from when she worked here last summer. Giselle spotted it right away, but assumed it was for one of our off-the-books situations, so she didn't mention it until I requested a check this morning that would have overdrawn the account. It looks like Tiffany Lynn wired the money to a cash advance place downtown. When we called, they said it was a stopover transfer—that the funds were being transferred to the recipient somewhere else, and maybe transferred again after that. They wouldn't say where." He shrugged. "Privacy act stuff. She could have been anywhere. You said she was in Florida, so..."

Ashley shook her head. "You covered for her."

"I didn't. She knew we were all looking for her. She certainly had to know we'd catch thirty thousand dollars going missing. She wanted to be found."

"By *you*."

"Even if that's true, does it matter?" Aaron held his hands out at his sides. "Do you think I was going to hide her from you?"

"No, it doesn't matter." Ashley looked down. "Not anymore."

"Why are you staying here? You've suffered a terrible loss. We all have." He stepped toward the

TIFFANY LYNN IS MISSING

kitchen. "You should be with family. Come stay at the house."

"No." She turned away.

"The girls would—"

"I can't!" Ashley wheeled around, her eyes filled with anger. "I couldn't before, and I especially can't tonight. I've made special arrangements for a funeral home director to meet me here in a little bit. He's helping me take her home. If you had knocked, I'd have thought you were him."

"Tonight?" Aaron looked at his watch. "It's almost eleven."

"I'm leaving tomorrow afternoon." She brushed past him. "I can't be here, Aaron. I can't. I can't be with your perfect family, and see the faces of your two beautiful girls still alive and breathing when my daughter is dead."

She stopped in the hallway, lowering her head and putting a hand on the wall. "I know that's horrible to say, but I can't do it. Please don't ask again."

Aaron took a deep breath and let it out slowly. He understood. There was pain behind the words, but also truth.

"The coroner," he said. "Was there any report? Did they do an autopsy?"

"I'm not letting them cut up my child. For what? It won't bring her back."

"To find out if anything else happened."

"Everyone said the same thing," Ashley said. "She slipped."

"And you're okay with that?" Aaron went to her. "What if someone's lying? It all just seems so... final. It's strange."

"Life is strange, little brother. You of all people should know that, growing up in our family." The light from the bedroom cast shadows over Ashley's face. She stared into his eyes, lifting her hand and stroking his cheek. "You have the look of our mother in this light. No wonder she liked you better."

Aaron turned his face away, looking down.

"Do you still have the nightmares?" Ashley said. "The door opening and—"

"Stop."

"They're the only nightmares that go away when you go to sleep." Ashley nodded. "You still have them. I know you do—same as me."

"I wouldn't say *exactly* as you."

"No." She put her hand to her side. "You had two monsters. I only had the one."

"You shouldn't meet this funeral director tonight," Aaron said. "Not when you've been drinking and definitely not after getting such bad news. I wish you'd have called me. I could have gone with you to the coroner."

"Why?" she whispered. "Do you think you could have brought her back? Things *look* final because they *are* final, Aaron. The sheriff said it was an accidental drowning. The coroner agreed. It doesn't get more final than that." She waved a hand at him, continuing down the hallway. "You did the obligatory hand-holding with me, so your conscience is clear. Now, I have to get dressed. The funeral director will be here any minute."

He clenched his jaw.

And you wonder why people think you have an iron heart.

Turning away, he reminded himself that she was grieving.

Let it go. People react to emotional stress in different ways, and sometimes the hardest exterior is hiding the softest interior.

Aaron turned back to see Ashley at the doorway to the bedroom. "Do you want me to stay here?" he asked. "I could help you with some of the arrangements."

She shook her head but didn't stop moving. "Go, little brother. Everything's been arranged, so go home to your family. I leave tomorrow afternoon. I'm not staying here one minute longer than is absolutely necessary."

DAN ALATORRE

CHAPTER 11

Aaron gripped the steering wheel with one hand and dialed his phone with the other as a nonstop stream of big, wet snowflakes landed on his windshield. The wipers cleared away the white blotches almost as fast as the next ones appeared, but it would soon be a losing battle. His headlights cut through the dark night, illuminating the inch of fresh powder that had already accumulated on the road.

Despite the late hour, his call was almost immediately answered. "Hello?"

"Collie." Aaron switched the car's hands free calling on and turned onto the highway. "It's Aaron."

"Aaron?" Collier Bristol grunted. "What time is it?"

"Eh, it's probably better if you don't check. We need to talk about the situation with my niece." Aaron fumbled around in the sedan, feeling for the cup holder to place the phone in without taking his eyes off the road. "My sister plans to leave town tomorrow, and take Tiffany Lynn with her, but... I don't like it. Something doesn't smell right. Does an uncle have any rights in a situation like this? Can I stop her from taking the body out of state?"

"No, not really," Collier said. "I could ask a friendly judge for some sort of emergency probate injunction, but don't count on getting one. It would get struck down pretty quick anyway, and no judge is going to appreciate being embarrassed. Even Judge Stein or Judge Laughlin wouldn't be very friendly after something like that."

Aaron rubbed his chin, frowning. "Okay, skip that, then. We have better connections in Florida, anyway. Make some calls first thing in the morning. Maybe we can get the Orlando PD to request an autopsy when Ashley touches down."

"Okay, but... what seems to be the issue?"

"Nothing definitive, but..." Aaron bobbed his head back and forth, tapping his teeth together. "It just smells funny. For one thing, Ashley ignored thirty grand going missing like it was nothing. That dog don't hunt—my sister wouldn't ignore a dirty nickel at the bottom of a public toilet. She's also getting out of Dodge pretty fast, which bothers me... I know she has business to take care of, but that excuse seems a little cold, even for her. I just want someone to look into it. Someone good, not like Renko."

"I'm sure Mr. Renko did his best," Collier said. "Sometimes it's complicated for people like him."

Aaron pulled up to a stop light. The top was covered in two inches of snow, and it was still

TIFFANY LYNN IS MISSING

coming down. "I'm not saying I don't like the guy, but this wasn't his skill set, and it showed. You did fine by hiring him. I'm the one who gave it the green light. But Renko probably planned on being a private investigator for a long time after he finished working for us, so he wouldn't go all in or push hard when things got uncomfortable. He was afraid to upset anyone. I can understand that, but we need someone who's willing to play by... looser rules."

"Or break a few rules?"

"If necessary."

"Okay, Aaron. I may have a few ideas."

"Good," Aaron said. "And call Matt Philson for me, would you, Collie? Arrange for him to come to my house for a meeting. Just you, me, and him—no associates. Matt will know some tech-based investigators, too. We need somebody good on the job, fast. Ashley plans on leaving tomorrow, so we need to drop everything and focus on this."

"No problem, Aaron. What time should I tell him to meet us?"

Drumming his fingers on the steering wheel, Aaron glanced at the clock on his center console. "I'll be at my house in ten minutes. I'd like you and Matt there by the time I can get a pot of coffee made."

* * * * *

Aaron stood in his massive kitchen, with an unopened bag of Café LaVazza in his hand. Reaching into the lower cabinet for a measuring cup, he knocked over a stack of stainless-steel mixing bowls, sending them clattering onto the tile floor. He grabbed at them wildly, but one rolled to the center island and flipped on its top, wobbling noisily for a few seconds before he could grab it.

Maybe I should let Collie make his own coffee.

Sighing, Aaron refocused his attention on the coffeemaker.

"Dad?"

He turned around to find his daughter Mattsie in the doorway to the kitchen, wearing a long t-shirt and flannel socks.

The sixteen-year-old squinted in the bright light, her disheveled hair falling around her shoulders. "What are you doing?"

"Making coffee. Why are you up?" Aaron said, rising. "It's late, sweetie."

"I heard a crash and thought it might be a home invasion." She crossed the room and took the bag of coffee out of his hand. Mattsie methodically pulled a paper filter from a drawer and scooped the ground beans into it, then opened the front of the coffee maker and dropped the filter and coffee in. Popping the plastic water receptacle from the side, she filled it at the sink and snapped it back into place. "There." The sixteen-year-old pressed the button on the front of the machine. "All set."

Aaron smiled. "Thanks. How'd you know it wasn't a home invasion?"

"It had to be you." Mattsie yawned. "Thieves would have been quieter."

"I'm sorry I woke you. Is Monie still asleep?"

"Snoring away. You don't drink coffee. Who's it for? The police?"

TIFFANY LYNN IS MISSING

Aaron recoiled. "Why... would it be for the police?"

"Other people don't have meetings in the middle of the night. Police do—when it's something bad. Is it about Tiffany Lynn?"

"Let's not get into all that right now. It's late, and—"

"You got bad news." Her face fell, her gaze going to the coffeemaker. "You wouldn't be making coffee in the middle of the night if it was good news."

"I'm sorry sweetie." Aaron swallowed hard. "Tiffany Lynn fell while she was hiking at Lake Brimstone, and she went into a lake and drowned."

Tears welled in Mattsie's young eyes.

"I know. I don't get it, either. She slipped, and the water was really cold, and it shocked her. The muscles just locked up. Mr. Renko told us that after a week, we should hope for good news but be prepared for bad news. Remember?"

She sniffled, tears running down her cheeks. "I could tell you knew something at the game tonight." She looked at her father. "When I'd look into the stands, you seemed stressed. You looked like you had a secret you wanted to tell someone, but couldn't. I wanted to ask you, but..."

Aaron closed his eyes, pulling his daughter to him.

The girls were close. They grew up playing together in Florida, and they FaceTimed a lot since the move to Colorado. It coincided with Tiffany Lynn going off to college, so her absence wasn't felt the way it might have been, but she was always the cool older cousin, and the twins looked up to her. Going missing changed that. A lot.

"Tiffany Lynn is missing? What does that mean, Dad? What can we do to find her? She wouldn't just leave. Something's wrong..."

A tense week became a tense two weeks became... a sense that the worst had happened. They'd get a call in the middle of the night saying there had been a car wreck...

Worse things crossed Aaron's mind, too. A long-haul driver finding a body by the side of the road, after being put through who knows what atrocities.

Aaron held his daughter, letting her cry on his chest.

"You teach your kids to do the right things," he said quietly. "To study hard and work hard, and you show them how to defend themselves and how to be alert... you watch as they grow, and they make friends and go out on their own... and they're doing it. They're becoming an adult and doing all the right things... and it can all go away in the blink of an eye because of something stupid."

Mattsie peered up at her father, her eyes red in the fluorescent illumination of the kitchen. "Dad, do you think Aunt Ashley—"

A bright light washed over them. Aaron looked through the large kitchen window. A car pulled into the snow-covered driveway. "That's Collie and Philson." Aaron faced his daughter. "My meeting's with them. Think you can go back to sleep? Or..."

She nodded slowly. "I'll be okay."

TIFFANY LYNN IS MISSING

The back door opened. Collier Bristol and Matt Philson stood in the doorway, flakes of snow covering the shoulders of their coats.

"Aaron," Matt said. "Should we…"

"Come in. Have a seat. I'll be right back." Aaron turned to his daughter.

"I should go back to bed," Mattsie said.

"You sure?"

"Yeah." She swallowed hard. "I was kind of expecting this, but…"

"I know." Aaron kissed her on the forehead. "Go back to bed. I'll come check on you in a little while."

He followed Mattsie into the dining room and watched her go up the stairs, his heart in his throat. "Hey, you were going to say something earlier. You had a question."

She stopped, gazing at him. The clink of coffee cups and spoons came from the kitchen. "It'll keep," she said. "Talk to your guys. I'll see you in the morning."

Rubbing his temples, Aaron walked back to the kitchen. He'd wrestled a lot of questions for the last three weeks. Now, he'd probably never get the answers.

* * * * *

Collier Bristol and Matt Philson were sitting at the table when Aaron returned, coffee cups and a pile of folders spread out in front of them. Bristol had his laptop open, scrolling through a spreadsheet. Philson sat with his hands on the table, his eyes on Aaron.

"Okay, guys." Aaron pulled out a chair and sat. "What have you got for me?"

"There are a number of qualified candidates," Collier said. "I made folders and printed out the pertinent details. Matt and I more or less agree on three investigators, and each of us has an additional suggestion for you to consider."

"So, five options." Aaron folded his hands in front of him. "Okay. Playing things straight didn't do much good, so let's start with the wild cards." He glanced at Philson. "Tell me about yours."

"I like this one." Matt slid a folder across the table. "Jeff Hawthorne. He has a decade of experience as a private investigator and was in the military before that. A friend used him on a special case a while ago. He said that Hawthorne is the type to… color outside the lines, shall we say. He's hard-nosed and determined, with a good track record of success, but he might embarrass his client. He's done a few high-profile cases that made national news, so he can deliver, but he's rough around the edges. He bends rules to the breaking point."

"I like the sound of that." Aaron flipped through the folder. "Why weren't we using him three weeks ago?"

"He served time," Philson said. "I didn't want to use someone with a record. Frankly, I was a little worried about what a man like that might do if he were working for us."

Aaron hooked an arm over the back of his chair. "But now you like him better than the others?"

"He's an additional option," Philson said. "The three we agree on all come from established

TIFFANY LYNN IS MISSING

firms and have solid reputations, but that's their downside, too. They have bosses to answer to and reputations to protect. If you want someone to bend rules, they won't be the right choice. Not now. Hawthorne might be your man, though."

Aaron took a deep breath and let it out slowly. "Collie, what have you got?"

"I'd like you to look at something." Closing his laptop, he pulled his phone out of his pocket and tapped the screen. "Bear with me."

The lawyer turned his phone around and leaned across the table. On the screen was a video that had been queued up—a television talk show or some sort of news round table. A crowd of over a dozen blurry people were frozen in place on the screen.

Collie lifted his chin and peered over the top of the phone, pressing the play button. The video went into motion.

On the little screen, a crowd exploded into a riot. Fists flew, men grappled, insults were hurled. A moment later, a chair sailed across the set and hit a young, female newscaster in the head.

"What is this crap?" Aaron winced. "Why are you wasting my time?"

"Just watch."

The host reappeared, jumping between a young white man and an older black man. They lunged at each other, but she kept them apart. With blood dripping from her nose, she worked to get the crowd under control, pointing and yelling at individuals while pushing the fighting factions apart.

The camera cut back and forth to different angles. The melee was intense, but it soon subsided.

The host walked back and forth across the set like a panther, not running away from the chaos and not losing her cool, but getting the situation under control—and keeping it that way.

Bristol stopped the video and looked at Aaron. "That's Jett Thacker."

"She looks familiar," Aaron said. "Who is she?"

"She's an award-winning investigative journalist. Remember that nursing home scandal in Florida a while back? She spent six months digging into abuses and dropping bombs all over south Florida each week."

Aaron sat up, snapping his fingers. "That's where I know her from. She's on TV in Miami."

"She was." Philson sneered. "She staged a race riot that cost her the host job on 'The Jett Set.' It was a panel discussion show that just started. Those first two guys she broke up were a Nazi and Florida state senator Kendall Marks."

"They started it, but she finished it," Collie said.

"She's a train wreck, boss man." Philson rifled through his folders. "I have another candidate we both like. Did some work with the secret service."

As the debate continued, Aaron put his elbows on the table, folding his hands together and extending his index fingers to massage his chin.

"Jett won a Florida Association of Broadcasters Award," Bristol said. "They don't give those away to just anyone. And I watched some of

TIFFANY LYNN IS MISSING

her exposé pieces. She has a determined air about her."

Philson rolled his eyes. "That's just TV, Collie."

The lawyer shook his head. "I don't think so. Her series on the nursing homes ended a lot of political careers and sent a few people to jail. That's no small feat in Miami."

"And then she put a race riot on live TV," Matt said. "I vote no. She's reckless. She could embarrass you the way she embarrassed her TV station."

Collie looked at Aaron. "If she turns out to be reckless, we cut her loose."

Philson tapped the table with a finger. "And how much damage does she do to this firm *before* we get that chance?"

"Well..." Bristol sat back and loosened his tie. "Obviously it's your call, Aaron."

Staring at the table, Aaron kept massaging his chin with his fingertips. "Matt's right, she's a little reckless."

Philson smiled.

"But I think she's got what it takes." Aaron dropped his hands onto the table like a judge's gavel. "Get her on a plane and get her out here. The sooner the better. Offer to pay her whatever it takes."

Philson winced. "Aaron..."

"I understand your concerns, Matt." Aaron stood. "Really, I do. But... she's a TV person. She'll understand things about this family better than anyone else we can find." He slid his chair under the table. "We're going to need that."

DAN ALATORRE

CHAPTER 12

The sound of the doorbell woke Jett up from a deep sleep. She lifted her head from her pillow and peered across her bedroom to the window. The angle of the bright light streaming in around the corners of the shade told her it was still early morning, but not her usual waking time of five AM.

The doorbell sounded again. Jett sat up, pushing her blonde hair out of her eyes to glance at the clock.

7:55AM.

She groaned.

Leah must have lost her key again. But she should be at school.

Unless Mrs. Dearmont didn't show.

Crap. She needs a ride.

Jett glanced at the lavender-eyed bartender lying next to her, leaning over to kiss her bare shoulder. "Hey, I need you to get up."

Maria sighed, rolling over onto her back. "Mmm? What is it?"

"I have a visitor at the door—the kid from across the hall." Jett crawled over her guest and pulled a t-shirt over her naked torso, removed a pair of jeans from the dresser drawer and slipped them over her long, tan legs. "I might have to take her to school. I'm really sorry." Tugging the jeans over her bare bottom, Jett fastened the button and zipped the zipper. "Can you get dressed?"

"Yeah, sure." Maria threw back the sheets and sat up, stretching her toned, nude figure. Her dark hair fell over her shoulders as she reached for her clothes. "Gotta admit—a school run? That's a new one for me."

Jett walked out of the bedroom and headed toward her front door. On the kitchen counter, her phone buzzed. She grabbed it, checking the screen.

Rico Torres.

Well, I'm popular this morning.

A jolt went through her gut.

Unless somebody took pictures of me with Maria last night on Second Avenue.

Heart pounding, Jett put her eye to the peephole, half-expecting paparazzi to be gathered in the hallway.

It was Rico. He had a backpack over his shoulder and two Starbucks cups in his hands.

Her heart settled back into her chest.

He doesn't look like a crisis is happening.
But why's he here?

She unlocked the door and pulled it open a few inches. "Hey. What's up?"

TIFFANY LYNN IS MISSING

Rico gazed at her, then smiled. "Your nose looks better—the swelling's going down. But the eyes are definitely headed toward raccoon."

She just looked at him.

"Forgot about our appointment, huh? We're supposed to be working on your video reel this morning." He handed her one of the tall, green-and-white paper cups. "Pretty sure you told me eight o'clock."

"Oh, uh..." Opening the door, she glanced toward the bedroom, cradling the Starbucks in her hands. "Yeah. Just... give me five minutes to go brush my teeth."

"No problem. Take your time." Rico walked to the kitchen and slipped the backpack off his shoulder. "I'm glad to see you slept in. That's good. You should be relaxing after yesterday." He lifted his backpack to the counter. "I didn't bring anything for breakfast because—"

Rico pushed Jett's little black purse toward the toaster, and picked up a second, lavender-colored purse. As he set the second bag next to the first one, he glanced toward the curved white couch in the living room. Two pairs of ladies' heels lay next to it.

His gaze went to the bedroom door, then to Jett. "Should I come back in a few minutes?"

"No," Jett whispered. "She's leaving."

"She doesn't have to go on my account."

"No, it's fine." Jett set her coffee on the counter, turning it slowly. "You and I have work to do."

"Okay." He opened his backpack and pulled out his laptop. "I guess you changed your mind about Martin hiring detectives to dig into your past."

Jett's eyes met Rico's. She opened her mouth to speak.

"Good morning," he said, looking over her shoulder.

Maria strolled out from the bedroom, fluffing her hair. She was dressed in her outfit from last night. "Good morning." She smiled. "I'm Maria."

"I'm Rico. Sorry to barge in like this," he said. "We're supposed to work on some interview clips this morning."

Maria sat on the edge of the couch and put her shoes on, then walked to the kitchen counter to grab her purse. As Rico busied himself with his computer, Maria put a finger to Jett's chin and gave her a long, deep kiss. "I'll see you later."

"Okay," Jett said.

"Nice to meet you." The beautiful brunette swung her purse over her shoulder and walked to the door.

Rico waved without looking up from his laptop. "You, too."

As the door shut, Jett put her hands on the counter and lowered her head. "That was really stupid of me."

"What?" Rico typed on the keyboard. "I told you, nobody cares."

"Yeah, well… I appreciate that you were cool with it when we were dating, but I don't need to give Martin and Mr. Nesmith an easy way to—"

TIFFANY LYNN IS MISSING

Jett's phone rang. "Collier Bristol, DAW Holdings, Colorado" appeared on the screen. She held the phone up to Rico. "Any idea who this is?"

"Answer it. Then we'll both know." He stopped typing and reached for his coffee. "It's probably a wrong number—you just got the phone."

Jett scrunched up her face, staring at the screen. Taking a deep breath, she tapped the green button. "Hello?"

"Ms. Thacker? This is Collier Bristol. I hope it's not too early to call."

"No, it's fine. What can I do for you?" Holding her phone in place with her shoulder, Jett turned Rico's laptop around and opened a search engine, typing in "DAW Holdings Colorado."

"My employer would like to retain your services for a private project. His name is Aaron Wells. Are you familiar with him?"

She was, and more than a little.

The laptop said DAW Holdings was part of Ashley Wells' budding Orlando-based empire, but Jett knew Ashley's handsome brother from the businesses he ran with his sister. She also knew he was affiliated with a private college near Tallahassee that Ashley Wells had started, and that Aaron had moved to Colorado a year ago to handle the family's real estate development.

Most of the powerful movers and shakers of south Florida were known to TV types. Their paths would cross during charity fundraisers or political events, and occasionally as the subjects in their news stories—for better or for worse. But Jett had never run into Aaron or his sister in person. Ashley Wells and her brother were Orlando personalities; Jett was a Miami news person.

Or was, until yesterday.

But a job at Ashley Wells' small network would be a definite step backwards for Jett's career, and one she wasn't ready to entertain quite yet. Not before finding a new agent and testing the waters.

My reputation can't be that damaged.

On the other hand, her bank account was almost empty, and an agent might take months to find her a new job.

Play it cool.

"I'm flattered that the Wellses would reach out," Jett said, "and I have great respect for their network."

"Oh, I'm not calling on behalf of the network, Ms. Thacker. This is a personal matter. Aaron Wells would like to hire you to look into the disappearance of his niece."

Great, it's not even a job offer for their crappy network.

"Mr. Bristol, I... First of all, thank you, but I'm not sure I'd be right for something like that. It sounds like a police matter, and if Mr. Wells would like to supplement the efforts of law enforcement, there are any number of qualified private investigation firms that should suit your needs."

Bristol cleared his throat. "Ms. Thacker, if I may... Mr. Wells could hire almost anyone in the country to do this project for him. He wants you. Now, I understand that you've recently been the subject of quite a few unpleasant headlines and some negative media attention, as well as being released

TIFFANY LYNN IS MISSING

by the Miami 5 TV station. Perhaps this would offer a nice distraction away from all that. Do you ski? Colorado is quite nice this time of year, and Mr. Wells has authorized me to pay you double what you were making with the station."

Jett clutched her phone with both hands. "Can you hold for a second, Mr. Bristol?"

"Of course."

Jett knew Aaron Wells was a successful businessman and real estate developer. He had been part of Ashley Wells' network until his move to Colorado—which some people said was because Ashley got tired of his mishandling of deals.

She lowered the phone and put her hand over the mic, looking at Rico. "They want me to do some investigating in Colorado."

"Tell them no," he said. "We need to find you an agent and start setting up some interviews."

"They're offering double what I made at the station."

"For a week or two of internet surfing. Then what?" Rico frowned. "That's time spent not interviewing."

"Yeah, okay." Jett returned the phone to her cheek. "I'm sorry, Mr. Bristol. I'm afraid my answer is going to have to be—"

"Would fifty thousand dollars be enough to get you to come for the day? Aaron would like to explain his request in person. We can get you on a noon flight that lands at three this afternoon. After that, if you say no, the money is yours—no strings attached—and you'll be on the nine PM flight back to Miami. If you agree to take the assignment, we'll consider the fifty thousand a guaranteed minimum payment."

Jett's jaw dropped. She lowered the phone again, looking at Rico.

"No!" he said. "We need to get to work."

"Yeah." Jett stared at the phone. "But I'm broke and they're offering fifty thousand dollars to fly me out there for one day."

Rico sat upright. "Ask if you can hire me as your assistant."

CHAPTER 13

Jett stared up at the white peaked ceiling of the Denver airport as she walked with the crowd toward the baggage claim. The roof's many high, curving triangles bent upwards like a row of tents, probably to appear as the tops of the Rocky Mountains from outside. Adjusting the strap of her overnight bag, Jett spied a young man in a dark grey suit near the exit, holding a small whiteboard with her name on it.

She stopped in front of him. "I'm Jett Thacker."

"Nice to meet you, ma'am. I'm Curtis, from Wildfire resort. May I take your bag?"

"Sure." Jett slid the strap off her shoulder and handed it to him.

A short, but very cold, walk took them to a Lincoln Town Car limousine in the parking garage, with a Wildfire resort logo on the side. The dry mountain air irritated Jett's sore nose and made her eyes water, but it was a temporary inconvenience. Curtis opened the rear door, allowing Jett to ease onto the soft leather of the back seat and the Lincoln's warm interior.

He placed her bag next to her. "It will take about ninety minutes to reach the Wildfire resort, Ms. Thacker. If you'd like to relax with a drink on the way…" Curtis pointed to a woodgrain panel. "This section opens the bar. Soft drinks, ice and mixers are underneath."

Jett had ridden in limousines many times for her work, accompanying celebrities to a private airplane while conducting an interview, or hitching a ride with a politician who was trying to appear impressive, but she still enjoyed the experience. She opened a bottle of water from the bar and took a sip, then stared at the phone sitting in her purse.

The desire to check in on her social media accounts was overwhelming, but reading the lies being spread by Martin's minions wouldn't help her. In her experience, celebrity storms tended to last about two weeks, and then the wolves moved on to other prey.

I can last two weeks.

I could stand on my head for two weeks, if I had to. So, I can do this.

She had posted a simple message online, in her best lawyerly fashion, and then quit the socials cold turkey:

"The many statements being put out about me and my departure from Miami 5, allegedly espoused by people who know me, are untrue and demonstrably false. I will not participate in the game.

TIFFANY LYNN IS MISSING

The public will learn the truth at a time of my choosing. Martin Brennan, Parker Nesmith, and the other parties responsible for this insulting charade need to clear my name and reputation with the same energy with which they are attempting to ruin it, or they will pay the consequences."

Eighty-three words that basically said, "no dice." She dropped the bomb and walked away.

Stating publicly that she wouldn't play was one thing. Naming Martin and Mr. Nesmith directly, with a veiled threat, was another. They wouldn't like that, and probably weren't expecting to be mentioned. Jett especially liked using Mr. Nesmith's first name, something that was strictly forbidden at the network, and a jab that would get under his skin. It was a little petty, but so what? It would cause a few media hounds to bark at Nesmith a bit, something he'd hate—and he might even try to deny any involvement.

And the likely result of that would be a lawsuit, but that was fine. The truth is the best defense. None of the smear could have happened without his approval.

The public might be a different matter. Didn't they understand she had the same concerns as everyone else? That fame didn't remove the doubts people carried inside themselves? The confidence Jett displayed on TV was real, because she worked hard and did her homework, but she still walked into a party concerned that people in the room didn't like her.

Just let it go. Focus on something else for two weeks.

Like maybe this story in Colorado.

She and Rico did some preliminary research on Aaron Wells, but it basically confirmed what she already knew. He worked at the network since its start, and moved to Colorado to do real estate development. But the stories divided there. Some said he was pushed out of Ashley Wells' network; others said he was expanding the empire. Ashley had created a private college in Tallahassee, and Aaron was on the board. Was she allowing her inept brother to maintain a respectable profile while others did the actual work?

Does it matter? I'm broke and he's giving me fifty grand.

If he's a bozo, I'm back in Miami tonight doing video cuts with Rico.

Outside the window, the white and massive Rocky Mountains spanned the horizon. The cloudless blue sky contrasted sharply with the blinding brilliance of each snow-covered tip. The mountains were crisp and clean in the dry air, from their icy tops to their brown bottoms, and dominated the landscape in a seemingly endless line.

It was easy to let the scenery move her thoughts away from her troubles.

As they drove past the massive fiberglass statue of a mustang stallion adorning the Denver airport's front lawn, Jett pulled out her phone to dial Rico. "Uh, Curtis... do you mind if we raise the partition? I have some calls to make."

"Of course. If you need anything, knock on the glass or put the window down. There's also an intercom. The buttons are on the door panel next to

TIFFANY LYNN IS MISSING

you." Curtis pressed a toggle on the dashboard, and the internal window separating him from his only passenger rose to seal itself against the car's plush, padded roof.

Rico answered on the second ring. "Got a job out there for me yet?"

"You have a job," Jett said. "Find any new info for me?"

"A few things. First, watch your negotiations. A techie friend of mine says two years ago he was working for a company that bid on a contract for Aaron Wells—to make a big, mahogany conference table, but under the wood veneer, it's a receptor grid of sensors for every different frequency of phone, computer, Wi-Fi... you send a text or make a keystroke on a laptop, he'd know what you said or did. And there are cameras and microphones everywhere. If you're staying in one of his guest suites at the resort, it's bugged. If you're in any of his buildings, you're on video and audio—so be careful what you say."

"What a great guy." She shook her head. "Listening in on private conversations during business meetings and when people are relaxing?"

"Night and day," Rico said. "I'm sure it doesn't hurt to know your opponents' internal strategies. The funny thing is, supposedly Wells doesn't need that kind of stuff. People who dealt with him ten and twelve years ago said he knew what was on your mind by the way your face would react. He's a real people reader, kind of like those big-time poker players in Vegas—everybody has a tell, and he can spot it from a mile away."

Jett chewed her lip.

Maybe the rumors about him being a figurehead are wrong.

"So why does he do the other stuff?' she asked. "It's gotta be illegal."

"No point in leaving anything to chance, I guess."

Jett glanced around the limo's interior.

That probably applies to his company cars, too.

I'm probably being recorded right now.

"You in a car from his resort?" Rico asked.

"Yep. A limo."

"And you put up the partition, so you would lower your guard, thinking you had privacy, and talk away. See how it works?"

Jett smiled. She didn't like the tactic, but she appreciated a challenge. "I may have to watch my step with this guy. What else did you find out?"

"Not much," Rico said. "Basic stuff anybody would find in a quick internet search. He still does a lot with his sister's company in Orlando and the private college she started in Tallahassee... he has two kids in high school—sixteen-year-old daughters—and he's divorced, but his wife passed away. Oddly, reading beyond the fluff pieces in the papers, he's kind of quiet—unlike his sister. My source said people who know Wells say he's a really nice guy and a good dad. Like, legit nice, too. He's absolutely shrewd at business, but he's not a cutthroat. He wants everybody to do well in the deal, and he gives a ton of money to charities but doesn't

TIFFANY LYNN IS MISSING

make a splash about it. No spotlight stuff, just writes the checks."

"Huh." Jett rubbed her chin. "A mogul who's generous and humble. I'm not sure I've seen one of those before."

"But there are still rumors that he's a figurehead—that other people do the deals and he just takes the credit. Either way, he probably ended up getting that mahogany table built—among other things—so he's no saint. Let me know if you need anything else, but watch your step out there."

"I'll do better than that." She sat up straight, assuming that Mr. Wells was hearing every word as she scrutinized each seam, tuft, and button of the upholstery in the back of the Town Car. "I did a lot of interviews as a reporter. I'm pretty good at reading people, too."

I'll get eye to eye with Aaron Wells and call him out on his little spy tactics—and then we'll see what happens.

* * * * *

The entrance to Wildfire Resort was elegant and breathtaking. The rugged, rustic exterior of Swiss-style tudor and exposed wooden beams soared ten stories into the air, a dazzling array of quaint, shutter-framed windows and green-shingled dormers that blocked the chilling wind from the great mountains beyond. The lower sections of the structure were trimmed in light yellow wooden panels; the upper floors wore a rich, burgundy red. Rather than overtake the surrounding landscape, the resort seemed to grow out of it, with rock wall facades on the sides and small, flowing waterfalls at the corners. Giant fir trees hugged the front elevations, and lush wintery gardens nestled at their base. Every spotless sidewalk was edged in stone; every bush, shrub, and blade of grass appeared to have been trimmed and manicured. It was a massive enterprise, filled with a constant stream of people coming and going, but all with an air of luxury, and all under the blanket of the resort's immaculate, green gabled roof.

Curtis stood next to Jett, holding the door as she exited the limousine. "Welcome to Wildfire, Ms. Thacker."

Jett's mouth hung open as she took in the massive resort, the crisp scent of pine trees filling the air.

All this belongs to one family?

More than one male guest stopped his activities to watch Jett walk toward the front door. A middle-aged bellman came for her bag. "May I show you to your room, Ms. Thacker?"

"Yes." Mesmerized by the architecture and the landscaping, she continued toward the entrance, following the bellman. "I mean, no." Jett shook her head. "I have a meeting with Aaron Wells. I'm not staying at the resort. I'm... not staying at all, actually."

"I see." The bellman smiled. "I'll just tuck this away in a guest suite for you, then. When you're ready to go, just give us this tag." He offered her a yellow claim check.

Jett glanced at the man's nametag.
Tonnie.

TIFFANY LYNN IS MISSING

"Uh, Tonnie, maybe I'd better take my bag with me."

"As you wish, ma'am." Tonnie maintained his smile. "But I'd catch the devil from the boss if I don't at least carry it for you. Mr. Aaron wouldn't like me letting a guest lug around her own bag."

Jett nodded. "And where would I find Mr. Wells?"

"His office is just inside, miss. This way." Tonnie turned and walked to the grand entrance. A uniformed doorman opened the tall, glass door, allowing another welcome rush of warm air to greet Jett's chilly cheeks.

The busy lobby of the Wildfire was adjacent to its four-story tall dining room, where floor-to-ceiling windows framed the spectacular mountains in the distance. Rows of tables dressed in white linen dotted the wood plank floor, with high, sparkling chandeliers casting the room in a warm yellow glow. At the far end, a towering stone fireplace kept a roaring flame in its iron berth, as rough-cut cedar beams framed the green ceiling.

Jett stopped walking and stared at the iconic architecture. "Tonnie, is everything in the resort this beautiful?"

"Nothing here is as pretty as you, miss." Tonnie chuckled. "Even with that shiner you're sporting, if you don't mind my saying."

She did and she didn't. Unsolicited remarks about her appearance were often inappropriate, but Tonnie seemed genuinely friendly and reassuring, as if he understood Jett might be worried about how her bruised eyes looked, and wanted to put her at ease.

She was relieved to know her appearance wasn't horrifying. She was from the TV world, after all, where looks mattered—and were constantly commented on. The right skirt made you look svelte; the wrong one made you look hippy. One extra strap took a shoe from alluring to slutty. Earrings were always too big and too gauche for Jett's tastes, but the ones she liked were too small to appear on camera. And of course, all necklines needed to plunge and accentuate the bust without appearing to do so. Tans were sprayed on, fake eyelashes were stuck on, hair extensions were glued on, and a rouge brush constantly found its way between her breasts to create just the right enhancing shadow and perkiness.

A woman on TV was subject to nonstop poking, prodding and critiquing until the cameras were on, and then it was all about confidence and personality—if anyone could have confidence or a personality after all that.

So when a nice man stated that her eyes looked human and not like a raccoon's, she took it in the spirit she felt it was intended. Jett knew she was attractive—almost everyone on TV is, especially in Miami—but she didn't mind being reminded in the real world on occasion. And to exaggerate the compliment beyond her to the four walls of the palatial hotel was something Tonnie would probably have said to his own daughters, if he had any—and they would probably like the compliment as much as Jett did.

TIFFANY LYNN IS MISSING

Tonnie guided her to the executive elevators and pressed the button to the top floor, happily holding her bag as promised.

"Mr. Aaron" would notice if Tonnie hadn't, I guess.

Jett surveyed her appearance in the elevator's shiny doors. She had dressed casual for the meeting, wearing skinny jeans with knee-length, buckskin-colored riding boots, and a white, faux-fur trimmed, cropped waistcoat.

She straightened her spine and tossed her blonde hair over her shoulder.

Casual, upscale, and professional.

Get him to relax and then ambush him about the rigged mahogany spy table.

When the doors opened, Tonnie held them for her, then followed her out. "Special delivery, Miss Giselle," Tonnie said. "This is Ms. Thacker, here to see Aaron." He faced Jett. "I'll just put your bag here, ma'am." He set the overnight bag on a chair in the lobby and folded his hands in front of him. "Will there be anything else?"

"No, Tonnie—and thank you for your help." Jett reached for her purse.

"Here, now—none of that." Tonnie shook his head. "Mr. Aaron pays me very well. Wouldn't do to have me begging tips from business associates, ma'am."

Giselle stood and walked out from behind her desk. "May I show you to Aaron's outer office, Ms. Thacker?"

Jett nodded. "Yes, please. Thank you." Clutching her purse, she followed the slender assistant through two carved wooden doors to a sleek conference room and a gorgeous, oval mahogany table.

This must be the spy room.

"That is a lovely jacket." Giselle's voice was soft as velvet. "Would you like something while you wait?" Her tone was friendly, too, like Tonnie's.

Must be part of the training. Disarm people through compliments, then rob them blind.

Jett glanced at a water pitcher on the table. "Water's fine. Will Mr. Wells be long?"

"No, ma'am." Giselle offered a warm smile. "He's just finishing up a call."

As Giselle exited, she closed the doors.

Jett walked around the conference room, inspecting the mahogany shelves filled with awards and pictures of Aaron Wells at construction sites, posing with people who were probably local politicians. A brass plaque read "Vincit Qui Patitur"—translated underneath with the words "He who endures, conquers." The inscription on the frame attributed the Latin quote to Persius, a Roman scholar.

Next to the plaque was a silver-framed wedding photo of a dashing, young Aaron Wells and a beautiful brunette. And next to that was a smaller, matching frame with a black ribbon over one corner—and an image of the same woman from the wedding photo, but this one could have been from a modeling shoot.

Odd, to keep a picture of you and your ex-wife in such a prominent place. He probably sees that picture every day. And the other one.

TIFFANY LYNN IS MISSING

He didn't want to divorce her.

Strolling to the rear wall, Jett gazed through a wide, three-panel bay window and viewed the resort's many ski slopes. The bright midday sun reflected off the white of the snow. Skiers appeared in a nonstop flow from the various mountain trails; children bounded down the lower hills in colorful innertubes. The massive hotel was constructed in three slightly angled sections, so Jett could see the shops, cafés, and restaurants that lined the building's backside, as well as the steel towers of the ski lifts that carried refreshed patrons back up the slopes. In the center, a large, stone circle served as a bonfire pit, with a low fire burning within its ring. Clusters of people surrounded it, sipping cocktails and consuming refreshments. As she watched, a small ATV with a trailer full of logs pulled up. Its driver tossed some cut wood into the bonfire's yellow flames, then drove away toward the ski trails. Between the curving white paths rose the dense, green forests of pines and fir trees, eventually giving way to the stark, icy peaks that cut across the sky.

The view was impressive, as everything about Wildfire had been so far.

I guess this is what you can accomplish when you spy on people in your business meetings.

DAN ALATORRE

CHAPTER 14

A side door to the conference room opened, and Aaron Wells appeared. He flashed a brilliant smile, extending his hand. "Ms. Thacker. Thank you so much for coming."

Aaron Wells was handsome—more so than pictures online indicated. He was tall and fit, with broad shoulders and the graceful, natural movement of an athlete. He had a strong chin and a well-tailored blue suit that covered a crisp, white shirt, but he wore no tie. A few gray hairs appeared among his dark brown locks, but not enough to show up in any of the pictures Jett had reviewed. It was just the right amount of silver accent that allowed a man to appear distinguished without looking old.

Mr. Wells could have stepped off the cover of Esquire magazine—and might have actually appeared on its cover at one time or another.

Jett crossed the room to greet him. She had met many men in her line of work. Some were powerful, some were rich, some were fakes. A few were handsome enough to be models. Aaron Wells appeared to be all of those things, but without any of the usual bravado that came with it. His voice was gentle and kind, and his demeanor was friendly.

But it was his eyes that said the most about him.

She had imagined a cold businessman with a phony warm façade, the kind of operator who knows all the angles of a deal and can't wait to exploit them. The person before her was a man in pain. He smiled, but his warm, brown eyes seemed as if he might cry, or recently had.

Of course. He lost his niece, and he was close to her.

Hiring me isn't a business deal to him. This is much more important than that.

Jett's cheeks warmed with embarrassment at her preconceived notions. Recovering, she took Aaron's outstretched hand and shook it. His fingers were soft and warm, with a firm yet gentle grip. This man didn't quite seem to jive with Rico's description of a business cheat.

But there's a quick way to find out.

Jett continued shaking hands as she glanced at the large mahogany table. "Mr. Wells, I've heard that this table is rigged with electronic surveillance equipment. That the whole place is bugged."

The light in his eyes switched, and she instantly regretted the comment. Wells went from whatever he was a moment ago to a businessman in a negotiation. His eyes narrowed slightly, but *only* slightly; almost imperceptibly. He could probably

TIFFANY LYNN IS MISSING

play poker with the best of them in Vegas and never give anything away, but she was good at this game, too.

He looked at the table. "Would you be more comfortable talking outside or somewhere else?"

"I just want you to tell me the truth." She kept her tone even. "Is it bugged?"

His gaze went to her, his eyes focusing on Jett's as if she were the only thing in the universe, like he was studying her face for a sign of her intentions. Outside in the lobby, beyond the thick doors that guarded this private world, phones rang and fingers clattered on keyboards. On the slopes outside, the sounds of a young child laughing were carried on the wind. And somewhere under that pale blue Colorado sky, a snow mobile hummed back and forth between the trees, driving over the new inches of fresh fallen powder.

"Is it bugged?"

Her abrupt words hung in the air like the clang of a Sunday morning church bell.

"It is," Wells said.

Jett's stomach lurched. That admission could land Aaron Wells in jail—yet he was brave enough or trusting enough to admit it to her.

Why would he just... do that?

"You asked for my help," Jett said. "If I'm going to work for you, we have to be completely honest with each other. No doubt you've seen what happened to me when I trusted the wrong people. I can't go through that twice."

"Fair enough." Wells crossed his arms, looking down and clearing his throat. "The situation

I need your help with is more important than any bad habits I've allowed this company to adopt over the past few years." He smiled. "You look good, by the way. I mean, your eyes. I saw the video where that chair hit you, but really, if I didn't already know… It's not obvious."

"The headaches and sinus pain keep me from forgetting. The cold, dry air out here doesn't help."

"Hmm. I'll see what I can do about the weather." He gestured to a chair. "Would you like to sit down?"

"I'd…" Jett swallowed hard. "I'd like you to post a bond of $1 million, that if you lie to me or cheat me in any way during our business, or if I find out that you did, the bond defaults to me."

She didn't know why she said it. She knew he wouldn't accept.

But she couldn't stop herself.

That was too big of an ask. An amateur move.

"I'm not going to do that." Wells' voice was calm and even, like a patient parent with a good child who'd simply asked to stay up a bit too late and had to be told no. "And you're not really in a position to ask for that." He walked to the bay window, leaning on the thick frame. "I can get a new investigator, but I don't want a new investigator—I want you. So, I promise, I won't cheat you or lie to you." Turning, Wells looked into Jett's eyes, without displaying a hint of anger or insult. "Now, I've given you my word, and I won't break it. You're the person I want looking into this. Please." He leaned back against the windowsill, peering at the conference room floor.

TIFFANY LYNN IS MISSING

"Your researcher should have discovered that I don't break my word."

Rico hadn't mentioned that, but Wells seemed firm enough about it.

He definitely wasn't acting like a figurehead. Aaron Wells seemed like a competent operator, and Jett liked that he genuinely seemed to care about not breaking his word. The tone was right. Convincing.

But a good liar would say that anyway, wouldn't he? With the right tone and conviction?

Still, fifty grand for one day's work will be fifty thousand dollars more than I had yesterday. Just proceed with caution.

Wells stood upright. "Giselle."

His assistant's voice came through the conference room door. "Yes, Aaron?"

"Would you ask Randy and Juan in maintenance to do me a favor and remove my conference room table, please?"

"Of course, Aaron. Right away."

"Thank you." Wells looked at Jett. "Now, where do we begin?"

Satisfied, Jett moved to the table and set her purse down. "I suppose we should arrange my fee before we start."

"It's already in your account at Miami Federal, if you'd like to check. I told you, I don't want some other investigator looking into this. I want you."

"Your lawyer told me a few things over the phone." Jett pulled a chair out and sat down, taking a small notepad from her purse. "Care to get me up to speed on the rest?"

Wells summarized the situation for her. His niece had disappeared after an argument with her mother the weekend before spring break, and turned up dead three weeks later. The authorities concluded it was an accident, and the case was closed.

"But there's one other thing." Wells leaned forward in his chair, folding his hands on the table top. "Tiffany Lynn sent letters. I'm not supposed to know about this, but my brother-in-law—Ashley's husband Jake—let it slip, and when I pressed him on it, he thought it might be a good idea for me to know. He doesn't trust Ashley with everything."

Jett stopped writing, mid-sentence, and looked up at Wells. "He doesn't trust his own wife?"

"When you get to know my sister, you'll understand why. Only a select few members of the Orlando police force and the Orange County sheriff's office know about these letters. Their existence is not common knowledge outside of that. They're in Tiffany Lynn's handwriting, basically asking her mother to stay away. 'Don't worry, and don't look for me.' That's it. Each letter is the same. They appeared about once a week, starting a few days after she disappeared. At first, we thought maybe Tiffany Lynn had been kidnapped and her abductors were forcing her to write them—which I still think is possible, by the way—and then Jake mentioned she might be writing them herself as a way to get at Ashley. It could also be that someone was copying her handwriting, looking for a payday somehow, or any number of other things." He sighed, leaning back and gazing out the window. "The police mostly thought it just seemed like a childish prank, but that's

TIFFANY LYNN IS MISSING

why we thought she must be in Florida—because Ashley kept getting letters *postmarked* from Florida. The only problem is, Tiffany Lynn appears to have not been in Florida when the last one was mailed."

Jett tapped her pen against her lower lip. "That's interesting. You don't buy the story about slipping while hiking with friends?"

"I..." Aaron shrugged. "I don't know the kids she was with. Money causes things to happen."

"Did Tiffany Lynn *have* any money?" Jett said. "Most college kids don't. Her mother did, though. Was a ransom note ever sent to Ashley?"

"My niece had thirty thousand dollars, which she took from a Wildfire company account. That's still missing. She got the... well, I *gave* her the access codes for the account when she worked here last summer. That money could have been to pay her ransom and get herself free from whatever she was caught up in. Drug addicts who wanted cash, or whatever—and after she gave them the money, they killed her."

"And hung around to talk to police? That doesn't make sense—not for kidnappers." Jett made a note on her pad. "And then they sent another letter—after she was dead?"

"Two." Wells put his hand to his chin. "Jake called this morning. The latest letter arrived at the house today—postmarked yesterday—from Christmas, Florida. That's a small town just east of Orlando, about—"

"I know where Christmas is."

"Oh. Okay. Well, the letter was identical to the others, with a 'Christmas' postmark stamped yesterday. That's at least a few days after Tiffany Lynn died."

"So..." Jett set her pen down and reviewed her notes. "Her kidnappers had her write out a dozen or so letters before they took off on a cross-country joy ride, and a partner in Florida mailed them on a regular basis not knowing she died." She looked at Aaron. "Or she faked a kidnapping and mailed them herself."

"Not after she died." He shook his head. "And she didn't need to fake a kidnapping to get access to money. She took it from the account. I'd have given it to her if she'd have asked."

"But then she would have had to face you. She obviously didn't want that. Were you two close?"

Aaron frowned, massaging his hands. "Yes. Definitely. She had to know I'd see the thirty grand go missing—that's like announcing her presence. I moved here to oversee construction around the time she went off to college in Tallahassee, but we saw each other all the time before that. Beach vacations, ski trips, cruises." He looked at Jett. "A person needs a family. Tiffany Lynn and my girls were like sisters. They were tight. More than tight. They didn't go three days without FaceTiming or playing an online video game together, even after she went off to school."

Jett tapped the pen against her lip again.

Tiffany Lynn had a family—her mother, for starters. Why wouldn't that be enough? And if it wasn't, why would she run away from everyone else?

TIFFANY LYNN IS MISSING

"What about her birth father? Any links there?"

"No," Wells said. "Canon died a long time ago. Tiffany Lynn was just a kid. She didn't really know him. My sister has remarried several times since then. I don't see that as a factor. Her husbands have never been... very important in her life."

Nodding, Jett made another note. "And about the argument? Do you know what it was about?"

"School. Tiffany Lynn wanted to drop out."

"Of the private college her mom built!" Jett raised her eyebrows. "Yeah, I can see how that might cause a stir. Did she say why she wanted to drop out?"

Wells shrugged. "I... wasn't really privy to that, but from what I gathered from Jake, the argument was a symptom. Tiffany Lynn was very angry at Ashley over something, and leaving college was the first step in some bigger thing."

"What's so big it turns you against your mother?"

"You'll understand that when you meet my sister." He sighed, staring at the shiny oval table. "I love Ashley, but... she's definitely overbearing. There was always a power struggle between her and Tiffany Lynn about being in show biz—among all the other things family members chose to fight about." He lifted his gaze to peer at Jett. "So? What do you think?"

Jett set her pen down and leaned back in her chair. "The fifty thousand is mine no matter what I say here, right?"

Wells nodded. "Yep."

"Mr. Wells, you seem—"

"Please, call me Aaron."

"Mr. Wells, you seem like a nice man... despite the custom-made spy table. But this has all the appearances of a family dispute gone wrong. There's really not much for me to find. Your niece had an argument and then ran off. She had an accident and died—that's sad and tragic. She was just a kid. But if the authorities are good with the explanation that it was an accident... I think you need to be, too. I'm sorry. I appreciate you flying me out here, but I have to say no."

"What if I offered to pay you twice what you were making at the station in Miami?"

"No. Not for a few weeks' work, just to end up right back here with the same story we have now. I can't do that in good conscience."

He tapped the table. "I'll guarantee you a year's pay at twice your Miami 5 contract. I'm part owner of the TV station in Orlando. We can leak that we're hiring you to host our new nightly news program there, and to spearhead the entire news division, as well as create a series of in-depth investigative reports—the first of which is my niece's case."

Jett shook her head. "Sir—"

"I'm not finished." Aaron leaned forward, his voice falling to a whisper. "My sister left town today with the remains. Our information was that Ashley was confirmed on an afternoon flight with Delta Airlines, the other half of a round trip ticket she bought to get out here. When I met with her last night, she said she was about to meet with a funeral

TIFFANY LYNN IS MISSING

director. I assumed it was to make arrangements to fly the body home. It wasn't. At the very moment I was talking to her, Ashley was having the body moved from the Brimstone County morgue—and cremated. Then today, at sunrise, she got on a private chartered aircraft and left Colorado. She didn't cancel the Delta ticket, to make sure we thought we still had time."

Jett cocked her head. "Time to do what?"

"To find out what she was up to and stop her."

"Mister—*Aaron*—no." Groaning, she put her hand to her temple and closed her eyes. "It's a family feud. It's a bunch of infighting among rich siblings topped off with a mother-daughter tiff that went wrong."

"How did my niece mail a letter after she died?" Aaron tapped the table again. "And why did my sister want to make sure no one would ever inspect the body? Where's the thirty thousand dollars, and where's Tiffany Lynn?"

"You just said it—she was cremated."

"*Someone* was. I never identified Tiffany Lynn at the coroner's office. I certainly could have. But Ashley did it, flying all the way out here in secret before I even knew what was going on. And Ashley made sure I couldn't identify the body now, by having it cremated. That no one could. Doesn't that intrigue you just a little?"

It did.

The situation was odd at best, and she felt for the uncle who was wrestling with the sudden death of his niece.

But it was his eyes that really set the hook in her.

Something in Aaron Wells' face said there was more to the story. There was a pain there that Jett couldn't describe, but it meant something.

Maybe it meant everything.

He suspects something, that's for sure. He's a smart guy who doesn't seem prone to wild allegations. Maybe there's more to this story than the simple explanation everyone's giving.

And I don't actually have a job to run back to.

Aaron folded his hands on the table. "Help me, Ms. Thacker. Please. I—I think I *need* you to learn what happened, and to hold the responsible parties accountable. And something did happen. I know it."

Jett stared at him.

What would Rico say? How is doing this advancing my career as a TV journalist?

By helping the owner of a TV station and taking down a Florida celebrity. Darling Ashley Wells was a Florida icon. If she was up to something nefarious, she had a lot to lose.

A kid died under some strange circumstances. That's worth looking into.

And breaking a story like this—if there is one—could put me right back on top.

Jett stood up, going to the bay window. The setting sun caused the snow to take on a blue hue. Soon, it would be dark out.

TIFFANY LYNN IS MISSING

If I do this, I have to do it for the right reasons. The stakes are too high for me and for the family to launch some half-baked witch hunt.

It could get very high-profile, very quickly—and very hot for me if there's nothing to find. Orlando news stations will be showing it as their lead story every night if word gets out.

In the reflection of the glass, she checked Aaron's face. He stood, putting his hands in his pockets and looking at her.

It was a risk. If it didn't pan out, she might be a laughingstock. Her TV career would be over.

But she smelled a story. There was something to what Aaron said. Ashley might be a grieving mother, but she was acting like someone with something to hide.

And I'd at least like to know what that something is.

And then it hit her. The pained expression made complete sense.

Aaron Wells was a man trying to decide if the sister he professed to love had somehow caused the death of the niece he and his daughters also loved—a gut-wrenching possibility that would give most normal people an ulcer—and he had no clear way to get to the answer.

Not without hiring someone who didn't care what the answers were and would find the truth, no matter what.

Jett nodded. That was a powerful reason to take the job.

She wheeled around to face Aaron. "Double my annual contract rate at Miami 5. Guaranteed, no matter what I find."

"Done." He nodded. "Anything else?"

"Yes. No spying on me, here or anywhere else. And I need a ticket on the next flight to Orlando. I want to talk to the people who work at that post office in Christmas, Florida."

"The next flight is tomorrow morning at ten." Aaron reached into his suit pocket and pulled out a boarding pass, setting it on the table. "I also took the liberty of booking a suite here at the resort for you—Presidente three. It's not bugged, unless you count the security camera in the hallway."

CHAPTER 15

Aaron picked up a manilla folder from his desk, leafing through it as his corporate counsel entered the private office. A cardboard box of video discs rested on the corner of the large mahogany desk. "Well, Collie?" Aaron sat back, holding the folder on his lap. "What do you think?"

"I like her." Collier nodded. "I think she's the real deal."

"I think so, too. So, I want you to do me a favor." Leaning forward in his chair, Aaron tossed the folder onto the desk. "Her former employer has been quietly shopping the Miami TV station for years, but he's always wanted an outrageously high price—close to twenty percent above the station's market value. I think it's time to put in an offer."

"Okay." Collier took a small bottle of soda from the mini fridge, cracking open the top. "For how much?"

"*Thirty* percent above market," Aaron said. "All cash, so they'll come to the table quickly—but I want two things in the contract. First, Parker Nesmith and Martin Brennan built that station, so I want them both under contract to stay on for five more years. Second, I need a rebate penalty in the deal. If the two main players violate any morals clause in the contracts, the purchase price reverts down to half of the cash price." He checked his watch.

"They won't go for that." Collier scoffed. "No one would."

"Yeah, they will." Aaron got up from his desk, smoothing his suitcoat and adjusting his cuffs. "They're hot to sell, and the station's in trouble. They won't give a clause like that a second thought. Set up a corporation in the Cayman Islands to broker the deal, so nobody knows it's me buying the station."

"Will do." Collier took a sip of his soda. "But I have to warn you, thirty percent over market sounds like a really bad deal."

"Let me worry about that." Aaron returned to his desk, picking up the box of video discs and heading for the conference room. "You just handle the noncompete agreements. Make sure Nesmith and Brennan are both signed to stay for five more years. That needs to be iron clad."

* * * * *

After splashing some water on her face in Presidente three—and resisting the urge to check her social media accounts and gage the thrashing she no doubt was still receiving there—Jett strolled

TIFFANY LYNN IS MISSING

downstairs to grab a bite at the restaurant that had impressed her so much on her way in.

And it was completely empty.

The lights were on—a dozen crystal chandeliers, all beaming their yellow light onto the warm wooden walls of the enormous dining room and the crisp linens covering the tables below. Through the tall windows, the darkening skies of the Colorado landscape glowed with ski lift lights and roaring flames from the stone bonfire pit.

But not a single person graced the elegant interior of the Wildfire dining room.

As a slender, golden-haired woman approached, Jett leaned forward, her voice carrying through the empty hall. "I'm sorry—are you closed for the evening?"

"No, Ms. Thacker." The woman smiled. "Aaron asked us to reserve the hall for you."

"The..." Jett clutched her stomach, looking up at the high ceiling. "The whole hall? The entire dining room?"

"He said you might need to review some things, and that you might want privacy."

Jett nodded.

It's definitely private... in a very odd way.

She glanced at the woman's name tag. *Cheyenne.* "Do I just sit anywhere?"

"Wherever you'd like." Cheyenne swept her hand toward the front of the hall. "Our most requested table is the round one near the front. It allows you to enjoy the fireplace, but you can still see outside. May I seat you there?"

Jett shrugged. "Lead on."

As they weaved around the other tables, Jett considered how nearly every female employee she'd met at the resort was relatively young and attractive. Cheyenne's plain makeup and standard server's attire—black pants and long sleeve white shirt—didn't hide her good looks.

Mr. Wells must have an eye for the ladies.

Jett cleared her throat. "Have you worked as a server here for very long, Cheyenne?"

"Oh, I've managed the dining room and the resort's ancillary restaurants for just about five years now."

"Managed?" Heat rose to Jett's cheeks. "You don't look old enough to... you look very young."

"Thank you, Ms. Thacker. Aaron stole me away from a competitor at Copper Mountain when I was barely a year out of Le Cordon Bleu."

As Cheyenne spoke, a row of uniformed servers appeared, carrying silver trays. Each set their platter down in front of Jett and lifted the cover while Cheyenne described the courses inside. The aromas filled Jett's nose.

"I have prepared a delightful Caesar salad for you," she said, "followed by a local, delicate goose liver *pâté de foie gras*. For your entree, we have Rocky Mountain rainbow trout almondine, sauteed in a lemon butter herb sauce, and mixed vegetables from our proprietary farms in Boulder. I recommend the 2012 Bollinger *La Grand Annee* champagne. It's very nice—stands up to the *pate* without overpowering the trout—or would you prefer to see a menu?"

TIFFANY LYNN IS MISSING

Before she could answer, a server popped the cork on the champagne and poured some into a fluted crystal glass.

The delicious aromas were more than enticing. Jett sat back, dropping her arms to the sides of the chair and smiling at the feast before her. "This looks amazing, everyone. Thank you."

"It's my pleasure," Cheyenne said. "*Bon Appetit.*"

As the servers departed, a gray-haired woman dressed in a charcoal business suit walked up to Jett's table. "Ms. Thacker?" She had a British accent and held out a tablet computer, displaying leggy models in long coats and stylish boots. "I'm Alexis, the manager of Callendale's ladies' shop downstairs. Aaron asked that I make sure you have whatever winter clothing you may need during your stay. Marceau from our Jenclairre sleepware shop will be up shortly."

Jett looked up at the shopkeeper. "Um… I'm not sure how much winter wear I need, Alexis. I leave tomorrow."

"But surely you'll be back, dear. Aaron said you're doing some very important work for the family. I assumed it could take some time. Now, you look to be a size six in dresses and a seven in shoes, is that about right?"

"That's… exactly right."

"And Giselle described your lovely jacket to me. It sounds very stylish, miss, but please allow me to fix you up with a proper coat and gloves, in case you should need to go out in our weather. It gets very cold here this time of year. We get most of our snow in March and April, so a nice pair of boots wouldn't hurt, either."

As Jett opened her mouth to object, a man's voice boomed through the hall.

"As for sleepwear, some warm, soft flannel pajamas will do the trick. The uglier, the better." The short, portly, middle-aged man was balding, appearing somewhat stuffed into his blue suit; his collar was askew on one side, and the knot in his necktie was too small, but his refined French accent allowed Jett to disregard the other shortcomings. "I will bring to you the ugliest pajamas we carry," he said, wagging a finger. "But I do not enter the style into my ledger. The boss does not need to know what you wear to bed."

Jett smiled, impressed with the level of attention. A moment later, the clothiers had departed, and two tall, young ladies walked toward Jett's table. They wore jeans and sneakers, and North Face sweaters—one in red, the other in yellow. "Ms. Thacker?"

And the parade continues.

They were twins, and obviously they were Aaron's daughters. Jett stood to greet them. "Hello. You're Aaron's children, is that right?"

"Yes ma'am." The one in the yellow sweater nodded. "I'm Matisse and this is my sister Monet, but we go by Mattsie and Monie. Dad said it would be rude to let you dine alone, so we're here to keep you company."

"He said that, did he?" Jett smirked. "But he didn't extend the rule to himself."

TIFFANY LYNN IS MISSING

"Oh, he's on a business call," Mattsie said. "He wanted us to tell you he'll be down shortly."

Monie rolled her eyes. "But that can be an hour for Dad when it's a business call—which it always is."

"Well, please, have a seat." Jett held her hands out, lowering herself back into her chair. "I probably have enough food here for the three of us."

Mattsie placed her hands in her lap. "No thank you. We already ate in Dad's conference room."

"We had to use a folding table," Monie said. "The regular table was missing."

Jett lifted a forkful of salad to her lips. "I see."

Mr. Wells likes to deliver on his promises quickly.

But I bet that table is back in the conference room the minute I leave town.

Monie lowered her head, peering at Jett through her bangs. "You're here to look into what happened to our cousin, aren't you?"

"Tiffany Lynn was our favorite cousin," Mattsie said.

"Even though she was our only cousin."

Mattsie frowned at her sister. "And so she was our favorite." She faced Jett. "Please tell us how we can help you with the case."

"Hmm. Well." Jett covered her mouth with one hand and swallowed, gently waving her fork back and forth with her other hand. "I hate to disappoint you, but I'm not really at liberty to discuss any business I may be doing with your father. Not unless he gives me permission."

"He told us you're looking into why Tiffany Lynn is missing," Mattsie said. "Or... why she was."

Jett looked around. She didn't want to continue discussing—or not discussing—the situation without knowing from Aaron that it was actually okay. "I can see you're both very sad. I know what that's like. I lost somebody very close to me when I was young—my older brother died in an accident. I was younger than you, but my heart hurt so bad, I thought I would never recover. It's like you're hollowed out inside and you're at the bottom of a deep, dark pit at the same time, and it's never going to feel better, doesn't it?"

"Yes," Monie said. "It's terrible."

Mattsie nodded.

"I know how much it hurts." Jett gave them a smile. "But I promise, things will get better. You two seem to be handling it much better than I did. One day soon, you'll be remembering some fun thing you did with your cousin and you'll realize the empty part has gone away. I know it seems like that day would take forever to arrive, but it *will* come. You'll think of her and smile. And that's good. I don't think your cousin would want you to think of her and be sad. Not if she loved you."

Mattsie looked down.

Maybe that wasn't the right tack.

Change the subject.

"Um... so you ate with your dad upstairs?"

"Yes," Mattsie said. "He was helping plan for the volleyball match this weekend—we're playing Andalusia High School in the championship. Dad got some videos of them for Coach Vellmer, and we

TIFFANY LYNN IS MISSING

were watching them while we ate. Andalusia's really good."

"Sounds exciting." Jett sliced into her fish. The girls seemed to be moving on with the conversation. "I played volleyball in high school during my freshman year, but my team wasn't very good. I was the worst one of the team, too. I hope you win."

"Thank you," Mattsie said. She studied Jett's face. "You're very pretty."

Monie gasped. "Mattsie!"

"What? Dad always says we should acknowledge beauty in the world when we see it."

Monie huffed. "He didn't say to be rude."

Mattsie's cheeks turned red. "I wasn't being rude. Was I, Miss Jessica? I've always heard that you have to be pretty to be on TV."

"It's fine," she said. "Please, call me Jett. And thank you, you're very pretty yourself—both of you." She took a sip from her glass.

The comment was out of place, but kids did things like that. Especially stressed kids, and Aaron's daughters were grieving the passing of their cousin. That counts as stress times two.

Poor things. Their emotions are out of whack and they're trying to act normal—and trying to act like adults, too, but they aren't quite there yet.

Let's try another subject.

Jett set her glass down. "And may I say, I'm glad to see you aren't burying your faces in phones like everyone your age seems to do these days."

"Yeah." Mattsie nodded. "Dad says that's rude, too. We're not allowed to have screen time until our homework's finished."

Jett smirked. "Except for watching volleyball videos, apparently. Do you two do everything together, like the twins in TV commercials and movies?"

"No, not everything." Mattsie shook her head, keeping her hands in her lap. "I play tennis and she runs track. Volleyball is the only thing we do together."

"The only *sport*," Monie said.

"Yeah. The only sport." Mattsie looked at her sister. "We used to have all our classes together, too, but not anymore. Not once we started high school."

Aaron Wells' voice echoed through the dining hall. "Are these urchins bothering you?" Carrying a ski jacket in his hand, he walked to the table and patted his girls on the back. "Time to head home, ladies. It's getting late. Curtis will take you tonight."

Mattsie stood, smiling at Jett. "Goodnight, Miss Jessica—I mean, Jett."

"Goodnight," Monie said.

Jett waved. "Goodnight, ladies."

They stood on tiptoe to kiss their father on the cheek—one daughter on each side—and walked to the front entrance, where the limo driver from this afternoon stood waiting.

Leaning on the back of a chair, Aaron peered over his shoulder at them. "And be sure to leave your homework on the kitchen table so I can review it when I get home."

TIFFANY LYNN IS MISSING

"Okay." The girls said, following Curtis through the glass doors to the waiting car. A stream of thick, white exhaust barely escaped the vehicle's tailpipe before being swept away by the wind.

Jett picked up her champagne glass. "Must be nice to have a chauffeur to drive you everywhere."

"Oh, the girls drive," Aaron said. "Trust me, I've paid their speeding tickets. But they're not allowed to drive after dark." He pulled out a chair and sat down. "They both have terrible night blindness, just like their mother had." He glanced at her plate. "How was your dinner?"

"Delicious." Jett took her napkin from her lap and placed it on the table. "Thank you."

Two bellman approached, carrying several boxes tied with string.

"These must be the selections you made from our stores." Aaron pointed. "I'll have them sent upstairs—unless you want to try the coat. I thought… maybe you might enjoy finishing your drink outside by the bonfire. It's scenic, and it'll be warm by the fire pit, but transitioning from Florida's climate to Colorado's can take a little while."

"I'm sold. I'll risk the cold with the coat Alexis picked out for me." Jett stood, taking her glass and the champagne bottle. "I have some additional questions for you anyway."

Standing, Aaron pulled the string off the largest box and removed an elegant coat, slipping it over Jett's shoulders. "Comfy?"

"Oh, yeah." Jett closed her eyes, brushing her cheek over the coat's soft collar. "Mmm. This will do nicely."

* * * * *

The bonfire radiated heat to at least ten feet away, despite the gusty wind. The pit's wide, stone terrace was dotted here and there with clumps of snow. Aaron grabbed two metal wire chairs and placed them close to the pit's raised stone perimeter. "That should be close enough to keep you toasty without melting your shoes."

Jett sat, setting the champagne bottle in the snow. The fire's heat warmed her cheeks. "Are you drinking?"

"Let me get a glass." Aaron lifted his hand at a passing server. The young man immediately stopped.

"Hi, Aaron. Need a drink?"

"Just a champagne glass, Jonah. Thanks."

"You got it." Jonah faced Jett. "Ma'am? Anything I can get for you?"

She held up her glass and the bottle. "I'm good. Thank you." Settling into her chair, she pulled the coat close around her. "This is nice."

"I love the fire pit." Aaron folded his arms and propped his feet up on the edge of the stone wall. "I got the idea from a place I stayed at in Breckenridge, back in the... oh, probably 2005, 2006. They had an awesome fire pit, and everyone gathered around it after they finished their ski runs. They got drinks from the bar and sat around the bonfire singing songs like it was an Irish pub." He nodded. "Good stuff."

"And you wanted that camaraderie here?"

TIFFANY LYNN IS MISSING

"Their bar revenue was twenty percent higher than the surrounding resorts. Heck, yes, I wanted it here."

Jett smiled, taking a sip of her drink. "Why don't I believe that was your only reason?"

"Well..." Aaron grinned. "Let's say it was part of the reason I wanted a bonfire here that everyone would gather around."

"I bet the other part of the reason was those two girls that sat with me at dinner."

He rested an elbow on the chair and rubbed his chin. "I didn't know I'd hired a psychologist. Go ahead. Let's hear your theory."

"Your daughters are very sweet," Jett said. "It's obvious how much you care for them. You all moved here, but it's not home to them, and they'll be going off to college soon." She cocked her head and narrowed her eyes, raising her glass to point a finger at him. "Maybe you created an atmosphere so they'd want to visit Dad a little more often after they leave the nest. Part of that is this bonfire pit."

"Wow, you're good. I'm totally busted." Aaron peered into the fire. "I had no idea my plan was so obvious."

Jonah returned with a fluted champagne glass and a stand for the bottle. "Here you are, Aaron. Is there anything else I can get you?"

"No, thanks." Aaron took the glass. "Didn't your shift end about an hour ago?"

"I'm meeting friends to ski twenty-seven tonight. It's supposed to snow again."

"Okay." Reaching for the champagne bottle, Aaron glanced over his shoulder at his employee. "Be careful. Twenty-seven is steep."

"We'll be okay. Goodnight, sir."

Jett grinned. "I almost expected him to say, 'Goodnight, *Dad*.'"

Aaron poured some champagne into his glass. "I may be a little overprotective around here after what happened to my niece. Sue me." He held the bottle up to Jett. "More?"

"Sure." She held her glass out, and Aaron filled it. "You know, I noticed something." Jett lifted her glass to her lips. "Everyone calls you 'Aaron' around here."

"They should. It's my name." He put the bottle back in the stand. "I'd be upset if they called me George."

"I'm just saying, I like that. It's friendly, like family. Most bosses wouldn't allow that."

Aaron snorted, looking toward the fire. "A real boss doesn't have to remind the employees who's in charge. They know. Why not call people by their first names and have them call you by yours? Make sure they know they aren't just employees?"

Jett took another sip of champagne. The warmth of the fire and the cold of the surrounding air was an enticing combination of contrasts. "The owner of my station—my old station—would never allow that. He was Mr. Nesmith, all the time."

"Then he had other issues. Insecurity, for one. I don't suffer from that particular affliction."

TIFFANY LYNN IS MISSING

Jett looked at him over her drink, her breath turning white as she exhaled over the glass. "Do you suffer from any?"

Aaron shifted in his chair. "Everyone has weak spots. I have two. You met them earlier."

"Mattsie and Monie," Jett said. "They seem very sweet and polite. Very well spoken for their age. They might be a blind spot, but they're not a weak spot. Your family isn't a weak spot. It's a strength."

"Remind me to ask if you still feel that way after you meet my sister." He turned to her. "Speaking of which, you said you had some questions."

"Back on the clock, huh? Okay." Jett sat up, setting her glass on the stone deck. "I'm going to need to access your niece's computer, to see who she was talking to before she disappeared. Email, social media accounts, phone texts, all that. A probate court would grant your sister access. Can you get Ashley to let me into Tiffany Lynn's computer?"

Aaron shook his head. "No chance. Ashley's too much of a control freak. She wouldn't let us see anything that she didn't inspect first, and even then she'd say no. But I have a technician who can probably get into my niece's computer. The one that made the table you don't like, if that won't run afoul of your sensibilities."

"Hey, I only said don't spy on me." Jett held her drink between her forearm and her abdomen while she opened her purse to get her notepad. "I use a special tech person on occasion, too. Sometimes we investigative journalists have to bend a few rules to get to the truth, you know? Now... what do you think the significance of Christmas, Florida was?"

"No idea." Aaron sighed. "Maybe just some sort of twisted joke."

"Is that the sort of thing your niece would normally do?"

"No—but..." The bonfire's flickering flames cast an orange-yellow light across Aaron's face. "People do all sorts of things when they find themselves beyond what they can handle. When someone is truly scared and intimidated, or when they're trapped and threatened... the best of people can do something reprehensible." He turned to Jett. "That's been my experience, anyway. What else?"

"Well, I need to start conducting some interviews. As an investigative reporter, my best angle was telling someone that talking to me was their best way of getting their side of the story out. It has a better effect if they think a subpoena or a civil suit might be coming right behind me, though. I'm sure you've made friends with a few prosecutors and judges out here. We might need to call in a few favors."

He nodded. "Who needs to be interviewed?"

Jett stifled a laugh. "Everybody." Aaron didn't necessarily have faith in the work the locals had done looking into his niece's case, but he hadn't exactly done anything to probe further, either.

I guess that's my job.

It made sense, though. People tended to know the version of law enforcement they saw on an hour-long TV show, which wasn't how it worked in real life. Hours of interviews and days of staring at a computer screen, pounding the keyboards to find links that might or might not add up to a version of events that was different from what was already known—that was where the real investigative reporting took place.

It was tedious and time consuming, but even that wasn't the hardest part of the job. Getting people to talk, confronting the people with something to hide, persuading innocent underlings to risk their job or their security, sometimes even their lives, all in exchange for the ethereal benefit of the truth becoming known, even if justice might never be done… it was a lot to ask of strangers, and it took a lot to win them over. But it was Jett's specialty, because they seemed to know she honestly cared about the truth.

Whatever people knew about Aaron Wells' niece—a runaway, a homicide victim, a suicide—she'd find out. And she'd deliver the truth to the person asking her to.

"We need to talk to the two friends that witnessed the accident, for sure," Jett said. "That hunter, whoever he was, and the kids that were ice fishing. Your sister, but we'll save her for last if we can."

Aaron cocked his head. "Why? She probably knows a lot about the situation. I'd start with her."

"It's…" Jett shifted in her chair. "She's the key player right now. Fairly or unfairly, Ashley would be my main focus in an investigation. We still pursue all the evidence, wherever it leads, because she can be totally innocent, but when I was a practicing lawyer, it was better to get as much information as possible before sitting down with a key player. That way we know what all the people in the chain have said, and we can box in the top dog. An interview goes a little differently when you already know the truth."

"You won't get any of Ashley's underlings to talk."

"Yes, I will. But we also need to talk to your niece's college friends, your brother-in-law…"

"Better let me talk to Jake for now," Aaron said. "That's a lot of people to interview."

"And that's just the first round." Jett looked through her notepad. "Each of them could send us to three or four more people, so I'll need help. I know some folks in Florida I can ask."

"And I know some out here." Aaron set his empty glass down. "Whatever you need, let me know. If you have to hire somebody, hire them. Call Collier to get them on board, call Giselle to get them paid. Whatever they find, they report only to you—I don't want anything getting out. But you report only to me." He stood, reaching into his coat pocket and pulling out a business card. "This is my private number. Call me any time, even in the middle of the night. I'll email you an employee directory tonight when I get home. Desk extensions and home numbers for the DAW Network people."

Jett reviewed the card before slipping it into her purse. "Then I suppose the next thing would be to look at where the accident happened." Standing, she bent over and set her glass at the base of the champagne stand.

TIFFANY LYNN IS MISSING

"Okay," Aaron said. "I'll take you. We're going to get more snow, so the sooner we go, the better. We'd have time before your flight tomorrow, if we go early. Maybe around six?" He turned toward the hotel.

"Fine by me." Jett walked with him, staring at the imposing structure he'd built on the mountainside. Each breath sent a thin stream of white over her shoulder. "Does this place have a gym? My membership in Miami was on the company plan."

"Lower level. Opens at five." Aaron put his hands in his coat pockets and hunched his shoulders against the cold.

Jett stopped, putting her hand on his arm. "Aaron, there's one more interview I'll need to do."

"Who's that?"

"The uncle. You. I need to know what you know, in detail. No business secrets, like how someone can just walk away with thirty thousand dollars. No family secrets, like the relationship between you and your sister—or anything else. If I ask you a question, I'll need you to answer it fully. It'll be the quickest way to figure out what happened to your niece."

Aaron pursed his lips, turning toward the bonfire pit. He took a deep breath and let it out slowly. "Okay. Whenever you're ready." He took a step toward the hotel, then turned back to her. "Why don't you stay and enjoy the fire a little longer? I'm only leaving because I need to review some high school chemistry homework."

Jett put her hands in her pockets. She'd reviewed plenty of homework for her young neighbor across the hall in Miami. It usually needed to be looked at the night it was completed, but this felt more like an invitation to part ways for the night.

"Okay, Aaron. I'll see you in the morning." She felt bad inside, as if she had insulted him.

"Goodnight."

I probably did insult him. Suggesting that someone's sister was your chief suspect in the death of their family member... Even if Aaron thought that himself, it couldn't be easy to hear it said out loud by someone else.

As Aaron continued to the resort, Jett went back to the metal chairs beside the fire pit. Aaron's chair had a small, melted spot in the snow next to it, like a tiny dog had snuck over and relieved itself there without anyone seeing. She squatted next to the chair, letting the light from the fire illuminate the spot.

A resort server came to the empty chairs and stood with her hands behind her back. "May I pour you another glass of champagne, ma'am?"

"No," Jett said, glancing at the bottle. "I think we finished it. Thank you. It was very good."

"I'm happy to hear that. I'll let our manager know you enjoyed it." The server picked up the bottle in one hand and grabbed the champagne stand with the other. "Would you like anything else from the bar?"

Jett stared at the little melted spot in the snow. "Hold on." She took the champagne bottle from the server and rocked it back and forth. A tiny bit of champagne sloshed around in the bottom of the bottle. Jett slowly poured it out next to the chair,

TIFFANY LYNN IS MISSING

creating a second spot in the snow that was identical in color to the first.

It was the champagne.

Aaron quietly pretended to drink with me while emptying his glass into the snow, little by little.

Jett drank, but Aaron did not.

Very crafty, Mr. Wells.

Standing, she handed the empty bottle back to the server. The wind picked up, carrying a small dusting of snow off the hill and down over the patrons below. Jett tugged her collar closer to her neck as an ATV rolled up next to the bonfire, toting a small trailer behind it. A worker in navy blue coveralls jumped out and picked up pieces of dark red wood from the trailer, tossing them onto the glowing coals. The pieces were squares and rectangles of varying sizes, with rough edges, not like the cut logs she'd seen feeding the fire from Aaron's office suite earlier.

Each chunk of wood landed in the pit and sent a burst of tiny, glowing embers upwards into the night sky, zigzagging as they ascended, like a miniature swarm of orange-colored fireflies.

"What are you burning?" Jett asked. "It looks like… wooden tiles."

Across the crackling of the fire pit, the worker held up another dark red rectangle and showed it to Jett. "It burns like tiles, too—not well. Weird, how it's got little wires in it. I guess that was for reinforcing or something."

Jett brushed a strand of hair from her eyes. "Where'd you get it?"

"This morning, this was Aaron's conference table." The worker tossed another chunk onto the flame. "I guess he's getting a new one."

CHAPTER 16

Jett dug through her makeup bag as she stepped out of the steam-filled bathroom. An early workout and a hot shower had done a good job of starting her day, and the arid mountain climate helped her hair dry quickly. She munched on a Wildfire Resort room service bagel as she dressed, sipping coffee and gazing into the mirror over the dresser—and frowning at the two bruised eyes staring back at her. The purple-blue rings weren't any bigger, but they had taken on a deep black tint.

Groaning, Jett reached into her makeup bag.

There is not enough concealer in the world to keep this charade up.

The large, wall-mounted flatscreen TV displayed the local news broadcast. High winds and heavy snow were predicted for the afternoon, but through her window in Presidente suite three, the first rays of dawn displayed a calm, snowy landscape. The skies over the resort grounds looked clear; small gusts of wind lifted delicate waves of fresh powder off the tops of the manicured shrubs, hurling them away.

Dabbing on moisturizer with one hand, Jett picked up her phone and dialed Rico, calculating the difference in their current time zones.

If it's five-thirty here, it's seven-thirty there.
Yeah, he should be up.

Rico answered, sounding wide awake. "Hey. What's up?"

Pressing the phone to her cheek with her shoulder, Jett squeezed a blob of concealer onto her fingertips and gently smoothed it under her eyes. "I've decided to take on this contract with Aaron Wells. Can you make some preliminary phone calls for me—to DAW network employees? I'm hiking to the site of the accident this morning, so I won't be able to do it."

"Sure, no problem," Rico said. Static and road noise came over the line. "I'm doing some remotes with Derek for the next few days, so I can work in some calls. What am I looking for?"

"I'm told the employees won't talk, so keep it basic. By now, they all know about Ashley's reaction when she learned about Tiffany Lynn being found and the call from the morgue. Start with that and build—some receptionist must've taken the call, a bunch of office workers saw Ashley fall to the ground... Try to get any kind of dialogue going. Talk about their pets if you have to."

"And I should direct these conversations toward..."

TIFFANY LYNN IS MISSING

"Well, I doubt any of them will be stupid enough to say anything negative about Ashley while they're at work, but I'm curious to know what their gut reactions were to all this." She peered into the mirror, unhappy with results of the concealer, but moved on with her makeup regimen. Pouring a small amount of foundation onto the back of her hand, Jett picked up a thick, soft brush. "Prod the employees to see if they think Ashley could have played any role in her daughter's disappearance. Do they think there was something more than just an argument with her daughter? Some of them have been around Ashley for years. How was she acting during the disappearance, and during the week or two before that?" Jett ran the brush across her soft skin, blending the colors. "Her reputation is, on-screen she's a sweetheart, off-screen she's a tyrant—but did she act worried about Tiffany Lynn, the way you'd expect a worried mother to act in that situation? Her brother emailed me the network employees' extensions and home numbers. I'll forward it to you. Maybe one of them knows something and will take the chance to get it off their chest."

"You got it," Rico said. "And I want to ask you a question about your new employer—this Mr. Wells."

"Fire away."

"Do you think there's any chance he might have molested Tiffany Lynn somehow?"

Jett took a deep breath and let it out slowly, resting her hand on the dresser.

It was a thought that had to be considered in such a case. The girl had gone missing and ended up near her uncle; that much looked okay for Aaron. But Tiffany Lynn turning up *dead* near her uncle? That didn't look good. If Aaron created the impression to anyone that he'd lured Tiffany Lynn to Colorado, it would be a very different story.

Was Tiffany Lynn running to Aaron for help, or could she have been coming to confront him?

Did she steal the $30,000 or was he paying her off for something—like her silence? It was his word against... no one else's at this point. The money was taken using *his* access codes; maybe he was setting someone up. Creating an alibi about a runaway before he got rid of her.

Aaron said Tiffany Lynn visited his family a lot. Maybe something happened. Something a young woman can't—or won't—tell her mother about her uncle.

Or something that, if the mother found out, could cause the girl to run off.

If Aaron Wells and his niece had grown inappropriately close, and Ashley found out, that would definitely set off some fireworks in the family. Some lingering rumors had it that Aaron was sent to Colorado in disgrace, that he didn't go of his own accord, and did a poor job in his roles at the station. But maybe those rumors were a convenient explanation as Ashley interrupted some unseemly activity.

But...

Other than cheating at business deals, nothing had really come to light indicating anything negative about Aaron so far. All aspects had to be considered, though. He listened in on the conversations of

TIFFANY LYNN IS MISSING

business associates and hacked their texts and emails during deals—but he'd admitted that right away to Jett. That was it, so far.

He was very honest about his dishonesty.

But I don't have any evidence to support a theory of abuse.

"No," Jett said. "I don't think he molested her. It seems... not his style, if that makes sense."

"Consider asking him directly. Watch his reaction."

"I'll think about it." She set down the makeup bottle and dug for another brush.

What would an innocent person's reaction be to an allegation that they had abused their niece? Anger? Embarrassment, that people could think of you that way?

That'd be my reaction.

Jett shook her head. She wasn't doing that to anyone on a whim. "Anything else?"

"Just this." Rico took a deep breath. "Wells' ex-wife Kate died about six months after they got divorced. She was by herself, at night, in a one-car accident, on a lone Florida highway."

Jett held her brush in midair. "Okay..."

"The alimony was pretty substantial. Maybe Wells didn't like paying it."

Exhaling sharply, Jett swiped the soft bristles of her brush across a red rectangle in her makeup palate. "Eh, Aaron isn't..."

She leaned closer to the mirror, raising the brush to her cheek and lifting her chin. She recalled the picture of Aaron's wife in the conference room, the framed print with the black ribbon on it. That seemed like a loving remembrance, not a trophy. And his daughters were in that room a lot. It was there for them, too.

It doesn't fit.

That's not my take on this guy.

"No. Aaron wouldn't take his girls' mother away from them."

"He's Aaron now, huh? Well, remember—we've misjudged people before, haven't we? Like Martin Brennan and Mr. Nesmith. Maybe what happened to Kate Wells is just as the record said, but be careful until you know for sure. I mean, he didn't exactly deny bugging the place when you called him on it, but he still did it."

She stopped applying blush and glanced around the room. "Good point."

"Just be a little paranoid, okay?" Rico said. "For my peace of mind."

The phone vibrated against her cheek. Jett held it away where she could read the screen—it was a text from Aaron.

"I'm here. Are you ready to go?"

She glanced at the time display chyron on the bottom of the TV screen. Six AM on the dot.

Jett texted a quick reply. *"Yes."*

It wasn't completely accurate. She still needed to finish up and put her hair in a ponytail, but an elevator ride to the lobby would take a few minutes anyway.

I'm close enough to being ready that Aaron won't know the—

There was a knock at the door.

TIFFANY LYNN IS MISSING

"Hey, Rico, I'd better go," Jett said. "I'll call you later."

"Okay. Are you still flying back to Florida this afternoon?"

"Yeah." She ended the call and went to the door. Aaron Wells stood in the hallway, wearing a bright red sweater.

Jett winced, grabbing the doorknob.

I guess "I'm here" didn't mean the lobby.

Flipping the deadbolt lock, Jett opened the door for her new employer and stepped back, turning her face to the wall. She lifted her arm halfway over her eyes. "Sorry, I'm not quite camera ready yet. I… thought we'd be meeting downstairs."

"Well," Aaron said, "Alexis asked me to bring these by for you." He held up a small, Wildfire Resort gift bag as he entered the room. "What's wrong? Why are you hiding?"

Jett lowered her arm. "I look like Rocky Raccoon. I need a few more gallons of concealer."

Aaron smiled. "I guess that's why I was dispatched with this stuff." He reached into the bag and pulled out a small makeup bottle. "This worked miracles when Mattsie took a line drive to the arm in softball last fall—right before the homecoming dance, and she had gotten a sleeveless dress. You couldn't even tell she had a bruise in the photos." He removed a pair of large-frame oval sunglasses from the bag. "Alexis also suggested these."

Jett took them and walked back to the mirror, trying them on. The sunglasses hid all of the bruised area around her eyes but still looked fashionable. She turned her head back and forth, viewing the glasses from various angles. "Think it's too much?"

"Nope. Let's go."

As she reached for her room key, Rico's thoughts about Aaron's surveillance tactics came back to her.

Maybe the room's still bugged, and the disposal of the conference room table last night was all for show, to get me to drop my guard.

Let's find out.

Jett held up her phone. "I'll be done with this call in a minute. Can I meet you downstairs?"

"Oh, absolutely." He turned around and headed toward the door.

Jett picked up the makeup bottle. "Thank you for bringing this. And please thank Alexis for her kind consideration."

"You're welcome." Aaron opened the door, looking back at her. "Your eyes look fine, by the way. They're... very pretty." He smiled, then looked down, his smile disappearing as fast as it had come. "Anyway, I think you notice the bruising a lot more than other people would."

"Yes, I do. Now, shoo." She waved a hand at him. "I'll be down in five minutes."

The door clicked shut behind him. Jett stared at it, tapping her finger on the lid of the concealer. Aaron Wells did not seem like a nefarious person. He seemed nice. Wholesome. A generous business owner and a good father.

Rico's other warning echoed in her head.

"We've misjudged people before..."

TIFFANY LYNN IS MISSING

Jett walked to the closet and took out her new, heavy coat, laying it on the bed. "Okay, Rico," she said, lifting the phone to her ear and pretending to continue her conversation. "Aaron left, but I need to go now. Keep probing into…"

Think of a name. Something innocuous.

"Keep probing into Project Red Fern. It will blow the Wells case wide open. Okay? Got it. Thanks." She tossed the phone onto the bed and disappeared into the bathroom to finish getting ready.

* * * * *

With her hair in a ponytail and a thick white sweater to brace against the cold of the coming hike, Jett stepped out of her suite and boarded the elevator. The doors glided shut in front of their sole occupant, and the elevator started its descent, forcing Jett to pop her ears.

We are a long way from Miami and our sea-level elevations.

She shoved her hands deep into the warm pockets of the coat, enjoying its soft lining. As she did, her phone rang.

Ashley Wells' name appeared on the screen.

Jett held the phone in front of her, pursing her lips. The lawyer part of her didn't want to take the call—it was better to speak to a target in an investigation after interrogating the subordinate players—but the investigative reporter part of her said never turn down the big interview. It might not come again.

Her thumb hovered over the green button as the phone rang again.

Ashley Wells has a harsh reputation. This isn't likely to be a social chat.

But it has to happen sooner or later.

Maybe she wants to know how things are going. Let's hope that's it.

Jett didn't like confrontation any more than anyone else. She did it because it was part of her job, first as a lawyer and then as an investigative reporter—but that didn't make her immune to the discomfort of verbal clashes with people. She did it because she had to. She was good at interviews because she did her homework and forced herself to ask the tough questions—the kind of questions other reporters wouldn't ask. But she hadn't done much homework on Ashley Wells yet.

I guess you have to answer anyway. Never let the big interview slip away.

Swallowing hard, she tapped the screen and put the phone to her ear. "Hello?"

"Leave my employees alone."

It was roughly the greeting Jett expected. "And a good morning to you, too, Ms. Wells."

"Don't be snide," Ashley said. "I don't know what you're up to, but I am in no mood to have some diva TV reporter poking around in my family business in an attempt to get some headlines for herself. I lost a child, my employees did not. Leave me alone and leave my employees alone. They have nothing to do with any of this."

Jett's heart was racing, but she tried to maintain a calm demeanor. Years of training made it possible, even if was still an act. "Thanks, but I'll run my investigation the way I see fit."

TIFFANY LYNN IS MISSING

"I see. Well, if your minions continue to interrogate my people, I'll slap you with an injunction and file a suit for harassment. You want to play hardball? Let's play. I have things to lose, but I'll bet you do, too."

"Is that a threat?"

Dozens and dozens of interviews had taught Jett that angry people like to vent and bluster, but in doing so they occasionally let something slip.

Let's wave the red flag at the angry bull.

Let's see what you might spill, Darling Ashley Wells.

"I don't make idle threats," Ashley said. "I am telling you directly, if you don't stop, I will burn your house down with you in it. You think those amateurs at Miami 5 hurt you with their little clown show? Did their little smear game bruise your ego? Wait until I get started."

Jett had gotten innuendos like that hundreds of times—typical bluster, to keep a celebrity's or politician's odd actions out of the public eye. Ashley seemed no different.

Ashley may be a professional TV persona, but right now, she's still just a person who's venting.

Press her.

Jett adjusted her grip on her phone. "You certainly sound like someone who has something to hide."

Ashley laughed. "Don't try to play the antagonist game with me, sweetie. You're out of your league. Go home to Miami, and stay there. I work with TV people for a living, but preying on a grieving mother? Even the tabloid reporters would find that despicable. And it won't play well. I'm a Florida icon. What are you? An unemployed, temper tantrum-throwing drunk. A local TV star who wants the big time but has only succeeded in getting a good address and a mediocre reputation—before getting fired."

Jett nodded. Insults were part of the bluster game.

Typical celebrity stuff.

"I'm sorry you don't feel my credentials are up to par," Jett said. "My new employer thinks otherwise."

"Who hired you? Aaron?"

"I'm not at liberty to disclose that."

"Of course my brother hired you. You like him, too. I can tell. Everyone likes Aaron."

Jett sighed to demonstrate her disinterest in Ashley's attacks. "From what I know, your brother seems like a nice man, but that's not relevant to this conversation."

"Don't lie. I can always tell when someone's lying to me. Of course it's relevant. Don't be so naïve. Now, you *will* cease calling my employees, immediately. And you will stop any discussions about this 'Project Red Fern.' There's no such thing. Don't try to associate me or my businesses with it. Do you hear me?"

Jett's head snapped upright.

Project Red Fern?

How could Ashley know about that already? I just invented it!

"You're just trying to make trouble for me, Ms. Thacker," Ashley said. "It's an obvious stunt to

TIFFANY LYNN IS MISSING

gain a cheap headline and get back on the air. Don't mess with me or my people again."

Jett was only half listening. She had laid out a trap for Aaron, but snared his sister.

My room is bugged. It has to be. There's no other explanation.

Ashley and Aaron work together on everything, so Aaron probably set it up. Rico was right. I need to watch my step.

And I don't need to keep talking to Darling Ashley Wells right now.

Jett tried to keep from displaying any surprise at the mention of the fictitious Project Red Fern. "You're repeating yourself, ma'am. Maybe that's a sign that we should end this conversation."

"I'll end *you*, sweetie. Everyone has secrets they don't want exposed. I do, but so do you."

Jett's stomach lurched.

If Ashley has been listening in on all my conversations, what else have I been talking about?

What else does Ashley know?

Is she having someone research me? A private investigator wouldn't have to work too hard to learn about the extracurricular activities that ended my marriage...

She shifted her weight from one foot to the other, her heart racing.

I don't need any more negative headlines right now, either. Not while I'm trying to get another job on TV.

"Miami is a fun town," Ashley sneered. "So many clubs and bars... it can be quite a small town, too. Tell me, Ms. Thacker... who do you think will suffer more when our secrets finally come out—me, or you?"

Jett gripped the phone, swallowing hard.

"That's what I thought." Ashley chuckled. "I'm glad we understand each other."

CHAPTER 17

Tonnie, the bellman, was standing in the lobby when the elevator doors opened. "Miss Thacker!" Tonnie smiled. "How are you this morning?"

"Great!" Jett lied. She forced a smile, her stomach still in a knot from Ashley's phone call.

Rico's right, my private life isn't a big deal.

But... it's a big deal to some people. National networks might have anchors who live nontraditional lifestyles, but smaller markets have owners like Mr. Nesmith, who'd never—

"Ma'am," Tonnie said, "Aaron is waiting at the snowmobile rental stand. May I show you the way?"

Jett tried to put Ashley's call out of her head.

What did Ashley know, anyway?

Meanwhile, who am I really going on a hike with? Aaron lied about bugging the room, or Ashley wouldn't have known about the fictitious Project Red Fern.

But I can't bail out on the case. I need the money.

"Ma'am?"

Why fly me out here and play games?

The frustration mounted, as it always did when she was investigating something with contradictory stories.

"Ms. Thacker?"

Jett shook her head, bringing herself out of the chasm of her thoughts to look at the middle-aged bellman standing in front of her. "I'm sorry, Tonnie. What did you say?"

"Not a problem at all." Tonnie put his hands out. "Takes a while to get used to the time change from Florida. It's probably very early for you, miss."

Jett rubbed her forehead. "No, Florida is two hours later. I'm just... I have a lot on my mind."

"Then a nice hike will do you good." He smiled and gave her a wink. "Fresh air and all. Aaron will be outside, getting ready. I'm happy to take you. We can walk most of the way indoors. This way, please, ma'am."

She followed Tonnie down a long, sloping corridor, trying to get the uneasy feeling in her abdomen to subside.

"Welcome to the team!" Martin smiled broadly from the other side of his big desk as Jett signed her employment contract with the station. He glanced over her shoulder toward the door. "Mr. Nesmith, we got the talent you wanted." Martin stood as the station's owner entered the room.

TIFFANY LYNN IS MISSING

"Nice to have you on board, Jessica." Mr. Nesmith was a large man, both in stature and girth. He towered over most of his employees.

"Thank you, sir." Jett stood and shook his hand. *"Please, call me Jett."*

Mr. Nesmith laughed. *"I'll call you expensive. I saw that contract."*

"And worth every penny, sir." Martin beamed. *"This lady is a rising star."* He sat back in his chair, putting his hands behind his head. *"Do you know what I think it was that put you over the top for this job? Your credentials are top notch, but it was a story Rico told us. You were both prepping for a live shot near Biscayne Bay—some sort of drug thing—and a member of the drug gang started firing a gun."* Martin grinned at Mr. Nesmith. *"Rico said when he looked up, Jett was the only person running toward the bullets."*

Nesmith smiled. *"Is that right?"*

"Well, it was very generous of Rico to say that." Jett folded her hands in her lap, keeping her eyes focused on the station owner. *"The truth is, I was scared silly. But that's where the story was, so that's where I went."*

"You see?" Martin rocked forward and slapped the desk. *"That's the kind of instincts we need around here."* He pointed at Jett. *"That mindset will take you straight to the top, Jessica. And our station with you."*

Run toward the bullets. It had made her a star.
Then do it now.

As Jett continued down the sloping corridor, guests came and went, opening doors and letting the icy wind blast its way into the building. She clenched and unclenched her hands in her pockets.

Focus on the task at hand and trust your gut about the other stuff—and your gut says Aaron's not involved in his niece's death. He just listens in on conversations and then shares them with his sister—so watch it.

When the time's right, let loose with the accusation about molesting Tiffany Lynn. Watch his reaction.

And if the chance comes up, let it slip about Project Red Fern and see what Aaron does in person.

Meanwhile, you are being paid to do a job. A young woman is dead, and some of the people around her are acting very strange. That's what you focus on. Just assume all your conversations on Aaron's properties are being listened to, and be more careful.

And for now, don't let on that you know about the bugging—or are bothered by it.

"Here we are." A large set of double doors opened automatically as Tonnie approached. "Aaron is right over at that shack."

Jett peered across the snowy ground to a small building with wooden siding, with a "rentals" sign mounted on its roof. A thick stream of white smoke rose from its chimney pipe; a young man and woman in coveralls wheeled tall propane heaters out from the back door. Several other workers roared forward on brightly-colored snowmobiles, parking them next to the heaters.

As Jett crossed the short, cold span of ground, the fragrant scent of pine trees swept over her with the breeze. She spied Aaron in a blue and white ski

TIFFANY LYNN IS MISSING

jacket. He waved to her from the front counter of the shack.

"Good morning." Aaron stood next to a young woman in a red snowsuit that covered her from neck to ankles. He grinned at Jett, his breath drifting away in white puffs. "I should have asked you—do you know how to ride a snowmobile?"

Jett put on her oval sunglasses. "I thought we were hiking."

"We are. But it's about five miles to the Lake Brimstone trail head, and another five up to the site of the accident. Overdo it at this altitude and you'll be gasping in no time. You just came in from sea level. You need time to adjust to the thinner oxygen up here. Didn't you notice during your workout?"

Jett shrugged. "I didn't do any cardio because I thought I'd be hiking."

Lighten up. You're acting angry.

She didn't like the change in plans, but didn't recall the specifics being mentioned, so maybe it wasn't a change.

"Well, don't worry." Aaron smiled. "You'll still work up a sweat. I know I will." He pointed at the mountain. "The trail is that way. It slopes gradually upward most of the time, but some parts get pretty steep. How are you on a motor sled? Ever ride one?"

Jett shoved her hands deep into the warm pockets of her new coat. "On vacation once. When I was about twelve."

Aaron recoiled, his eyebrows raising. He turned to the rental shack employee. "Uh... we'll take the tandem snowmobile, Lucinda."

"Okay, Aaron." The young woman walked to a large blue snowmobile with a long, two-level seat. She threw a leg over the machine and sat down, turning a key and pressing a button on the dashboard. The engine roared to life. "Hold the rail around the back seat, ma'am." Lucinda turned around, patting the thin, stainless-steel piping that surrounded the second seat. "Feet go on the running boards, and you just lean forward going uphill if it's steep." She shut off the engine. "This sled's all gassed up and ready to go, Aaron. Let's get you two some gear."

They followed Lucinda into the building, to a long rack of snowsuits. "You can put your coat over in the locker, ma'am. I'll get you a snowsuit that will keep out the cold. Your boots look good for today."

Aaron approached, carrying two helmets. He handed Jett one. "These have two-way radio communication, so we can talk while we ride." He took off his ski jacket and climbed into a snowsuit that was hanging on the wall. The legs had zippers to allow for oversize hiking shoes and boots; the arms had elastic at the wrist to shut out the wind. Aaron stood up and reached for some mittens, then zipped the front of his suit over his red sweater. "There."

Lucinda appeared with a smaller suit and some mittens for Jett. "This one ought to fit you pretty good, ma'am."

Aaron grabbed two bottles of water from the counter, dropping them into his helmet as he headed outside.

Slipping into her new attire, Jett checked herself in the rental shack's full-length mirror. The top of her white sweater stuck out from the collar of

TIFFANY LYNN IS MISSING

the thick snowsuit, but the suit itself was a bit bulky for her satisfaction, like she'd gained twenty pounds.

She scrunched up her nose. "I look like... the Michelin tire mascot!"

"The helmet radios get good reception." Lucinda continued her preparations. "But only over a short distance. If it goes out or you can't hear over the engine noise, just tap Aaron on the shoulder and yell. Cell reception at Lake Brimstone is spotty at best, and nonexistent when you get up on the mountain, but if you get in trouble, there are emergency flares in the cargo bag. And Aaron took some water, so... that's about it, for safety, I guess. You're all set."

Jett stretched the elastic sleeve bands over the ends of her mittens. Two people riding one snowmobile was a little closer than she wanted to get to Aaron Wells at the moment.

He said the trails were steep. Maybe that's not true.

She faced Lucinda. "How difficult would you say these trails are that we'll be going on?"

"The one you're going on has several inclines that are much steeper than we'd let our guests ride, and you can always hit a pocket of powder that's three or four feet deep, but Aaron knows what he's doing. He can be a speedy driver, though, so if he gets going too fast..."

"Tap him and yell." Jett nodded. "Got it."

"Yes, ma'am. You'll be fine. We'll see you in a little bit."

Jett put her purse in the locker, unzipping her snowsuit to slide her phone into the pocket of her jeans before walking toward the exit.

"Hold up. Let's secure that helmet before you go outside." Lucinda took Jett's helmet and eased it over her head. "It's cold out there, and it'll be a lot colder when you're underway. Don't let any chills get inside the suit, and it'll keep you nice and toasty. You'll need that today." She adjusted the collar for Jett. "Looks good. Try the radio."

Jett automatically prepared to do her standard spiel for a mic check at the TV station.

I'm Jett Thacker, and this is The Jett Set, live from...

She caught herself, her cheeks growing warm. There was no Jett Set. Not anymore. She shifted her weight from one foot to the other and cleared her throat. "Testing, one, two, three."

"Come on out, co-pilot." Aaron's cheerful voice crackled over a tiny speaker in the bulky helmet. "Your chariot awaits."

Outside, Aaron was already atop the blue tandem snowmobile, a steady stream of white exhaust blowing from its tail. Jett put her hand on his shoulder and stepped onto the running board, the machine's springs bouncing as she straddled the rear seat.

"Hold those rails," Aaron said. "They're pretty firm."

The fumes from the snowmobile's exhaust pipe assaulted her sore nose. Gripping the steel rails at her sides, Jett stared at Aaron's waist, which was more or less between her knees. She leaned against

TIFFANY LYNN IS MISSING

the motor sled's tiny backrest for maximum distance. "Lucinda says you're a speedy driver. If the snowmobile feels too light, check to see if I fell off."

Aaron chuckled, easing the machine into motion. "I won't lose you. You're important cargo."

The snowmobile gave a smooth ride as it left the packed snow around the resort, and didn't get much bumpier over the virgin snow beyond. The wind was strong though, especially when Aaron sped up in the open areas. It pulled at her constantly, like a thousand cold, invisible hands trying to snatch her off the big machine.

I don't like how it makes me look, but this snowsuit is a lifesaver.

Jett looked around at the whiteness of the landscape. Florida was always very green, even in winter. Here, the colors were few and stark. Blindingly white snow that sparkled like tiny diamonds close up. Deep, dark green pines. Gray rocks and brown dirt.

The swath of trees at the base of the mountain grew closer and closer, but until then, the ground was relatively flat and smooth. The immaculate white tips of the Rockies loomed in the distance, and the scent of evergreens filled the air. Before long, the knot in Jett's stomach had subsided. The scenery was too gorgeous to harbor bad feelings.

"This is really pretty out here," she said.

"You can see why everyone loves it." Aaron waved a hand toward the snow-white horizon. "Such a great view."

The motor sled bumped over a patch of rough terrain. A few small, thin fir trees zipped by.

"Which do you like better," Jett asked. "Colorado or Florida?"

"Well… If I could have this scenery without the cold weather, I might choose Colorado. But I think Florida will always have my heart."

She settled into the ride, relaxing more as the scenery rolled by. A deer perked its ears up and looked at them before darting off into the brush when they got too close. She let her eyes wander upward to take in the sheer massiveness of the mountains. It was like a postcard every time she looked at it.

"Why'd you move?" Jett asked. "Just for business?"

She knew the answer, but was testing him. The reports demeaning Aaron were always based on "a well-placed source at the station" or "someone close to the situation." Sometimes, the source in such a story was a disgruntled employee with an axe to grind, but occasionally the source was merely a figment in the imagination of a creative instigator looking to exact a vendetta—as Jett well knew, based on her recent Miami 5 experience. But even the best rumors about Aaron's reassignment to Colorado were always based on the idea that Ashley was putting him someplace where he couldn't harm her growing network, and he had never refuted them.

The gossip didn't seem to jive with reality, though. According to Rico, Aaron's reputation was that of a savvy negotiator and solid deal maker, a quiet and skilled deal maker who was in it for the long haul, not the headlines. He certainly appeared to be more than a figurehead or screwup to Jett. A lot more.

TIFFANY LYNN IS MISSING

"I moved here because we saw an opportunity," Aaron said. "We knew we could make money. Ashley's audiences are very loyal. If she mentions a book on her show, it sells ten thousand copies that day. If she says she likes a restaurant, it's packed for the next three months. Why wouldn't we capitalize on that? So we started talking about developing a beach resort in Florida, but prices were crazy. Then, on a family ski trip out here, we noticed properties that were available and that weren't too far from the popular ski spots—and they were cheap. Building a luxury resort in the mountains suddenly seemed like a very attractive option."

Jett stared at the back of Aaron's helmet. "The Smoky Mountains are a lot closer to Florida."

"Oh, I love the Smokies, but if you're going to build a resort…" He turned his head toward the jagged white peaks of the Rockies. "That's the view to have when it's done. We scored a ton of land options through a private LLC, so nobody'd know it was DAW doing the buying. We had the architect waiting in the wings, the builders… it was organized down to the nanosecond. The resort went up in record time and was profitable almost overnight. Now, we're expanding to phase two."

"We? Ashley oversaw all that from Orlando?"

Aaron sat up a little straighter in his seat. "As far as the press is concerned. She's the face of the organization."

As they reached the base of the Brimstone Lake trail, Aaron slowed the snowmobile to a stop.

A wooden sign had been erected, courtesy of the Brimstone County Sheriff.

"Warning. Police crime scene ahead. Trespassing is a federal offense."

Jett peered around Aaron to glimpse a thin, snowy space between the trees that weaved its way up the mountain before disappearing into the brush. The trail—what there was of it—was untouched white snow a few inches thick, discernible from the rest of the forest because it was a slightly wider patch of white, and slightly straighter—but that was all. If the signs designating it as a trail head hadn't been erected, the path wouldn't appear to exist at all.

"The accident site is a few miles up," Aaron said. "It's supposed to be marked by some cones and police tape."

"Okay." Jett gripped the rails again. "I'm ready when you are."

The snowmobile crawled up the trail, branches and brush lashing out at the travelers as they ascended. The path zigged and zagged, coming close to the edge of a few very scenic—and very steep—drops, but only getting tricky in a few places. One incline caused Aaron to rev the engine hard, as the snowmobile ascended a section that was practically straight up. Jett squeezed the stainless-steel rails, leaning forward into Aaron's back. His muscles rippled through the thickness of the snowsuit as he forced the machine up the trail.

As the engine whined, gravity seemed to want to pull Jett off the back of the snowmobile. She threw her arms around Aaron's middle and pressed her knees into his hips. "If I go, you go, buddy."

TIFFANY LYNN IS MISSING

At the top of the tricky ascent, he eased off the engine, his firm back relaxing as he breathed hard. Jett relaxed her grip on Aaron's torso, but didn't let go the rest of the way.

The trail flattened out. Aaron drove the snowmobile between the tall pines and firs, finally stopping in a semi-open area. "I think we have to hoof it from here."

Jett looked around. "Where's the police tape?"

"Further up the trail, I guess." Aaron pointed to another steep incline. The path was like a makeshift staircase, with rocks and exposed tree roots as the steps. The bark of small trees had been rubbed smooth where hikers gripped it to help themselves climb. Aaron stepped off the snowmobile. "The sheriff said we couldn't miss it."

"Yeah, but has it snowed since then?" Jett dismounted, her legs tingling from the engine's nonstop vibration.

"I think he took that into consideration." Aaron stared at the steep grade, removing his helmet and placing it on the motor sled seat. "Come on. It can't be far." He pulled a wool cap from his outer pocket and slipped it over his head, turning to her. Another thick wool cap was in his hand. "We'll have better visibility without the bulky helmets."

Cap in place, Jett followed Aaron to the hill. The dirt around the rocks was cold and hard, still frozen from the Colorado winter. She climbed, grabbing skinny tree trunks and firm branches where necessary, hauling herself up the icy trail toward the scene of a young woman's unfortunate death—possibly with someone who had played a role in it.

CHAPTER 18

At the top of the incline, Jett looked around, breathing hard. The climb hadn't been more difficult than her regular session on a StairMaster at the gym, but she couldn't catch her breath. Heart pounding, she trudged after Aaron, sucking the cold air into her lungs.

High altitude sucks. I work out! This is embarrassing.

He stopped, placing his hands on his hips. A ribbon of yellow tape flickered near his shoulder. Jett walked forward, inspecting the site.

It looked too small.

The trail widened to maybe twenty feet, in a flat circle, with trees all around. Snow covered the area, but the tips of frozen grasses and small plants peeked through. Between the lush trees on the slope, the ground fell away, allowing a view of the morning sun as it cast its glow over a frozen lake and the gorgeous mountains beyond.

The scene was majestic, as if a photographer had created the perfect image of a mountain lake, but had somehow managed to allow all the images to remain in motion. A cluster of gray specks was a distant flock of birds soaring across a clear blue sky; dashes of snow drifted from treetops now and again, slowly gliding down to the cold, hard surface. The surrounding forest was dark, with its green pine needles and brown bark, calm and quiet under a thick white blanket of fresh powder. Across the frozen lake, the blue tint of the shaded mountainside looked out over the world.

If this hadn't been the site of a terrible accident, it would make for a beautiful park or scenic overlook.

She looked at Aaron. He had been silent the entire time since reaching the taped-off section. "You okay?"

"Yeah, I'm... it's just hard to imagine someone falling from here, especially my niece. It's flat. There's a good view without going near the edge. She was an athlete, with great balance and coordination. She—"

"Aaron..." Jett clasped her hands in front of herself, lowering her voice. "She was a kid, playing around, and she slipped. Kids do things like that."

"No." He frowned. "Not Tiffany Lynn. It doesn't figure."

The sound of barking dogs carried over the top of the hill, their long howls piercing the stillness. Jett turned toward the noise, peering into the trees. They sounded like large animals—and angry ones. "Is hunting allowed up here?"

TIFFANY LYNN IS MISSING

Aaron stepped toward the edge of the cliff. "I just can't see it. Not Tiffany Lynn." He peered into the abyss. "Look at it. There's hardly a branch disturbed."

The knot returned to Jett's stomach.

I can see it fine from right here.

But that wouldn't cut it. Not for the reporter who ran toward the gunshots.

Jett crept toward the edge. The slope dropped away dramatically, veering down to the ice below. The curve of the shoreline dipped inward, almost creating a pocket. Chunks of ice rested on the surface; a rectangle of yellow tape was held in place with orange cones. Aaron stood at the edge of the cliff, frowning, his hands on his hips.

And he was right.

There was new snow on the side of the gorge, but it didn't look like anyone had passed through there at all—much less the tumbling body of a grown young woman who had fallen accidentally. A descent like that would be awkward and cumbersome, rolling and sliding, flattening smaller plants and breaking limbs from shorter trees. It might not look like an avalanche had happened but it would not look like a pristine wilderness.

"Maybe they got the location wrong." Jett looked further up the path. "Let's have a peek that way."

She walked ahead, huffing and puffing again in the thin mountain air, with Aaron following. After a few curves, the trail took a sharp turn away from the drop-off.

There, the side of the cliff looked broken in places. Jett stepped closer. A clear path of flattened brush and foliage showed what looked like someone's quick descent.

It was here. Tiffany Lynn fell here.

At the bottom, the ice of the frozen lake and the police tape.

The wind blew hard into Jett's face, searing her cheeks. "I think this was the spot, Aaron. I think... it happened here." She turned to him, his face grim. "Could this have looked similar to the marked spot before the recent snow?"

"Maybe." He scowled. "I'd think if you're a sheriff in these parts, you'd know the difference."

Jett peered down the steep slope. "The kids were scared. They just lost their friend. Nobody's going to think straight in that kind of situation. And the slope seems to end up at the same place—the curve in the lake."

He studied the ice, the chilly gusts pulling at the collar of his snowsuit. "You know, they didn't recover her coat. Not for three days." Aaron faced Jett, his voice growing softer. "The boy who jumped in to rescue her, he said it was too... too heavy, too *waterlogged*, for him to get her out with it on." He shook his head. "She was a Florida girl. That's a Florida mistake—heavy outerwear that soaks up the water... like having a twenty-pound weight tied to each arm and leg. No wonder she... People out here, they know. They dress in material that doesn't..."

Aaron turned away, putting his hands on his hips as he stared into the tree line. "A stupid coat."

TIFFANY LYNN IS MISSING

The wind pulled another soft wave of powder off the treetops and sprinkled it on them.

"She was out here for a reason, Jett. She took money that she knew I'd notice. And you know why we didn't spot it sooner? Because I bribe politicians to get land variances. Giselle thought that's what it was, and she didn't say anything. We only found the discrepancy after it was too late." Aaron turned to her, his faced etched in pain. "If I were an honest man, my niece might be alive."

Jett's heart sank as she watched the tortured man in front of her.

This is not a man who was involved in causing anyone's death.

She went to him, putting her hand on his arm. "Come on, Aaron. I've seen what I needed to see. Let's head back."

He nodded, taking a deep breath and letting her guide him down the trail toward the snowmobile. In the distance, someone whistled, and the dogs started barking again. A far away gunshot carried through the trees, and the dogs stopped their howling.

Jett peered down the trail. It all looked the same—snow and trees—like the rest of the forest. Somewhere over the ridge, the dogs started barking again. This time, they sounded closer. "Do you remember how far it was to the snowmobile?"

Aaron pointed. "It's right around this bend and then up about—"

A man in a ski mask stepped from behind a tree, holding a rifle across his body and blocking the path. His plaid jacket was dirty and worn, his boots frayed. The stranger narrowed his eyes, his long black beard sticking out from under his mask and swaying in the cold mountain breeze. "What y'all doin' up here?"

He had an angry tone, thick with the drawl of a hillbilly, and the dirty hands and fingers of a person who hunted for their meals. The gap in the ski mask over his mouth displayed a scowl that said he wasn't happy about having company on the mountain this morning.

Fear gripped Jett's insides.

"I'm talkin' to you, boy." The man pointed his rifle at Aaron, baring a mouth of sparse black teeth and gaping red gums. "Put yer hands up, both y'all. What you doin' up here?"

Aaron and Jett raised their hands. The sound of the dogs came closer.

"We came to look at a crime scene," Aaron said, his voice firm and even.

"Crime scene?" The stranger spit a streak of brown onto the snow at Aaron's feet. "Ain't no crime scene up here."

"Okay, then. There's not. So, we'll be on our way." Aaron took a step.

The man jumped into Aaron's path, frowning as he leveled the gun at Aaron's waist. "Y'uns can go when I say you can, not before. This here's private property." He stared at Jett, licking his lips, a small string of drool escaping where his front teeth should have been. "Is what he said right, girlie? You looking for a crime scene?"

"Yes." Jett's voice quivered.

"But I just told you! There ain't no crime scene up here! Are you calling me a liar?"

TIFFANY LYNN IS MISSING

"No. I mean, I don't..." She shook her head, the knot in her gut growing. "We—we may have been mistaken."

The man reached over with a mud-stained finger and flicked Jett's hair. "You'd better believe you was mistaken. I done told you, this is private property. My cousin and me been hunting all morning and we ain't spotted no crime scene. Lessen you're sayin' we're stupid and missed it. Is that what you're saying?"

The barking and howling got louder.

"No." Jett kept her eyes down to appear submissive. "Nobody's saying that."

Years of crime scene reporting had taught Jett that confrontations usually ended in one of two ways—a fight or a negotiated settlement. The stranger had the gun and was acting aggressive; that put him in a momentary position of power. Provoking him might end in tragedy. But coming off as meek could invite a disaster, too. It was a fine line; a tricky hand to play. Jett and Aaron hadn't passed another soul on their trip. If the stranger was determined to get hostile, there wouldn't be a lot of ways to avoid it. No one might ever even know.

Appear agreeable without coming off as weak and submissive.

Jett's gaze darted over the snowy ground, searching for a rock or heavy stick to use as a weapon.

"Look," Aaron said. "We told you. We came to inspect a crime scene. It's marked in tape right over there, around the bend."

His tone is perfect. No anger or weakness.

Aaron glanced at the trail. "You can go check it out if you—"

The rifle fired, filling the woods with the deafening sound of its blast.

Jett cringed, her ears ringing as pine needles fluttered to the ground between her and Aaron.

"I'll do the talking here, boy." The stranger glared at Aaron. "I'm telling you folks for the last time, there ain't no crime scene. Or maybe you and your woman's too deaf to hear good. Is that it?"

Aaron stood still, his hands in the air. Jett trembled as she watched the interaction. The barking dogs came closer.

Whatever this guy is thinking, right now he might be like a bear that's been surprised—making himself big to scare us, but probably not actually intending to do us any real harm.

Unless he's a psychopath.

Either way, he needs to put us down so he can feel dominant. Then he'll either go away or try to do something.

Aaron's no fool. He knows that's what we need to do—without submitting too much.

The man poked Aaron with the rifle. "I asked you a question, boy!"

A second man came out of the woods, carrying a shotgun and leading two howling dogs—one pit bull and one rottweiler. He wore a ski mask, too, and a long riding coat that was just as threadbare and dirty as the other man's. His animals strained at their makeshift leash, a rope tied around each animal's neck. They clawed the snow and dirt to get

TIFFANY LYNN IS MISSING

to the strangers, snapping and growling as they flashed their massive yellow teeth.

Jett's heart pounded.

Those are not hunting dogs.

How do we get out of this? There are two now, and maybe more.

Negotiate, but be ready to fight. A rock, a stick, fingernails—anything to let the attacker know a fight will cost him something.

The knot in her abdomen lurched.

Fight two men who have two guns and two big dogs?

The second man stood on a short ridge, about twenty feet away, holding the barking dogs, his shotgun resting on his forearm. "Whatcha got here, Lem?"

"This here's some folks come to see about a crime scene, Jarvis." Lem grinned, exposing his black gum line as he shifted back and forth on his feet. The dogs barked nonstop behind him, their eyes fixed on Jett and Aaron. "This city fella and his woman don't hear good. I done told them, there aint no crime scene up here."

"Y'all are lost." Jarvis' hillbilly accent was as thick as his cousin's. "Ain't no crime scene 'round here."

"Have it your way." Aaron's voice continued to be firm and even. He looked Lem right in the eye. "We'll leave. We have a snowmobile around that ridge. Let us get to it, and we'll be on our way."

Jett's heart pounded, the fluidity of the scenario changing.

Aaron is not going to submit.

Is he going to provoke a fight and try to get the weapon?

Two of us against one of them could get the rifle. That changes things. The other man won't shoot into the three of us if we're clumped together, wresting for the gun.

Be ready.

Lem turned his head toward the other man but kept his eyes on Aaron. "What do you say, cousin? Should we let them take their snowmobile and be on their way?"

The dogs pulled at Jarvis' hand. "I reckon we need to check out that snowmobile."

"It's fine," Aaron said.

"Oh, y'all are mechanics now?" Lem growled. "Well, I know you ain't. Got no grease under them fingernails."

"You're right. I'm not a mechanic." Aaron clenched his jaw. "Now, what do you want? Fun time's over."

"You think so?" Stepping back, Lem waved the gun toward the trail. "Let's take a walk down and see that snowmobile. Maybe the fun's just starting."

The wind picked up. Large flakes of snow fell from the sky.

Aaron looked at Jett, lowering his voice. "Walk ahead of me, Jett. I'll be right behind you. He won't hurt you."

Swallowing hard, Jett glanced at the mountain man.

He grinned his semi-toothless grin. "Don't you be so sure, girlie."

TIFFANY LYNN IS MISSING

As Jett walked toward the snowmobile, Aaron followed close. "Be ready," he whispered. "If this goes bad, jump right over the edge and grab something to stop your fall. There are too many trees to get a clean shot off, and they won't risk following us down."

She winced, peering at the ice at the bottom of the cliff. "*If* it goes bad?"

"Shut up!" Lem shouted.

Jett stopped at the snowmobile. Lem walked around to the front of the group; his cousin and the dogs stayed behind.

"Why we stopping here?" Lem said. "This can't be your snow machine." He pointed the gun at Aaron again. "This here one's mine. Yours must still be down the trail a piece. Maybe you should go look fer it."

"No, this one's mine." Aaron's voice was flat, displaying no emotion, even as he continued to defy the hillbilly.

Jett held her breath.

Aaron's obviously had enough.

"It's a rental," Aaron said, his eyes on Lem.

"A rental! From one of those fancy resorts." He grabbed the handlebars and turned the snowmobile toward the frozen lake, then walked behind and tucked his rifle under his arm. "I reckon y'all are about to lose your deposit." Chuckling, Lem put his hands on the rear frame, shoving the snowmobile toward the cliff.

Do we jump him now, with a shotgun pointed at our backs?

"Hold up," Jarvis said. "Check that saddlebag."

Lem stood up, pulling the straps of the bag under the rear seat. He took out the two water bottles and the flare gun, laughing. "This is a real nice pea shooter, boy." Staring at Aaron, Lem stopped smiling and tossed the flare gun off the cliff. "Oops."

Jarvis chuckled.

Returning his attention to the snowmobile, Lem threw his weight into the frame. Grunting and groaning, his feet churned the soil, advancing the machine to the edge of the cliff.

It tottered a moment, bits of snow and ice dropping down the cliff, and then he gave it a final heave.

The snowmobile crashed through the underbrush, smashing plants and small trees as it bounced along. Halfway down, it rolled over on its side and slamming into the dirt, turning over and over, as it kicked up rocks and snow. It plummeted down the slope and hit the ice with a loud bang, breaking straight through the frozen surface in a frothy, white splash. The tail bobbed up and down a few times, then it disappeared under the waves.

Lake water sloshed around the hole, waves spilling over onto the ice.

"All right," Aaron growled. "You've had your fun. Let us go."

"You can go right now, boy." Lem pointed the rifle back at Aaron. "But I'll be having that pretty set of coveralls you're wearing.

Jett gasped. "He'll freeze out here without his snowsuit!"

TIFFANY LYNN IS MISSING

"Yours, too, girlie. And both y'all's mittens." He faced Jett. "Get 'em off. Then start walking."

The snow came down harder.

Jett glanced around. "It's too cold to be out in this snow in regular clothes!"

"Then you'd best walk fast." He glared at Jett. "Now strip out of them fancy britches or I'll shoot you in the head and take 'em off for you."

Her stomach lurched.

Strip? That's a specific word.

Is he going to force himself on me? Would he take Aaron out of the equation by shooting him or tying him to a tree, and then...

The thought of his sparse teeth and black gums coming close to her face made Jett's stomach churn.

"Get out of your britches," Jarvis said. "Then get to moving."

Frowning, Aaron glanced at Jett and nodded. *"Get to moving."*

Maybe it's over, or almost over.

Odds are they still just want to push us around to show who's in charge. It could be a trick to make us relax a little, then attack with surprise.

Aaron's being smart, though. If these hillbillies don't know how to end this, he's making suggestions.

As she unzipped the suit, the wind sliced through her sweater and jeans like they weren't there.

If they just want the snowsuits, it'll end here.

If they want something else, we need to fight for our lives.

Aaron tossed his snowsuit to Lem. Wrapping his arms around himself, Aaron's red cable-knit sweater was a sharp contrast to their white surroundings. He rubbed his arms.

Shivering, Jett kicked her snowsuit to Lem's feet.

"Are we done?" Aaron said. "Can we go?"

Smart again—asking permission while suggesting.

It's probably the best we can do at this point.

Lem leered at Jett. "Maybe... we ain't quite finished yet." Another stream of brown drool spilled from his toothless mouth as Lem smiled at her, patting his rifle barrel.

Here we go.

Jett balled up her fists, her pulse throbbing in her ears.

Fight, Jett. He doesn't get what he wants without a fight—and without paying a price.

Aaron's hand darted out, seizing the gun barrel and jerking it upward. He stared into Lem's eyes, not blinking. "You finished what you came to do. We're leaving. And you're going to let us leave."

Lem tried to jerk the gun away, but Aaron kept his grip, stepping sideways so that Lem's body blocked Jarvis' line of fire. The rifle stayed pointed at the sky, each man clenching one end.

Grunting, Lem jerked the rifle a second time. Aaron didn't let go. He kept his eyes fixed on their harasser. Lem pulled again, unable to get the gun free.

Grab Lem's ankles and bring him down. Maybe Aaron can get the gun away from him.

TIFFANY LYNN IS MISSING

Jett took a step toward the two deadlocked men.

A blast from Jarvis' shotgun rippled through the air, sending a cascade of leaves and branches down between Jett and Aaron. The gunshot's echo bounced off the frozen lake and hillside.

Aaron looked at Jarvis on the ridge and slowly released the barrel of Lem's rifle.

Free of Aaron's grip on his weapon, Lem hauled his rifle back—and swung the butt hard into Aaron's ribs.

Jett screamed. Grimacing, Aaron fell to the ground, clutching his side and groaning.

"Who's a tough guy now, city boy?" Lem hovered over Aaron, raising the weapon above his head. "You and your big mouth are layin' on the ground, ain't ya!"

"Stop!" Jett leaped forward, grabbing the rifle. "Stop it!" She clawed at Lem's face through his ski mask, yanking it up over his ear.

As Lem twisted away, his mask came off in Jett's hand. Streaks of red lined his cheek. He put a hand to his face, dabbing at the wound and inspecting his bloody fingers.

Jett leaned back, swinging a leg at Lem's ribs. He caught her foot before it hit him.

"You…" Gritting his teeth, Lem shoved Jett backwards onto the cold, rocky dirt.

"That's enough!" Jarvis shouted. He aimed his shot gun at Jett and Aaron. "You two—get up and get moving."

Jett wrapped her cold fingers around an icy rock, holding it to her side as she got to her feet. She took Aaron's good arm and helped him stand. Aaron groaned, panting and holding his side.

Lem sneered at Aaron. "Maybe we should take your woman with us, so's she can see what a real man's like. How'd that be, boy?"

Aaron took a half step toward the hillbilly, his voice a low growl. "You try it, and you'll be dead in sixty seconds—no matter who's holding the rifles right now." He clenched his teeth, leaning into Lem's face. "I *might* die, but I guarantee, you *will* die."

Lem backed away, his face falling. With trembling fingers, he lifted his weapon toward Aaron. "You... you gonna do something, boy?"

"Yes. I'm going to stop you." Aaron narrowed his eyes and stood tall, as if he felt none of the pain that had been delivered to him moments ago.

Jarvis cocked his shotgun. "I said that's enough. Lem, you got the britches. That's good enough." He spit into the snow, wiping his mouth with the back of his hand. "Now, y'uns get on out of here before I change my mind and let the dogs loose."

"Yeah!" Lem crouched behind his rifle, shifting from one foot to the other. "Sic the dogs on 'em, Jarvis." He dabbed at his bleeding cheek.

Aaron put his arm on Jett and took a step toward the trail they'd taken up the mountain, keeping himself between her and their attackers.

"Not that way, mister. The other way." Jarvis pointed up at the high path.

Aaron frowned. "That way's another seven or more miles."

TIFFANY LYNN IS MISSING

"Best get to it, then." Jarvis looked at the sky. "Blizzard's coming. Be getting a lot more snow soon. Wouldn't want you to lose your way."

Aaron stared at Jarvis, the wind blowing his hair across his eyes. Turning, he moved to take the longer path.

"Lem," Jarvis said. "Don't forget their water."

"Good idea." Lem stooped to pick up the water bottles. "See? We ain't savages." He cradled his rifle under his arm and unscrewed the cap from one of the bottles. "Here."

He squeezed the bottle, launching a stream of water into Aaron's face and chest. Aaron recoiled, the water soaking into his red sweater.

Cackling, Lem jumped backwards, away from Aaron to grab the other bottle. "Can't forget you, girlie."

As Jett turned away, a stream of water hit the back of her head, running down her spine. She gasped, the shock of the icy water forcing her to double over, goose bumps covering her arms and legs. Pain rippled across her back as the liquid glued her sweater to her cold skin.

Before she could step away, a second shot of water hit her face like a cold slap.

"Well, lookie here." Lem tossed the bottle aside, walking toward her. He leaned over and inspected Jett's face from a distance, aiming the gun at her. "You got you some shiners on you, girl. Did your man give you them black eyes?"

Aaron glared at him. "Get away from her."

"Shut up!" Lem shoved the tip of his rifle under Aaron's chin and pulled a large pocket knife from his belt, flipping it open to expose the blade. "I'll take this here knife and slice you up, y'hear? Now stay quiet." He looked at Jett, breathing hard. "Now, y'all tell the truth, girl. Did that man hurt you?"

Pulse throbbing, Jett shook her head. "No."

She clutched the frozen rock in her hand, holding it near her hip, ready to smash it into the side of Lem's face if he moved an inch closer.

"No, you ain't hurt." He pulled the gun away from Aaron's neck and stepped backwards. "You probably like that kinda thing." He spit at her feet.

"Leave her alone." Aaron shoved Lem backwards. "If you try anything else, you'll follow that snowmobile over the cliff."

Lem backed away another step, pointing his shaking gun at Aaron. Jarvis laughed as his dogs broke into a fit of barking.

The snow came down harder, becoming a cascade of thick, white lace. Jarvis was only half visible from his perch on the ledge.

Clutching his gun, Lem scowled. "Y'all heard him. Get to walking."

Aaron continued staring at the man with the shotgun. Wet, white flakes gathering on his cheeks and shoulders.

Turning to Jett, Aaron nodded his head in the direction of the longer section of trail. "Let's go."

The shotgun fired again, sending a spray of pine needles and twigs onto their heads.

"Faster!"

TIFFANY LYNN IS MISSING

The hostages sprinted up the path. Somewhere behind them, the dogs barked and howled.

DAN ALATORRE

CHAPTER 19

Jett's legs pumped as she ran along the narrow trail, her gaze staying on the snowy, uneven ground. Moving quickly over the slippery surface was a lot different from walking on it—and one person had already gone over the edge on this trail. "Is it really seven miles to the exit this way?"

"Maybe more." Aaron huffed, leaning toward his injured side. Each footfall seemed to make him grimace harder, but he ran at Jett's pace. Coughing, he lifted his hand and pointed into the woods. "There's a cabin over there. The path to it crosses this one up ahead. Hurry."

"Okay." Jett peered into the trees. The torrent of falling snow hid everything more than ten feet away. "What about the dogs? Won't they follow us?"

"Those dogs," Aaron grunted, "have as much chance of tracking us as a goldfish. They're not hunting dogs, and the way this snow's coming down, our tracks will be covered in an hour. That's all the time we need."

Jett blinked snowflakes out of her eyes, her lungs aching. The high altitude was working on her again. Each breath wheezed through her windpipe, tightening in her throat, but didn't seem to get down to her lungs.

But she didn't dare stop running.

Her neck and back were wet and cold, her cheeks stinging in the frigid air. She glanced at the rock in her hand and tossed it into the brush. Every ounce of effort needed to go into moving.

"Right here," Aaron said. "Turn."

Gasping, Jett slowed down to let him lead the way. As Aaron turned to the right and headed down the offshoot trail, Jett stopped moving and put her hands to her knees.

She sucked the cold air into her lungs, but it wasn't enough. She couldn't stop gasping.

"Hey, you okay?" Aaron stopped and ran back to her.

Jett shook her head, fighting for a deep breath. "Just... overdoing it." Standing, she put her hands on her hips and took a few steps along the trail, getting a word out between gasps. "This is... embarrassing. I can't... catch my breath."

"You're doing fine." He went to her side and put his hand under her arm. "It's the thin air. You're not used to it. Can you walk?"

She nodded, wheezing.

"Just walk with me. Don't try to talk." Aaron guided her down the trail. "The cabin's not much

TIFFANY LYNN IS MISSING

further. We can slow down." He glanced over his shoulder. "I don't hear the dogs."

Jett forced herself to inhale each icy breath and keep moving. "This is... ridiculous."

"No, it's not. People do it all the time, even me. It's the sudden change in altitude. If I spend more than a few weeks in Florida, I have to readjust. I can barely get up the stairs, otherwise."

She kept her eyes focused on the ground. She didn't need to slip and fall, too. Her feet were warm; everything else was freezing except the top of her head.

"Lucinda... rocks," Jett gasped. Each breath was a knife in her chest. "These caps... are awesome."

Aaron smiled. "Just walk with me, okay? No talking necessary. I've got you."

She nodded.

"How's your breathing, Jett? Any better? Just nod or shake your head."

It wasn't better, but she nodded again anyway. Her chest felt like it was being squeezed by a python. Her throat felt like it had shrunken to the size of a soda straw.

Her foot slipped on the snow, sending her sideways. Aaron's firm grip kept her from falling, then he slid her arm across his shoulders. "You're doing great, Jett. Just a little further."

The falling snow was all she could see. Tall trees became faint brown shadows behind a blur of white. Landscape didn't exist unless it was smacking her in the face. It was all white flakes.

"We're almost there," Aaron said.

Jett's ears hummed. Aaron's breath was almost as labored as hers. She squeezed her eyes shut and shook her head.

"No, don't do that, Jett. Don't close your eyes. Keep breathing. I've got you."

Moaning, she tipped her head back and heaved her chest up to get a deep breath.

Aaron grunted, his breath blasting across her cheek. "That's it. Breathe as much as you can. You'll be fine when we reach the cabin and get some water into you. It's just another minute."

Each breath was capped with a short wheeze on its way in and another on its way out. She let her eyes close.

Only for a moment.

Immediately, she lost her balance. Wincing, she braced for impact with the frozen surface.

But she didn't hit the snow. Aaron's hands went under her legs and shoulders, hoisting her upwards.

He's carrying me.

Aaron's breath was warm on her face, his grip on her solid and firm. Reassuring. She couldn't help but relax a little as he trudged through the snow.

"You did well, Jett. Made it all but the last ten feet." The bottoms of her boots touched the ground, and Aaron held her upright. "We're here. Can you stand up?"

The sound of a creaky door met her ears, and then she was moving again, stepping with Aaron across a wood floor. As the door shut and closed out the noise of the wind, Jett opened her eyes.

TIFFANY LYNN IS MISSING

The ceiling of a small wooden cabin stared down at her—and Aaron's smiling face. "Welcome back."

He was strikingly handsome in the light of the cabin. Square jaw, bright eyes, focusing only on her.

A tingle shot through her insides.

This guy almost got himself killed to save me. He grabbed that gun without any weapon of his own to defend himself.

Heat rushed to Jett's cheeks. "'Welcome back?' I didn't pass out." She tried to sit up.

"Whoa, tiger. Don't try to get up. Just breathe." Aaron put one hand on her shoulder and one behind her head, easing her back down to the floor. "I know you didn't pass out."

Her heart rate lessened as her faculties returned to her. "Did I?"

"No, you're too tough for that. Close, though." His brilliant smile radiated through her. He rubbed his hands together, then massaged her upper arms, his breath streaming away from his lips in a puffy, white cloud.

The little bit of warmth from his hands felt like heaven.

"You're okay now," Aaron said. "I'm going to get a fire going for us, then I'll melt some icicles from the roof for water, so you can rehydrate. You'll feel a lot better in a sec."

"I can't believe I almost passed out." Jett cupped her hands to her mouth, blowing hot air over them. "This is so embarrassing."

"Well..." Aaron kneeled in front of the cabin's small fireplace, arranging some kindling from a stack on the hearth. "I'm not going to tell anybody, so your secret's safe." Standing, he opened what looked like an antique metal milk box and took out a box of matches. A moment later, a small flame was growing in the fireplace.

Aaron walked to the rear room of the small cabin, returning with a thin blanket and a worn-out sleeping bag, that had been rolled up and tied with rope. He spread the blanket out on the floor. "Can you slide over onto this? It'll give you a little insulation."

As she moved onto the blanket, he wrapped the sleeping bag around her shoulders and returned to the fireplace.

"Thank you." Jett settled in, laying on her side and resting on one elbow. Her head was still a little groggy, and her stomach clutched like she might need to vomit. "Uhh... Aaron, I feel a little sick."

"That's the altitude sickness trying to work on you. It'll pass." Aaron placed a few more split logs on the fire. "Drinking some water will help. I'll have that for you in a sec."

He opened the box again and took out a metal cup. Walking to the cabin door, he reached outside, snapping a long icicle from the roof. He broke it into sections and stood them upright in the cup, placing it on the hearth near the fire. "Now, let's get you warmed up some more."

Aaron walked behind Jett and sat down, putting one leg on each side of her and pressing his firm torso to Jett's back. She leaned close to the wonderful little flames in the fireplace as Aaron

TIFFANY LYNN IS MISSING

rubbed her arms. "Body heat," he said. "Let the fire work on you. I'll be a ninety-eight point six degree backstop."

His arms felt good. He was warmer than her, but neither of them was really warm yet. The close proximity on the floor was awkward, but... very welcome. Aaron had helped her, carrying her when she couldn't go on, and now he was getting her warm instead of himself.

Jett peered over her shoulder. "Share the sleeping bag with me. You're almost as cold as I am."

Jett pulled his hand from her shoulder and held it up to the small fire, massaging his fingers with hers in the fire's warm glow.

Aaron sighed. "That feels... very nice." He lowered his forehead to the back of her shoulder, letting out a long, slow breath. "Good thing you made it. I was getting close to passing out myself."

The fire crackled and popped, its little flames shining into the dim cabin. Outside, the steady stream of falling snow blotted out the light and shaded the windows in a gray hue.

Aaron pointed to the cup. "We should get some fluids into you. It'll make you feel a lot better."

Jett reached over and picked up the metal mug. Chunks of ice still floated inside, but the vessel contained enough water to drink. She lifted the metal brim to her lips and took several long, deep sips. Each gulp soothed her insides, slowly dissipating the tension in her lungs and neck. The queasy feeling subsided, and she took a few deep breaths. Normalcy was quickly returning.

She pressed the cup to Aaron's hand. "Your turn."

"Okay," he said. "Thank you."

He drank deeply, his firm chest warm against her back, and drained the cup. The ice rattled as he lowered his hand. "Sit tight. I'll get us a refill." Crawling out from the sleeping bag, he stood and went to the door.

Jett's entire backside immediately grew cold again. "Wow. Hurry back." Shivering, she clutched the sleeping bag to her neck and rubbed her upper arms.

Cold air blasted through the tiny cabin as Aaron plucked another icicle from the overhang. "Luckily, we already have a fire and there's more wood on the porch. Here." He handed Jett the icicle. "I'll grab some bigger pieces and get our little blaze up to room-warming level."

As Jett broke the icicle into the cup, Aaron stacked small logs onto the fire. He took a second cup from the milk box, along with a small, rectangular container, and sat down on the side of the hearth. "I think these might be crackers." He popped open the lid on the container and peered inside. "Yep." Shaking a saltine into his hand, he held it out to Jett. "Hungry?"

She accepted the cracker and took a bite. It was salty and a little stale, but it was a welcome morsel of food. She held her hand out for another. "How did you know all this was even here—this cabin?"

TIFFANY LYNN IS MISSING

Aaron shrugged, shaking a few more crackers into Jett's hand. "I saw it when we were doing aerial surveys for the new Passionfire resort."

"Phase two of your construction?" she said. "This cabin is on your property?"

"Technically. Why?"

Jett frowned. "Your niece died on your property, and you don't find that relevant to mention?"

"I don't think she knew we owned this." Aaron took a bite of a cracker. "Not many people do. But so what? If she came to check out the new site with friends, how is that important?"

"I don't know. Maybe it's not. But it might not look good."

"To who?" Aaron cocked his head. "You?"

"I just..." Jett pulled the sleeping bag closer around her. "I think it might matter at some point. You should have told me." She looked at him. "Honesty, remember?"

Aaron nodded slowly. "Okay, I'm sorry. I should have told you sooner." He popped the rest of his cracker into his mouth. "I wasn't hiding it, though. I've been straightforward with you, like you asked."

Jett sat upright. "Really? What about Red Fern?"

He pushed his hair off his forehead, his expression blank. "What's Red Fern?"

"After you left my room this morning, I pretended to be discussing Project Red Fern with my associate in Miami. I said it would blow this investigation wide open, and five minutes later your sister called, asking about it."

Aaron's jaw dropped. "Ashley called you?"

"Yep. She told me to stop harassing her employees and that Project Red Fern didn't exist. Now, if you aren't bugging my room, how did you know about Project Red Fern?"

"I didn't." Aaron shrugged. "I just heard of it—when you mentioned it right now."

Jett watched his face in the light of the fire. "Then how did Ashley know about it?"

"I don't know."

"The room is bugged," Jett said. "Did you lie to me?"

Aaron put his elbows on his knees, taking another cracker from the box and handing it to her. "I didn't lie to you, and I didn't bug the room. I got rid of the conference room table for you, didn't I? That thing cost a lot of money, but I got rid of it... because you... because..." He clasped his hands together. "Anyway, I got rid of it. I've been straight with you, whatever you've asked, and I'll continue to be straight with you. That's our deal, and I keep my word. You can watch my security guy scan your suite when we get back, or we can have it checked by whatever company you want. Then we'll both know what the deal is." He sat back, resting his back against the hearth. "We're on the same team, Jett."

The wind picked up, rattling the cabin windows.

"Maybe Ashley bugged the room," Aaron said. "She stayed there a few nights ago. Maybe she

TIFFANY LYNN IS MISSING

thought I'd have someone stay there to work on the case. Which I did."

"So she'd know what I was saying? She doesn't trust you?"

"She trusts me."

"Does she?"

You think she may have bugged your hotel rooms and sent people out here to threaten and possibly shoot you. You think she might also have played a role in your niece's death.

But you're still partners with her, and you still trust her?

Jett adjusted the sleeping bag. "What's the deal between you two, anyway?"

"We're business partners," Aaron said. "We always have been."

Jett watched Aaron's eyes as she asked her next question. "Did she kick you out of the station in Orlando?"

A thin smile crossed Aaron's lips. "That old story. It never goes away." Shaking his head, he sat upright on the hearth and looked into Jett's eyes. "She... the press likes a story, right? When we decided to expand and build a college, it became a big tax on Ashley's time, and she needed to be focusing on her show. My sister is as smart as she is beautiful, but she has her limits. The public sees Darling Ashley Wells as the driving force behind the business, and the TV sponsors started to worry that she might be spreading herself too thin. And she was. That's her style. But the sponsors thought programming might suffer—though it never did, I'm proud to say—and if they thought Ashley was focusing on real estate development in addition to a private college and a fledgling TV network, that would *really* make them worry. So she came up with a cover story that she leaked to a reporter during a fluff piece interview. A rumor, allegedly, from a staffer close to the source, you know?"

"Close to the source." Jett nodded. "My understanding of that phrase has taken on new meaning recently."

"The story got a little skewed when it came out. Ashley was trying to assert that she was still principally in charge of everything, but delegating some new projects to others so she could focus on improving ratings. That came off as me getting moved out of the TV station because ratings were slipping. The *concerns* of the sponsors were taken as actually having happened, and she couldn't get the regular press to report the story correctly. They liked the version that suggested maybe the starlet was juggling too much. In Ashley's eyes, the only way to fix it was to feed the press an even juicier tidbit—that I'd never been anything but a figurehead all along. The second story knocked the first one off the front page and into oblivion."

Jett took a sip of water from her cup. "So, it was a power grab?"

"It was a *publicity* grab. And so what? She needs headlines, I don't. So I went with it because refuting it wouldn't have changed public perception. I mean, how could we convince people we were *both* running everything when the sponsors preferred to think there was only one decision maker? I knew how valuable I was to our company. Ashley certainly

TIFFANY LYNN IS MISSING

did—we aren't fifty-fifty partners in everything because she's generous. But the company isn't called 'Darling Ashley Wells And Her Really Smart Brother, Too.' We had a lot of money at stake with the expansion, so we kept it simple for the sponsors—let everybody think Ashley is a whiz at everything she touches. It turned out to help marketing, too. I was able to raise our advertising rates ten percent just a few weeks later."

Jett considered that. She didn't know the intricacies of running a resort hotel, but from outward appearances, Aaron definitely seemed to know what he was doing. He knew all of the employees by first name, down to waiters at the bonfire pit *and* that their shift had ended. According to his daughters, he worked late all the time. The managers spoke well of him, and seemed genuine and competent in their jobs. They were more than competent; they were experts, and they exuded a satisfaction at being part of the Wildfire establishment.

That kind of thing comes from the top, and no one at Wildfire has even mentioned Ashley.

"Okay, Aaron. You're no figurehead."

He grinned. "Why, thank you."

"But why did she do that?" Jett put her hand out. "Lots of companies run with different people in charge of different departments. Coca-Cola does. Nabisco does, General Motors… The vice president of GM's marketing department isn't also the head of engineering."

"We aren't Coke, Nabisco, or GM," Aaron said. "It's Darling *Ashley* Wells. That matters. And we aren't as big as those other companies, either."

Jett stared at the fire.

Maybe ego played a role, too. Ashley seemed to have too much ego, and brother Aaron had too little—which she knew.

But did he?

It hadn't seemed that way with the hillbillies a moment ago.

She looked at Aaron. "How did you know those two guys wouldn't kill us back there? The hunters."

He shrugged. "I didn't."

"No? You sure acted like you did."

"People watch TV and think guns are magic wands—you wave one, and everyone has to do whatever you say. That only works if the attacker actually intends to shoot or kill someone. If the victim tests that, or doesn't comply, and the gunman hesitates... in that instant, the magic is gone from the wand and the whole situation has changed."

He picked up a stick and poked the fire.

"Someone sent to commit a murder needs to get it done quickly. Those clowns took a long time to do things. Taunting, heckling... We mentioned a crime scene. They had no way of knowing if the sheriff was coming to meet us, or another group of people looking to inspect the site. So, killing us didn't seem to be on their agenda. They just wanted us out of there."

TIFFANY LYNN IS MISSING

"Guess so." Pulling her legs up under her, Jett rested her chin on top of her knees. "Friendly crowd you get out here."

"I don't think those guys were from here. They weren't dressed for the kind of cold we get here. And the one guy said a *blizzard* was coming. People in Colorado don't throw around the word 'blizzard.'"

"That was Jarvis, yeah. There weren't any footprints in the snow when we started onto the trail. Think they came the other way?"

"Probably," Aaron said. "There weren't footprints around the cabin when we got here."

Jett sat upright. "Something struck me about their clothes, too. Their coats and shoes were old and worn, but not the ski masks. Those looked brand new. I'd bet they bought them just for our little encounter. And I did a TV report about hunting in Florida. Hunters usually bring something to field dress their kill and carry it back. Aside from the knife, I didn't see any of that. And nobody uses rottweilers or pit bulls for hunting dogs. So…" She looked at Aaron. "They were sent here? By who?"

"Who bugged your room?" he said. "I know I didn't."

You didn't react like you bugged my room, either, unless you're an Academy Award winning actor. You definitely weren't faking it when Lem hit you with that rifle.

Speaking of which…

Jett nodded to Aaron's ribs. "How's your side feeling?"

"Not great." He lifted his sweater. His side was cut and bleeding, with a bruise the size of a dinner plate.

"Aaron!" Jett jumped up, rushing to him. "You are really hurt! Sit down on the blanket." She pulled him off the hearth, stripping off his t-shirt and sweater.

"We trading roles?" He winced as he sat down on the floor. "You're the nurse now?"

"Shh." She threw the sleeping bag over his waist. "Lie back and let me look at you." She knelt next to him, gazing at the injury in the light of the fire. Aaron's rippled torso shined in the orange glow.

We are in this mess together. It's happening to both of us.

He's injured because he stopped that maniac from hurting me.

"I'm so sorry." She shook her head. "I was so busy worrying about me that I didn't even think... Can I do anything? Should we put ice on it?"

"No ice, please—I've had enough cold for a while." He smiled at her, his deep brown eyes shimmering as the flames flickered in the hearth. "Besides, it looks a lot worse than it feels. I think I'd be very happy to just lay here for a bit and get warm. I'll be fine."

"Okay." She pulled the sleeping bag up to his chin and crawled under, letting him be closer to the fire, pressing her body to his uninjured side. The warmth felt good.

The closeness felt good, too.

He'd been willing to sacrifice himself for me. He didn't even hesitate.

TIFFANY LYNN IS MISSING

Jett studied Aaron's face. Even now, he looked very handsome in the warm glow of the fire, laying back with his eyes closed, his toned chest rising and falling with the calmness of a sleeping lion.

She drew a deep breath. "You were going to attack him so I could get away, weren't you?"

"If I had to." Aaron turned his face to Jett, his eyes locking on hers. "You'd have done the same. I saw you grab that rock."

"No, I mean... I'm not sure I've ever known anybody who would do something like that for me."

"Now you do." He tucked his hand behind his head. "How does it feel?"

It felt good. Better than good.

She sat up, trying to ignore a different type of knot that was now growing in her stomach. "Does your side... uh, hurt bad?"

Lifting his head off the floor, Aaron peered down at his big bruise. "The hillbilly cracked a few of my ribs. Not much you can do about that but tape it up and suffer—and we don't have any tape."

Jett looked at the metal box on the hearth. "Does that milk crate have aspirin in it?"

"No." He closed his eyes and rested his head back on the floor. "Most cabins like this have a few things. Usually, it's matches and a little wood. This place did well for us, with those crackers."

Pulling back the sleeping bag, Jett leaned over him to inspect the injury again. "It looks awful. We're getting you to a doctor when we get off this mountain—whenever that is."

"I'll be okay. The snowstorm will pass in a few hours, and then we'll walk out. I'll get my ribs looked at then. But it's really going to suck hiking out of here without snowsuits. We were able to hang onto our boots, so that's good, but the blanket and sleeping bag are going to have to keep us warm until we can get to a phone signal—which is probably a mile or two past the trail head." He sighed. "If we try to walk out now, with it snowing this hard, we'll just get lost. I'm not letting anyone else die on this mountain."

"Deal," Jett said. "Except for maybe those hillbillies. I might be okay with them freezing to death out here." She looked at Aaron's face, the warm light of the fire shining on his skin. "You didn't seem too shaken up by Mr. Toothless Mountain Man and his cousin. Why?"

He shrugged, keeping his eyes closed. "I was nervous. I wasn't gonna let *them* see it."

"You didn't let me see it." Jett rested her hand on his shoulder. "Because it didn't happen."

"It happened." Aaron looked up at her. "I wasn't going to get killed over a motor sled and some snowsuits, but once that mountain man pointed his gun at you..." Aaron smiled. "I wasn't going to let him hurt you, Jett."

"Pretty gutsy, you grabbing his rifle like that." Jett let her fingers drift across Aaron's shoulder and up his neck, lingering on his chin. "You may have saved my life."

Aaron's voice fell to a whisper. "Think so?"

"Yes, I do." She leaned forward and slid her finger to the side of his chin, turning him to her and

TIFFANY LYNN IS MISSING

kissing him deeply, enjoying the warmth of his soft, full lips. "Thank you."

Aaron exhaled sharply. "You're, uh... you're welcome."

She laid her head on his shoulder, stroking his cheek. "So..." Her voice was a hush on his warm skin. "The storm should pass in a couple of hours, and the hillbillies' dogs would serve as an early warning system if they start heading our way. What do we do until then?"

"Drink water and stay as warm as possible. It's gonna be a very cold walk."

She lifted her head and brushed her nose across his ear. "I have another idea." Sitting up, Jett pulled her sweater and t-shirt over her head, her blonde hair falling across her bare shoulders. She pressed her lips to his again, swinging a leg over his hips and straddling him.

Aaron put his hand on her shoulder. "Jett, I..." He swallowed hard. "I don't think we should..."

"No?" She kissed him again, moaning softly as his hands slid over her thighs and came to rest at her hips. She let her hair fall around his face, looking into his brown eyes. "Why not?"

"Well, uh... you're an employee of mine now, and—"

"Shh." Jett crushed her mouth against his, exploring him with her tongue, her body tingling as he put his hands on her back and pressed her into him. Sitting back, she grabbed the edges of the sleeping bag and pulled it over them. "Body heat. We need to get as warm as possible for that long walk."

DAN ALATORRE

CHAPTER 20

Aaron kneeled next to the hearth, the blanket wrapped around his toned waist as he placed more wood on the fading red embers. His muscles rippled in the dim glow of the fireplace. Clutching the sleeping bag around her naked figure, Jett slid two metal cups of icicle chunks across the hearth.

Clapping some bark fragments from his hands, Aaron stood and walked to the window.

"How's it look out there?" Jett asked.

"Better. We'll be able to leave soon." He picked up her phone and checked the time. "Keep an eye on your battery—it'll drop like a rock when we get out in the cold again. With any luck, we'll get out and be picked up before it gets dark, but we'll take some matches to start a signal fire if necessary."

Jett reclined on the floor, propping herself up on one elbow. "You don't worry much, do you?"

"Sure, I do." Aaron walked back to her, sliding under the sleeping bag. His firm, naked body felt good on her skin. "I just try not to obsess—which I'm really bad at—but I try not to let it show. I guess when you've actually had bad things done to you, lesser things don't mean much by comparison. You're more... numb. Less threatened."

Jett rolled over to face him. "What bad things were done to you, Aaron? Did Ashley do something?"

He shook his head. "You don't want to get into all that. I don't see how that could help your investigation."

"Let me decide what helps my investigation." She looked into his eyes. "You said you'd be honest about everything." Jett took his hand in hers, intertwining their fingers.

"Ashley never hurt me." Aaron sat up, giving Jett's hand a squeeze. "Karen used to be rough on my sister and me when we were kids, okay? Real rough."

"Karen is your mother?"

He looked away.

"Just tell me, please," Jett said. "I want to know. And I want to know *you*. Your family business is tangled up somehow with a missing niece who ended up dead. I need to learn about the family dynamics. Maybe it will help me understand what went on with your sister and your niece."

Aaron took a deep breath and let it out slowly. "Karen's our mother. When we were young, she was a broken-down woman with twin babies and no money, barely scraping by... often, not even scraping by—and she was a pretty bad alcoholic. We lived in a trailer with holes in the floor and a tarp over the roof to keep the rain out, and we wore clothes that

TIFFANY LYNN IS MISSING

other families threw away. Karen was beautiful—men all over town were always chasing after her. But she was... unstable, and as kids we took the brunt of it."

He stared into the fire, as if his eyes were seeing a place in it from long ago. "Karen felt we were the reason for her problems. No money, no food, no life." His voice grew soft. "For as long as I can remember, Ashley and I would stay outside for as long as possible before going home, so we wouldn't be on the receiving end of whatever Karen was upset about that day. Our neighbor, Mr. Farrow, had a small farm, so we played there, in the back pasture. When Karen called us for supper, we could usually tell by the sound of her voice if she'd been drinking or not. If she had, we were going to get hit."

"What did you do?"

"Go home, eat fast, keep quiet, and get to bed." He looked at Jett. "If we did it right, we'd be okay. If we didn't—and there wasn't really any way to know for sure, because the rules always changed—then we were in for a rough night." He sighed, folding his hands in his lap. "After a while, we knew anything could set Karen off. In the morning, she'd cry and apologize... sometimes, anyway. But that night, it'd be the same thing all over again. She'd lay into Ashley, screaming and yelling..."

Jett furrowed her brow. "Your mother didn't hit you?"

"She did, yeah. Sometimes. But, with me, it was... different." He swallowed hard. "She'd yell at us and threaten us with all kinds of stuff, and then she'd slap us around. The trailer was small, so you couldn't really get away. Karen would eventually get tired and go sit on the porch to smoke and drink, and Ashley and I would go to bed. We were twins, so we shared almost everything, including sharing one tiny, crappy bedroom in that dirty trailer until we were almost fourteen. Sometimes in the night, when it was real dark and the cigarettes were gone… our bedroom door would open and Karen would come in… and she'd wake me up and make me go to her room." He shook his head, his eyes shining in the glow of the fire. "I don't know how old I was the first time. I just remember smelling cigarettes and alcohol, and my mother taking off her clothes and making me get into bed with her. In the beginning, when I was little, I think we'd just sleep. Later on, it changed. I had to get undressed, too. By the time we were eleven or twelve, Karen was threatening to beat Ashley a *lot* more, and had almost stopped beating me at all. Instead, Karen took me into her bedroom almost every night."

Jett's voice was a whisper, gently prodding to make the words come. "You were eleven?"

"I think so. I remember seeing my fifth grade Easter project on the dresser, from Sister Alexis' class. It was a wood cross that I painted purple and gold. I just tried to focus on that cross while it was happening."

The wood crackled and popped in the fireplace.

"I don't mean to be gross," Jett said, "but how… how did Karen…"

TIFFANY LYNN IS MISSING

He pursed his lips, gazing at her. "You got hit in the nose, right? By that chair?"

"Yes."

"Your nose, it swelled up—even though you didn't want it to." He shrugged again. "It was like that. Grabbing, squeezing... And when someone is bigger and stronger than you, you can't really stop them from forcing you to do things. She would just... hold me down and climb on top of me." He sat back, running a hand across his neck. "But when I got to be about fourteen, she wasn't stronger anymore. A little while after that, it all stopped."

"Did you tell anyone?" Jett asked. "Or see a counselor?"

"I told everyone." Aaron lowered his face, shaking his head. "People don't listen too closely when a boy complains about sex. A lot of guys had the hots for Karen. Deep down, I think they wish they could have traded places with me." He sighed, returning his gaze to the fire. "They talked to Karen and they believed her lies, case closed. But Karen let me know if I ever said anything again... she'd kill Ashley. I believed her. And she beat Ashley on a regular basis after that just to make sure I never forgot."

His voice grew quiet, drifting off. "One day, the trailer burned. Karen was supposed to be home and would have normally been passed out on her bed. We found out later that she got drunk and she missed the bus. She got the message, though."

"You burned the trailer?"

"Not me. Ashley." He leaned forward, taking the edge of the sleeping bag in his fingertips. "She was trying to save both of our lives, and maybe she did. But not before trying to understand why our mother hated her so much. I think it was simple. In pictures when Karen was younger, she looked just like Ashley—beautiful, with those high cheek bones and big eyes. I think every time Karen looked at her daughter, she saw what might have been, and she hated Ashley for it. Looking back as an adult, I think that was obvious. But it wasn't then, not to kids. All Ashley knew was, Karen hated her and seemed to love me." He stared at the hem of the old sleeping bag, twisting the end. "So, one day before Karen got home, Ashley told me there was a rabbit having babies under the trailer, and that we could see the baby bunnies through one of the holes in the master bedroom floor. I went in there, into my mother's room, and while I was trying to see... my sister started taking off her clothes. She got on the bed and asked me to help her learn how to be special, the way I was. The trailer was hot. I was sweating. She put her hand on the front of my shorts, not grabbing or squeezing, just touching, and she said, "You love me, don't you, little brother?" Then she kissed me." He looked down. "My head was humming, that trailer was so hot. She pulled the waistband of my shorts away and slipped her fingers inside, and she said it was okay, that she'd done it with other boys." His eyes met Jett's, a pained expression on his face. "She laid down, and she took my hands and pulled me on top of her. She started kissing me, and... I heard the bus pull up. I panicked, thinking Karen would catch us in her bed, naked and everything. I jumped up and went to run out of the room, but my foot went

TIFFANY LYNN IS MISSING

through the hole in the floor. That ended it." He raised his eyebrows, taking a deep breath. "I was crying in pain, trying to get my foot out... Ashley got dressed in a flash and helped me get my shorts on. Karen wasn't home—the bus came and went—but I couldn't walk. I couldn't put any weight on my foot, and Ashley thought it was broken. She ran next door to Mr. Farrow's, and he took me to the hospital. The whole way, Ashley was crying and saying she was sorry, that she'd never do it again. Mr. Farrow asked what happened and she said she pushed me too hard on the tire swing in our back yard, and I fell. He didn't believe us, but he didn't want to know more. There weren't any grass stains or dirt on us. All I had on was a pair of shorts, and Ashley's shirt was on backwards."

Frowning, he gripped the fraying material between his fingers. "Mr. Farrow told the doctors that he was in his garden and saw us playing on the swing, and he saw me fall. He took Ashley's story and made it sound better, like it had actually happened. She just pushed me too hard on the swing. Everybody could see how upset Ashley was. She cried more than I did. I don't think she stopped crying until Mr. Farrow drove her home. Maybe not even then."

A gust of wind rushed across the roof of the cabin, making the old boards creak and groan.

"They kept me overnight to make sure the bone would set," Aaron said. "And Father Mills, from Karen's work, said he'd take care of the hospital bill." He looked at Jett. "When I got home, the trailer was burned—and Ashley was gone."

DAN ALATORRE

CHAPTER 21

When the wind finally died down, Aaron got dressed and looked out the snow-laden window again. "Looks like only a few inches of snow actually stuck. The rest must've been carried away by the wind."

Jett pulled her boots on over her jeans. "What's the plan?"

"I think we go for it and walk out. We could wait here—quite a few people knew where we were headed. By nightfall, they'd be looking for us with the helicopter, and we could light some signal fires. But it won't take more than four or five hours to walk out, and it'll still be light when we get to the end of the trail."

Bending over, Jett peered out the window.

"I wouldn't worry about those hillbillies," Aaron said. "If they aren't long gone, they're frozen stiff somewhere on the mountain. Even a snowsuit can't keep you warm forever." He handed Jett the sleeping bag. "You wrap up in that. I'll take the blanket."

She glanced at his side. His ribs had to be aching. "You sure?"

"Yep." He smiled and kissed her. "I got you into this. I'll get you out."

She believed him. Everything about Aaron Wells was done with confidence and certainty. It relaxed her to be in his presence. It was reassuring in a way she hadn't really known before. Inspiring. Motivating. Definitely something she didn't feel at the TV stations she'd worked for or the Greenman Trotter law firm. Those businesses were cutthroat. Aaron was different that way. So was the resort he ran. It was like a big, loving family.

Aaron picked up the short length of twine that had tied the sleeping bag shut and slipped it through the handle of the milk box, making a loop that he tied with a knot. "There. A backpack. We can drink water from melted snow as we walk—if my body heat gets through the blanket—and the metal is reflective enough to signal someone if we need to." He slipped the loop over his shoulder.

"Just watch those injured ribs of yours." Jett threw the sleeping bag around her. "I don't think I could carry you."

Pressing open the door, Aaron stepped outside and peered at the sky. "Looks good. Let's get started."

It was slow going at first, but mostly downhill. The wind had died down, so it wasn't brutally cold. Aaron maintained a slow and steady pace, walking side by side with Jett.

TIFFANY LYNN IS MISSING

"Keep your fingers wrapped up in the sleeping bag," he said. "You don't want them getting too cold."

Her nose was a different story. Lucinda's knit caps kept their heads tolerably warm without the added protection of the snowsuits, but the icy wind made Jett's cheeks and nose sting.

They passed the site where the snowmobile had gone over the cliff. One of the water bottles stuck out of the snow. Jett grabbed it, scooping up snow and shoving it into the bottle to melt for water.

"Check it out." Aaron pointed to fresh paw prints in the snow. There were two sets.

The mountain men's dogs had gotten off their rope leash.

"I bet we see those dogs at the trail head," Aaron said. "And I bet we don't see their masters."

Jett winced. "I'd be okay with not seeing any of them."

"Oh, I don't think they were mean dogs. They just wanted off that rope."

As they started walking again, Jett stared at the prints in the snow. Not seeing any human footprints next to them didn't bother her much.

"So," she said, "how did you and Ashley meet back up?"

Aaron picked through the fallen twigs and branches, picking up a long, smooth stick. "I didn't see her again for about three years, until she turned up on *Reverend Hadley Hemmins' Gospel Hour*. By then she'd been married, had Tiffany Lynn, and was a rising singing star on TV." He poked the ground with the stick as he walked, keeping Jett by his side.

"I'd been working for a local accountant for a few years, and helping take care of Karen—the school put her on disability a few months after the fire, and moved her to a halfway house. Mr. Murphy let me stay in the spare room over his garage. This was in Kissimmee, and it didn't have air conditioning or a TV or anything, but I didn't care. Mr. Murphy drove a brand-new Lincoln every year, and I figured if I could learn to do like him, I might be able to own a Lincoln one day, too. One night, Mr. Murphy yells for me to come into the house—and there's Ashley on TV. When I saw that, I almost fell over." He shook his head, smiling. "My sister, on TV! Well, I got the TV station's number at work the next day, and I left a message for Ashley—and she called me the day after, asking me to come get her. It was almost like we were kids again, but without the bad stuff, like the whole thing had never happened. Karen was out of our lives, and Ashley had been offered a contract by Reverend Hemmins. They wanted to sign her to a ten-year deal. I told you, Ashley's pretty, so sometimes people forget how smart she is."

Jett nodded. She'd grown familiar with such biases, ever since she'd been a teenager. Being a blonde on TV hadn't made people's ignorant assumptions any better, either.

"Ashley knew what her segment's ratings were every week." Aaron strolled through the snow, wearing his threadbare blanket like it was a Roman toga and he was Caesar. "When Reverend Hemmins' performers weren't on stage, he had them doing office work for the station. Ashley did bookkeeping, just like me, and she saw how popular her segments

TIFFANY LYNN IS MISSING

were because sponsors could request their commercial come on before or after certain acts aired on the show. Ashley's segments were always the most requested ones, so she figured if Reverend Hemmins was offering a ten-year deal, somebody else might, too—and for more money."

Aaron looked between the trees to the towering white mountain peaks in the distance. "Mr. Murphy let me borrow his car, and I drove nonstop from Kissimmee to Jackson, Alabama, to get Ashley and Tiffany Lynn. We had landed a six-minute spot on the Kissimmee station's *Friday Night Family Hour* because they owed Mr. Murphy a favor, and after that, we were on our way. Six minutes and two songs was all Darling Ashley Wells needed to work her magic. I negotiated her contract the next day. Two years later, we got Ashley her own show, and three years after that, we were putting together the DAW television network. Ashley was a bona fide star."

He was proud of his sister, and it showed—despite what she tried to do to him as a child, and how the gossip reporters maligned him in the press.

"The stories in the press always make it sound like she did it all by herself," Jett said.

"Like I told you, some people need the spotlight more than others. Ashley does. And she's better at it than I am, so it all works out. The people in the press can think what they want."

Jett slipped her arm into Aaron's, holding onto him as she worked her way down a steeper section of the trail. "The two of you built quite an empire."

"And we aren't finished yet." The trail flattened again. Aaron put his arm around Jett. "It's an empire Ashley wanted Tiffany Lynn to be a part of. My niece was just as talented as my sister, but she didn't want any part of show business. She tried it. It wasn't for her."

"Maybe she didn't want to work with her mother."

"She didn't. Ashley was pushing her too hard, and I guess she rebelled."

"Pretty big rebellion."

"Are there small rebellions?"

The trail head finally loomed in the distance—a wide-open space out from under the cover of the trees.

Aaron pointed. "See? I told you we'd make it off the mountain. And look."

Parked under a fat fir tree, two dogs were visible—a rottweiler and a pit bull. They trotted toward Aaron and Jett, wagging their tails.

Aaron held one of the cups out, letting the dogs drink some water. "I can't say what makes me happier, seeing the dogs or not seeing the hillbillies." He continued walking, the dogs staying by his side.

Her nose and cheeks were stinging, but most of the rest of her was reasonably warm. Her butt hurt a little, and her fingers, but the walking was generating heat. Wrapping her arms around herself, Jett trudged through the snow after Aaron and his two new friends. "If you don't mind, I'll be happy to celebrate later—when I'm in a nice warm bath sipping hot chocolate."

TIFFANY LYNN IS MISSING

"I may know a place that has hot chocolate and warm baths. Come on. Your phone should be able to get a signal soon."

They marched over the flat ground. The wind had all but died.

"My researcher looked into the charities you donate to," Jett said. "It's almost exclusively children's shelters and adoption agencies."

He held a branch out of their way as they passed, the dogs following. "Guess I'm trying to right some past wrongs."

"I think you turned out okay. From where I sit, it looks like you did. That stuff with Karen had to make for some rough adjustments after."

"It did. I knew our situation wasn't like other families. Other kids didn't come to school with bruises all over them, or sleep at the playground. We just... for Ashley and I, it was like we were holding our breath for ten plus years. Somehow, we got each other through it. You go through that with somebody, you're always going to share a special bond. We knew Karen was messed up. Father Mills even said Karen was partially crazy. He said I should try to forgive her."

"Did you?"

Aaron sighed, walking across the snow. "It's hard for any kid not to love their mother. No matter how bad things get, a kid will hold out hope. Deep inside, they want that connection—a good, loving connection with family. One they know is how it's supposed to be. I just decided, Ashley and I were out of the house, Karen couldn't hurt us, and we didn't have to dredge up painful old memories if we didn't want to."

"What about Ashley? Was she able to forgive your mom?"

"Ashley doesn't forgive." He shook his head. "She gets her pain out in her songs... and in some other ways."

They came to the trail head, the sun sinking low in the sky. Jett lifted the plastic water bottle to her lips, taking a drink. "You thought things were getting better until Tiffany Lynn announced she was dropping out of college?" She offered the bottle to Aaron.

"Yeah." He took a drink. "Why?"

"Curious timing."

Jett walked on through the snow, the wheels turning in her head.

The fighting and abuse had been going on for a while. It lessened, then it resurged. Why?

Maybe there was something Tiffany Lynn learned about Ashley that pushed her too far. Something she found out at the college.

Jett's phone pinged in her pocket. "Holy crap, I think I have a signal!"

The dogs ran to her, barking and nuzzling her legs.

Digging into her jeans, she held her phone up. A dozen texts and voicemail notifications flashed on the screen. The signal indicator barely registered any reception. Jett grinned, cradling the phone in both hands. "I've never been so happy to see one bar on my phone."

TIFFANY LYNN IS MISSING

"That ought to be enough." Aaron held his hand out. "If you'll let me use that, I'll call the resort and have the helicopter come and get us."

She handed him the phone and he dialed Wildfire. He pressed the phone to one ear and held a hand over the other, shouting to be heard. "That's right. Maybe half a mile from the trail head." He nodded, looking at the snow. "Yeah, two people and two dogs. Okay. We'll be watching. Thanks."

He gave the phone back to Jett. "They'll be here in five minutes. Think we can last that long?"

"Maybe." She clutched the sleeping bag. "I'm not going hiking for a long time after this, I can tell you that."

"Me, either," Aaron said. "And until we get your suite at the resort debugged, you'll need a more secure place to stay. You're welcome to the guest room at my house. I guarantee it's not bugged."

She narrowed her eyes, smiling. "You've guaranteed that before, but I'll take it anyway. Thank you." Wrapping her arms around him, she lifted her lips to his and gave him a kiss.

He held her close, putting his cheek on hers.

Jett ran her fingers through the hair over his ear. "What if I sneak across the hall after the kids go to sleep?"

He kissed her again. "That wouldn't be the worst idea ever."

DAN ALATORRE

CHAPTER 22

In his bath robe, Aaron paced back and forth across his large bedroom, holding a phone to his wet head. "Long beards, medium builds. They might be lucky enough to end up behind bars, but they weren't dressed for the weather. My guess is, if they didn't have horses or a snowmobile stashed somewhere, they didn't make it off the mountain. One of the Wildfire employees is taking the dogs to a veterinarian, so we'll see if there's a microchip that will help us get a phone number—but I doubt it, and there's no signal on the mountain anyway. If those hillbillies are still alive, they're probably in bad shape."

Jett walked out of Aaron's bathroom rubbing a towel over her hair, one of Aaron's old robes covering her torso. Her overnight bag and other belongings stood stacked against the bedroom wall, moved out of Presidente three at Aaron's request.

Sitting down at his computer, Aaron nodded. "Use the Wildfire Resort helicopter to look for them, sheriff. You'll cover more ground that way. I'll tell the crew to have it ready for you."

He ended the call and looked at his computer, frowning. "There's a flight to Orlando in three hours. We can make it, but we'll have to hurry. The next one's not until ten, and lands after midnight."

She dug through her bag. "Any word on the de-bugging of Presidente three?"

"Matt Philson tried to call while I was talking to the sheriff." Aaron lifted his phone. "He must have completed his check of the suite."

He placed a call to his tech guru, pressing the speakerphone button. As the phone rang, Jett picked her phone up off the wireless charging pad on the dresser. During their long, regenerative shower, Jett's phone had gotten almost fully charged. She scrolled through the missed texts as she listened in on Matt Philson's report.

"I went in with housekeeping," Philson said. "They changed the bed sheets and bathroom towels as a matter of routine while I kept silent and ran a full-range scan."

Jett peered at the phone. "What about video?"

"I scanned the video frequencies from the hallway before I went in. It was clean. But the room is definitely bugged, Aaron, and not too secretly. I found some stuff inside, if you wanna come look."

Aaron shook his head. "No time. Can you remove it?"

"Yeah. It's a very sophisticated system with a really amateur installation. You'd probably have

TIFFANY LYNN IS MISSING

spotted it if you were looking. I can shut it down and have it out of there in about ten minutes."

Jett moved toward the desk. "Hold on a sec, Matt." She looked at Aaron. "Maybe we should leave it up. We could plant phony information to flush out the spy."

"You sure?"

"Yeah," she said. "I might have some ideas we can use."

Aaron nodded. "Let's leave it up, Matt. Any idea who it's sending information to?"

"Not right now," Philson said. "The sensors transmit their data to a small receiver I found in an air conditioning vent. It's beaming a signal out to an encoded remote server somewhere, and from there, my software indicates the signal gets bounced around over a dozen or more encrypted sites. At some point it lands at the computer of whoever wanted the information, but it could take a year for me to trace your room's specific data through that much encryption."

Sighing, Aaron lowered the phone. "Okay, pal. Thanks."

"Hey, boss man," Philson said. "Please be careful with that room. Leaving the equipment up is a bad idea. You don't want to forget the bugs are there and accidentally say something, you know? Let me uninstall it."

Jett frowned. "They'll see that it's uninstalled or that it stopped working. That will just tip off whoever's doing the bugging."

Philson huffed. "Aaron—"

"She's right, Matt. Leave it as is."

"Okay." Matt sighed. "You're the boss."

"Nice work as always, Matt. I really appreciate it. Thanks." Aaron ended the call and set the phone on the desk, removing his robe and tossing it onto the bed. Jett took a moment to admire Aaron's naked backside before returning to her messages. As he turned, the huge bruise over his ribs became visible.

Jett stifled a gasp. It looked much worse than before. "Aaron, your ribs! We should really get you to a doctor."

"Or we can have one come here and save some time." He winked. "I told you I'd get it looked at. The resort has a physician on call. He's on the way, so relax."

Reassured, Jett settled back onto the pillows and viewed her missed texts. One was labeled "unknown name," containing an equally cryptic message.

"You're looking in the wrong place."

Jett bolted upright on the bed.

Not a lot of people knew what she was doing in Colorado, but of those that did, she had their phone numbers. They weren't "unknown."

Could it be Ashley?

No. This message is trying to help me. She wouldn't do that.

But whoever sent it knows something about Tiffany Lynn's disappearance or they wouldn't know I'm looking in "the wrong place."

The message could also be a bluff.

TIFFANY LYNN IS MISSING

She tapped the screen to bring up the sender's information. It didn't say anything, but she could call the number that had sent the text.

Her finger hovered over the phone.

Does this tip them off to something?

Am I being a sucker, falling for the bluff and about to be given information to send me on a wild goose chase?

Aaron put on a pair of pants and stepped into the bathroom, running a comb through his hair. Jett pressed the send button, listening.

Before it rang, an automatic message came on. "This device has not yet been set up for voicemail. Please try your call again later."

Pursing her lips, she typed out a text. "Who is this?"

A moment later, an automated reply appeared on her screen. *"This device is not authorized to receive text messages."*

Jett's shoulders sagged.

I can't call you and I can't text you. Then what can I do?

Switching to the "recent calls," she took a screen shot of the number and texted it to Rico.

"See if you can track this," she typed, and switched the phone to silent mode.

His reply came a few seconds later. *"Okay."*

Moving to the bathroom, Jett slipped her phone into the pocket of the robe and picked up the hair brush.

"Everything all right?" Aaron asked.

"Yeah. Just thinking." She leaned over, running the brush through her golden locks.

If I'm looking in the wrong spot, doesn't that mean the sender of the text knows where the right spot is?

One of the people who witnessed the accident is reaching out.

Why?

Aaron put a t-shirt on and walked out of the bathroom as Jett reached for the hair dryer.

"Dad!" One of Aaron's twin daughters raced into his bedroom, throwing her arms around her father's waist and almost knocking him down. "After tennis practice, Curtis told me you were lost in the snowstorm and they picked you up in the Wildfire helicopter." She buried her face in his chest. "I drove straight home. Are you okay?"

He kissed his daughter on the top of her head, closing his eyes and hugging her. "I'm okay. I got a few bruised ribs but otherwise, I'm fine."

"Oh, my gosh!" She dropped her arms, her hand flying to her mouth as she stared at his t-shirt. "I'm sorry! Did I hurt you?"

"No, it's my ribs, not my waistline. Where's your sister?"

"Track practice. You went out to the trail this morning with Miss Jett. Why didn't anyone tell us you got lost?"

Jett's stomach lurched.

I'm wet and naked, wrapped only in a robe, in this girl's father's bedroom.

She held the hair dryer in her hand, inching away from the bathroom door.

"I guess they didn't tell you sooner because they didn't want to scare you," Aaron said.

TIFFANY LYNN IS MISSING

"Is Miss Jett okay?"

"She's fine." He glanced toward the bathroom. "She's uh…"

His daughter followed his line of sight, peering into the bathroom and locking eyes with Jett. The girl's jaw dropped.

She turned and ran out of the room.

"Mattsie!" Aaron shouted. He glanced at Jett, a blank look on his face. Down the hall, a door slammed. Aaron put his hand to his forehead. "I'm very embarrassed about this awkward… Um, please get dressed. I need to talk to my daughter."

He stepped toward the door.

"Aaron." Jett rushed out of the bathroom, putting her hand on his arm. "Why don't you let me talk to her?"

"What? No. She's my daughter. It's my responsibility to explain why… why I have a woman in my bedroom."

Jett smiled.

Chivalrous to the end.

"Your girls aren't babies, Aaron, and you've been a widower for more than ten years. Haven't the girls seen an occasional woman in your room before?"

"Uh…" Aaron tugged at his collar. "No."

"Oh. Then I'd definitely better be the one to talk to her."

Aaron looked her over. "Don't you think you should put some clothes on first?"

"Ideally, yes." Jett moved past him, stepping into the hallway. "But she already saw me like this."

DAN ALATORRE

CHAPTER 23

At the end of the hallway, still dressed only in the robe, Jett stood by the closed bedroom door. She had no idea what to say, she only knew it was probably best to address the awkward situation quickly. Leaning close, she knocked gently on the door. "Mattsie? Can I come in?"

She held her breath, listening for any sound of movement on the other side of the door. After an eternity, the door opened. Mattsie stepped back, staring at the floor, her cheeks glowing bright red.

Jett tiptoed into the bedroom, clasping her hands in front of her. Sports trophies decorated every flat surface—tennis, swimming, softball—and of course, volleyball. A poster of Olympians Misty May-Treanor on a sand volleyball court, leaping into the arms of teammate Kerri Walsh Jennings, had been plastered to one wall.

It's all warm weather sports. They're still Florida girls at heart.

There was a desk, a computer, two phones, two iPads... a few stuffed animals—but only one bed.

The twins don't share a bedroom.

Mattsie's wall also displayed a small poster with a variation of the Persius quote her father had on the shelf in his conference room—"Those who endure, conquer"—under the image of an eagle.

This apple didn't fall far from the tree.

Jett cleared her throat. "Hey, so... thanks for letting me in." She lowered herself onto the edge of the bed. "I wanted to apologize for surprising you like that."

Mattsie nodded, keeping her hand on the open door. "It's... okay." The teen's voice was barely a whisper.

What do I say next? She's obviously embarrassed.

Just keep going. Address the awkwardness head on and hope for the best.

"Well..." Jett wrapped her robe sash around her finger. "I'm sure it was still an awkward surprise for you, and you didn't deserve that, so... I'm sorry. Your dad mentioned he doesn't have a lot of lady friends visit the house."

A thin smile tugged at Mattsie's lips. "No, he doesn't. Dad never dates. He doesn't even go out to dinner unless it's with Monie and me, or some kind of business dinner." She raised her eyes. "He thinks it's disrespectful to my mom's memory."

Jett nodded slowly. "What do you think?"

Sighing, Mattsie eased the door shut. "Mom died a long time ago. I love the memory of my mom,

TIFFANY LYNN IS MISSING

and I love my dad, and I want him to be happy." The teenager walked toward her desk, picking up a phone and setting it down again. "It's not fair that he has to sacrifice everything and watch over us."

Jett's phone vibrated in the pocket of her robe. She reached in and checked the screen.

Rico's attempt at tracking the mystery phone had been unsuccessful.

"Can't track through my connections. Might be too new."

Jett put the phone back in her pocket and looked at Mattsie. "Is that what Aaron says? That he has to sacrifice for you and your sister?"

"Dad? No." The teen turned around to face Jett. "He'd never say that. He probably doesn't even think it. I do, though. I know he sacrifices a lot for us. He's allowed to have a life."

"That's a pretty grown-up observation." Jett patted the mattress. "Come sit down."

Mattsie took a seat on the bed.

"So..." Jett folded her hands in her lap. "I know I only just met your dad—and you and your sister—but..." She took a deep breath. "I guess what I'm trying to say is, if I were you, I might think some lady who just met my dad was being less than respectful, turning up in his room like that. And you'd be right to be upset. Your dad is special to you."

The teen's eyes went to Jett's. "Is he special to you?"

Jett smiled. "In the last twenty-four hours or so, I've come to discover that your dad is an amazing guy. And..." Pursing her lips, she nodded. "I think, yeah, he might be pretty special to me. I'd like to spend some more time getting to know him and find out, if that's okay with you and Monie."

"Dad's allowed to be with someone if he wants—I mean, with you, if he wants. He just..." She shrugged. "He never does. So... don't hurt him, okay?"

It was hard for Jett to imagine the man on the mountain that grabbed their attacker's gun as needing a teenager to watch out for him. It was a heartwarming display of emotion.

"Okay," Jett said.

There was a knock on the door.

"Everybody still alive in here?" Aaron opened the door an inch. "Is it safe to come in?"

"It's safe." Mattsie jumped up off the bed and went to the door. "We were just saying how when Monie comes home from track practice, we should all go out to dinner. What do you think?"

Jett stood, glancing at Aaron's side. "And we should get you to a doctor."

"Sadly, I have to decline the generous offer of dinner. It sounds very nice." Aaron put his hands in his pockets. "But, Dr. Neil is on the way over to look at my ribs, and then Jett and I are catching a flight to Orlando."

"You're going to Florida?" Mattsie said. "Today?"

"Yep." Her father nodded, adjusting a button on the cuff of his shirt. "We have a lot of stuff to look into."

"Are you going to talk to Aunt Ashley?"

"I'm sure I will. Why?"

TIFFANY LYNN IS MISSING

Mattsie put her hand on the edge of the desk, as if she needed the support to carry on the conversation. "Do you think she had something to do with Tiffany Lynn's death?"

Aaron stopped, looking at his daughter. "No."

His reply was flat. Plain. Unequivocal. Decided.

He does not believe his sister caused the death of her daughter.

Mattsie's gaze did not move from her father's face. "But... if she did?"

Aaron sighed. "She didn't. I know people. I know how they can be. Under the right circumstances, anyone could do almost anything—I've seen it happen. Ashley's done regrettable things. I know she hit Tiffany Lynn sometimes, and I know it scared you when your cousin told you about it. But deep in my heart, do I think my sister could have done something really bad... something that ended up in the death of her daughter? No, I don't."

He shifted his weight from one foot to the other.

"But..." Aaron shook his head. "I also know I'm not impartial when it comes to my family. Part of me feels like... like even *allowing* a thought like that is a betrayal, like I stopped loving my sister and turned on her. I'm not the kind of person who gives up on a family member." He looked at Jett. "So I hired someone who's stronger than I am, to look into it. I don't know what happened to Tiffany Lynn on that mountain trail, but my gut says it's not as simple as a slip and fall. I don't know why she was out here, or why she didn't reach out to us. That's not like her." Aaron's gaze returned to his daughter. "But I *will* find out what happened to your cousin. And whoever's responsible will be held accountable."

His eyes drifted to the window, and the white-tipped peaks of the massive mountains. "I'll find out the truth. I owe her that."

CHAPTER 24

Jett slid across the back seat of the limousine as Aaron climbed in behind her.

"Curtis," Aaron said, "would you mind putting up the divider while we drive? I have some business to discuss with Jett."

"Sure, Aaron." The glass partition went up, separating the limo driver from his passengers.

Aaron unfolded the tray table from the seat in front of him and pulled his laptop out of his carry-on bag. "When we touch down in Orlando, I want you to go talk to the postmaster in Christmas. I'm taking a puddle jumper to Tallahassee. I want to talk to Tiffany Lynn's friends."

"Okay," Jett said. "Rico will have done some more interviews by then—unless Ashley scared all the employees into not talking to us."

"They'll talk to us." Aaron set the computer on the tray table and powered it up. "They aren't *her* employees, they work for me, too. Remind them of that. It'll loosen a few mouths." He turned to Jett. "Now, you've had a curious expression on your face since we were in Mattsie's room. You have something you want to ask me. What is it?"

Jett looked at Aaron. "You weren't honest with Mattsie. If you didn't think your sister could have played a role in your niece's death, I don't think I'd be here."

"I didn't lie to my daughter. We don't do that."

"Well..." Jett sat upright. "You didn't tell her the whole truth—but we have an agreement that you'll tell it to me. So..."

Aaron held up a hand. "Okay, I admit, I may have been less than completely forthright with my daughter. But there's a reason. Until we know what actually happened, how does it benefit her to hear wild allegations about a member of her family? You can't un-ring a bell."

His face glowed in the light of the computer screen. Pursing his lips, Aaron lowered his hands to his lap. "I don't suspect Ashley because I *can't*. It's like... if you were a Jew in a Nazi prison camp—Auschwitz, say—and a guard let you out but then borrowed five dollars from you, would you ever ask for that money back? She saved my life."

"A person is worth a little more than five dollars."

"I'm worth over a billion dollars." He frowned. "So what? I'm not here without her."

"I didn't mean you," Jett said. "I meant Tiffany Lynn. She's not a five-dollar debt."

TIFFANY LYNN IS MISSING

Aaron opened his mouth, but said nothing, averting his gaze to his window.

"But I get it, Aaron. That's why it has to be me."

Because your world has been turned upside down, making you question people you've trusted your whole life.

Her thoughts went back to the Greenman Trotter law firm in Miami, when Jett was a first-year associate. Tate McNeil, a partner at the firm, and half a dozen of Jett's first-year colleagues were poring over a conference room table stacked with documents.

"It's here," Tate mumbled, running a hand through his thin, gray hair. He peered over his reading glasses, setting aside one folder and opening another. "I know it's here. We just need to find it."

It was well past midnight and the trial would start first thing in the morning, their schedule upended from a last minute deposition of a Criminal Informant that went bad earlier that same evening. Opposing counsel asked the CI to explain how the arresting officers searched her prior to the exchange.

She stood up, lifted her shirt and said, "Like this—and then you jiggle..."

McNeil turned white, his whole strategy upended by a CI less than twelve hours before trial.

All the evidence pointed to the client's son-in-law. Jett—along with the other assisting attorneys—were convinced he did it. But McNeil kept looking elsewhere. While half the team worked on the new strategy, McNeil dug through the mountain of papers in search of his white whale.

Jett glanced at the clock again. The pressures on a young associate were plentiful. Trying to be perfect for the partners while keeping up on her own files... There wasn't enough caffeine in the world sometimes. One colleague had already started to dabble in pills to keep him going; others alleviated the long hours and cutthroat stress with heavy drinking. So far, nonstop Starbucks and hourly eye drops had allowed Jett to keep her workload almost manageable, and working out every morning helped vent her stress. It was hard work, and detailed work. Several people who started when she did had already quit.

But there was something about the last-minute intensity in a trial case, where all the chips had been pushed to the center of the table and things could still go wrong... it was a real rush, and Jett loved it—when it worked out in their favor.

"This!" McNeil jumped up from the table, brandishing a tiny, faded, thermal-paper receipt. "I knew I remembered this from somewhere." He carried the white sliver to the note-filled dryboard on the wall. "The son-in-law was in Tampa on the fifteenth, at nine in the morning. This receipt proves it." McNeil turned to face the group. "That means he couldn't be in Miami on the fifteenth at ten in the morning—and he can't be the culprit."

The group of attorneys groaned.

McNeil didn't show it in his face or words, because he didn't have to, but his discovery indicated

TIFFANY LYNN IS MISSING

that things were about to start over again, and they were all going to get zero sleep.

Jett slouched in her chair, awaiting a reprimand. The son-in-law had been her assignment in the pre-trial research.

McNeil rubbed his eyes. "Let's all take a five-minute break, then we'll regroup to hammer out a new plan."

Jett didn't have to be asked to stay behind as the others filed out of the conference room.

The partner sat down next to her, dropping the receipt onto her notepad. "Sometimes all the collected evidence points in one direction, but it's the wrong direction. Whether someone's feeding us information to misdirect us or we just get tunnel vision because we're so convinced things are a certain way, one extra piece of the puzzle—just one—can change the whole picture. And it happens more often than you'd think."

She nodded, readying her apology and knowing it wouldn't do any good. Weeks had been spent preparing and only hours remained before the trial started.

"Pursue every lead with equal intensity, Thacker." McNeil extended his long, thin index finger, tapping the conference room table. "It's the only way to avoid embarrassments like this. We want the truth. Lives may hang in the balance."

Jett kept her gaze focused on her notepad, swallowing hard and trying to keep her voice from wavering. "Thank you, Tate."

He stood, walking toward the door.

"Resist the urge to run after only the hot lead," he said. *"Tunnel vision is what happens to people before they black out and fall on their face. It's probably best to avoid that."* Her gray-haired mentor folded his arms and leaned against the door frame. *"And just so you know, I made a similar mistake about six months ago. Had to redo our whole trial strategy in fifteen minutes."* He winked at her. *"You're a lot smarter than me, so I'm confident it won't happen to you again."*

In the Wildfire Resort limo, Jett inspected Aaron's face. It revealed nothing—which revealed everything.

I have to help you learn the truth because you're afraid you won't do the right thing when you find out—and for some reason, you desperately want to do the right thing.

He turned to her, their eyes meeting. "I trust you, Jett. This situation involves my family. If I didn't trust you... well, you're right. You wouldn't be here. I saw something in you when I watched that video—when the fight broke out. How you stood your ground. It was more than bravery. It was... honesty of purpose. You were scared but you hung in there."

"Like you, on the mountain, when you grabbed the hillbilly's rifle."

He nodded. "I guess so. You're someone who does the right thing in a tough situation. That's rare. When I look at you, that's what I see."

Reaching across the seat, she took his hand. "You're a good man, Aaron. That's what I see."

TIFFANY LYNN IS MISSING

"I'm... a business cheat. And I bribe public officials." He smirked, opening a spreadsheet. "It's nice of you to look past my faults."

"No." She tugged on his hand until he looked at her. "You're not a business cheat. You decided to burn the conference room table. Every day you choose not to cheat at business, that's not who you are anymore."

DAN ALATORRE

CHAPTER 25

Jett pulled her rental car out of the hotel parking lot, maneuvering through the morning's rush hour traffic until she got on Interstate 4—where everything slowed almost to a standstill. Sipping her Starbucks, she gazed at the commuters in other vehicles, the morning air already thick with humidity.

It's gonna be a hot one.

She reached to the dashboard and cranked the air conditioning to its maximum.

The flight from Colorado had been quiet, and she and Aaron each got some sleep on the plane, but in-flight sleep was never as good as regular sleep. Aaron's second flight departed an hour after they landed, and Jett managed to get a few more hours of shut-eye at a downtown Orlando hotel before heading out.

"Two investigators," Aaron said. *"Twice as much ground getting covered."*

Jett's phone rang with Matt Philson's name appearing on the screen. She reached down and hit the speakerphone button. "Hi, Matt. What's up?"

"Hey, I heard you were heading to Florida. Just wanted to get a status update from you."

Jett recoiled. "Uh... excuse me?"

"An update. Get me up to speed on what you're doing in Orlando."

"Matt... Aaron was pretty specific with my instructions. I'm to report only to him."

Philson chuckled. "Well, that doesn't mean you can't share information. We're on the same team."

"We are, but unless he directs me to tell you something, I can't. I'm sorry."

"Yeah," Philson mumbled. "I'm sure you are."

She gripped the wheel, glancing at the phone. "What's that supposed to mean?"

"It means you didn't have to slam me yesterday about taking the surveillance equipment out of Presidente three. You already had Aaron put a match to the conference room table he had me custom make for him, and by leaving that equipment still in your suite, you can't stay there—so now you're conveniently sleeping at Aaron's place. You think I don't see what you're doing? I see it. Everyone does."

Jett bristled. "Look, Matt, I was hoping we could be friends. Aaron obviously thinks very highly of you, and—"

"Does he?" Philson said. "I wonder for how much longer, with you in his ear. You think you're

TIFFANY LYNN IS MISSING

the first to try this act, Thacker? There are a ton of pretty women who work for Aaron, and a lot of them have their hooks out with their eyes on his wallet. You lost your TV job and now you're trying to take over my gig. Not happening, sweetheart. I'm not some hack Miami nursing home director."

Office politics were the worst thing about most jobs; Jett wasn't sure why she expected Wildfire Resort to be any different. Philson felt put out. Threatened. But that was his problem—his insecurity. His issue really wasn't with Jett.

He's scared. Just defuse the situation and move on.

Jett took a breath, keeping her eye on the traffic so she didn't wreck the rental car. "How about we both do the job Aaron's paying us to do and act like professionals? Like you said, we're on the same team."

It was an offer she'd had to make before to an insecure co-worker. Half the time it worked out; half the time it didn't—but it was all she cared to muster at the moment.

"Matt?" Jett said. "We good?"

Philson didn't respond. When Jett glanced at the phone, the screen said "call ended."

"Nice." She huffed. "What a great way to start the morning, *teammate*."

* * * * *

The town of Christmas, Florida, took less than thirty minutes to reach from Jett's hotel. The post office was a nondescript, one-story brick building with a peaked gray shingle roof and an empty, oversized parking lot. It could have been a small public library or maybe even a bank; it had the same generic look—austere and unassuming. The type of building a person could drive right by and never notice. Oak trees surrounded the structure on all sides, and a huge forest spanned outward behind it. The only other visible building was an old church across the street and down the road a hundred feet or so. Otherwise, the little post office was all on its own, nearly swallowed up by the dense, green oaks of central Florida.

Jett parked, a light sweat threatening to break out on her forehead during the short walk to the post office's front door.

Inside, the lobby was bright and clean—but just as small as she'd expected. A tall, lanky uniformed man with dark brown hair and a bad haircut stood behind the counter, busily counting or stacking some large envelopes.

"Excuse me." Jett approached the counter. "Is the manager of the branch here?"

"Sure." The employee set the envelopes down. "He's in the back."

They stared at each other, neither moving.

"Uh, may I *speak* with the manager, please?" Jett said.

"You don't want no stamps or nothing?"

"Not at the moment. I'd just like to speak with the manager, if that's all right."

He nodded, looking her over. "What's this about?"

The man was maybe thirty years old, but with the bad skin and poor posture of a teenager, and a

TIFFANY LYNN IS MISSING

slight Florida redneck twang—and he was in no rush to bother his boss.

Might as well start with this guy. He may know something.

His nametag read "Dave."

Jett put a hand on the counter, glancing toward the large clock on the far wall. "Well, a friend of mine has been getting some letters postmarked from here." She turned her attention to Dave. "We were hoping to find out who's been mailing them."

The man ran his tongue around the bottom of his gums as if he'd gotten some of his breakfast stuck down there and had just discovered it now. "You mean the letters from the Wells girl."

Jett smiled. "That's right."

"I can help you with that."

"That would be great. So—any idea who's mailing them?"

"Yep. The cameras recorded it. She came inside each time."

"She?" Jett took a pen from her purse. "Do you know her? Does she live around here?"

A gray-haired man with a large beer gut emerged from the back room, his uniform shirt straining at the buttons. "I'm sorry, ma'am." He spoke with a more southern drawl, like they had in Titusville, on the coast, or Lakeland, on the other side of Orlando. "Federal law prevents postal employees from disclosing information without a warrant or a directive from the Postmaster General."

"Oh, I don't want anyone to break the law." Jett held her pen to her side, out of view of the older man. "I just want to help the family. You know, they received another letter a day or so ago."

Dave raised an eyebrow. "You working for the Wells family?"

"Yes." Jett nodded. "For Aaron Wells."

The older man waved a hand at Dave. "That's enough." He turned to Jett. "Miss, we'd all like to help, honestly—we don't like to see a nice lady like Darling Ashley Wells suffer. But—"

"When she came in, she looked a mess," Dave said.

"Ashley Wells came in here?" Jett gripped her pen. "When?"

Dave rubbed his chin. "Oh, probably three weeks ago—the first time. Her and the sheriff."

"—but we can't talk to you." The older man leaned back, scratching his shoulder. "Not without a warrant. It's the law. You understand."

"I understand." Jett cocked her head, peering at the gray-haired man.

Let's try something.

"Sir... I mentioned I work for Aaron Wells. He lives in Colorado these days, with his two daughters—they're twins, about fifteen—and they were very close to their cousin, Tiffany Lynn, the young lady who went missing." She sighed, letting a little southern drawl slip into her speech. "They're such *sweet* girls, and they are just broken up to pieces about what happened. And now, to see the family still being tortured like this, with these letters that keep coming... well, it just breaks your heart." She blinked a few times, gazing up at the older man. "Now, if you *could* talk—I mean, if I went to a judge

TIFFANY LYNN IS MISSING

and got a warrant—would I be wasting the time of those sweet young teenagers by coming back here? I mean, what kind of things could you tell me if I had a warrant?"

The two men stared at her, the large clock ticking on the wall.

"Such sweet little dears." Jett swallowed hard. "And just *so sad*, not knowing what's happened to their beloved cousin."

The senior postal employee frowned, his lip twitching.

"I just..." Jett shrugged, lowering her head. "I hate to go back to them with news like this."

Stepping back from the counter, the older man cleared his throat. "Dave, I'm going to lunch."

Dave looked at the clock on the lobby wall. "It's only ten thirty, Frank."

"I know when I'm hungry." Frank scowled. "I'm taking my lunch break. Go grab some supplies from the back and restock the lobby displays."

"Yes, sir," Dave said, disappearing into the back room.

Frank looked at Jett. "Sorry I couldn't help you, ma'am, but if you're hungry, there's a grocery store down the street. They make a great Cuban sandwich, and you can sit out back at a picnic table under the oak trees and have a nice quiet lunch. That's where I'm headed."

Jett nodded.

It's working.

"I love Cuban sandwiches," she said.

"Well." Frank smiled. "Maybe I'll see you there. Out back, at the picnic tables."

He walked into the back room. Jett opened her purse and took out her key fob, heading for the exit. When she was halfway to her car, a brown pickup truck drove slowly through the lot. Gray haired Frank sat behind the wheel.

"It's this way," Frank said, pointing down the road.

Jett nodded, pressing the remote and unlocking her car.

She checked her messages while following the pickup truck. A few friends had called, and Rico—leaving several messages asking for a return call, and one that divulged a bit more.

"Hey," Rico's message said. "After working the phones all day, I finally found a few people over at DAW network who were willing to talk to me. A clerk in accounting had a few things to say—Emily Becker. She's new, so I guess Darling Ashley didn't work her over yet. I'll be talking more with her tonight, and a receptionist, too… I'll email you an update. Call me when you can."

As Frank's turn indicator flashed, Jett ended the call and slowed down to turn onto a dusty, gravel parking lot.

The old grocery store was in dire need of a paint job, but it was clean enough inside and it smelled amazing. The deli counter had roast pork, rice and beans, spicy chicken empanadas, and fried plantains. Although Jett enjoyed bananas, she never developed a taste for their relative, the plantain—and more than a few of her friends in Miami never forgave her for it. She did, however, have a taste for *pastelitas*, a Cuban-style pastry stuffed with fruit

TIFFANY LYNN IS MISSING

fillings like guava. Rows of the delicious desserts called to her from a shelf on the deli counter.

When Frank had received his order, he paid and walked out the back door. Jett stepped up to the counter and ordered a Cuban sandwich and a bottle of water, taking her mid-morning lunch outside as soon as it came off the hot press.

Half a dozen wooden picnic tables filled the grassy area under a grand old oak. Frank sat at a table on the far side of the massive tree, opening the parchment paper wrapper on his lunch. As Jett approached, he gestured to the table behind him. "That'd be a good spot, miss. Lotsa shade and a fair bit of breeze. I noticed you looked a little warm."

Jett sat down at the table behind Frank. "So, did you want to tell me something?"

"Nope." Frank picked up his sandwich. "Can't. That's against the law. I might work for the post office now, but before that I was twenty years with the sheriff's office. I like to follow the law, and I like others to."

Her heart sank.

"But," Frank said, "I might talk to myself while I eat. Can't help if someone overhears."

She smiled to herself, settling in on the wooden bench seat. "The sheriff out here dropped the case when Tiffany Lynn turned up dead, right? Because it was declared an accident. Now, I get it that the police are busy, but—"

"Miss, law enforcement officers have enough to do working real crimes." Frank took a sip of his soda. "If a missing person is no longer missing, and the death is officially ruled an accident, what more can they do? You don't keep looking for your lost car keys once you find them."

"But…"

"Now, there's a church down the road from the post office," Frank said. "They installed security cameras after they had a few break-ins. Put 'em on the front of the building, the back, the sides, the interior… On the recommendation of a certain parishioner who was formerly in law enforcement, they got high quality gear installed, and a good recording system. I've heard it said that one camera is pointed right at the post office driveway—so it would have gotten a license plate of the person delivering the letters, day or night. It's not illegal to record public access areas of a federal building, and I'm told the church keeps the discs for three months, just in case. Might be they'd share it, if they were asked, no warrant needed. You might see who you're looking for about those letters that keep coming."

Jett beamed.

Thank you!

Picking up her sandwich, she peered at the old man at the next table. "This is a really good Cuban—much better than I expected. I'm indebted to the person who recommended this place to me. I wonder how I could thank him?"

"Oh, I'm sure seeing the completion of a difficult, uh, *meal*—is thanks enough. But I always wondered—why would a nice girl like that just up and disappear?"

"Why do you think?" Jett cracked open her water, taking a sip. The shade from the big tree was

TIFFANY LYNN IS MISSING

nice, but the heat and humidity still enveloped her from all sides.

Frank tore open a bag of chips. "There was a woman who worked as a receptionist for Ashley Wells a long time ago. Big stars don't realize that the little people, like the ones who take the phone calls to a business, they can know a lot about what's going on because of who they see calling. This receptionist was always saying that what you see on TV isn't half of the picture with Darling Ashley Wells. That the real Ashley is as crooked as a hound's hind leg and as greedy as they come." He shook the bag, selecting a chip. "I'd look into that if I were you. Maybe there's a life insurance claim."

"You think Ashley killed her daughter?" Jett said. "The police said it was an accident, and there were witnesses…"

"Then I guess it's so." Frank popped a chip into his mouth. "One way or another, the girl is dead and Ashley Wells is alive."

Jett frowned, lifting her water bottle to her lips. "But you believe that receptionist."

"Well, I guess so." Frank chuckled. "I married her, so I'd trust her about this." He set the bag of chips down, staring toward the line of trees at the end of the grocery store's gravel parking lot. "It's a funny thing about people who cross Ashley Wells—like her first husband, or her brother's wife, or their mother…"

Jett's stomach jolted.

She held the water bottle in mid-air, her heart racing.

I thought their mother was alive.

I thought Aaron's ex-wife died in a car wreck. I thought...

"Nobody much talks about it," Frank said, "but a fair number of folks who disagree with Darling Ashley Wells end up dead."

CHAPTER 26

The lady sweeping the entrance of the old church directed Jett out the back door, to a tiny vineyard filled with posts and wires. Green plants of varying sizes appeared to be attempting to grow up the wires; an old man in blue jeans overalls and a sweat-soaked t-shirt stood at the far end of the weedy patch, watering the base of his vines with a hose.

Walking between the rows, Jett fanned herself with her hand as the moist grass soaked through her shoes. A chorus of cicadas hummed from the tree line.

The temperature must be headed for ninety today. What happened to spring? Did we just skip it and go straight to summer? Miami isn't even this muggy.

"Reverend Parce?" She raised her hand, waving. "I'm Jett Thacker. I'm told you might have some security video that would be helpful to a case I'm working on."

The old man squinted in her direction. "Jett Thacker? From the TV?"

"Yes, sir—well, I *was* on TV. I hope to be again one day."

He nodded. "Gave it up and decided to pursue an honest living, did you?"

"No." Jett smiled. "I did that when I quit being a lawyer."

"A TV reporter and a lawyer." The old man frowned, walking over to a weed-covered spigot and shutting off the water. "Hard to say which profession is less honest. I'll pray for your soul."

"Uh, thank you." Jett grabbed the collar of her shirt, lifting it a few times to pump air to her sweltering, damp torso. "Your videos might be important. I'm looking into the disappearance of Tiffany Lynn Wells."

He wiped his hands on the front of his overalls. "Ashley Wells didn't hire you, that's for sure. What do you think happened to that poor daughter of hers?"

"That's what I'd like to find out. Someone's been mailing letters in Tiffany Lynn's handwriting and sending them to her mother. As you can imagine, that's causing the family a lot of pain."

"Pain is a tricky weapon," the reverend said. "We may punish our target, but we can damage others as well—sometimes ourselves. But if there was ever a person who deserved punishment, it would be Ashley Wells. 'Vengeance is mine, sayeth the Lord'—but even He might look the other way if somebody wanted to settle a score with that witch."

TIFFANY LYNN IS MISSING

Jett nodded. "I understand some people don't find much 'darling' in Darling Ashley Wells."

"She got her start in TV on a religious show in Alabama, but you won't hear her speak of the Lord unless she's on TV. Maybe not even then. But she sure rakes in the donations."

"Uh huh. So—do you think I could see the security videos?"

Lifting a leaf on a yellowed vine, Reverend Parce peered at its underside. "Do you know anything about grapes?"

"I like wine," Jett said. "Grapes can be a nice snack."

"There's a saying." The reverend wagged a finger at her. "The more stressed the vine, the sweeter the grape. I think that was the situation with Darling Ashley. She had a hard childhood, and she turned it into a music career filled with songs about heartache and pain. Then, she hurt her daughter—but her daughter ran away. Tiffany Lynn is dead because of what she learned when she tried to stop taking the hardship Ashley was dishing out on her." He grabbed the base of the plant and jerked it from the ground, tossing it into the grass. "There'll be no fruit from that stressed vine."

He moved to the next plant, picking off a few small leaves but leaving the larger ones. Taking a screwdriver from his pocket, he poked around the soil at the base of the vine, then peered into the holes.

"Running away is a temporary solution." Reverend Parce stood, wiping the mud from the screwdriver. "Because everybody can be found. Your cell phone tracks you, your credit cards…

social media says you 'checked in' at places." He dropped the screwdriver back into his overalls. "You'll be found. Chick-Fil-A will text me if I drive by one of their restaurants. A smart girl like Ashley Wells' daughter would figure that out—and maybe she *did* figure it out, before she disappeared. Then it becomes a matter of stopping your tormenter. So how do you do that?"

"I don't know," Jett said. "How?"

"Girl, you spend too much time on TV and not enough on the playground. Sure, you know. What do people say to do to a bully?"

Jett shrugged. "Punch him in the nose?"

"Right. Fight back. Take a stand. So here, when the bully is your own mother, you hold your breath if you can, picking your battles until you leave the house—you go off to college. Then, if things still don't improve, you fight back on a different level. Once provoked, a woman tends to attack another woman with severe, unrelenting, irreversible force, where her opponent is most vulnerable—her reputation and her past." He picked a leaf off another plant, holding it under his nose before discarding it. "Everybody has secrets. Rich folks have as many secrets as anyone else, they just think their money will hide it better. You want to get Ashley Wells off your back, you look into her past. That's where everybody's secrets are buried. Tiffany Lynn would have known that better than most." He put his hands in his pockets, staring at Jett. "I think that girl got too close to whatever Darling Ashley Wells didn't want known, and she's dead as a result."

TIFFANY LYNN IS MISSING

A bead of sweat rolled down the side of Jett's face. She wiped it away with her shoulder. "Ashley Wells doesn't seem to have a lot of friends out here in Christmas."

"She doesn't have a lot of friends, period." The reverend spit into the grass. "Just the people who watch her TV show, and she only acts like she cares about them because they bring in advertising dollars. That lady is all about the money. She forgets, some people in Florida knew her when she was growing up—and we've seen what she's turned into since she came back. She was a twisted little snake then, and she's a money-grabbing big snake now. About the only decent work she's done is with the prisons, finding jobs for hard-core criminals after they get released—and I even question her reasons for doing that. Probably gets a kickback from the state or something."

"Well, as I said, the letters are hurting the family, not just Ashley." She wiped away another drop of sweat. "Getting a peek at your videos would help me move along in my work."

"Stickler, aren't you?" The old man grinned. "Gotta see things with your own eyes."

Jett shrugged. "It makes for a more honest report when I talk to my boss."

"I've seen the videos. I can tell you exactly who's been mailing the letters." Parce pulled a clean white handkerchief from his back pocket and handed it to her. "Hope Carmichael, Doctor Carmichael's granddaughter. She's living over on Elm Street now. Drives a light yellow Volkswagen Beetle." He nodded at Jett. "Every time a letter gets received, we check the recordings and there she is, a day or two before. Never comes to the post office before that or after that, always one to two days before we hear a letter arrived at Darling Ashley Wells' house."

Jett wiped her brow with the handkerchief. "That's pretty specific. How could you be so certain?"

"I have a few friends at the post office. I worked there for quite a while before I came here, and we still talk on occasion—like every Sunday after services."

She peered down the street at the post office. "Do you think your friends might have talked you into aiming a camera at the driveway of the post office so it could read the license plates of cars as they entered the property?"

"You're smart. I like that. Miss, after this business with the letters started, we upgraded the system. Got a high-definition camera zoomed in right on the post office entrance. You can read the license plates, plain as day—and you can see who's behind the wheel."

"I'd like to look at that."

"I'll bet. Let's get some lemonade."

Reverend Parce walked toward the old church building, taking a red handkerchief from the chest pocket of his overalls and wiping the back of his neck. Jett followed, sweat running down her spine.

"This post office is only busy before the holidays," he said. "People wanting a postmark that says 'Christmas' for their cards and such. After December, traffic drops way off. There are only

TIFFANY LYNN IS MISSING

about a thousand people in the whole town, and the post office gets less than fifty customers on a typical day—which means the employees know the customers. All packages and letters get postmarks the same day they are received. They're trucked out the same day."

Jett did the math. "So if Ashley Wells gets a letter postmarked from Christmas on a Thursday, it was at the post office Wednesday, Tuesday at the earliest."

"That's right." The old man nodded, smiling at her. "Like I said, you're a smart one. Whoever hired you made a good decision."

* * * * *

Jett drained the last drops of lemonade from her glass, taking a seat next to the reverend at his computer. He moved the mouse to a file icon labeled "security" and clicked on a file.

An image of the Christmas post office driveway appeared on the screen. A yellow Volkswagen Beetle drove onto the property and parked, its heavyset female driver exiting the vehicle and walking toward the front door.

In her hand was what appeared to be an envelope.

"That's Hope Carmichael," Reverend Parce said.

Jett jotted down the license plate of the car. On the screen, Hope entered the post office.

"Here." He fast forwarded the video. "Watch when she comes out."

Hope exited and got back into the car, driving away. Nothing was in her hand when she left the building.

"That's it." Reverend Parce leaned back on his chair. "She's never there any other time except for a day or two before a letter arrives for Ashley Wells from her daughter. I checked."

"Could I get a copy of the file?" Jett set her empty glass on a coaster on the desk. "I'd like to watch the rest of the footage to be sure she doesn't come any other time or that no one else could be dropping off the letters."

"You can have this copy." He ejected a DVD and handed it to her. "No one's come looking for it, and if they do, I know who I gave it to. But you'll be wasting your time. The fellas in the post office know Hope. She handed them the envelopes with that cursive handwriting every time."

Jett sighed. "I don't get it. Why wasn't this mentioned before?"

"Because someone didn't want it mentioned. Someone didn't want people looking into why someone's mailing letters for a missing girl who's now dead. And there's only one person in the world who doesn't want that looked into. Darling Ashley Wells."

Standing, Jett put her hands on her hips and paced back and forth in the small office. "She stopped the investigation by making sure the guys at the post office knew the rules and followed them. They said 'warrant' ten seconds after I asked my first question."

TIFFANY LYNN IS MISSING

"I told you, lawyers are evil." The reverend took a sip from his glass. "Her attorneys told them they couldn't discuss anything without seeing a warrant first. Then they'd need to get permission from their public relations person. A post office is federal property. That means a federal judge has to agree to a warrant—"

"And the Wells family is politically connected." Jett nodded. "Ashley slowed everything down until the missing person wasn't missing anymore. No federal judge is going to waste time with a case that's already resolved."

"The police don't have time to poke around into resolved cases, either. It all comes to a stop."

She shook her head, staring out the window. The little grape vines waved in the breeze.

The question is, why?

What did Tiffany Lynn know that was so important that she had to run away or be killed over it?

Maybe the lady delivering the letters knows.

"Reverend..." Jett faced the old man. "Would you give me Hope Carmichael's address on Elm street?"

DAN ALATORRE

CHAPTER 27

Rico pulled a heavy tripod from the rear compartment of the Miami 5 news van, setting it on the crumbling, broken asphalt. "Derek—which microphone do you want?"

The newly-promoted reporter walked to the rear of the van, peering over his boss' shoulder. "It's a two-shot, so... the Bose mic, if that's okay."

"Whatever you want, rookie." Taking a hard plastic case from a shelf, Rico looked at his trainee. "This is your story. You can have your choice." He opened the box and checked the battery life on the microphone inside.

"I like the Bose. It makes my voice sound deeper."

Technically, postproduction mixing did that, but the Bose mic captured a fuller range of sound. The former videographer sounded like a more polished reporter when he used it.

Holding a hand to his brow, Rico glanced at the sky. "How do you like this light?"

"It's fine for the setup shot," Derek said. "Nice and hazy, no harsh shadows… we won't need any bounce reflectors." He turned to the dirty alleyway, pointing at a burned-up dumpster and the faded rags that hung on the laundry lines overhead. "I'd like to get all this in there. Start tight on me, then pull out and show the red brick walls, the chipped paint…"

"Good." Rico mounted a camera on the tripod. "But let's not overdo it. The images are important, but the content is the story. Gangs, drugs, violence." He held up a finger for each item he counted off. "Scared residents will tune in. Bored ones will switch over to Channel 13 and watch Lisa Preager's beach report."

Praeger. The pretty brunette that wore blouses two sizes too small.

"Yeah." Derek snorted. "That's fair."

"That's Miami news. Get aggressive and get viewers or get left in the dust."

Rico knew the process. He started as a segment reporter and worked his way up, with eyes on the station manager gig as soon as Martin Brennan announced his retirement—which rumor said would be soon. And Rico had done all the leg work to earn the job. He recruited talent, he trained employees, and he managed production schedules. He put in whatever hours were necessary—and then some—so he would be Mr. Nesmith's obvious choice whenever Martin decided to hand over the reins.

TIFFANY LYNN IS MISSING

From there, he might land a job at a national network, or possibly at an up-and-coming Florida station, running their entire TV operation. News, features, entertainment, the works.

Taking his phone from his pocket, Rico checked the time. "I need to make a phone call. Your interview will be here in a few minutes, but a guy's coming to meet me about another story—so keep your eyes open, but let me do the talking when my guy gets here." He walked toward one of the empty shops, stepping over the broken glass that apparently used to be windows. "You good?"

Derek nodded. "What's with you and all the secret phone calls all of a sudden?"

"Just working on a different story." Rico put his phone to his ear.

"Is there a part in it for me?" Peering around the large, mounted camera, Derek raised himself onto his tiptoes. "Is it a better story than mine?"

"It's different, that's all. It's about Ashley Wells. I can't give you a piece of it, and trust me, you don't want a piece of it." Rico disappeared into the dark interior of a former shoe shop.

"Oh, man! Darling Ashley? I bet that's juicy." Shifting from one foot to the other, Derek raised his eyebrows. "Throw me a bone. Let me in on it. I'll make your story shine."

His words faded into the storefront as a seagull swooped down to perch on a nearby overhang. The bird looked around, cawing loudly.

"Try the dumpster," Derek said.

* * * * *

As the new reporter put his eye to the camera and lined up his shots, a gray van came toward him in the alley. Its wheels sent splashes up from the desolate backstreet's many mud-puddle potholes as the van rolled along. Stopping about thirty feet away, the vehicle's side door opened and a large, musclebound man in a black polo shirt got out. His dark sunglasses shaded his eyes, his thick arms barely swinging at his sides as he walked toward Derek.

"Hey, how ya doing?" Derek forced a smile.

The man kept a firm face and didn't slow his stride, pulling on a pair of black driving gloves. When he was about ten feet away, he stopped and nodded at Derek. "Are you Rico?"

The reporter cocked his head, eyeing the large stranger.

"A guy's coming to meet me about another story..."

"Uh... yeah," Derek said. "Yeah, I'm Rico." He squared his shoulders. "You the guy with the Ashley Wells info?"

"Sure." The man hooked a thumb over his shoulder. "It's confidential, though. Why don't we talk in the van? It's hot out here." He pinched the material stretched across his wide chest, pulling it away from his bulging pecs a few times and sending waves of air through the dark fabric. "We don't want nobody listening to our conversation, you know?"

Derek gazed at the vehicle. The paint was faded and there were dents in the sides. Rust poked through around the car's fenders.

An uneasy feeling welled in his stomach.

TIFFANY LYNN IS MISSING

"C'mon." The stranger took a step toward the van. "You want some inside details for that big story you're working on, right? And I'm here to deliver the message. Let's you and me talk."

Swallowing hard, Derek eyed the stranger. "In... in the van."

"Yeah. Come on." He took the reporter by the arm, his thick fingers wrapping around Derek's bicep. "I don't wanna be seen out here in broad daylight, you know?"

"Uh, yeah..." Derek stopped, pulling his arm away. "But just let me make a phone call real quick first."

"You can make your phone call in the van."

"I think I'd better do it out here." He backed away, moving toward the news vehicle. "There's... better reception out here. But you can go ahead and give me your update."

The stranger sighed. "Fine. You wanna take the message out here? Okay by me."

The big man balled up his fist and rammed it into Derek's gut.

Derek's breath hissed out between his teeth as he doubled over and dropped to his knees. Gasping and holding his abdomen, he stared at the ground.

"What I got to tell you is this." The stranger swung his foot into Derek's side, sending him sprawling over onto the asphalt. "You need to stop calling Ashley Wells' employees, see? She don't like it."

Derek rolled onto his side, trying to force a breath of air into his lungs. His ribs and abdomen blazed in waves of pain.

The big man squatted over him, pummeling his fist into Derek's back. "No more calls to Ashley's people..." He punched the reporter, delivering a blow like a sledgehammer. "No more messages left at DAW..." Another painful blow.

Derek flopped onto his back, wheezing as the sides of the old alley swayed back and forth over him.

"No more anything. Ashley Wells doesn't exist for you."

Another kick to the ribs. Derek's side exploded in pain.

"You got it, TV man?"

Unable to speak, Derek squeezed his eyes shut and tried to nod. The stranger grabbed him by the collar and yanked him upward. Forcing an eye open, Derek saw the attacker rear his fist back. As Derek turned away, his mouth and jaw received the impact, slamming his head to the side. His ear rang with a high-pitched tone, his head throbbing.

"No more of that big mouth of yours, understand?"

The stranger shook him. Small, hard objects rolled across Derek's tongue. Bolts of pain shot up the side of his face.

Punches landed on his cheek and jaw a few more times, his mouth filling with warm, coppery fluid.

Derek slumped to the ground. A cough sent a thick, gooey spray of red out from his lips. Barely able to focus, he stared at several of his teeth laying on the asphalt in front of him.

TIFFANY LYNN IS MISSING

Gasping and wheezing, Derek's vision grew cloudy, his entire body aching. The piercing tone reverberated through his skull, his head pounding in excruciating pain.

Groaning with each sliver of humid Miami air he could suck through his windpipe, the reporter lay there with his head on the ground. Red streaks smeared over his vision with each blink of his eyes. He pushed himself across the hard ground, trying to crawl away.

The van door opened again. A second man stepped out, walking forward as he cocked a gun.

The reporter closed his eyes, awaiting the gunshot that would end his life, and unable to prevent it. He whimpered, clawing the asphalt as the crotch of his pants turned warm and wet.

Derek's rear pocket jerked open, his wallet sliding out.

"Mack, this here's not Rico. The wallet says—"

"Not Rico?" The stranger growled. "What do you mean?" Squatting, he waved Derek's driver's license back and forth in front of his face, then dropped it to the ground. "Well, what do you know about that?" He leaned close and whispered in his victim's ear. "But you know Rico, don't you, Derek?"

Summoning all his remaining strength, Derek moved his head up and down, groaning.

The stranger used Derek's shirttails to wipe the blood off his hands. "Then Rico will still get the message."

* * * * *

Rico ended his first phone call when the unmistakable sound of squealing tires echoed off the burned-out walls of the abandoned shoe store. He turned, staring into the alley outside.

The news van was visible; the TV camera was still mounted on its tripod—but Derek was nowhere in sight.

Rico raced outside to see a gray van at the far end of the alley, racing backwards onto the main street. A big guy, like a body builder, sat in the passenger seat; the driver was a small, thin, dark-haired man.

On the ground, Derek lay unconscious in a pool of red, his swollen eyes and split lip turning black with bruises under the raggedy laundry lines. Dirt and blood covered his shirt.

Rico ran toward his friend, his gut clenching. At the other end of the alley, the gray van sped away.

The business end of the new reporter's favorite microphone protruded from the lips of his blood-soaked mouth. As Rico removed it, Derek groaned and rolled onto his side, blood pouring over his lips.

Rico's phone rang in his hand.

Unknown name, unknown number.

He pressed the green button and put the device to his ear.

"Is this Rico from the TV station?" The stranger's voice was deep and gruff.

Holding his breath, Rico put a hand on the red-splattered shoulder of his friend.

TIFFANY LYNN IS MISSING

"I left a message for you with your pal Derek," the man said. "Did you get my message, TV man?"

Rico's pulse throbbed in his ears.

"Did you get my message?"

"Yes." Rico swallowed hard, his heart racing. "I got your message."

"Good." The stranger laughed. "Now, just because you're thinking you're some kind of hotshot TV detective—let me help you out. The van was stolen and this phone's a disposable. So don't try tracking any of it, that'll just be a waste of time. You should forget all about me and my friend, and you should forget about Ashley Wells—but you're gonna remember that message I delivered, aren't you, Rico?"

"Yes."

"Say it, TV man."

Rico gritted his teeth and squeezed the phone tightly. "I'll remember the message."

"Good. Leave Ashley Wells and her employees alone, or I'll have to deliver that message again—and this time, I'll take my time. Same process, same result—but it won't be quick like your friend got. It'll be slow and awful for you, Rico. For *days*. Understand?"

Rico clenched his fist. "I understand."

"Okay," the stranger said. "Good talk. Have a nice day."

DAN ALATORRE

CHAPTER 28

Hope Carmichael's residence on Elm Street was a weather-worn, single-wide trailer, surrounded by big oak trees and a rusty chain link fence. The small yard was mostly dirt, likely compliments of the three huge dogs that lay under the green-stained, wooden porch. Tongues hanging from their mouths in the midday heat, the canines' heads lifted as Jett's rental car pulled to a stop, but the animals did not venture out from the shade.

Jett put her hand on the car door latch, taking note of the light yellow Volkswagen Beetle parked next to the oversize aluminum mailbox.

Opening her door, Jett stood and peered over the top of her rental car. "You dogs are friendly, right?" She picked up a long, heavy stick from the ground, holding it behind her back as she approached the gate. "Hello, dogs. You're good dogs, aren't you? Yes, you are."

You'd better be.

She put her hand on the rusted gate, the big dogs watching her every move.

Do I want to be as quiet as possible so the dogs don't get startled, or do I want to make noise to announce myself so if they're going to be aggressive, they'll do it before I get inside the fence?

How did Aaron know the dogs on the mountain were friendly?

One of the dogs turned his large, brown head in her direction and licked his lips.

She exhaled sharply. "You're, uh... not drooling over me as your lunchtime appetizer, right?"

The animal continued staring at her.

"You're a good boy, right?" Jett swallowed hard, easing the gate latch upward. "Or girl? A good *dog*."

The hinges squeaked as she moved the gate forward, keeping the stick by her side.

"Okay, I'm going to come in now, doggos. You guys just... be cool under the porch."

It was about ten steps to the porch, along a narrow path in the dirt, marked by a dozen garden stones.

Walk to the porch, ring the bell, wait for someone to answer... If the dogs are going to take a bite out of me, it'll be between here and the porch. Once I'm up there, I can defend myself a little. The yard is their territory.

She eyed the nearest tree.

Worst case, I can make a run for that oak and start climbing.

TIFFANY LYNN IS MISSING

"But you're good dogs, aren't you? And you know I'm here…" She put a foot inside the yard. "It is way too hot to come out from under that nice, cool porch." Gripping the stick, she inched across the yard. "Don't mind me. I'm just going to walk to the front door and talk to your owner. You guys can stay right where you are."

She neared the raised porch—and the three large dogs underneath.

Point of no return. If the dogs decide to attack, they'll get to me before I can get to the porch or the tree.

Just gotta run toward the bullets, Jett.

One of the dogs stood up, his tail hanging low as he growled. The other two dogs got to their feet.

Jett held her breath, her eyes on the animals as she lifted a foot to climb the rotting wooden steps.

Almost there…

The biggest dog turned its head, looking out over the sandy yard. It didn't appear any more interested in Jett than anything else inside the fenced area. Jett tiptoed up the remaining stairs, reaching out to push the cracked, yellowed doorbell button, keeping her eyes directed through the gaps in the deck boards to the big dogs below her.

As the sound of heavy footsteps came from inside the trailer, Jett took a step back so she didn't appear too in-your-face when the owner opened the door—but held her stick tightly behind her back in case the dogs decided to change their minds.

* * * * *

Aaron stood next to the dean at her office window, gazing out at the lush, green lawns of the

Crestview College commons. A maintenance worker entered the office and handed him a laptop computer. "Here you are, Aaron."

"Thanks, Theo." Aaron took the computer and slid it into a backpack. "How'd the room look?"

The maintenance worker shook his head, looking down. "Like she'd be home any minute. Text book open on the desk, bed was unmade... it was kind of eerie. And sad, knowing she'd never be coming back." He raised his gaze to Aaron's. "But I was happy to get that computer for you."

Aaron shook the worker's hand. "I appreciate it."

"There he is." At the window, the dean pointed toward a group of students walking across the grass. "He's the one in the dark blue shirt, carrying the red backpack."

Aaron peered out the window, nodding. "Thanks, Lyra." He turned toward the exit. "And don't tell anyone I was here, would you?"

"Might be too late for that." She returned to her desk. "The whole staff knows you. Most of the students, too..."

Pulling a baseball cap over his eyes, Aaron put on his sunglasses and adjusted his t-shirt. "You mean my elaborate disguise won't hold up under scrutiny?"

"No," Lyra said. "But from a distance, you could fool some students—for a while."

"Good enough." Aaron picked up his backpack and slung it over his shoulder. "I just need to fool one."

* * * * *

TIFFANY LYNN IS MISSING

The trailer door opened an inch, and a heavyset woman stared at Jett through the gap. "Can I help you?"

"Ms. Carmichael," Jett said, "I'm here to ask you about some letters you've been mailing. The ones from Tiffany Lynn Wells to her mother Ashley."

The woman put a hand to her mouth. "You know about that?"

"I think a lot of people know. Can we speak inside?"

Hope stepped back, opening the door.

"Thank you." Jett leaned her stick against the exterior wall of the trailer and walked inside. "You have a lovely..."

The inside of the trailer was piled high with magazines and cardboard boxes, stacked waist high. Mountains of newspapers and plastic bags occupied every visible space, with a single, dim lamp shining over the sea of clutter. Sunlight peeked in around the room's drawn shades, illuminating the arm of a threadbare brown couch that stuck out from a mound of unfolded laundry. The kitchen cupboards sagged on the walls, doors hanging open; the garbage can overflowed with fast food wrappers. In the corner, an old tube-style television played a daytime drama from atop a dry, empty aquarium. Only a narrow path led from one room to the next, a cavern among the debris, and the air was thick with the stench of used kitty litter.

Jett cleared her throat. "You have a lovely home."

"I don't." Hope shook her head. "But it's very nice of you to say that."

A calico cat emerged from somewhere between the stacks, brushing across Jett's ankle. Hope Carmichael wrestled an armful of laundry up from the couch and relocated it to an ottoman that had been serving as a table for a half-finished jigsaw puzzle. "Please, sit down."

An inch of cat hair covered the brown cushions. Stifling a wince, Jett moved to the sofa as her host sat down.

If you don't sit—and act like nothing's wrong—you'll alienate this interview.

And this lady is too important to let that happen.

Jett seated herself, placing her notepad on her knee. The calico followed, rubbing its nose against Jett's shoe.

"Pepper, you leave her alone." Hope waved at the cat. Pepper ignored her owner and continued her fascination with Jett's footwear.

"I'm a cat lover, too," Jett lied. "How many of these cute little critters do you have? I saw some dogs outside."

Hope smiled, leaning back. "Oh, we have the three dogs and seven cats, a parakeet and a goat."

Jett nodded, debating whether to ask why anyone would have a goat. "That's a lot of mouths to feed."

"Yeah, I do the best I can. It's harder since my program didn't get renewed at the grade school. I was a language arts specialist, and a federal grant paid my salary. It didn't get re-approved for this year,

TIFFANY LYNN IS MISSING

so they had to stop the program temporarily." She glanced around the trailer. "I started taking jobs on Fiverr and Upwork to help out."

Looking around, Jett spied an unlit, fully-decorated Christmas tree standing next to an overloaded dining room table—but no chairs. She faced her host. "Is that how you connected with Tiffany Lynn? Through Fiverr? Was she paying you to write letters for her?"

Hope pressed her knees together, wringing her hands. "I hope I haven't done anything wrong."

"No..." Jett kept her tone soft. "No, I don't think so. Just... Maybe you can tell me how you got involved with Tiffany Lynn." She leaned down to peer up into Hope's eyes. "You *are* sending the letters, aren't you?"

"Yes." Hope nodded. "I sent them. A letter would come every few days, maybe once a week."

"The letters would come? Tiffany Lynn brought them to you?"

"No, I'd get a big envelope, and inside would be a sealed letter that was all ready to be mailed—the address was on it, the postage... all I had to do was take the letter to the post office and mail it."

Jett rubbed her chin. "The envelopes that came—did you see where they were postmarked from?"

"They came from all over." Hope sighed. "One came from Tallahassee, one was from Colorado... one was from right here in Orlando. But there wasn't ever a return address on the envelopes they came in. Just postmarks."

"Can I see them? Did you keep any?"

She shook her head. "The instructions were to burn the envelopes after I opened them, so I did."

"That didn't strike you as strange?"

Hope looked away, wringing her hands. "It did, but what could I do? I needed… I needed the money."

"You were in a tough spot." Jett nodded. "I understand. So, how did you get paid? Every time you mailed a letter?"

"I got paid in advance. Three thousand dollars to mail whatever letters came. Take them to the Christmas post office, mail them from the lobby counter—and not say anything." She sniffled, wiping her eyes. "I thought she wanted secrecy, but I guess that didn't work, because here you are."

Jett eyed the subject of her interview.
She's softening, but she's breaking, too.
Go easy or you'll lose her.
She wants to tell you. Let her.

Jett sat upright. "It was smart to supplement your income with jobs on Fiverr. Stuff like that is the way of the future. Did you set everything up online with Tiffany Lynn? Were you ever able to talk to her in person or over the phone?"

"We talked on the phone once. She called me so I'd know what she sounded like and to tell me a code word—well, her *safety* word, she called it." Hope smiled. "But I saw her on TV a few times, on her mother's show, and on the YouTube videos they used to do, so I knew what she sounded like. The lady on the phone sure sounded like Tiffany Lynn Wells to me. I never had a doubt about that, I just—"

TIFFANY LYNN IS MISSING

"Excuse me," Jett said. "Did you say she told you a code word?"

"A safety word, yeah. I was supposed to keep mailing letters as long as they arrived unless she called and said the safety word. I guess it doesn't matter now, since the news said she died. But there must've been someone else like me in the chain, because I still got letters. Even after the news said Tiffany Lynn had passed, the letters kept coming."

"And you kept mailing them."

She nodded. "That was the arrangement. I try to keep my word, because I need the money."

It was an interesting point. Tiffany Lynn might have written a dozen letters and sent them to an intermediary to re-mail once a week to Hope.

If she paid that person in advance, they'd do their job, too.

But why would Tiffany Lynn do it at all?

It's a way to punch without being punched back. Intermediaries who can't trace the chain back to you—but they already knew it was you. They just didn't know where you were.

That's a lot of effort just to let your mother know you're mad at her. What would make someone so angry? What's behind the urge to vent that bile?

But at some point, it would stop. Then what?

"Ms. Carmichael, how long did Tiffany Lynn say she'd keep doing this?"

"She didn't." The woman slouched in her seat.

Guilt.

She feels bad about taking money from a dead girl and hiding secrets from the police.

"I figured it would be for about nine months," Hope said. "She told me on the phone call that at Christmas we'd look at another deal, and she asked if I could do this until then. I said I wasn't going anywhere, and she said okay. She sent the money that day." She peered toward the street. "I don't know if I'm supposed to return some of the money now—I bought that used Volkswagen with some of it." Turning to Jett, Hope's eyes brimmed with tears. "What do you think?"

Jett looked around at the shabby dwelling. "You said the agreement was three thousand dollars for mailing the letters as long as they came, and you did that. I'm not sure you owe anybody a refund."

"I'm still doing it. A letter came yesterday."

Jett cocked her head. "Yesterday?"

We didn't see that on the church video.

"Did you take it to the post office and mail it?"

Hope nodded. "Yes."

"Hope, the post office..." Leaning forward, Jett clutched her notepad. "There's video surveillance cameras that record anyone who drives onto post office property. Your yellow Beetle didn't go there yesterday."

"Wow, no. My car was low on gas, so I took my sister's and delivered the letter. You guys record everything and watch it all?" Hope wrapped her arms around herself. "That's kinda creepy."

Jett shook her head, putting her hand out. "That's not quite the deal. Nobody's spying on you. The guy who reviewed the security video just pointed your car out to me. I'm trying to help the family."

TIFFANY LYNN IS MISSING

"You said people know I'm mailing the letters. Should I be worried?"

Exhaling slowly, the former TV reporter stared at her interviewee.

What do I say here? Yes, you should worry—and add to a situation you're already barely managing? Or lie and say no, possibly putting you in danger?

"If it were me," Jett said, "I might find a place to stay for a few days. You said you had a sister. Could she put you up for a while?"

"She is." Looking around the trailer's filthy living room, Hope waved her hands over the debris. "This is her place. I moved in last August when they cut my job. She can't manage on her own right now, so I'm dealing with that, holding onto every nickel, and trying to get back on my feet—and then get her back to seeing her therapist. She had to stop going when the grant got denied."

Jett pursed her lips. "I'm sorry. Looks like you're doing things the right way, taking care of her."

"Trying to." Hope sighed. "Around these parts, people take care of family."

Taking her phone from her pocket, Jett scrolled across the contacts screen. "Listen, let me give you my friend Rico's number. Tell him I asked you to call. He manages the production team at a TV station in Miami, and he always needs odd jobs done—research, editing for news stories... You said you were in language arts. Maybe he can hook you up with a few gigs, you know?"

"That's very generous of you, Ms. Thacker. I really appreciate it." A slight blush came to the woman's cheeks.

"We're friends now. My friends call me Jett."

Hope's blush reddened. "Okay… Jett."

Bringing up Rico's information, Jett air dropped it to Hope's phone. "There. Call him, okay?"

"I will. Today." She pressed her phone to her bosom. "Thank you."

"You're welcome." Jett walked to the door, opening it and stepping outside. The three dogs were at the bottom of the porch steps, wagging their tails.

"There's my security system," Hope said. "These big ol' Teddy bears wouldn't have the sense to scare off Al Capone if they knew who he was, but they might lick him to death."

"They're sweet." Jett maneuvered between the canines as she descended the stairs and they raced up. "By the way…" She turned around to face Hope. "What was the code word Tiffany Lynn gave you? Can you tell me?"

Squinting in the bright sunlight, Hope shrugged. "I guess it won't matter now, since she passed on." She bent down, rubbing each dog behind the ears, one at a time. "The safety word was 'Aaron.'"

* * * * *

Bubbles rose to the surface of the canal as the stolen gray van disappeared under the waves. Mack tossed the disposable phone into the rippling water and walked to Buzzy's waiting car, taking out another phone and pressing a number.

TIFFANY LYNN IS MISSING

After two rings, the call connected. "Hey, boss. I got something for you."

"Talk," the man on the other end said.

Mack climbed into the car, and the pair drove away from the abandoned produce processing site. "The little bird whose phone ID we hacked in Colorado—she just started singing again. She air dropped the phone number of our Miami news guy to a lady in Christmas, Florida."

The boss chuckled. "She is regular as rain. I love modern technology. Okay, I'll have someone handle it."

"Me and Buzzy could drive up and do it. We could be there in about four hours."

"Buzzy might have a different appointment, Mack. The client just called in another job. Finish up in Miami, then pack a bag and go to the airport tomorrow morning."

Mack grinned. "We're getting awfully busy. Where am I headed?"

"You might need to pay a visit to a private college near Tallahassee. I'll tell you more tomorrow."

DAN ALATORRE

CHAPTER 29

"Remy!" Aaron scampered up the dormitory stairs after the athletic young man. "Hey, Remy. Hold up."

With one hand stuffed in the pocket of his jeans, Remy Delphine stopped in the middle of the staircase and turned around. The wind lifted the edge of his tennis shirt collar. "Sorry, do I know you?"

Scowling, Aaron climbed the stairs two at a time. "Yeah. You know me. I'm the uncle of your girlfriend, Tiffany Lynn. You remember her?"

The young man smiled, pointing a finger at Aaron. "You're on the board of the school. Aaron Wells, right?"

"Right," Aaron said. "I give the readmission speeches you attend out there on the commons every year during the first day of school—glad to see you were paying attention. I have a question for you. Where's Tiffany Lynn?"

"What—what do you mean?" Remy recoiled. "She's... she died, sir. In Colorado."

"Did she?" Aaron gritted his teeth. "Then why does her mother keep getting letters from her? And what happened to the thirty grand she stole from me before she disappeared under the ice at Brimstone Lake?"

Remy's jaw hung open.

"Remy?" A curvy, petite young woman with long brown hair appeared at the top of the steps, her short-shorts riding up her rear end like they had been painted on. "Is everything okay?"

He nodded. "Everything's fine, baby. Go on back to your dorm room. I'll be there in a sec."

"You sure?" She snapped her chewing gum, glaring at Aaron.

"Yeah," Remy said, eying the school founder. "It's cool."

The young woman disappeared.

"Baby, huh?" Aaron frowned. "No, I guess you're not grieving too hard for my niece."

"Baby is her nickname," Remy said. "Her real name's Barbara."

"And you're helping her with freshman calculus? This is the freshman dorm, isn't it?" Heat rose to Aaron's neck and cheeks. "I mean, I built the school, but I might be wrong."

Remy leaned away. "What's it to you?

Aaron grabbed Remy by the collar, shoving him against the stone stairwell wall. "I'll tell you what it is to me. The sheriff in Colorado says my niece died in a lake. He says you were there—you and some girl named Brandy, a local out there—and

TIFFANY LYNN IS MISSING

I'll be talking to her next. But maybe you can answer a few questions for me, like what you were doing in Colorado in the first place. The sheriff seemed amazingly incurious about that."

Remy held his hands up. "Spring break, man. Partying. Weed's legal out there. 'CO for a DO,' you know? *Day off.*"

Aaron leaned forward, shoving him into the wall again. "So you went out there and partied. How'd you pay for the trip?"

"Tiff paid. She had lots of money."

"Where'd you stay?"

"Look, Mr. Wells..." Remy gently put his hands on Aaron's. "Giving me a hard time isn't going to bring your niece back. She's gone, and I don't care who you are, that's the end of it. We're all sad, bro, but life goes on."

"Remy..." The brunette reappeared at the top of the steps. "Come on."

"Yeah, I can see you're all broken up about it." Aaron released him, scowling. "Go on. Calculus is waiting."

As Remy went up the steps, Aaron stormed down them, heading for the administration building parking lot. When he reached his car, he got in and started the engine, turning the air conditioning up to full and wiping his brow.

Then he called Matt Philson.

"How'd I do?" Aaron held his phone to his ear with one hand and reached under the passenger seat with the other, retrieving his laptop.

"Not bad," Philson said. "I thought you brought a 'pissed off father' vibe to the role, which was a nice touch. Did you place the device?"

"Yeah." Aaron glanced at a cardboard box full of Philson's surveillance equipment on the back seat. "I placed it when I grabbed him. It's on his shirt—a tennis shirt, under the collar."

"Perfect." The sound of fingers typing on a keyboard came over the line. "Okay, so that's gonna fall off eventually, but if he makes any calls in the next hour or so, we'll—" Philson chuckled. "And there he goes. Hold on a sec, Aaron. I gotta segregate the signal for clarity."

Aaron fanned himself. More keyboard noises came through the earpiece.

"Okay," Philson said. "I'm receiving him. Where'd you put the transceiver unit?"

"Outside the freshman dormitory. He's upstairs in some girl's dorm room, and the transceiver's right outside. I stuffed it into a backpack and put it at the bottom of the stairs."

"Good place to hide a big box like that, especially on a college campus. Make sure maintenance picks it up for you before someone calls in a bomb threat... Okay, I've locked in on his phone ID. We can track him now, and in a second I'll have both ends of the call."

"You're recording him, though, right?"

"Yeah. Here we go, boss man. The link is live. Check your laptop."

"Okay." Aaron clicked the link. A window opened on the screen, displaying a digital wavelength that moved when anyone on the call

TIFFANY LYNN IS MISSING

spoke, followed by a second window showing the location of the college on a street grid. A green dot blinked on the far-right side of the little map—the freshman dormitory.

Remy's voice came through Aaron's laptop speakers loud and clear. "I'm telling you, the freaking guy knows something. Why else would he be here?"

"Because," the other man on the call said. "He wants to know what happened to his niece, like he said."

"Dude, he was pissed." Remy breathed hard, speaking in hushed tones. "He was asking about the money. He knows something's up."

Philson chuckled. "Aaron—something's definitely up."

In the background of the call, a young woman expressed concern. Her voice was muffled, like she was talking through a closed door.

"Remy, ya gotta chill," the man said. "He didn't say you got paid ten grand, did he? Wells is guessing. He doesn't have any more authority than the police, and they didn't pursue anything."

"I don't care. I'm coming to your place." Remy's voice grew strained. "We need to come up with a plan."

"We *have* a plan, stupid. Stay home. You got paid ten grand to do a job. This is part of that job. Don't come here."

"Nope. We need a face-to-face," Remy said. "I'm already on my way."

"Remy, don't—"

The call ended. A short burst of static blasted across the laptop speakers as the audio link went offline. The green dot remained on the computer screen.

"Aaron," Philson said, "now that we've hacked his phone ID, that signal locator on your laptop will move when he moves. You can follow this kid wherever he takes his phone—which will be everywhere."

"Good. Thanks, Matt."

"Sure—happy to help, as always. You and me go way back, boss man. I always have your back. You know that."

Aaron stared at the laptop. The dot hadn't moved—yet.

"You got paid ten grand to do a job."

And what job was that, Remy? To make my niece disappear? Why?

He gripped the steering wheel, watching the dot. "Matt, what about the other guy? Can we follow him, too?"

"Sure, but you might want to hop on a plane first. He's in Miami."

CHAPTER 30

Jett sat in Orlando's I-4 traffic, her car moving at about one inch per minute. She leaned on the car door and drummed her fingers on the steering wheel.

What do we really know about this case?

Tiffany Lynn had a fight with her mom, went missing, and ended up dead.

But she's still mailing letters to her mother because she wrote them ahead of time and gave them to Hope to mail.

Mom is acting strange.

Is it actually Tiffany Lynn who wrote the letters? Seems like it. Her mom thinks so. Aaron does.

Did she send the letters to Hope? Maybe. We don't know for sure if it was actually Tiffany Lynn who contacted Hope in the first place. It sounded like her, but that could be faked...

Tiffany Lynn may have already been dead by then and someone was creating a smokescreen with the letters, to keep the police away from what was really happening. Could that be kidnappers? But then where was the ransom request? And why keep sending the letters now that she's dead?

Jett shook her head. The kidnapping scenario got too crazy too fast.

It all did.

Okay, not kidnappers. Start over.

Tiffany Lynn sends the letters to Hope herself, possibly through an intermediary. Let's say that's legit. Why do it?

Just to piss off her mom? Or...

Or what?

Why would someone do that?

And why would her mom act so strangely afterward?

Jett's old lawyer self emerged.

Don't look at why. Look at who benefits.

Who benefits from these actions?

She ran her fingers through her blonde hair, gazing over the steering wheel. On the side of the road, a billboard displayed a local attraction featuring knights in armor on horseback, jousting with long wooden lances while the nearby king feasted on a large drumstick and a cup of ale.

The car in front of her pulled forward a few inches; Jett eased off the brake and let her vehicle creep forward.

TIFFANY LYNN IS MISSING

Who benefits from Tiffany Lynn disappearing?

Who benefits from Tiffany Lynn writing letters to her mother?

So far, no single solution had answered *all* the questions. When something *did* answer them all, it would probably be the only option that did—and it would lead to whoever was behind the whole thing.

In the rental car's cupholder, Jett's phone rang. "Leah," the name of her ten-year-old neighbor across the hall in Miami, appeared on the screen.

Jett reached over and hit the green button, putting the phone on speaker. "Hey, Leah." She tried to sound upbeat and casual, not irritated over her current case. "How'd we do on that math quiz?"

"I got an A," Leah said. "I thought you'd be home yesterday."

"Yeah, sorry. I got delayed." Jett eyed the bumper-to-bumper traffic, her mind rolling through suspects and options.

If things are not what they appear to be, then who benefits from how things are being presented?

She shook her head, refocusing on the call. "Good job on the quiz, though. That's really—"

"I heard the door slam on your apartment, and I thought it was you, so I went over…"

Jett's stomach tightened.

"There were two men inside your place," Leah said. "A big giant guy, like Randy Orton, the wrestler, and a little scrawny guy. They were looking around. They took your computer and stuff—just yanked it right off the desk and pulled out the wires… Is everything okay? Do you know them?"

Wincing, Jett glanced at the phone. "Crap. Sounds like my apartment got robbed."

"I'm sorry," Leah said. "I wasn't sure what to do. I didn't call the police because sometimes you let Rico or Derek come over and borrow stuff when you're not home, so I thought they could be friends of yours... even though they weren't acting like it." She sighed. "I should have called 911. Do you want me to call 911 now?"

"Uhh..." Jett adjusted her sunglasses. "I think I'm heading back to Miami today, so I'll take care of it. Are you okay? Were you scared? And where's your dad?"

"Dad's still in Puerto Vallarta. I wasn't scared, though. Good journalists run toward the bullets."

"No, no we don't. Not always. Not when—"

Her phone beeped with another call. The screen showed Rico's name.

"Hey, Leah, I'll have to call you back. If the burglars come back, you stay in your apartment and stay quiet. Let them take whatever they want. That's why I have insurance, okay?"

"Okay."

Jett clicked over to Rico. "Hey, what's up? Any progress on your end? Because I feel like I am spinning my wheels over here."

"Jett, I have some bad news..."

"I mean, I'm getting really solid information, but I can't figure out where any of it fits, and—"

"Jett, I—"

"—it's really starting to drive me—"

"Jett!"

TIFFANY LYNN IS MISSING

She looked at the phone. "What? Rico, I'm right here."

"I have some bad news," he said. "It's about Derek. He... went to the emergency room. He got beat up pretty bad."

"Derek from Miami 5?" Jett's stomach lurched. "What—what happened?"

"He and I were setting up for a remote, and while I was making some calls, he met with a guy I was supposed to meet. They... really went to town on him."

"Oh, no." She put her hand to her forehead, closing her eyes. "Oh, poor Derek..." The reporter had been a good workmate when Jett was new at the station, and he'd become a friend during her time at Miami 5. His friendly smile flashed across her mind. Derek had always been cheerful and friendly. Trustworthy.

And now he was in the emergency room.

Rico's words echoed in her head.

"He met with a guy I was supposed to meet."

Jett bolted upright. "But, Rico, that means they were looking for you."

"Or you," he said. "The guy was supposed to give me information about Ashley Wells, for your case. Somebody doesn't want us looking any further into it."

Jett gritted her teeth. "Like Ashley Wells."

This has gone beyond being an aggressive corporate CEO. This is madness, bordering on homicidal lunacy.

"Darling Ashley would sure be my guess for this. The guy called me after he... when I found

Derek. He said to leave Ashley Wells and her employees alone."

Holding her breath, Jett stared at her phone. "Are you going to do that?"

"No way. You know me. The best way to have me on your back is to tell me to keep away. What's the plan?"

"I'm not sure yet." She glanced around. The traffic was finally moving. "My apartment got robbed. That's no coincidence. Leah said two guys stole my computer."

"She get a description?"

"Not really." Jett frowned. "A real big guy, like a pro wrestler, and a scrawny guy, that's about it. She—"

"Jett! That's them!" Rico said. "That's the guys who attacked Derek. I saw them. A big bodybuilder type and a little skinny guy. That cannot be a coincidence, Jett."

Her jaw dropped. "Geez. No, it can not."

"And you said *Leah* saw them?"

A ten-year-old girl, all alone in an apartment.

A lightning bolt of fear flashed through Jett's insides.

"I gotta go." Jett ended the call, driving with one hand and scrolling for Leah's phone number with the other. She laid on the horn and mashed the gas pedal, swerving around the other cars.

Airport. I have to get to the airport.

Leah's phone rang, but she didn't pick up. A recorded message came on. "The owner of this number has not activated the answering system."

TIFFANY LYNN IS MISSING

Jett pounded the red button to end the call and dialed again.

Come on, Leah. Answer.

After a few rings, the recorded message came on again.

Crap!

She ended the call, redialing.

Please just be playing video games. Please be playing video games.

Please, please, please, please, please...

Swerving around an irate motorist, she sped down the off ramp, holding her breath as the phone rang.

Leah's voice came over the line. "Hey, Jett."

"Leah! Listen to me. Where are you right now?"

"I'm home."

"You need to get out of your apartment. Right now. Is there somewhere you can go?"

"What? Why do I need to leave?"

"The two burglars you saw in my apartment, they're really bad men. They might come back, and if they find you, they might hurt you." She swallowed hard. "I think they *will* hurt you."

"But," Leah said, "we run toward the—"

"No! Not every time, we don't." Jett's heart pounded. "We need to be smart about that. Now, can you... can you go to Mrs. Dearmont's?"

"If it's an emergency."

Huffing, Jett squeezed her eyes shut. "It's an emergency, kiddo. Tell her I said it is." She zigzagged through the streets, racing toward the airport. "Get over there. Go down to the lobby right now and ask Mr. Rutherford to call you a cab. Don't even stop to pick up your toothbrush, okay? Just go. Are you going?"

"I'm going."

"Good. Call me back when you get there."

The traffic light ahead turned yellow. Jett stomped the accelerator, bouncing her car as it sailed over the cross street.

Her phone rang again. She pulled a hand away from the wheel long enough to hit the button. "Leah, are you in the cab?"

"Thanks for the info on the kid." The man's voice on the other end of the call was gruff.

Adrenaline gripped Jett's chest.

It's the guys who attacked Derek. They got Leah.

"I didn't know we were being spied on from across the hall," he said. "Now, take a hint and stop looking into all this Ashley Wells stuff."

Jett's heart rate dropped a notch.

If he'd have gotten Leah, he wouldn't talk about her vaguely. Didn't Rico say they called to taunt him right after attacking Derek?

They don't have her.

Jett tried to keep her voice even. She slowed the car and pulled into a restaurant parking lot.

Focus. Details will matter here.

"Who are you?" she said.

"I'm the guy who could put your nosy little neighbor's face on the side of a milk carton—if she's lucky. A lot of kids die in the hull of those freighters when we ship them overseas. Or you could walk away."

TIFFANY LYNN IS MISSING

"Child trafficking?" Jett said. "You're all class, mister. Just know this—you touch that kid, you die."

"Maybe. Maybe not."

His tone was casual, like he was making a grocery list. No determinable accent.

That means he's probably from a main city in Florida, like Tampa or Orlando... or possibly somewhere in the Midwest.

And if he had Leah, he'd act like it. He'd say things like "I will," not "I could."

Jett's blood pressure eased a little more.

He doesn't have her.

"Killing isn't easy," he said, "but between the two of us, I bet I'm the only one who's served time for it, so I'll take your comments as the idle threat that they are. But you and your associates should stop bothering Ashley Wells' employees and move on to some other investigation. I hear Jimmy Hoffa's still missing. Maybe you could fly to New York and check out Giants Stadium. Might be a big scoop for you."

If he did time for manslaughter or murder, he'll be in the system, and he'll be traceable because he'll probably have a parole officer.

If he's out on parole, he can get locked back up if he had any part in Derek's attack.

Leah, Rico, and a sketch artist could get this guy off the street pretty quickly.

Jett gripped the wheel. "I'm not afraid of you."

"Well, you should be, news lady. But some dumb people have to learn the hard way."

"That's me." Jett nodded. "Dumb as they come. I run toward the bullets."

"So brave." The man chuckled. "Braver than Derek. My friend Buzzy was about to show him a few bullets, and your friend wet himself. Me, I like to work with my hands—and I'm all ready to work on you, news lady. Unless you do what I said and walk away."

Convicted felon. Big giant guy, like a wrestler. Buzzy is an associate.

That might be all I need.

"You and I are going to meet sometime." Jett kept her voice low, growling into the microphone. "We're going to have a little conversation about my friend Derek. And when we do, only one of us is going to walk away."

"If you don't leave Ashley Wells alone, we'll meet real soon—I promise. And trust me, I'm looking forward to that. Until then... have a nice day."

The call ended.

Jett pounded the steering wheel, cursing as the adrenaline pulsed through her system. Her fingers shook as she gripped the wheel.

How did he get this number? No one has it!

They're listening to my calls. They have to be.

Her mind raced, connecting the dots.

That means they're getting information on other people I call, and potentially tracking any of them. They're getting every piece of information I get!

Leah, Rico, Aaron... any interview subject I spoke with, any text I sent...

TIFFANY LYNN IS MISSING

Making a fist, she pounded the seat. "Crap!"

Okay, okay. Think. How do I let people know not to call me? I can't just turn the phone off—I need to hear back from Leah first... and everyone else will still call, which might be enough to track them. Plus, they'll worry when I don't pick up, then they'll start to make mistakes because they'll assume I'm hurt or dead...

I could get a disposable, but whoever I already called has probably been compromised, so I have to let them know or they're in trouble. They could track Leah by her cell phone. Rico, too—and they already beat up Derek... They might have my texts, my emails, and maybe my notes...

"Crap!" She pounded the steering wheel. "Crap, crap, crap, crap!"

Think.

What's the smart move?

She stared at the phone.

They'd know my location, too. But I can't just ditch this phone and get a disposable without telling people the new number, or they might not even answer when I call to warn them.

So...

I have to assume every call from this phone is under surveillance. I just need to get a clean contact established somehow. Then maybe I can use this phone to lead the bad guys in the wrong direction.

The phone rang. Jett stared at it, unwilling to answer.

Aaron's name appeared on the screen.

She reached for the phone.

Choose your words carefully, because someone may be listening—and don't let him give any information away, either.

Pressing the green button, she put the phone to her ear. "Hey, this phone's been hacked. They may have everything, so don't talk if you don't have to—and don't use any names. We…" She chewed her lip. "We need to switch to burners—both of us—but I won't be able to call you and tell you my new number or the hackers will get it, and then we'll be right back where we started—you follow?"

"Yeah…" Aaron said.

Jett nodded, taking a deep breath. "So, here's what we're going to do. I'll create a Hotmail account that we'll both be able to access. The email address will be…"

She tapped the steering wheel.

What's something I can reference—but not actually say directly—that Aaron and I both know?

A name of one of the mountain peaks? No. Others could guess that.

An employee? The color of the snowmobile?

She envisioned his office, where they had first met.

The plaque. The one on his shelf, with the quote.

"Hey." She snapped her fingers. "That Roman soldier who you have a quote from on your conference room shelf—you know the guy?"

"Yes," Aaron said.

"The email address will be his name—twice in a row, no spaces. And then… the password will be the nicknames of your daughters, alphabetically, and

TIFFANY LYNN IS MISSING

the first word in the Roman soldier's quote. In Latin." She exhaled, her heart still not fully back to normal speed. "That last part's not super secret, but it'll buy us enough time to establish a clean contact with each other. As soon as I can, I'll send an email *from* the account *to* the account, with my new burner phone's number in the body of the message. We'll go from there."

"Got it."

She pursed her lips, looking out over the road. "We should be able to talk freely after that. Until then, assume..."

Her gut clenched.

Is it possible Aaron is unwittingly a part of this? He's the only person I've met on this case who has a reputation for hacking. Him and his tech guy, Philson.

She gasped.

Could Philson be part of it?

As quickly as the thoughts flooded in, she dismissed most of them.

Aaron can't be part of it. That doesn't add up. The mountain, the cabin—he's not part of it. You can trust him. But Philson...

"Hello?" Aaron said. "You still there?"

But Philson had the chance—more than once. He could have gotten my phone ID pretty easily, with all that high-tech surveillance stuff, and started trying to break into it.

Or am I just becoming a raving paranoid? Would Philson go behind Aaron's back?

"Hey... Can you hear me?"

Trust your gut, Jett. What does your gut say?

It says Aaron isn't in on it. Philson might be. Okay, then.

"Did I lose you?" he said.

"No." Jett took a deep breath and let it out slowly. "No, I was just... I'm here. Just watch out when you use your phone. Assume someone's listening. I need to get to Miami."

"Me, too," Aaron said.

Jett scrunched up her eyebrows. "You do? Why?"

"One of my Tallahassee contacts is headed there. I intend to be there when he arrives. Get on the first flight you can. I'll meet you in Miami."

Doubt crept back into her gut.

Are you going there to get information from them, or to make sure they can't give out any more information?

Jett swallowed hard. "I... might drive. It's almost as fast, and I already have the rental car."

Which could have a tracer on it, too...

"We don't have that much time," Aaron said. "Fly. I'll meet you at the airport."

"Okay." She ended the call.

I have to get word to Rico, too.

And a lot of other people.

And if they attacked Derek, they might go after whoever else they know has pertinent information on Ashley Wells. Our interviews will dry up—or die.

* * * * *

In his Miami apartment, Rico frowned at his computer screen. A legal pad and a pen sat on his coffee table, and three empty soda cans.

TIFFANY LYNN IS MISSING

More and more DAW employees were refusing to talk to him. They had never actually been willing, but now they were impersonating clams. He called two dozen employees, trying to keep his mind off what happened with Derek—or possibly because of what happened to Derek—but few answered the phone.

The routine was simple. He'd call; they wouldn't answer. He'd leave a message, hang up, curse, and dial the next person on the employee roster.

Setting the phone on his couch, Rico went to the refrigerator for a beer.

The phone rang from the cushions.

He walked back, sighing. "With my luck, it's probably a telemarketer." He picked up the phone and read the screen.

Unknown name, unknown number.

"Yeah, no kidding." He pressed the green button. "Sell me a timeshare, friend. I'm ready."

"Is this Rico Torres?" a woman asked quietly. "From the news? The one who's asking about Ashley Wells?"

"Yes, this is Rico." He grabbed his pen, flipping the notepad to a clean page. "Who is this?"

"You just called me," she said. "I can't talk to you."

She sounded like she could be in her midforties. Not a child or teenager, with the higher pitch and the casualness of speech that younger people tended to have, and she didn't sound elderly, either. Her words were certain and solid, even though her voice was tenuous, and had a slight Florida-style Spanish accent.

Rico dropped a little Miami Latin flavor into his words. He could speak in Spanish, if necessary. It helped break down barriers and establish rapport. "You called to tell me you can't talk to me? Did Ashley Wells tell you not to say anything?"

The woman's voice was quiet, but she exhaled into the phone like it was pressed hard up against her cheek.

"I've worked for Ashley Wells a long time," she whispered. "That's not how it's done. I won't talk to you, but there's someone who will. She has details that I don't. I'll call her and tell her to talk to you. You're in Miami, right?"

"Right. Who is it? Who's the friend?"

"She's not on the roster you're using," the woman said. "She's new. Can I give her this number?"

"Please do." Rico made a note on the pad. "But can I get her name, too? So I know I'm talking to the person you asked to call me?"

"Is anyone else calling you?"

He sighed. "Good point."

"She made the funeral arrangements for Ashley's daughter. Start with that." Static came over the line. The woman kept her voice low. "I don't want to say anything more. She should call you soon. And don't call me back on this phone, it's a disposable."

Dropping the pen, Rico sat back on the couch. "I appreciate your help, ma'am. What if your friend doesn't call me?"

TIFFANY LYNN IS MISSING

"Then they've killed her, too," the woman said, ending the call.

DAN ALATORRE

CHAPTER 31

Rico paced back and forth across his living room, his hands on his hips, staring at the phone on the coffee table. He sighed, putting a hand to his forehead. "For Pete's sake. Ring, would you?"

The screen illuminated with an incoming call.

He leaped over the back of the sofa and grabbed it immediately. "This is Rico Torres."

"Mr. Torres... my name is Emily Becker. A friend of mine said I had information that could help you. I work for Ashley Wells."

Her voice was pure Alabama honey, a sweet southern accent with all the right drawls.

Checking the time, Rico grabbed his notepad. "I really appreciate you calling. Emily, is it? Our mutual friend says you did the funeral arrangements for Ashley's daughter's service, is that right?"

"Yes, but Olivia said I can't talk about any of this over the phone."

Olivia. Okay. That'd be the Spanish lady...

He scribbled the name down on the pad. "Well, that's fine. You're in Orlando, right? I'm, uh, actually going to be in Orlando early tomorrow morning! How's that for a coincidence? I could meet you any time. Before you go to work, if you'd like. I wouldn't need more than fifteen minutes, maybe less."

It was an old reporter's gimmick. Everybody can meet for fifteen minutes—or ten, or five; whatever ruse the reporter offered. Once the subject agreed to meet, the meeting would go on for as long as they kept talking. Usually, an hour would sail by if the interview didn't take place at their work.

"You're too late," Emily said. "I can't see you in Orlando."

Rico squeezed his eyes shut. *Crap!*

"I'm not there. I'm in Miami."

He bolted upright, smiling. "Well, hey—I am, too. That works even better."

"Really? Miss Ashley gave me a hotel room," Emily said. "And three days off, just for helping make all her flights to Colorado and then set up all the funeral arrangements for her daughter. I got called into her private office and sat right at her desk, for about three hours—and for that I get to stay on Miami Beach, on the top floor of the Fountainbleu. Isn't she the best? I've always been such a fan of hers, and now all this!"

"She is the absolute best—and the Fountainbleu is right around the corner from me," he lied. "Tell you what. I'll stop by before I head to Orlando, and we can chat. Then you can get back to

TIFFANY LYNN IS MISSING

your vacation. Would fifteen minutes interrupt your plans too much?"

"I don't really have any plans," Emily said. "I'm here by myself. I was just going to go down to the pool and work on my tan, then maybe go for a walk on the beach."

Rico pumped his fist. *Perfect.* "Hey, I can talk at a pool. I'll even buy you a margarita for your trouble. They have a great bar at the main pool."

"That sounds real nice."

"Good. I'll wear a red bandana around my neck and I'll be the only dorky guy at the pool with a pen and a notepad. How will I recognize you, Emily?"

"I'd recognize you, Mr. Torres. I've seen you on TV lots of times before—you're real cute."

He laughed. "Sounds like you've already dipped into the margaritas."

"Mimosas. Miss Ashley had them sent up."

A twinge went through Rico's belly. For a moment, he was a rookie reporter again, trying to land an interview after hours of cold calls. In reality, Emily might be in danger. She was nearly the only DAW employee to talk to him, and she was being put up in a suite at the Fountainbleu in Miami Beach—by Ashley Wells—far away from Orlando and the DAW empire...

For what? Ashley's not known for being generous. The last person that was supposed to talk to me about Ashley Wells wanted to hurt me and ended up almost killing Derek.

Maybe I'm the one being set up.

He stood, pacing back and forth across the living room.

We've scheduled the meeting for a public place. Nobody's going to shoot me at the pool. Keep it public and see what she knows.

He'd wanted a meeting. Now he was almost afraid to take it.

Just stay in a public place, with lots of people around.

"Well, don't drink too much before I get there." Rico rubbed his abdomen. "I'll change clothes and head your way. See you soon."

He ended the call but continued pacing.

Ashley wouldn't try anything in a suite reserved by Ashley Wells. But a lot of bad people are doing a lot of things for a secret Ashley doesn't want found out. What's that important?

And if Emily's being set up... Small town girl parties it up in the big city and overdoes it, then disappears?

It had happened before. He knew. He'd covered those stories.

Sighing, Rico tossed the notepad to the couch and ran his hand over the back of his neck.

The phone rang again. *Martin Brennan.*

Rico put the phone to his cheek. "Hey, Martin. I was just about to call you."

"Really!" The Miami 5 station manager sounded irritated. "Where are you?"

"I'm home." Rico shrugged. "You know, trying to recover from that thing with Derek and all."

"Is that right? So if several people from the DAW Network left messages that you've been

TIFFANY LYNN IS MISSING

calling their employees all afternoon, they'd be lying?"

Rico grimaced.

"You were supposed to be doing remotes all week," Martin said, "but now I'm starting to wonder what you've been up to. There should be a ton of B-reel footage that you shot with Derek before he was assaulted. How about we sit down soon and see what your story looks like so far?"

"Sure," Rico said. "I've got time tomorrow afternoon, and—"

"I was thinking about sooner than that. I was thinking right now."

"Uh, well..." He swallowed hard. "I have a meeting I'm headed to..."

"Have someone else cover it," Martin said. "You're so busy trying to get my job, you're forgetting to do yours. Be in my office in thirty minutes. Do I make myself clear?"

Rico opened his mouth to reply, but the line was already dead.

* * * * *

He was on his way out the door, working on excuses for why he didn't have much footage to show his boss, when Rico's phone rang again.

This time, it was Jett.

"Hey, partner," he said.

Jett quickly repeated the warning she'd given Aaron: don't talk, her phone may be hacked—and his, now, too. The covert email codes were easier for Jett to relay to Rico—the color of the blanket they used to share on the couch when they lived together, plus the name of the dog he said he'd had when he was in college. The password was their old alarm code PIN number, twice, with her middle name sandwiched in between.

Jett had been able to relax and think after a call from Mrs. Dearmont said Leah was safe—and Mrs. Dearmont's brother was a cop, so he'd gone over for the night as well. It helped a lot, knowing that Leah was out of harm's way.

As Jett waited, the sound of Rico typing on his computer came over the phone. "I'm in," he said. "And I see your new phone number."

"Good." Jett nodded. "Get a burner phone and call me ASAP."

* * * * *

Great beaches, great architecture, fine dining and exclusive nightclubs are everywhere in Miami—as are low-rent, seedy electronics stores. Rico obtained a disposable cell phone in less than ten minutes and still got *en route* to his meeting with his boss, for what he assumed would be a career colonoscopy of epic proportions.

When he called the phone number Jett had placed in their new covert email account, she answered on the first ring.

"Hey," she said. "I need a favor."

"Me, too." Rico raced his convertible BMW down Biscayne Boulevard. "Any chance you can do an interview in Miami Beach for me this afternoon? I finally got someone from DAW to talk—a new office person named Emily. I can push it back, but based on the Derek factor, I think we should move fast and see her today."

TIFFANY LYNN IS MISSING

"I'm getting on a plane to Miami right now," Jett said. "We'll land in less than forty-five minutes. I could be at Miami Beach in about an hour, depending on traffic. How good is the lead?"

He sailed along the roadway. "Emily allegedly has info on Ashley Wells' travel plans to Colorado, and she made the arrangements for Tiffany Lynn's funeral. But the real scoop is, someone else thinks she might have information that's of interest to us. I'd go see her, but Martin is demanding to see the B-reel footage I haven't been shooting all week. I'm heading in to meet with him now."

"Oof, that's going to suck," Jett said. "Well, here's my issue. I'm supposed to meet Aaron when I land, but..."

"Are you having second thoughts about Aaron?"

Palm trees whizzed by as Rico turned onto Northeast 36th Street, the wind pulling at his hair.

"Hey, it's me," he said. "I'm having second thoughts, too—about everything. Seeing a friend beaten to a pulp will do that."

"I don't think I doubt Aaron, but a few of his associates are making me jittery."

"Jitters?" Rico said. "Tell me about it."

Jett sighed. "Rico... you know you don't have to do any of this stuff for me. I don't want to—"

"Stop that. I'm still on board. Your story has legs. Let's see where it leads."

"Okay," Jett said. "Call your interview and tell her to sit tight. Don't tell her you aren't coming, but if you can get over there after your appointment with Martin, you and I need to meet up. We have a lot more to talk about, and we can't do it at my apartment. Not anymore."

CHAPTER 32

Jett tightened the safety belt around her waist for a second time, looking out the small oval window at the endless stream of fluffy white clouds streaming by. Over the intercom, the Southwest Airlines flight attendant made her post-takeoff announcement. "The captain has turned off the 'fasten seat belt sign.' You are now free to move about the cabin and use any approved electronic devices."

Settling back in her window seat, Jett pulled out her laptop and lowered the tray table. She inserted the disc from Reverend Parce, and the image of the Christmas post office driveway appeared on the screen. A few taps on the keyboard sent the video into fast motion.

The reverend was right. Very few customers visited the Christmas post office.

Several passengers stood up and went into the aisle, making their way to the restrooms at the front and rear of the large, half-full plane.

Sighing, Jett slouched down in her seat, keeping her eyes on the screen. Not many cars went on or off the property, but the yellow Volkswagen was like clockwork. Maybe fifty vehicles pulled into the post office driveway, but every few days, Hope Carmichael's VW was one of them. Always in the early morning, around ten—which was within thirty minutes of when her mail at the trailer had been delivered.

What did Tiffany Lynn discover that made her angry enough to turn against her mother?

This isn't a child. Tiffany-Lynn was an adult. Something impacted her recently. What could do that?

She was away at college. She escaped Ashley, more or less.

What could you discover at college to make you turn against everything you know?

"Whatcha looking at? Movie?" A man with black dreadlocks and a colorful knit cap sat down in the aisle seat. He smiled at Jett through a fuzzy black beard and mustache.

She turned her gaze back to her work. "No, just a project for my job."

The stranger reeked of smoke. Jett scrunched up her nose, peeking at his clothing.

Blue jeans, a red Bob Marley t-shirt, sandals.

It was an investigative journalist's habit to note details, sometimes to round out a story and make it more 3-D; sometimes to aid police detectives in an identification. The stranger's long toes had slightly yellowy nails, but otherwise he looked well kept—except for the foul stink of the smoke, which clung

TIFFANY LYNN IS MISSING

to him like a blanket. He wore a stylish wristwatch, and his clothes, while casual, looked to be in good shape. The watch was the oversize kind that were coming back in style, like a diver's watch, but bigger. She saw them a lot on guys when she and her friends went to South Beach or the clubs.

He wasn't assigned to a different seat—because Southwest doesn't do that—so she couldn't ask an attendant to ask him to go back to his original spot, but it wasn't unusual for people to get out of the cramped confines of their window seat to snag a roomier one on the aisle, even on short flights. Normally, Jett preferred an aisle seat, but watching the video from the window seat seemed like it would garner more privacy.

So much for that, with this smelly busybody.

Jett reached up and turned on the overhead fan, sending a blast of air down over her. She aimed it toward the stranger in hopes of dissipating his smoky odor.

The man rubbed his chin like his thick beard itched. "So—what kind of work do you do?"

Small talk was either welcome on a flight or despised. Jett traveled a lot, so she could go either way, but she was too stressed and antsy to be good company at the moment. She shifted in her seat, turning the computer slightly in the direction of the window. "It's just... research."

"Research? Huh." The stranger rubbed his chin again, leaning toward her. "I thought it looked more like... an investigation."

A chill rippled through Jett's spine. He was too close, and his tone was less polite and more direct. Jett kept her eyes on the screen, turning the laptop a little bit more toward the window.

"Yeah, if I were a betting man, I'd be thinking you were looking at a post office."

Jett tensed, her finger hovering over her keyboard.

His eyes stayed fixed on her. "Post offices have that appearance, being plain brick and kinda dull-looking. They don't care much for people taking movies of their facilities, though. Not after the terrorist attacks. It might even be some sort of federal crime." The man leaned on the armrest, lowering his voice. "Of course, there probably aren't a lot of bad guys in a place like Christmas, Florida."

Her gaze darted to him.

The stranger's dark eyes were focused directly on her, flashing wide as Jett's gaze locked on his.

"Or are there?" The corners of his mouth turned upwards, his putrid, stale breath reaching her nostrils.

Jett gasped, her stomach forming a knot. The lingering odor of smoke wafted from him.

"Interesting place, Christmas." He grinned, showing a mouth of yellow-stained teeth. "Lotsa forests out there. Big trees everywhere. Always catching fire. Did you know Florida is the lightning capital of the world? We get a lot of trees burning all the time."

She squirmed on the thin cushion, pressing herself away from the man sitting just inches away.

TIFFANY LYNN IS MISSING

"I saw a nice little place get burned up that way. Tree probably got hit by lightning and next thing you know, the whole place was burning."

Jett held her breath.

"Her home, her pets..."

He's taunting you. What does he want?

He wants to intimidate you. Don't react.

"See that pretty yellow VW Beetle you're staring at in that video?" he said. "That car burned big and bright, flames so high and hot you'd think they'd melt your eyeballs. They couldn't put it out in time. Whole trailer went up. Those three dogs, too. Even the pet goat."

Jett winced, balling her hands into fists.

It's a lie. He's lying. There wasn't time to burn her place and make the flight. He'd have had to go there the second I...

The second I left.

The knot in her stomach lurched.

"Every stack of magazines and boxes..." He chuckled. "Poof, all gone. Dreadful sight, but there was nothing that could be done." He sat back, shaking his head. "Don't see how anybody could survive a thing like that, all those terrible flames. Heck, you can probably still smell the smoke on me."

Jett's pulse throbbed in her ears.

Details.

Black dreadlocks. Brown eyes. No scars or visible tattoos. No discernible accent. His head is in the middle of the headrest, so he's average height. Blue jeans. Red t-shirt with Bob Marley logo. Sandals. Long toes. Big watch, like a diver's.

"Well, you take care, miss." The stranger got up from his seat. "Remember, though. Accidents like that can happen anywhere, even in a Miami high rise."

She kept her eyes locked on the computer until she was sure he had moved away, then swallowed hard and turned to get any additional details.

Okay. Get a flight attendant over here.

She reached for the panel over her head, then stopped. Her hand hovered in midair, her finger on the "call attendant" button.

And tell them what? That some guy talked mean to me? I don't have any proof of one word he said.

Lowering her arm, she folded her hands in her lap.

Even if they believe me, if they call the air marshal or the captain, I'll never make that interview Rico set up.

In fact, this guy probably knows about the interview. He wants me not to go.

Jett turned slowly and peered over her shoulder. The stranger walked toward the rear of the plane, slow and casual, his long dreadlocks dangling in the middle of his back like he didn't have a care in the world. Near the bathrooms, he stopped walking and stood in the aisle behind a man in a suit.

If he goes into the bathroom, I can get a picture of him when he comes out. Maybe a video. There won't be too many guys in dreadlocks on this flight. Later, I can show his ugly mug to some friends

TIFFANY LYNN IS MISSING

on the Miami Dade police force and see if they recognize him.

We don't need an air marshal. Just play it cool, get a picture, and get to your interview.

A bathroom door opened, and an elderly man came out. The man in the suit stepped inside. A moment later, a woman and her small child came out of the other bathroom, and the stranger went in.

That's my cue!

Jett jumped up, grabbing her phone. Several seats near the bathrooms were empty.

I might be able to hide there and get a good picture. He won't expect that.

She crept down the aisle, her phone in her hand. At the rear of the plane, the flight attendants milled around in the galley area, getting a last drink for a passenger or disposing of gathered trash.

Jett fixed her gaze on the bathroom door, her phone camera open and ready.

If you need to fight him off, it'll only be for a few seconds. The air marshal or the flight attendants will be pretty quick to pull him off.

He'd get arrested after that. At least he'd be detained.

But he can't really risk that, can he? So he won't attack.

She stood up straight.

He can't attack. He'll have to let me take as much video of him as I want, and he won't be able to do a thing. He can't risk being taken into custody.

Nodding, she inched toward the door, her heart pounding. Holding her camera up, she pressed the button to record.

When that door opens, we are rolling. Nonstop. I only need one good image...

She looked up around. No one else was waiting in line for the bathrooms.

"Miss," the flight attendant said. "We're about to prep for landing. Please go back to your seat."

"Oh." Jett lowered her phone to her side. "I'm, uh—waiting to use the—"

The right-side bathroom door opened, and a gray-haired woman walked out.

Jett's jaw dropped.

What? He was in there!

She craned her neck to peer around the woman.

Empty?

Where did he go?

The overhead speakers cracked. "We are preparing to make our final approach to Miami International Airport. Please return to your seats and fasten your seatbelts, and return your tray table to their upright positions."

The flight attendant in the galley looked at Jett. "Miss, are you going to use the restroom? If not, I need to ask you to return to your seat, please."

Heat rushed to Jett's cheeks. "No, I was... I mean, yes, I'm going to use the restroom."

The attendant pointed to the open restroom door. "This one is available."

The one on the right.

"Yes," Jett said. "Okay."

She stepped into the tiny space, looking across the short aisle to the other restroom door.

TIFFANY LYNN IS MISSING

Could he have gone in there?
I looked away for a second. It's possible. But...

She peered at the little sign above the door knob.

Vacant.

No one's in there?

Grabbing the other bathroom door, she pushed it open.

It was empty.

What! How? He was here!

She stepped back, looking around the inside of the tiny compartment.

I saw him. He went in this one.

She inspected the walls, the toilet, the sink.

There isn't a secret door to another room, and he didn't just disappear.

She squeezed her eyes shut, putting her hands on the tiny counter and exhaling.

Think. Where could he have gone?

Did he crawl out of here when you were waiting to come down the aisle?

She pounded the counter, taking a deep breath and letting it out slowly—and the foul odor of smoke filled her lungs. Opening her eyes, she backed away from the sink.

The panel on the counter had a spring-loaded trash lid, shutting it off from the collection bucket below. It was a small opening, about six inches by four inches, marked with a red circle with a line through it over the white image of a cigarette.

Leaning forward, Jett put her hand on the lid and pressed it open.

Long, black strands of dreadlocks stared up at her, sitting atop a colorful knit cap. She pulled them out, the fake wig reeking of smoke. The sandals were there, too, and the red t-shirt.

Jett leaned back against the wall, holding the wig up to the mirror. A fake beard dangled from the tangled weaves.

Cursing, she shoved her phone into her pocket and jammed the costume back into the trash, returning to her seat.

The stranger could look like anyone now. Fifty men on this plane could be him. Maybe a few of the women.

He went into the bathroom carrying a change of clothes, and came out looking just like everyone else. He probably put the dreadlocks on in there after we took off, right before he sat down with me, so there won't be any video footage at the airport of him in the wig and beard if I gave the description.

Well, the joke's on me right now, but I'm going to make that interview in Miami Beach, and then we'll see who's laughing.

She slid into her seat, shoving her laptop into her bag.

Games. You're just playing games, trying to scare me and see where I run.

Folding her arms across her chest, she stared out the window. The grounds of Miami International Airport sped by, coming closer and closer.

Well, I'm not scared now. Not anymore.

And I'll be running right at you, jerk.

CHAPTER 33

The Fountainbleu hotel rose over the white sands of Miami's South Beach like a miniature city placed on the sand. Covering twenty-two oceanfront acres, the massive complex dominated the landscape for a mile in every direction, its many pools, bars and restaurants constantly rated among the area's best. Like much of Miami Beach, movies and television shows had been filmed within the resort's hallowed halls, and Hollywood royalty had made it their home away from home for more than six decades.

Ashley Wells hoped to be among that group one day, and her suite on the thirty-seventh floor was one of many steps she had taken to get there.

Jett spied the roses in front of the cabana on her walk up. It hadn't taken much to avoid Aaron at the airport—he hadn't told her what flight he was on; he probably figured she'd call when she landed—and normally, she would have.

But things had gotten pretty far away from normal lately. If he called, it might be best not to answer.

Glancing into her bag, Jett surveyed the disposable phones she'd labeled with a Sharpie to keep them straight—one for Rico, one for Leah, and one for Aaron—just in case.

Just in case I'm a raving lunatic.

A beautiful young woman with a large cocktail glass and a small bikini sat on a lounge chair next to the roses, her oversize sun hat casting most of her curvy body in shade.

Jett stopped at the woman's feet. "That's not the right way to get a sun tan." Smiling, she extended her hand. "I'm Jett Thacker. You must be Emily."

"Yes, that's right." Emily shook hands, looking around. She pulled a beach towel up over her bathing suit. "What happened to Rico?"

Rico hadn't mentioned Emily's Alabama accent. Jett liked it. The southern drawl made Emily sound more honest. That was useful on the witness stand—and in TV interviews.

"I hate to ruin the fun, ma'am." Jett sat on the adjacent chaise lounge chair. "Rico was called away. But this wasn't a blind date. My friend Derek was nearly killed, and Rico was with him. I think Ashley Wells had something to do with it. So does Rico—that's why he wanted to meet you. Your friend Olivia thinks you may know something that will help us. Can you think of what that could be?"

"No! Your friend was hurt?" Emily's hand flew to her mouth. "That's terrible."

TIFFANY LYNN IS MISSING

It was an old lawyer tactic, hitting someone between the eyes with an abrupt, harsh statement that could turn their world upside down—but it usually worked. People tend to look for safety when they're afraid. The interrogator can look like a safe haven if they say your life might be in danger, too.

But it has to be the truth. Otherwise, people tend to sniff out the duplicity.

Sadly, Jett believed Emily's life might be in danger, and so did Rico.

From the look on her face, Emily was starting to think so, too.

Time to press.

Jett leaned forward, placing her elbows on her knees. "I think your new boss had someone hack my phone and listen in on my calls. She's spoken to me directly and told me to back off of my current case—which is looking into her daughter's disappearance and death. So far, one person is dead and another one is in the hospital." She peered straight into Emily's eyes. "I want to be sure no one else gets hurt—including you."

"Why…" The young woman's fingers were trembling. "Why would anyone want to hurt me?"

"I don't know." Jett shrugged. "Let's talk a little. Maybe we can figure that out."

* * * * *

From a rental car in Miami, Aaron was able to locate the green dot on his computer and pull right up behind it on the street—a black Toyota Camry with Remy Delphine behind the wheel.

Aaron's phone rang. He glanced at the screen.

Office of Coroner Brimstone Cty CO.

He pressed the green button and put the phone on speaker. "This is Aaron Wells."

"Mr. Wells, this is Dr. Bennett from the Brimstone County Coroner's office. Your sister Ashley listed herself and you as the people to notify when the DNA results came back on the deceased woman we retrieved from the lake… I'm sorry to inform you, sir, but it was a match. The DNA confirmed the deceased woman as Ashley Wells' daughter."

"I, uh…" Aaron swallowed hard. The information wasn't unexpected, but it wasn't pleasant to hear. "Thank you for letting me know, Doctor."

"Yes, sir. I'm very sorry for your loss, Mr. Wells."

Aaron sighed. "Yes. I… I appreciate the update. Thank you, doctor."

"You're welcome, sir. Goodbye."

Ending the call, Aaron stared at the car in front of him, imagining the scenes portrayed in TV and movies. A dim morgue with a dead body laid out on an examining table, covered by a sheet.

Now, it was fresh in his mind again. His beautiful young niece, killed by her boyfriend—who was right in the car in front of him. Aaron didn't know what he was going to do when the car finally stopped, but he knew he was going to do something.

Slowing down, Aaron allowed Remy's Toyota to get a few blocks ahead of him. The roads narrowed and became a residential area. Remy was

TIFFANY LYNN IS MISSING

driving fast, and hadn't used his phone much during the long trip, but he looked like a man possessed.

Picking up his phone, Aaron dialed Philson and waited for his tech spy to answer. "Matt, how does it look?"

Philson's voice came over the earpiece of Aaron's phone. "I'm seeing what you're seeing. The Miami guy hasn't budged—or at least, his phone hasn't."

The brake lights of the Camry came on.

"Okay," Aaron said. "He's stopping."

Remy's vehicle pulled to the curb between two other parked cars. The houses were small, with tiny yards and big windows looking into the living room. Aaron stopped a block away.

"Hang back for now," Philson said. "When he goes into the house, you can drive up and park out front. Get as close as you can, and use the audio cone reception antenna like a directional microphone. Just point it at the room they're in, and it should pick up what they're saying."

Aaron pulled the device from the box. The cone was as big as a Frisbee, but clear, with what looked like the butt of a rifle attached to it. "You don't think this is going to attract attention?"

"It might," Philson said. "So you need to act casual, like you're waiting for a friend to come out. Put your arm on the door frame and put the cone right next to it, but you don't look at the house. You stare straight ahead or pretend to be watching a video on your phone. Unless someone's looking right at you, they won't really notice it."

Remy exited the vehicle.

"He's going up to the house," Aaron said.

Running across the yard, Remy didn't stop when he reached the front door. He threw it open and disappeared inside.

Aaron pulled forward in his car, stopping in front of the residence and shutting off the engine. He pointed the cone antenna at the large living room window, squeezing the microphone button and sending a crackle of static through his earpiece.

Inside, shadows moved on the hallway walls—then loud crashes filled the air.

"You ratted me out, you snake!" Remy shouted. "You told Aaron Wells I killed Tiffany Lynn, didn't you? You gave me up! We had a deal!" His voice was strained and his words came in broken sentences, like he was running or working out while he yelled.

Aaron squeezed the steering wheel with one hand, his grip tightening around the cone antenna with the other.

Remy killed Tiffany Lynn. He just admitted it.

"You told him, didn't you?" Remy's voice blasted through the earpiece. "You threw me overboard!"

"No!" The other man said. "I never said it was you!"

"You told him! Why else would he show up like that? We had a deal, you miserable snake!"

The other man screamed. Crashes came over the earpiece.

"You gave me up!" Remy grunted. "You told him I killed her!"

Groans and cries filled Aaron's ear.

TIFFANY LYNN IS MISSING

"Somebody's going to get killed in there." Aaron gripped the antenna and opened the door. "I'm going in there to break it up."

"That's a bad idea, boss man," Philson said.

"Yeah, I know. Call for an ambulance. That kid might be able to tell us something if he doesn't die first." Aaron jumped out of the vehicle and raced across the grass toward the little house.

I can't believe Tiffany Lynn's boyfriend killed her and then took a payoff! Who's behind all the—

A loud crash blasted through the earpiece. Aaron dropped to the ground.

Was that a gunshot?

A man's gruff voice came over the headset. "That's enough, tough guy."

Crawling over the grass, Aaron went to the side of the residence and pressed himself between a palmetto bush and the concrete wall of the exterior. He peeked around the corner to look into the large living room window.

A large bodybuilder threw Remy across the room like a rag doll. Blood streamed from the young man's nose and mouth as he slumped to the floor.

Aaron yanked off the headset and dropped the cone antenna, bolting toward the door.

I might get my head taken off by that big guy, but I have to stop him from killing Remy so I can find out what's happening.

Heart pounding, Aaron raced into the house, stopping in the tiny foyer. He looked around; the place appeared empty.

The tiny house's back door banged shut. A low groan came from the living room. It was Remy, sprawled out on the floor. Aaron rushed to the young man's side, dropping to a knee to lift his bloody head. "I have an ambulance on the way, Remy. You hang in there."

Peering up at Aaron through swollen eyes, Remy coughed, spitting red. "Mister... Wells?"

"That's right." Aaron nodded. "Who was that gorilla?"

Remy groaned, dropping his head to the side. His chest rose and fell weakly.

"Okay, just rest. You're going to make it." Aaron glanced at the back door. Distant voices came from the yard.

Is there still a chance to get a better ID on that guy?

He leaped up and ran across to the kitchen, leaning over the counter to peek through the open window into the small back yard.

A large man was visible through the dirty screen, walking across the grass. He was huge, like a body builder, and he pulled a small, skinny man by the arm.

"This is bad, Buzzy," the big man said. "You know the deal. Blood pays for blood. That's two now, because of you."

"It wasn't my fault," the little man whimpered. "I told him to stay in Tallahassee."

"Well, he didn't listen." The stranger fixed the collar of his polo shirt, and the two men disappeared between the neighboring houses.

* * * * *

Emily's mimosas were exchanged for two iced coffees as the sun slinked toward the horizon.

TIFFANY LYNN IS MISSING

When the coffees had been consumed, Jett ordered them both some water.

"What makes you different at the TV station, Emily?" Jett asked. "Why did Ashley specifically request it be you that she invited into her private office to make all those very personal arrangements?"

"I don't know." Emily had gone from nervous to worried, tearing up a few times.

Jett sat back in the lounge chair.

Time for a different tact.

She looked at her notes. "Who's Olivia?"

"Olivia is my supervisor at work. She's my trainer. She's the one who said I should talk to Rico."

"Olivia's a smart lady." Jett nodded. "She's right to trust Rico—and you should, too. He's my best friend, and he's as solid as they come." Jett looked at Emily. "Tell me... if Olivia were here and I could ask her, what would she say was the reason to talk to you? What kinds of things do you two discuss?"

"Well, work things, of course. But we talk a lot about Ashley, because I'm such a big fan. I told Olivia that's why I took the job—because I wanted to be in show business, too, just like Ashley Wells." Emily smiled. "You know, she started in the front office, just like I am. Over at the Reverend Hadley Hemmins' Gospel Hour. And Ashley's from where I'm from. Well, I mean Ashley was living in my hometown when she got her start on Reverend Hemmins' show."

Jett nodded, taking notes. So far there hadn't been a big connection.

But Ashley put Emily up in this hotel for a reason, and gratitude over clerical work isn't probably it.

"What else do you and Olivia talk about?" Jett squinted in the bright light. "Stuff related to Ashley? Like, what would Olivia know that I don't? What'd you tell her when you were training?"

Emily looked away, lowering her head.

"It's okay," Jett said. "You're not in trouble."

The young woman turned back to her. "Are you sure?"

This is it.

Holding her breath, Jett leaned forward. "You can tell me."

Emily sighed, looking over the grandiose pool. "I said I'm a big fan, right? Well, we were talking at the office one day—about Ashley—and someone mentioned how Ashley and Aaron are partners, and that Ashley always regretted that her only child didn't want to be in the family business."

"Right. And?"

"Well, I knew that wasn't right. She had two girls. Twins."

Jett shook her head. "Aaron has the two twin girls."

"He might, but Ashley did, too. I know, because I saw the birth certificates."

Jett bolted upright.

"At first," Emily said, "I thought it might be like Elvis Presley's twin brother, where he was stillborn but the family made him a grave marker anyway. But that wasn't the case at all. Ashley had twin girls at her house, with a midwife—but they

TIFFANY LYNN IS MISSING

didn't get birth certificates until a few days later when they went to a church hospital."

"How..." Jett gripped her notepad, her voice falling to a whisper. "How do you know all this?"

"My momma was a nurse at the hospital, and she knew the midwife. They talked..." Emily shook her head. "Using a midwife was kinda common in those parts back then—lots of people didn't have the money to go to a hospital to deliver their babies. Momma said Ashley Wells might be a singing star, but she must have had a heart as cold as ice to give away her child like that."

Jett recoiled. "Oh, I don't know... Putting a newborn baby up for adoption can be a selfless act..."

"She didn't give a *baby* up for adoption," Emily said. "In the middle of the night, she went to the hospital with a scarf pulled up over her face and dropped one of her two-year-old daughters off at the back door—and then just drove away."

DAN ALATORRE

CHAPTER 34

Rico's meeting with his boss had been short—and anything but sweet.

When Martin Brennan viewed the lack of footage from almost a week's worth of remote shots, he simply chuckled and stood up from the editing room desk.

"I don't think Miami 5 will be requiring your services any longer, Mr. Torres."

Rico drove back along Brickell Avenue much slower than he did earlier when he'd been going the other way. The wind messing up his hair, he stared out at the lights of downtown Miami and the darkening sky beyond, the abrupt termination hanging in his chest like a boat anchor.

Up ahead, the traffic light turned red. Rico rolled to a stop, not really in a rush to get home—or to anywhere else, for that matter. He sighed, leaning back and closing his eyes.

Oh, I really did it this time.

Now, instead of helping Jett find a job, I have to find myself a job.

Next to him, his phone rang. He cracked open one eye to look at the screen, not really in the mood to talk to anyone.

Unknown name, unknown number.

Groaning, he looked away.

But this might be that Spanish lady who called earlier.

He shook his head, reaching for the phone.

It certainly isn't going to hurt me to talk to her now.

Pressing the button, he held the phone to his ear. "Hello?"

"My friend said she talked to one of your associates. Good. I have one other person you should talk to." It was the Spanish lady, her voice calm and reserved. "His name is Bob Wencell, and he used to work security for Ashley Wells' TV station when I was new there answering the phones. He's lives in Miami now. He'll talk to you."

Rico stared at the red light as she gave him a phone number, the back of his head not coming off the headrest. "I really appreciate your help, ma'am, but I have to ask… why are you doing this?"

"It needs to be done. I've been quiet too long, and look what's happened as a result."

The call ended.

He let out a long, slow breath as the traffic light turned green. Instead of continuing to his house, he eased the BMW onto a side street and pulled to a stop, dialing the number for Bob Wencell.

* * * * *

TIFFANY LYNN IS MISSING

"I had been on the police force for about five years, so I was working on my own a lot by that point." The gray-haired man hung his head, holding a beer in dirt-stained fingers as he rested his elbows on his knees. The apartment building's small back yard was half grass and half weeds, surrounded by a rickety wooden privacy fence that looked like it had been constructed in a prior century. A long hose ran across the grass, attached to a nearby rotary sprinkler that threw water into the air in low, flimsy rings.

Rico sat back in the deck chair, holding a bottle of beer and letting his new acquaintance speak.

"I got a call one night." Wencell shook his head, his voice soft in the warm evening air. "I'll never forget it. It was a Thursday night and it had been raining. Dispatch sends me to a 911 call. An accidental shooting, they said. A woman phoned in, all hysterical, saying her husband had accidentally shot himself. I was two minutes away, so I go. I was the first on the scene." He turned the bottle slowly in his hands, the humid night air forming condensation on the bottle and dripping into the grass. "When I get there, she takes me and she shows me. Walks me straight back to the bedroom and says look what happened. She seemed almost like she was in shock, but not quite, like she was in a kind of fog. She's got these two little girls in the next room. Toddlers, about two years old. And she's not letting them see what's happened, you know? She says she came home from the grocery store, put the girls down in the living room to play, put the groceries on the counter, and then walked to the bedroom to see where her husband was."

Rico let the story come at Wencell's pace, each word a painful memory that obviously tortured the storyteller.

"I checked his pulse when I got there, but almost as a formality. You could see he was already dead. All that blood, and a big gunshot wound to the chest… his eyes staring up at the ceiling, and he's not moving… so, you just know. There's no signs of breathing, no blood pumping out of the wound. I took the lady into the kitchen for a glass of water, so we weren't in the room with the body and she could tell me what happened."

He sighed, looking up at Rico, but his eyes were far away.

"There was this grocery bag sitting on the counter. Well, she said she'd gone to the grocery, and there's some vegetables in the bag and some grapes, a gallon of milk. When she was getting me a glass for the water, I put my hand on that bottle of milk. It was room temperature. So I'm looking at her and I know she didn't just get home. She's been here a while. Right then, she turns to me and says, 'I think he killed himself.' Her eyes were sad. She says, 'Look at us. Me and my girls have nothing. If you report a suicide, there's no insurance payout. But if it was an accident, then those little girls don't have the shame of their father's suicide hanging over their heads their whole life, and maybe they can get a little bit of money so we don't end up on the street.' She's crying, and the tears are flowing. 'This trailer is a rental, I got no job…' She's begging me. Now, an ambulance is on the way. A coroner's gonna look at the body. But we're in the boonies. It's gonna be a while."

TIFFANY LYNN IS MISSING

He rubbed his chin, looking at the ground.

"I went back in the room. The husband was shot square in the chest. There are ways you can do that with a gun, but it's not very common if you're committing suicide and it's even less common if you're cleaning the gun. There's a dishrag on the floor and a can of gun oil on the dresser, but the rag was clean and the can wasn't open. I go back in the kitchen and she's begging me. She says, 'Wait here' and she goes over to the girls' bedroom and locks the door. Then she comes back and starts taking off her clothes. She says, 'I'll do anything.'"

He shook his head, wiping the back of his hand across his cheek.

"What did you do?" Rico asked.

Wencell looked up. His eyes glistened in the reflected streetlight from down the block. "I didn't sleep with her, if that's what you're asking. She was beautiful. Long hair, great body, big eyes... but I was pretty happily married." He lowered his head again, clutching the beer. "There are ways you can write up a report so it'll get looked into, and ways you can write it up so it won't. When the others showed up, I talked to who I needed to talk to, and I got the situation looked at a certain way... and I left. Now, I'm not saying anybody else didn't get made an offer from that pretty lady, or whether or not they acted on that offer. But I left that place, thinking one thing... that she killed him."

The story was as much an accusation as it was a confession—and confessions take time. Regardless of the forum—TV, jail house, back yard—they require a sympathetic ear, despite how stomach-turning the content of the admissions may be.

Rico took a sip of his beer, trying to keep his expression plain and non-judgmental. He knew Wencell would start talking again when the time was right, like a bucket under a leaky drainpipe. It would slowly fill up and then it would spill over.

"I had a bit of a drinking problem," Wencell said. "About a year later, I got let go from the police force. By then, I saw that the lady from the trailer was on TV, and she was making some good money. So I went to her looking for a favor and she helped me get on as a security guard at the TV station—you know, watch the equipment, walk with her to events, stuff like that. Well, I guess one day I was feeling strong—alcohol will do that—and I said I needed to talk to her again. We meet in the parking lot that night after the show, after everyone had gone, and I told her to get me a raise—a big raise—or I might talk about what I knew about her in the trailer that night."

"And?"

Wencell snorted. "She laughed. She said she wasn't admitting she was a killer, but if she was, how foolish would it be for me to try to shake her down? What would prevent her from killing again to keep the first story quiet? I'll admit, it scared me, the way she said it. Just… cold, like she was telling me what time it was. I knew I'd overplayed my hand, but she wouldn't just let it go. She had to make sure I knew never to bring it up again. And so she gets up close and looks me in the eye, and she says, 'It doesn't have to be you Bobby. It could be that wife of yours. Maybe she's driving home at night, all by herself on

TIFFANY LYNN IS MISSING

a dark road, and she loses control of the car and hits a tree and dies.' I got the message—and I stayed clear of her after that. Then, a few years later, I read in the paper about her brother. That he got divorced from his wife and then all of a sudden his wife drives off the road at night and hits a tree and dies."

Rico sat upright.

Wencell looked at his inquisitor, the distant streetlight illuminating half his face and the darkness claiming the other half. "That really put a scare into me—her brother's wife dying the exact same way Ashley said my wife might die if I tried anything."

DAN ALATORRE

CHAPTER 35

Jett slipped her credit card into the gas pump and inserted the nozzle into the fuel tank of the rental car. As the pump approved the card, she gazed through the open passenger window and studied the three phones in her handbag. One had "Rico" written on it in permanent marker, and another one was labeled "Aaron." Leah's was in the trunk.

And the last one's my original—the one that's been hacked and traced, listened to and spied on.

The warm Miami wind lifted a strand of hair and deposited it on her cheek. Reaching inside the car, Jett took out the phone marked "Rico" and sent him a text.

"I will call you from my old phone in 1 min. Answer and talk but divulge no secrets."

When the screen indicated the message had been delivered, she picked up her old phone and called him.

"Hey," Rico said. "We need to talk. I've got a bombshell for you."

Jett leaned on her car, absently watching the digital display on the gas pump as it climbed higher. "Yeah, I was thinking that same thing. You won't believe what I just found out. Let's meet at my place. How fast can you get there?"

"Are you sure you wanna do that? You said it had been broken into, so they—"

"I don't care." Jett narrowed her eyes, peering at the large towers of the Fountainbleu a few blocks away. "I'm tired of this game of Whack-A-Mole, and I'm not going to let some thugs make me afraid to go to my own home. So—how fast can you get there?"

Cars rolled by on the roadway as another warm breeze tugged at her blonde locks.

"Maybe... ten minutes," Rico said.

"Okay. See you in ten."

She ended the call, then texted him from the disposable.

"It's a setup. Stay put and keep an eye on my social media."

When his affirmative confirmation text came back, she picked up the third phone and called Aaron, requesting he also meet her at the apartment.

"I'm heading there now." Jett shoved the gas nozzle back into the side of the pump and walked around to enter the vehicle. "How fast can you meet me?"

"Pretty fast," Aaron said. "I'll leave right now."

TIFFANY LYNN IS MISSING

"Good. Thanks." Dropping the phone onto the passenger seat with the others, she started the engine and stomped the gas pedal, swerving into traffic.

* * * * *

The lobby of Miami Tower looked normal, as did the elevator. No one had pointed a gun at Jett in the parking lot, and nobody grabbed her in the atrium. When the elevator doors opened on the twenty-sixth floor, no shady characters were lurking in the hallway.

She approached her apartment, looking at the door lock. It appeared intact.

Maybe the burglars picked the lock. But then why make enough noise after that to alert Leah?

She unlocked the door and pushed it open, inspecting her living room from the hallway. White couch, white desk, white carpet. The evening Miami skyline filled the large panel windows.

Jett peeked around the corner to check the kitchen. The refrigerator compressor engaged, sending a low hum through the room. Otherwise, there was no sound.

Walking toward her desk, she dropped her handbag off on the kitchen counter. Wires rested on the desk where her main computer normally would have been.

Her bedroom seemed undisturbed, as did the bathroom and closet. Crossing the living room, she checked the empty guest bedroom on the other side of the apartment. Nothing seemed amiss.

The burglars came in, took my computer, and left. So, whatever they wanted, they thought it was on the computer.

Let's say they hacked it. After all, if they could hack a phone, a computer can't be much more difficult. What did they get? Not much more than they already had. And why break in for that?

She put her hands on her hips, staring at the desk.

To show you they can. To make me feel like no place is safe. Same reason you call me to mention Leah, but then don't actually go after her. It's all about intimidation. Power. Control. Keeping me off balance while you enforce your will on me and everyone else.

It's just one more game.

Well, no more.

Walking back to the kitchen, she glanced at the microwave display to check the time.

I have a few minutes before Aaron gets here.

Stroking her chin, she clutched her phone and stared at the two disposable ones in her purse. She slipped her main phone into her rear pocket of her jeans and walked around the kitchen counter, squatting to open the cupboard beneath the sink. Reaching past a container of bleach and some tile cleaners, she grabbed a bottle of Goo Gone and a roll of paper towels.

The men's names came off the disposable phones with relatively little effort, leaving an acrid solvent smell in the air. Jett wiped the phones down with a clean paper towel and shoved the cleaning supplies back under the sink, placing one of the

TIFFANY LYNN IS MISSING

disposables on the counter near her purse and the other inside, it. The third remained in her pocket.

In her bedroom, she took a lightweight blue blazer from the closet and put it on, checking her look in the mirror. The jacket fit snugly over her t-shirt—but not snugly enough. She pulled the fabric tighter and tucked it in again, accentuating her bustline and slender waist.

That ought to catch a few eyes.

A quick trip to the bathroom to apply some blush between her breasts, and she was ready. Taking the phone from her rear pocket, she slipped it into the breast pocket of the blazer and returned to the mirror.

Jett frowned. The top one-fourth of the phone was clearly visible.

Okay, then...

She yanked open her top dresser drawer and dug through a few silk pocket squares, selected one with a gray and silver checkerboard pattern, and returned to the bathroom mirror. The pocket square looked bad, tucked into the breast pocket of the blazer, but it camouflaged the phone.

There was a knock at the door.

Jett leaned out of the bedroom. "Be right there, Aaron." Standing upright, she smoothed the hem of the blazer and checked her hair.

Good enough for now.

Strolling out of her bedroom, Jett stopped, her jaw dropping.

A massive man, big enough to be a pro wrestler, stood in her living room. Next to him was a small man with dark hair who looked like he'd recently been beaten up.

The burglars.

"Hi, news lady." The big man smiled.

A shiver went down Jett's spine. She recognized the intruder's voice from the phone threats.

These are the guys who beat up Derek, too.

Heart pounding, she took a step away from the man.

"A friend of ours would like to chat with you," he said. "How about coming for a little drive?"

Turning, Jett raced back into the bedroom and slammed the door, pressing the little button lock on the knob. She heaved her back into the door, pushing her hair out of her eyes as she glanced around the bedroom.

There's not really anything to use as a weapon in here! The sharp knives are in the kitchen, my pepper spray is in my purse on the counter.

My old tennis racquet is in the spare bedroom, all the way on the other side of the apartment... in one of the boxes I haven't unpacked yet!

The intruder pounded on the other side of the bedroom door. Jett flinched, putting her hand over her ear.

"Open up, news lady. Open up, or I'll just break it down!"

Reaching into the breast pocket of the blazer, she grabbed her phone and opened a livestreaming function on a social media app.

The stranger banged on the door again. "I'm not kidding. I could break this door down in two seconds."

TIFFANY LYNN IS MISSING

"Then do it!" Jett slipped the phone back into her blazer pocket, the camera lens barely visible over the top edge.

"Okay, then," he said. "Have it your way."

She switched off the bedroom light and turned away from the door, backing toward the dresser.

The door burst open and crashed into the bedroom wall, splinters of wood flying everywhere. The shadow of the massive stranger filled the opening, blocking the light.

"There's no need for all this, Jett." The big man's voice was calm and even. "My friend just wants to talk to you."

He reached toward her.

"Who does?" Jett cringed, backing away. She banged into the dresser, knocking over the lamp and some books. "Who's your friend?"

The stranger chuckled. "Oh, I think you know who she is. Now, come on out and let's talk." He lowered his hand and stepped to the side. "We don't need to get rough."

Through the doorway, the curved white couch was visible.

"Come on." He backed up a step, moving into the living room. "Come see what's out here. Look."

He nodded to the kitchen.

Jett inched forward, her pulse racing. She could see half the kitchen—and the small man standing behind the counter. He held a gun in one hand and her pasta pot in the other.

"I know your buddy Rico Torres is on his way here," the big man said. "Aaron Wells, too. No sense in them getting hurt—right?"

Jett glared at the massive intruder.

You only know who's on the way if you're the ones who tapped my phone.

The little man in the kitchen picked up Jett's disposable phone from the counter. "I'll be taking this." He put the pot in the sink and dropped the phone in. Bending down, he disappeared behind the counter. "Aha. Here we go." He reappeared with the bottle of bleach, opening it and pouring it into the pot as well. "This stuff is mostly chlorine, and chlorine likes to absolutely devour phone circuitry." He smiled at Jett. "All the little electronics just go poof."

"Buzzy," the big man said. "Check the purse."

The little man nodded, grabbing Jett's bag and dumping it onto the counter.

"No weapons." He rummaged through the spilled contents, an even bigger smile spreading across the little man's face. "Well, what do you know? A backup phone." Buzzy looked at Jett. "You're gorgeous *and* smart. But..." He dropped the second phone into the pot, chuckling. "It's going bye-bye, too."

"She's smart, all right." The big man took a step forward. "Smart enough to know she should come with us, so we don't have to leave Buzzy here to shoot her friends when they arrive."

Jett's mind raced.

Us? Come with us and leave Buzzy? Who's us?

TIFFANY LYNN IS MISSING

Was that a slip of the tongue or is there someone else here?

The big man shrugged. "That seems like a good deal. You don't want to see your pals get hurt. Or..." He glanced at his accomplice. "Buzzy can just blast whoever knocks on your front door. That could be Rico, Aaron Wells, some poor pizza delivery guy—whoever."

Jett's stomach lurched. "You—you'd kill Aaron Wells?"

"Oh, in a heartbeat—so to speak."

She let out a long, slow breath.

If Ashley was behind everything, her partnership with her brother would be ending soon—with his death.

That never seemed like her scheme, but she's a performer. It's possible.

"Okay." Jett eyed the big man. "Okay, let's talk. But I'm not getting in a car with you." She took off her blazer and draped it over her desk chair, arching her back a little so her guests would focus on her cleavage and not the phone camera in the blazer pocket pointing out into the room. "If you just want to talk, we talk here."

The big man's eyes wandered over Jett's t-shirt.

Public service videos done during Christmastime to help shoppers safely get through a dark mall parking lot with an armload of presents had told her: if someone confronts you and says they want your car, say okay, toss the keys in one direction—and run away in the other direction. If you're *in* the car and they say they want it, say okay—and get out quickly on the passenger side. Car thieves don't want hostages. Predators do.

Jett kept her eyes on the massive intruder. There was no way she was leaving with him. If he only wanted to talk, leaving wasn't necessary.

"I told you she'd say no." A woman stepped out of the guest bedroom. "She's smart, this one."

Jett gasped, certain she recognized the voice as Ashley Wells. The woman wore a thin scarf over her head and a second one pulled up over her face, but the conversations on the phone gave enough detail that Jett knew the sound of Ashley's voice.

"Ms. Thacker's definitely smart." Glaring at Jett, the woman pulled the scarf away from her mouth. "Maybe too smart."

Jett swallowed hard.

It's her.

Hundreds of TV commercials and dozens of magazine covers left no doubt who was in Jett Thacker's apartment—Darling Ashley Wells.

I need to get her closer...

"Smart?" Jett looked Ashley in the eye. "I bet that's something nobody's ever accused you of."

"Hey!" The big man grabbed Jett's arm, his thick fingers like sandpaper on her skin.

"Mack—no." Ashley shook her head, twisting the scarf around her fingers. "There's no need for that." She sauntered along the panel windows, the Miami skyline glowing behind her. "This one's smart enough to come with us of her own accord. She doesn't want to see her friend hurt, or my brother, while you slowly strangle her to death."

Jett stared at Ashley, holding her breath.

TIFFANY LYNN IS MISSING

She's not in view of the camera.
She needs to go to the middle of the room. Near the couch.

The TV star strolled up to the desk, tugging the scarf tightly between her hands. "You still don't understand what's going on, do you, sweetie?" Reaching over the chair, Ashley tapped Mack's massive hand. He released his grip on Jett and moved back. Ashley stepped in front of Jett, lifting a finger to move a strand of hair from Jett's cheek. "You're very pretty. Did you ever do any modeling?"

Jett's pulse throbbed in her ears as she stared into Ashley's eyes.

"No?" Ashley tilted her head. "Pity. With a face and body like that, you could sell ice to Eskimos—and I should know. A pretty face is half the reason I'm a star." She lowered her voice. "Or maybe a third of the reason. The rest is talent and a rocking body—and a certain willingness to use that body during contract negotiations—which may have been what you had in mind when you were getting dressed tonight." She grabbed the front of Jett's t-shirt and yanked it out of her jeans, letting it fall loosely over her abdomen. "But it won't work on my boys. They're paid well, so they'll remain loyal—and I'm not some tramp bartender from Eighth Avenue."

Jett winced.

She knows.

"I told you." Ashley turned away, waving a hand in the air. "Everybody has secrets." At the edge of the white couch, she turned around and put her hands on her hips. "You made it too easy—although she *does* have lovely eyes. Lavender is such an intriguing eye color. I'm sure you couldn't resist. I wonder what your other female hookups had? Other than the fact that they weren't your husband." Ashley leaned on the back of the couch, putting one leg up and folding her hands on her lap. "Now, tell me, Ms. Thacker—what will it take for you to pack up shop and go away? I asked you nicely once."

Jett gritted her teeth. "I wouldn't say you asked nicely."

"No, I suppose not. But you can't expect a lot of courtesy when you're threatening to ruin an enterprise worth billions of dollars."

"You talk like you're the sole owner of the company. Your brother—your *business partner*—hired me to do this job. He can fire me, that's it."

"Otherwise, you stay hard at work, is that it?" Ashley nodded. "Nose to the grindstone—or nose to the flying TV studio chair, as it were? You like my brother, don't you? Everybody likes Aaron. He's been successful in business for many reasons, not the least of which reasons is his charm. He absolutely oozes it, and people eat it up. More than one pretty banker has been deluded into thinking he cared for them."

"I'm..." Jett looked away. "...not interested in him that way."

"Silly girl." Ashley smirked. "I can always tell when someone's lying to me, just like Aaron can. When children grow up with an abusive alcoholic that threatens their lives on a regular basis, they learn to become experts at detecting whether someone means what they say or not. You're lying to me right

TIFFANY LYNN IS MISSING

now. My brother is charming, handsome, and rich—what more does any woman want? He even loves his children, openly gushing over them. He probably thinks he loves you by now, too. But he doesn't. Not deep down. He might even want to, but he had his heart broken once and he won't risk it again. Not for you or any other woman."

Jett swallowed hard. "I understood his divorce was amicable and then a few years later she passed away, so—"

"Not his wife. Our mother. If you want to investigate something interesting, ask my brother about Karen. I'm sure you've already learned enough from my employees to despise me, but if you want to see real evil, look there."

"Is that why you tried to get Aaron to sleep with you before you burned up the trailer?" Jett said. "So he'd help you do it? Or was it the fact that Aaron rejected your sexual advances that made you want to kill your mother?"

Ashley recoiled, her eyes flaring. "Is—is that what he told you? That I tried to seduce him?" She stared at Jett, her mouth hanging open, then threw her head back and laughed. "Karen forced us to share a bedroom in that crappy, run-down trailer, but Aaron certainly didn't seem to mind. He... he couldn't wait to climb on top of me every chance he got—until I ran away to Alabama."

The knot grew in Jett's stomach.

"I'm sure his version of events was quite different." Ashley raised her eyebrows, a thin smile spreading across her lips. "I wonder... did he tell you that little fable after you slept with him? While the sweat of passion was still glistening on your gorgeous cheeks?" She sashayed toward the kitchen but stopped halfway there, her eyes fixed on Jett. "That would be the way to really seal the empathy, wouldn't it? I bet you fell even harder for him after he fed you that line. You'd do anything for him then. Don't feel bad. It's an old trick—I've even used it a few times myself. How do you think I got featured on Reverend Hemmins' show so quickly? I couldn't even play guitar."

Mack cleared his throat. "Ma'am, the clock's running. What do you want us to do?"

"Yes, the clock." Ashley approached her hostage, extending a finger and brushing it across Jett's chin. "Mack, Ms. Thacker has become the type of problem that requires a permanent solution. What options do you have in mind?"

CHAPTER 36

Mack stood at the large, panel windows, looking out over the balcony. "We can make it look like a murder-suicide." He turned back to Ashley. "Aaron hired her to look into the Tiffany Lynn thing. Jett comes on to Aaron while he's grieving, seduces him... Then he sees a few texts on her phone admitting she's only with him for the money. He comes here in a rage, murders her, then realizes what he's done and kills himself out of guilt." He hooked a thumb at the window. "We put the bodies on the balcony, so it'll seem like the neighbors wouldn't have heard the scuffle, and then get our boss to have someone plant a few backdated texts."

Jett's heart pounded, her gaze darting around the room.

"I know that look." Ashley smiled at her from the couch. "It's the look of surprise. The one people get when they realize they've made a terrible mistake. When they come to understand that people are capable of terrible, terrible things."

Panting, Jett forced herself to look at Ashley. "Was that the look you saw in the mirror after you tried to seduce your brother?"

The TV star's smile turned into a glare. "You're actually trying to get killed, aren't you?"

"Is this where you are now, Ashley?" Jett said. "It wasn't enough to put one of your two-year-old twins on the street, and then make sure she never found out you were her mother. Giving a two-year-old away?

"A grieving young mother with two children gets a lot of sympathy—but not a lot of help. I was broke, and children are so very, very expensive. So I cut those expenses in half." She shrugged. "It was a matter of survival."

"But even after you had money, you kept her away, letting her suffer in poverty and pain while you threw lavish parties at your estate and flew first class to resorts. You could have cared for her anonymously—you had enough money and lawyers for that. You didn't, because you only cared about protecting your bank account and avoiding anything that might tarnish the wholesome image you were building for Darling Ashley Wells. You'd protect that image at all costs—including now, going all the way to becoming a murderer."

Ashley narrowed her eyes. "I've heard quite enough. Mack, get rid of her—and make sure that pretty face gets a makeover in the process, especially that big mouth. When Aaron gets here, finish it. The way you said. Murder-suicide."

TIFFANY LYNN IS MISSING

Mack patted his fist, walking toward Jett. "I'll wear gloves and put them on Aaron's body afterward." Grinning, he reached into his pocket. "They'll both be so covered in blood, the cops won't even look to see whether the gloves fit him or not."

The front door flew open. Aaron stood in the entry, red-faced and scowling.

Mack whipped around, his jaw dropping. "Aaron!"

"Gun!" Jett yelled. "In the kitchen!" She leaped on Mack's back, clawing at his face.

Aaron rushed inside as Buzzy raised his weapon. Grabbing the barrel of the gun, Aaron jerked Buzzy's hand upward. A shot fired into the ceiling, sending a cascade of broken plaster down onto them.

The two men locked hands around the pistol, struggling as the gun swept back and forth. Ashley threw herself over the back of the couch and rolled off the seat cushions, crouching low by the coffee table as the melee unfolded.

Grunting, Mack grabbed Jett's hands and pulled her off of him, throwing her to the floor. He ran to the kitchen and grabbed Aaron around the throat, lifting him off his feet. "Time to die, pal!"

Aaron's face turned blue as the massive arm constricted around his neck. He forced Buzzy's hand left and right, gasping as Mack dragged him into the living room. Buzzy maintained his grip on the weapon, stumbling along with the others.

Getting to her feet, Jett darted to the kitchen counter.

The knife block.

She reached for the biggest blade in the set.

Mack jerked Aaron around, pulling Buzzy with him. Aaron's eyes went wide as Jett plunged a bread knife deep into Mack's forearm.

The big man howled in pain. Aaron wrestled himself free from one attacker, working hard to get loose from the second. He flung Buzzy's hand downward, another shot firing.

Buzzy screamed, the tip of his shoe exploding. He dropped the gun, grabbing his foot and falling over backwards.

Jett grabbed the weapon, picking it up and pointing it at Mack. "Stay put or you'll get one, too."

The big man's face turned into a scowl. He pulled the knife free from his arm, a string of red flying into the air. Raising the knife, he growled and stepped toward Jett.

She fired a shot past his ear. The wall behind him burst into a puff of drywall dust.

"Not so fast." Jett cocked the gun. "I did a segment on firearms with the Navy Seals for sweeps week, so I know what I'm doing. Get on the floor."

Mack groaned, glaring at her.

"On the floor!" She kicked Buzzy in the rear. "That goes for you, too, pipsqueak. Both of you, sit by the door and wait for the cops to arrive." Her eyes finally fell on the female guest cowering in the living room. "And you, Darling Ashley. You can sit right down next to your two thugs."

Ashley raised her hands over her head. "They... they forced me. It was blackmail." She looked at Aaron. "You know I'd never do anything to hurt you, little brother. I love you."

TIFFANY LYNN IS MISSING

Leaning on the kitchen counter, Aaron breathed hard, rubbing his throat. "You have a funny way of showing it."

Jett glared at Ashley. "You had Tiffany Lynn killed, didn't you? Your own daughter! You probably had Mack follow her. You had her met on that trail just like you had those mountain men meet Aaron and me."

"Your thugs," Aaron gasped, "threw Tiffany Lynn into the lake and you paid off her boyfriend so he wouldn't talk about what he knew."

Ashley gasped, putting her hand to her mouth. "What! Never!"

"It's too late, Ashley," Jett said. "The police will never buy your story."

"They—they will. They always do."

Her brother walked past her, massaging his neck. "I just want to know why."

"I... Aaron." Ashley fell on her knees. "Please help me."

He peered down at her, still breathing hard. "Help you? After you just told that steroid clown to kill me?"

"Aaron, please." She dropped to the floor, hugging his foot. "We—we love each other, little brother. We always did. Back in the trailer, when I'd come to you, just the two of us. We were all the other had. We saved each other from a hell worse than death."

"It's all gone on too long." His shoulders sagged. "Look into my eyes. We could always tell when the other was lying. Tell me—am I lying?

We're done, Ashley. Over—as business partners and as family. I'm done with you."

"Please, no..." Ashley sobbed. "Aaron..."

His face was grim. "I should've said no to you the first time you wanted to spy on people at the resort. Good people, who came to do honest deals with us. We didn't need to do that, Ashley. We never needed to, and I should have said no." His voice fell to a whisper. "I should've said no to a lot of things."

"Stop!" she cried. "I love you!"

He glared at her. "Did you kill my wife? Did you kill Kate?"

"Please, little brother, I love you." She reached up, taking his hand. "I'd never hurt you."

Aaron jerked his hand away. "Did you kill her!"

"She was a tramp!" Ashley shouted. "She was on her back with you just long enough to give you the twins and then she filed for divorce. Everyone could see that."

Aaron gritted his teeth. "What did you do?"

"I protected you! I worked hard to build an empire. I—I mean, *we* did. We worked hard to build an empire. I sang the songs and you made the deals. And it worked. You grew my singing into a TV network and a private college, a ski resort... But to just give a fourth of it away? Aaron, no..."

He nodded. "So you killed her."

"I didn't."

"No, you didn't. You had some thug do it for you. Probably one you met through your prison-jobs charity, like these two. Tell me you didn't, sister. Look into my eyes and tell me you didn't."

TIFFANY LYNN IS MISSING

She swallowed hard, her mascara streaking down her cheeks. "Aaron…"

"Just tell me you didn't do it!" He grabbed her by the collar. "Look me in the eye and say it isn't so!"

"Aaron, please…" She sobbed, her head sinking to the floor.

"You can't do it, can you?" He scowled. "Because you know I'd see you're lying."

"I'm… your sister…"

Aaron let her go, standing over her. "I have no sister. Just like you had no second daughter. You don't exist to me anymore, just like she didn't exist to you."

Jett readjusted her grip on the gun, keeping it pointed at the two men sitting by her door.

Ashley sat up, wiping her cheeks. "This isn't over. I… I can play this game, too. I'll tell everyone that Jett used you. How she slept with you for your money. I'll get my PR machine in motion. My fans will believe me. The public will, too. Darling Ashley Wells is a saint to them."

"Not anymore," Jett said.

Ashley looked at her. "What?"

Jett pointed to the blue blazer draped over the desk chair. "We've been on camera ever since Mack kicked in my bedroom door. You confessed to participating in one murder and conspired to commit two more."

Ashley's jaw dropped. "I'll—I'll… no one will believe that. I'll say the recording was doctored." She staggered to her feet, glancing around. "I'll say you manipulated conversations to make it sound like... like..."

"I don't think so. It's been livestreaming the whole time." Jett glanced at the phone in the blazer pocket and raised her voice. "Rico, call Aaron's phone and tell me how we're doing."

Aaron's phone rang. A confused look on his face, he pulled it from his pocket and hit the speakerphone button. "Uh... So? How are we doing?"

"We started with half a dozen of Jett's friends watching the livestream," Rico said. "And a few minutes ago we went over two million views. People all over the country have jumped onto the feed, and TV stations have started broadcasting it." He laughed. "It's everywhere, Jett. Miami, Orlando, Atlanta, New York... London, Berlin... I'm getting texts for permission to use it on the news in Tokyo. By tomorrow morning, you'll have over ten million views."

Jett gasped. "Ten million!"

"You're the hottest thing on the internet, Jett. A tough-as-nails investigative reporter. There's only one thing trending higher—hashtag DumpDarlingAshley."

As Ashley slumped down onto the floor, the sound of a two-way radio came from the hallway. Several members of the Miami Dade metro police stormed into the apartment.

Jett raised her hands, turning the gun around and holding it by the barrel as she offered it to the officers.

TIFFANY LYNN IS MISSING

A sergeant stepped forward, taking the gun. "No worries, Ms. Thacker. Your friend Rico told us the situation." The other officers handcuffed Mack, Buzzy and Ashley. "And we've been watching it on the live feed," the sergeant said. "Sorry we couldn't get here faster. There's a pretty big crowd downstairs."

"A what?" Jett asked.

He pointed to the window. "Look for yourself."

Jett walked to the balcony door, sliding it open and stepping outside. Twenty-six stories below, a massive mob filled 2nd street.

As she peered over the railing, they burst into cheers like they were at a rock concert.

"Jett! Jett! Jett!"

"Oh, my gosh!" She backed away, her hand on her stomach. "There are so many... people!"

Aaron went to her side and put his arm around her. "They're here because of you. Maybe you should say hello to your fans."

Trying to ignore the new knot in her abdomen, Jett stepped to the rail with him and waved. Below, the crowd cheered as thousands of cameras flashed.

"Jett!" Rico shouted over the phone. "The numbers are surging. We might get over ten million views *tonight!*"

"Well, put a chyron capper on it." Jett smiled. "And tell them to check in again tomorrow morning for an update, because I'm going to lay down and pass out—if I don't have a heart attack first."

"Will do," Rico said. "But first, tell me—who's the sharpest TV host in Miami? You are, Jett."

Aaron grinned. "I think he may be right. And since I still happen to be part owner of an Orlando TV station that seems to have recently lost its biggest on-air star, we could probably use a new one. Think we could talk about signing you?"

"We can—in the morning." Jett put her arms around Aaron's neck and kissed him. "Let's go to bed."

Below, the crowd went wild.

Aaron brushed his nose against hers. "I like the way you negotiate, Ms. Thacker."

"Just got three million!" Rico shouted. "Do that again!"

Smiling, Jett pulled Aaron close for another kiss. "We probably shouldn't disappoint all these new fans."

CHAPTER 37

Jett rolled over, pulling the bedsheets to her naked shoulders as she gazed at Aaron.

Her eyes drifted over his strong chin and his toned, bare chest as it rose and fell with each slow, deep breath. Smiling, she snuggled up to him, enjoying his warmth, his smell, the way his firm, naked body felt so good against hers.

Aaron Wells felt right in her bed, in a way other men hadn't.

She laid her head on the unbruised side of his muscular ribs, in blissful reverie.

Aaron sighed, stretching as he opened his eyes. His dark hair stuck up in the back, giving his masculine features a boyish playfulness.

"Good morning." He kissed her, his soft fingers stroking Jett's cheek. "I can't remember when I've slept so soundly."

She rolled over and propped herself up on her elbows, resting her chin in her hands. "Must be the mattress."

"Hmm." His eyes stayed on hers. "Are you always this beautiful first thing in the morning?"

She shrugged. "Depends on what I'm waking up to."

"It does, huh?" Aaron eased himself onto his side. "Well, today you're waking up to a guy who's gotta figure out how to put back together the pieces of the network he's half owner of, because its major star self-destructed last night. What about you, Ms. Action Hero Internet Sensation? What's your day look like?"

"I'm still pre-coffee. I have no idea."

He kissed her again, then rolled over to check his phone on the nightstand. Light peeked around the drawn shades of the bedroom windows. "Yeah, a hundred and eighty-eight missed calls. Employees at the TV station, the press... I'm guessing the employees want to know what they're supposed to do now. So will my board of directors. I can't wait to check email." He laid back, staring toward the ceiling. "I suppose I should also make sure Ashley gets a good attorney—but not one that's better than mine."

"She's a big girl," Jett said. "Let her find her own lawyer."

Aaron lifted his head to look at her.

"Ashley's going to prison for a long time, lover. Gotta cut the apron strings sooner or later."

TIFFANY LYNN IS MISSING

Sighing, he let his head sink into the pillow again. "I guess you're right. Still, there are a few other things that need my attention in Miami..."

"Aaron, I've been thinking about something. When we accused Ashley of killing Tiffany Lynn, I thought she acted surprised. When she looked you in the eye and said she didn't do it... did you believe her?"

He exhaled a long, slow breath. "I... I did. I don't think even she could lie about that. But she did so many other heinous things, that I don't know if—"

"And Tiffany Lynn's computer was just sitting there in her dorm room when you went to get it. Ashley flew all the way to Colorado to identify her deceased daughter's body, so why didn't she request her belongings get sent home from the college or go pick them up?"

"What are you thinking?"

"I don't know yet. Nothing solid. But there are gaps in the story that don't make sense. You trust Matt Philson, right? Why don't I take Tiffany Lynn's computer to him in Colorado? There's a flight at ten that'll get me there around noon. Let's have him break into it. There has to be information there, and it's time he and I had a chat anyway. We can't get tunnel vision right now. We're too close. We figured out half of the deal. We need to figure out the rest of it."

"Okay. Don't be too hard on him, though. He did a lot of computer stuff for the TV network. The board members will be hounding him to get into computers and look at files so they aren't embarrassed by what's in there." He closed his eyes and rubbed his forehead. "He's in for a rough day, just like me."

Jett smiled.

You're always trying to protect everyone, aren't you? You were ready to risk your life for me on the mountain and you did risk your life for me last night.

No one has ever done anything like that for me before, Aaron Wells, and you've done it twice in a week.

"A rough day, huh?" Jett climbed on top of Aaron, straddling him, her long hair falling across his face as she leaned in for a kiss. "Then let's start it as nicely as possible."

* * * * *

Philson's office in Colorado was a glorified warehouse. Two folding tables occupied one corner of the small building, with piles of strange-looking electronics and old computer parts lining the many shelves surrounding them. On the other side, a small shack served as an office.

Jett leaned back in an uncomfortable metal chair, pulling her hair into a ponytail as she propped her feet up on the folding table. "What do you think?"

Plugging in a power cord, Philson eyed the purple-haired young woman sitting in front of Tiffany Lynn's computer. Lance, the other employee present, opened a second laptop and started what appeared to be a diagnostics program.

"I doubt she had a super-complicated password," Daria said, typing. "I can probably gain

TIFFANY LYNN IS MISSING

access in an hour. If not, Lance and I will pull the hard drive. We can access a lot of the data that way if we have to, but it's a lot slower."

"Okay." Jett rocked forward and got up from the chair. "Thanks. Keep me posted."

"Hey, Jett," Philson said. "You, uh... got a sec?"

She turned to look at him. "Sure."

"My office?"

Nodding, she followed him into the shack.

Philson closed the door. "Aaron told me what happened between you and those thugs in your apartment last night. I watched it this morning on the internet—pretty amazing stuff." He cleared his throat. "Anyway, I'd just like to say I'm sorry. I gave you a hard time because I thought I was watching out for Aaron and I wasn't sure about your motives, but I was wrong. You're one of the good ones." He extended his hand.

Jett sighed, looking at him, then reached out and shook hands. "Okay. Just remember, we really are on the same team. We both want what's best for Aaron."

He nodded. "Yeah."

"Anyway, I gotta go." She pulled out her car keys and phone. "Ashley busted herself for her ugly past and her illegal activities, but there's a lot we still don't know about what happened with her daughter. Until you guys crack that computer..."

Jett glanced at her phone.

The mystery texts.

"Hey," Jett said. "My tech guy in Miami couldn't track down a phone number for me. Said it was too new or something. How'd you like to give it a try?"

Philson nodded. "Sure."

She opened the phone and scrolled to her saved screen shots. "It's this number. I've been receiving text messages from it, but I can't text it back or call it." Jett showed Philson the image. "Could you hack this number and undo the commands that make it not receive incoming calls and texts? And maybe track down the owner's location?"

"Probably. The setting data will be housed in a mainframe somewhere. It won't be easy—or fast—but I should be able to get in and force the phone to do a main system reset. That will usually make it default to factory settings, which would undo the block."

"What about locating the phone?"

"Depends." He rubbed his chin, sitting down at his desk and typing on his keyboard. "If it's coded or if it's bouncing its signal all over the place like that spyware we found in your suite at the resort, that'll be much harder."

"Okay." Jett headed for the door. "Do your best. Message me if you get something."

CHAPTER 38

On her way back to the Wildfire Resort, Jett called Rico.

"Hey," he said. "Your livestream with Ashley didn't get ten million views last night."

She steered the rental car onto the main road. "Don't care. I'm avoiding social media, remember? Wasn't that your suggestion?"

"Yeah, but I didn't have a video get ten million views—which yours did this afternoon."

Jett gasped. "I... guess I could reconsider my position on social media, then."

"I sure would. You're an internet star. Need an agent? I'm currently available."

"If you want to field calls for me, be my guest." She adjusted her sunglasses. "A few days ago nobody wanted me."

"That seems to have changed. Come back to Miami and let's capitalize on your newfound fame."

"I can't." Jett frowned. "I still have an investigation to finish."

"What's not finished? Ashley Wells killed her daughter and paid the boyfriend off to keep quiet about her involvement. It looks like she paid someone to kill Aaron's ex-wife fifteen years ago, and last night she was recorded conspiring to have Aaron and you killed. What's not finished about your investigation?"

"It's hard to explain." Jett sighed gripping the wheel. "And it's really just a hunch, but... Ashley seemed genuinely shocked when Aaron accused her of killing Tiffany Lynn. I don't think she did it, Rico. Aaron doesn't, either."

Rico groaned. "You just can't take yes for an answer, can you? She did it! The whole world says she did!"

"That's what bothers me. I've followed a hot lead before and ended up getting tunnel vision and falling on my face. That's not happening this time."

"Jett, all the evidence points right at her."

She pursed her lips. "Then it won't hurt to make sure nothing points anywhere else, will it?" She glanced at the phone. "This is how I do things, Rico. You should know that by now."

"Pursue all leads equally—yeah, I remember that story. But... where you gonna look?"

She sighed.

Sometimes all the collected evidence points in one direction, but it's the wrong direction.

"I was thinking I'd head back up to the site of the accident," Jett said. "See if anything jumps out at me."

TIFFANY LYNN IS MISSING

"Last time you went up on that mountain, something did jump out at you. Two hillbillies with guns."

"Okay, Mom. I gotta go."

"Hey, be careful," Rico said. "If you get killed, that's one less good referral I'll have for my resume."

* * * * *

Lucinda at the resort's snow mobile rental shack was more cautious than she'd been the first time Jett was there. Without Aaron along, the Wildfire employee seemed reluctant to let Jett take a snow mobile out by herself.

"Let me give you a quick lesson," Lucinda said. "It'll just take fifteen minutes, so I know you'll be safe out there. And I'll get you a two-way radio this time—with extra flares and some extra water, too. Maybe some food..."

Jett put her hands on her hips. "Would you make Aaron do all that?"

"Aaron isn't the boss's girlfriend, ma'am." Lucinda shook her head, wagging a finger. "You are."

Jett acquiesced, a warm feeling coming over her.

Girlfriend.

As Lucinda prepared a young couple for their tandem snowmobile ride, Jett walked back into the dressing area. She hadn't thought about being Aaron's girlfriend. It had been quite a while since anyone had referred to her as *anyone's* girlfriend, and she liked it.

Jett gazed out the window, over the snow-covered ground to take in the soaring, majestic white peaks of the Rockies.

I guess I could get used to this place if I had to.

She drifted between other guests as they put on snow suits or fitted themselves with helmets, taking a seat on the long bench in the back. A nearby woman helped a young teenage girl into a pair of insulated boots.

A man walked up to them, putting his arm around the woman and smiling at the girl. "Are you enjoying your birthday, Holly?"

"Yes," the girl said. "But I'm crossing my fingers for one more wish."

The man groaned. "Your phone?"

"Can we activate it, daddy? Please? I promise I'll only use it to call you and Mom, but if I could text, I could stay in touch with all my friends when school's out."

Her father grimaced. "Baby steps, kiddo. It took a long time for me to get comfortable with you having a phone at all. Authorizing it to receive incoming calls and texts is a big step. I don't want my credit card bill to come in with five hundred dollars' worth of calls to China on it."

Jett's stomach lurched.

The mystery phone doesn't get incoming phone calls or texts—because the owner isn't old enough to have a credit card.

It's a kid!

Her heart raced. She stood up, putting a hand to her mouth.

TIFFANY LYNN IS MISSING

A kid out here had knowledge about the accident. A kid that was close to Tiffany Lynn.

The twins.

"Tiffany Lynn and my girls were like sisters," Aaron had said. "They were tight. More than tight. They didn't go three days without FaceTiming or playing an online video game together, even after she went off to school."

Jett wrapped her arms around herself, breathing hard.

They are texting me because they know something. Maybe they saw what really happened on the trail that day.

A shiver went up her spine.

Tiffany Lynn didn't come out here to see Aaron. She came out here to see the girls.

She buried her face in her hands. The solution to the puzzle had been right in front of her all along.

They know what happened because they're involved. And now they're scared. They don't know what to do.

Lucinda walked into the rental hut. "Ready for your lesson?"

"What?" Jett jumped up. "No. No, I don't need a lesson."

"Ma'am..."

She shook her head. "I've decided to not go skiing today. I mean, I'm not going *snowmobiling*. I'm... I have to go."

Jett raced toward the door.

"It'll just take fifteen minutes," Lucinda called after her. "For your safety."

"It's fine." Jett threw open the front door, the icy wind hitting her like a slap in the face. She ran toward the hotel, waving at Lucinda over her shoulder. "It's... fine."

* * * * *

Jett sat on the edge of the bed in Presidente three, biting her thumbnail and staring at the wall.

The room key had been in her purse, and she didn't want any more Wildfire employees seeing her while she thought through the many scenarios that allowed Aaron's daughters to be involved in their cousin's death.

How are they involved?
Do I go to their school and talk to them there?
Do I...

She sighed, squeezing her eyes shut.

I wait.

They've been sending me clues, so they'll come to me. I'll just have to wait for them to do it.

Jett looked out the window at the snowy mountaintops.

A young woman had died there, and her new boyfriend's daughters were involved somehow. There was no other explanation.

She lowered her head.

They're smart girls. Too smart to have done anything stupid. Or wrong.

Clasping her hands in her lap, she hoped she was right.

CHAPTER 39

After changing clothes, Jett went down to the resort's gym. She was twenty minutes into a run on the treadmill when her phone rang.

Aaron Wells.

A warm feeling swept through her when she saw his name appear on her phone. The same feeling that had welled inside her that morning, while she watched him sleeping in her bed.

The feeling was immediately replaced by the awful sense that she might have to deliver bad news to him about his daughters.

Push that out of your head, Jett. You don't have any proof right now.

Act normal.

She picked up her phone, hitting the button on the treadmill and sending it from a run to a jog and finally a stop. Toweling her forehead and cheeks, she answered her phone and put it to her ear. "Missing me already?"

Aaron chuckled. "I have to admit, I really am."

"Good." Jett closed her eyes. "I miss you, too."

"Did you see Matt? Will he be able to get into Tiffany Lynn's computer?"

She almost didn't want Philson to get into it now. There could be secrets on the laptop that Jett would have to share with Aaron. Information about his daughters that he wouldn't want to know, and that she wouldn't want to tell him.

Stop thinking you know something you don't know. Wait for the proof.

Until then, deflect and change the subject.

"I haven't gotten an update from him yet." Jett stepped off the treadmill, dabbing the back of her neck. "But he felt confident he'd get into it and learn something. How are things going on your end?"

"Good, all things considered. I'm keeping the board under control with a whip and a chair, but the TV station employees know what to do, so it's a lot less chaotic there than it could have been. We're showing best-of re-runs all week while we look for other shows to make offers on. The advertisers are pulling out left and right, but that's to be expected. Nobody likes a scandal. When we have a new star signed, they'll all come rushing back—and then I can raise the rates, so we'll be okay in the long run. We just need to sign some new talent and we'll be fine."

"Sounds like you have your hands full."

"I'm used to it," Aaron said. "Orlando's getting all my attention right now, but I was still able to close a deal I've been working on in Miami. But

TIFFANY LYNN IS MISSING

you know how it is. Nothing in TV ever goes smoothly. I'm sure things at your old station didn't."

Jett nodded. "Tell me about it."

"Anyway, I was calling to tell you I'm flying back to Colorado tonight. And that I was serious about signing a contract to put you back on TV again. I emailed you a term sheet. Maybe we can talk about it over dinner."

Clutching the towel to her chest, Jett swallowed hard. "Actually, Aaron…"

"You aren't turning me down, are you? Did all those views on your livestream takedown of Darling Ashley raise your price above what I can afford? Have you even looked at my offer?"

"No, it's not that. I haven't checked my email. I just…" Jett shifted her weight from one foot to the other, hoping the next words that came out of her mouth weren't out of line. "I… was thinking we might have dinner with Mattsie and Monie. I feel like I should spend a little time getting to know them."

She put the statement out there and then she waited.

A girlfriend should get to know her boyfriend's children. That's all I'm doing, right?

He might think she was moving too fast. He might think she was reaching too far, or pressing too hard. He might not consider her as his girlfriend yet, even if people at the resort called her that.

Jett didn't know if she'd spent enough time with Aaron to start getting to know his children that way. But she felt like she did. And it *wasn't* just a feeling. She knew Aaron Wells. She knew what he'd let the news report about his past, but she knew the truth now, too. She saw the way he acted with his children and his employees. She saw where he'd come from, what he'd been through, and where he was headed—and she liked what she saw.

Anything she didn't know became unimportant when he grabbed that hillbilly's rifle on the mountain.

She knew Aaron Wells, and she wanted to know more—a lot more. Knowing him meant knowing his children.

They seemed like good kids.

Avoid suspecting them of anything bad and let the evidence go wherever it goes.

No tunnel vision—not to the bad, and not to the good.

"Well," Aaron said. "Why don't the four of us have dinner, then? Our newest restaurant at the resort opens later this week, so we're letting guests give it a test run before the general public, to iron out any kinks. It's by the stables, called Dressage, and it's very scenic there. Plus, the girls love checking on the horses."

Jett smiled at his answer—then immediately winced. She didn't like the duplicity, trying to build a relationship with the children of her new boyfriend while setting a trap for them at the same time.

"Yeah," she said. "That... that sounds good."

"You don't seem too certain."

"No, it's fine." Jett looked at the clock on the gym wall. "I'll see you tonight."

CHAPTER 40

The Dressage was fancier than Jett expected. Most of the male patrons were attired in jackets or suits, while the ladies mainly wore dresses. The wait staff was friendly and energetic, in crisp white shirts and impeccable black pants. Halfway through a delicious appetizer of wild boar sausage ravioli, the head chef went around to every table and greeted his guests.

It was a four-star service across the board, and when the reviewers got their chance to sample the menu in a few days, they would almost certainly rave about the place.

Jett convinced herself to relax and enjoy the dinner.

"You know..." Jett dabbed her lip with a silky-soft cloth napkin as she gazed at Aaron and his twin daughters. "When Aaron said he wanted to go to the new restaurant by the horse stables, I wasn't sure if my dinner would consist of eating hay and oats."

Mattsie and Monie exchanged glances, giggling.

Lifting his water glass, Aaron leaned back in his chair and looked at his girls. "These two have worked in just about every place on the property. Ski rentals, snowmobile rentals, front desk, accounting…"

"Bell hop, maid service," Monie said, rolling her eyes.

Matisse held up her hand and counted on her fingers. "Janitorial, maintenance, groundskeeping, mowing lawns, trimming trees, clearing trails…"

"Okay, okay." Jett laughed. "I get it. Your dad's a slave driver."

"Cleaning the horse stables…" Mattsie said. "Giving riding lessons…"

Aaron leaned forward, resting his elbows on the table. "I'd say you're making me feel bad, but you aren't. You learned a lot about running a hotel by doing those jobs. Maybe the most important thing."

Jett looked at him. "Which is?"

The girls answered for him, in unison. "The employees are the biggest asset of any company, and we need to make sure they know it."

"That's right." Aaron raised his glass. "And you learned that things like nice clothes or a reliable car, and the gas that goes in it—those jobs you worked can pay for that stuff." He took a deep swig of his water.

TIFFANY LYNN IS MISSING

Jett's phone pinged in her purse. She reached for it, tapping the screen to see a text had come in from Matt Philson.

"Uh-oh!" the girls said.

Jett looked up. The twins were looking at her with wide eyes and big grins.

"That's a ten-dollar fine," Mattsie said.

Monie nodded. "No phones at the table."

"Oh." Jett lowered the phone to her lap.

"Miss Jett doesn't know the rules." Aaron glanced at her and smiled. "Not yet, anyway. But she gets a waiver tonight, because this is supposed to be a business dinner, too. Jett's thinking about doing a TV show for the station."

"Wow," Mattsie said. "From here in Colorado?"

"No, from Florida." Aaron folded his arms on the table, leaning forward. "If she ever reads the offer. I think it's quite generous." He raised his eyes to meet hers. "Have you looked at it?"

She hadn't. She'd been too distracted by her plot to ambush Aaron's children to focus on a contract.

Far cry from when I used to do it twenty-four seven with trial dates looming and a nonstop parade of clients barking at the door.

"I'm sorry." She reached over and took his hand, giving him a squeeze. "I'll look at it tonight, I promise."

"I can hit the highlights for you right now," Aaron said. "It's roughly double your former Miami 5 compensation. Plus, you still get a car and a full gym membership, but the best part is, there's a ten percent kicker in the form of—"

Her phone pinged again.

She looked at Aaron, heat rising to her cheeks. "I'm sorry, do I get grounded now?"

The twins burst into laughter.

Groaning, Jett gave Aaron a crooked half-smile. "I really need to get this."

He looked away, leaning back in his chair and folding his arms. "Go ahead. It's a business dinner. Take your text."

"I'll…" She glanced at Mattsie. The teen pointed toward the ladies' room. "I'll be right back."

Jett stood and walked to the restroom. In the hallway, she stopped to check the texts from Philson, reading the second one first.

"We were able to access the phone number you gave me and reset it. You should be able to text it now."

Jett smiled.

That's good.

The first text did not contain news quite as good.

"Got into TL computer. Nothing there so far. Will keep you posted."

Sighing, Jett leaned into the wall and sent a text back to Philson.

"TL computer – nothing? What does that mean?"

His reply was quick.

"It looks like no one has touched that computer since she disappeared. No social media accounts accessed, no hard drive activity, nothing."

TIFFANY LYNN IS MISSING

Jett lowered her phone. The activity stopped when Tiffany Lynn disappeared. Her computer was a dog, sitting by the door, waiting for its owner to return, not knowing that she wasn't ever coming home.

She looked down the hallway to the dining room. A black-haired server walked over to their table, refilling the water glasses as Aaron and Monie smiled and made wild gestures. Mattsie sat quietly next to her sister, her hands in her lap, unengaged.

Jett reread Philson's text. The mystery phone could be accessed via text. Waiting only furthered the possibility that the phone's owner would discover the settings change and redo them, blocking her out again.

I can't let that happen.

She flipped back to her other texts, selecting the one from the mystery phone and typing a message, reading it without sending it.

"Who are you?"

It was the same message she'd tried to send days ago, the one that had never been received. Would it open a line of communication now?

Maybe. Maybe not.

She deleted what she'd typed and tried again.

"I might only get one shot at this," Jett mumbled. "What do I really want to know?"

She typed a new message.

"This is Jett Thacker. Will you talk to me?"

Frowning, she backspaced over the first part of her message. The owner of the phone already knew who Jett was.

And it shouldn't be such a straightforward request.

She thought back to Miami and her mentor.

"Ask people for their help," Tate McNeil told her. "People want to help. If you ask them, you'd be surprised at how many of them will say yes."

It was a simple idea she had used on dozens of interviews, just asking people to help her—Help me fix this injustice. Help me bring down this criminal enterprise. It had gotten her the Florida Association of Broadcast Journalists award three months ago, for her in-depth report on a nursing home scandal.

"Please help me stop the abuse of these elderly people," she had asked the receptionist—and the receptionist had delivered.

"Please help" carried a lot of weight. It had gotten her and Rico the information about Ashley Wells' past.

Jett typed a new message.

"Please help me. Talk to me."

Simple as it was, she read the message twice to ensure it was error-free and contained the right inflection. There might not be a second chance.

Without sending the text, she switched the phone to vibrate and lowered it to her side, walking back to the table and sitting down.

"Welcome back," Aaron said. "You missed a good story. Monie was just telling us about a funny thing that happened at track practice today."

Jett held the phone in her lap, staring at Mattsie, her finger hovering over the "send" button.

TIFFANY LYNN IS MISSING

Only one bar appeared on the screen, then it went to "no signal."

Crap!

"Cheryl Larkin pooted during stretches. Everybody heard it!" Monie laughed. "It was so funny! But not as funny as what I heard happened at tennis practice a few weeks ago." She turned to her sister. "I heard all about that."

"What?" Mattsie said, looking up. "What happened?"

"You know," Monie said. "Rebecca Cardin?"

Mattsie shook her head. "No, I don't know. What happened?"

"Ugh. You should know! You were there! Rebecca Cardin stepped on a stray ball while they were practicing serves. She hit coach Daltry right in the forehead with a line drive. You have to remember that."

"I, uh…" Mattsie said.

Jett glanced at her phone. One bar appeared again. She pressed the "send" button and held her breath.

"You *have* to remember." Monie put her hands on the table. "It was the same day we found out about Tiffany Lynn being out here. When they told us about how she fell through the ice."

"Oh. That's right." Mattsie's cheeks turned red. "Yeah, at tennis. That was funny."

Jett's phone vibrated in her hand. The screen showed "no signal" again. She checked the text status.

Not delivered.

Monie rolled her eyes in an overly-dramatic fashion. "You act like you weren't even there, Mattsie. I heard it was hilarious."

"I was at tennis practice." Mattsie frowned, her cheeks turning red again. "You know I never miss practice. And it *was* really funny. Hilarious."

The raven-haired server brought their entrees, delicious aromas filling the air, and placed them in front of her four diners. As the petite young woman stepped away, Aaron picked up his knife and fork, peering at Mattsie. "So? How did Rebecca manage to step on a stray ball?"

"She just…" Mattsie shrugged, looking down. "She was, you know, playing… and it got in her way…"

"Serving," Monie said.

Mattsie looked at her. "What?"

Her twin took a dinner napkin and placed it on her lap. "I heard she was practicing serves."

"Yeah. That's right." Mattsie's cheeks reddened deeper. "She was serving and she… she went to serve and stepped on the ball. I remember she was in a medical boot the next day. She was limping…"

"But she bounced her serve right off the coach's forehead." Monie laughed. "That's the funny part!"

"Yeah. She hit coach Daltry… in the forehead." Mattsie managed a smile. "I remember now."

"I don't know how you didn't remember that." Her sister took a sip of water, giggling. "I'd have been rolling on the floor."

TIFFANY LYNN IS MISSING

Jett sent the text again. This time, the screen showed two bars—and the text appeared to go through.

Across the small table, a phone pinged.

Mattsie looked up, her jaw hanging open. "I'm sorry, Daddy. I'll turn it off." She took her phone from her pocket, flipping the switch on the side. "I thought I powered it off before—"

She froze, staring at the screen.

"Okay," Aaron said. "Turn it off. You can text your friends after we finish dinner."

"Man." Monie chuckled. "Ten-dollar fines everywhere tonight."

Jett held her phone in her lap, quickly sending a second text.

"I'll help you."

The slightest hum of a phone on vibrate reached Jett's ears.

Mattsie raised her gaze from the phone, looking at Jett and swallowing hard.

"You know…" Jett picked up her fork and cut into her fish. "What you said earlier about employees is true in my business, too. The people I talk to are my biggest asset. I have to let them know they can trust me—and that I'll protect them." She looked Mattsie in the eye. "I always protect the people I talk to."

"That's good journalism," Aaron said. "A reporter should always protect their source."

Jett nodded. "They just need to know they can trust me completely, with whatever they have to tell me. That makes all the difference in the outcome."

Mattsie stared at her plate. "What if they're afraid?"

"Especially if they're afraid." Jett set her fork down, keeping her tone gentle and soothing. "Telling the truth when you're afraid might be the hardest thing in the world."

"But what if they did something really bad?" Mattsie looked up at Jett, tears welling in her eyes.

Aaron sat upright. "Hey, what's going on? Are you alright?"

Monie lowered her utensils, gawking at her sister.

"What if they did something that can't be fixed?" Mattsie cried. Her eyes stayed locked on Jett. "Something terrible, that can't be undone? What do they do then?"

The dining room fell silent, everyone staring at the sobbing teenager.

"Then they..." Jett's voice broke, her heart aching as tears came to her eyes. "They have to be brave, and talk to me," she whispered. "I can't help them if I don't know what's happened."

"Okay." Mattsie took her napkin from her lap and set it next to her untouched dinner. She stood slowly, taking a deep breath. "Wait here."

Wiping her cheeks with the back of her hand, Mattsie walked across the dining room in silence. The only sound was the faint clink of dishes behind the back room doors, as the bus boys and dish washers continued with their work, unaware of the teenager in her school uniform heading in their direction.

TIFFANY LYNN IS MISSING

When she neared the hostess stand, Mattsie stopped, extending her hand to the petite, black-haired server standing there. The young woman took Mattsie's hand, crossing back toward Aaron's table with her.

Aaron jumped to his feet, his napkin falling to the floor as he put his hand to his abdomen.

A few feet away from him, the girls stopped. Mattsie let go of the server's hand.

Aaron shook his head slowly, his mouth hanging open. "Is it… is it you?"

Standing still, the girl looked at him, her hands at her sides.

"Oh!" Aaron fell to his knees, holding his hands out to her. "Oh, it is you! You're safe!"

The server rushed forward to embrace him, her eyes brimming with tears. "I'm sorry, Uncle Aaron. I'm so sorry."

He wrapped his arms around her, holding her close. "You're alive! *You're alive!*" Sobbing, he rocked her back and forth, resting his chin on her shoulder.

Tiffany Lynn buried her face in her uncle's shoulder. "I'm so sorry I deceived you. I was scared. I didn't know what else to do."

The two of them stood there, in the middle of the restaurant, hugging and crying. The twins raced forward to embrace their father and cousin in a four-way hug.

Wiping the tears from her eyes, Jett joined them, stretching her arms around Aaron and Mattsie, her hand resting on Tiffany Lynn's arm.

She was alive.

Right now, that's all that matters.

Jett squeezed her eyes shut, her insides filled with joy. There could be no happier ending.

"I thought we'd lost you." Aaron held his niece at arm's length, smiling and looking at her before pulling her in for another long hug. "Thank heaven you're alive."

CHAPTER 41

By the time the emotional reunion had subsided and the tears had dried, the Dressage was essentially empty. Only a handful of servers and a few members of the management staff remained, busying themselves in the kitchen.

Aaron took a chair from an adjacent table, placing it next to his and patting the seat. His niece joined him and the others at the table.

His smile was unbreakable. "You cut your hair and dyed it. It's amazing how different that makes you look." He glanced at Jett. "I've known this kid her whole life and I didn't even recognize her. I feel like an idiot."

It was a remarkable transformation. In Jett's research, Tiffany Lynn always had long blonde hair like her mother, and a complexion that was closer to fair-skinned. Her radiant beauty and model-like posture had been substituted out for a shrinking stature that was quiet and withdrawn, and the wait staff attire, while not unattractive, was a far cry from the sleek designer apparel Tiffany Lynn had typically been photographed wearing.

It was as if the tall, confident young woman had been replaced by a shorter, timid one—and apparently that had been the goal. Hide in plain sight and draw no attention.

And it worked.

Tiffany Lynn pulled at her short, black locks. "There was a lot of makeup involved, too. I went much darker around the eyes, and put on a lot of face-bronzing cream." She lowered her gaze. "You weren't supposed to…"

"Yeah," Aaron said. "It… I… Really, I had no idea."

His smile slowly faded. Reaching out, he took his niece's hands, closing his eyes and taking a deep breath. "You're safe now. To me, that's all that matters. Okay?"

Tiffany Lynn nodded. "Okay," she whispered.

The room was silent. Aaron looked at his niece, his expression a mix of happiness, concern, confusion… She pulled her hands away, placing them in her lap. "You deserve an explanation, but honestly, I don't know where to start."

"How long have you been hiding out here?" Aaron asked.

"A few weeks."

"A few *weeks*." He leaned back, shaking his head. "Wow."

The young woman kept her eyes down, kneading her fingers. "When I enrolled at Crestview

TIFFANY LYNN IS MISSING

College, there was a paperwork issue." She sighed, shaking her head. "People think they can hide secrets, but they always let something slip. It's like a kid around Christmas time, when an adult asks if they believe in Santa Claus. It's the way they ask, like they're lying, and trying to get you to believe the lie."

"Christmas," Aaron said. "That's why you had the letters sent from there."

Tiffany Lynn nodded. "Inside joke. I guess I get my flair for the dramatic from my mother."

Leaning forward, the young woman placed her elbows on her knees and folded her hands, staring at her fingers like the words she was searching for might suddenly appear on them.

"There must've been a typo in my admissions information," she said. "Because the wrong name kept coming up. The admin lady was super embarrassed about it, since I'm the daughter of the school's co-founder. The registration screen showed a girl in Alabama, born on the same day as me, processed through the same hospital, and with the same Social Security number—only the last digit was different, a six instead of a five. Social Security numbers are almost always assigned randomly, so that got my wheels turning, and I couldn't let it go. It was like a voice calling out to me from the darkness, and I had to answer. I did an online request for a copy of my birth certificate, using my correct Social Security number, and it came up online. Remy's sister Barbara goes to Crestview, too, and she's good with computers. She was able to put in the *incorrect* number, and the other birth certificate came up. They were almost identical. Two baby girls, born on the same day, to the same mother—Ashley Wells. I had a twin sister named Tamara Lee."

The young woman looked at Aaron, then his daughters. "My whole life, I had a sister. A family member I didn't know anything about. Tamara figured it out, too, because after her mother died in March, Tamara wanted to refinance her mother's car. The loan was denied because Tamara's credit report showed she had been accepted to Crestview College. She hadn't even finished high school. After that, it was only a matter of time. She assumed that because she had been adopted, that the mother gave both of the babies away, but that I might want to discover a family member. They seal adoption records, so she never knew who her real mother was. Not until Crestview College pinged her credit report. She reached out through social media, and we met up during spring break. At the airport, in Alabama."

Sitting upright, Tiffany Lynn smiled and ran her hands over her thighs. "It was incredible how much we looked alike. We were a mirror. We talked and talked, and I realized how different our lives had been, so I tried to downplay things, like how glamourous it was to be a celebrity's daughter, or what it was like to be on TV. But Tamara was excited, and it was hard to hold back. She said she didn't have any other family but her mom, and now that her mom had passed away, finding me was a gift. That… that felt pretty good to hear." She sniffled, wiping her nose with the back of her hand "Anyway, the next day, we tracked down the nurse who took her in that night. She had moved on to a different job at another hospital, but the moment she opened her

TIFFANY LYNN IS MISSING

door, she knew who she was looking at and why we had come to see her. From there, everything just fell into place—and then it fell apart."

The words came slower now. Softer. The storyteller had reached the part in the story that is filled with heartache and regret, followed by guilt and anger.

"I'd heard bad rumors about my mom all my life," Tiffany Lynn said. "You try to dismiss them as gossip and other people's jealousy, but hearing the same kinds of stories, they add up over the years. You figure, maybe she did sleep with Reverend Hadley to get her big break, but you justify it by saying she was scared and desperate. You tell yourself the rumors about shooting her first husband can't be true, but you can't shake the feeling that maybe they are. You lie to yourself and lie to yourself, until you feel like you've eroded inside. When I met Tamara, the façade came crashing down. I didn't have all the answers, but I had one." She clenched her jaw. "Either way, I was done with Darling Ashley Wells."

Tiffany Lynn stared absently at the table, her eyes wandering over the empty water glasses and used napkins.

"Tamara grew up dirt poor. They had nothing. They were barely scraping by while we lived in luxury—and that's what I told my mom on the phone. We had a big fight, and she said she was coming up to school to get me and take me home."

Tears welled in the young woman's eyes.

"But she never denied one word of it, and that's when I knew it was true. I felt sick to my stomach. All my mother's horribleness, her disgusting blood, it flows through my veins, too. The cruel heart that gave away a two-year-old child gave me my heart. I couldn't stand it. I didn't want anything to do with her." She glanced at Aaron. "I wrote the letters that night and found a lady in Christmas to mail them for me. Then... I left."

She rolled the edge of a cloth napkin between her fingers, curling and uncurling it as silence filled the room. Sitting back in her chair, she closed her eyes, a tear rolling down her cheek.

"I walked out of my life just like Darling Ashley Wells walked out on her other daughter's. There were a hundred ways Ashley could have done something to help them, but she didn't."

"Tell me," Aaron said. "What happened on the trail at Lake Brimstone?"

Sighing, she lowered her voice again. "When Remy and I came out here, we met Tamara up on the trail. She acted different, then. She'd gotten a tattoo on her ankle, to match mine, but she brought this big rifle with her—and she said she was going to kill Ashley with it. I tried to take it away from her, but she started raging. We were both pulling on the rifle, and we slipped. I hit the ground, and when I went to grab the gun, Tamara did, too. I pushed her hand away... and when I looked over my shoulder, she was gone."

Her gaze moved to the floor.

"I don't get it," she said "I didn't push her that hard. I didn't think we were close to the edge. I just didn't want her to..." She swallowed hard. "I

TIFFANY LYNN IS MISSING

didn't want her to do something stupid with that rifle."

Tiffany Lynn drew a long breath and let it out slowly.

"Then you left," Jett said. "And Remy put a story together."

She nodded. "It was snowing, so we messed up the dirt so no one could tell how many people had been there. Then I went to the hotel while they stayed behind and talked to the police."

"They?" Aaron said. "Who's 'they?' Who else was with you up there beside Remy and..."

The group at Aaron's table had been silent the entire time, but now Mattsie was crying.

"I'm sorry, Daddy."

Aaron's jaw dropped. "What... what did you do?"

"She didn't do anything," Tiffany Lynn said. "She went there to give me some money so I could get an ID and a place to stay."

"The $30,000," Jett said.

Tiffany Lynn nodded.

"Mattsie." Aaron held his hands out. "Come here."

She rushed into his arms, burying her face in his chest. "I'm sorry. I lied to the police, but I had to, so Aunt Ashley wouldn't find out Tiffany Lynn was here."

"It's... I get it. You were scared." Aaron rubbed her back, tears welling in his eyes. He glanced at his niece. "When the police arrived, why did they identify the body as you?"

"Up on the trail it was really cold. Tamara's coat was thin and worn out, so we traded. My ID was in the pocket."

Jett chewed her lip. "The coat came off in the water when they pulled her out. It took a few days for them to retrieve it. When they saw the ID, they called Ashley."

Putting her hands to her face, Tiffany Lynn leaned on the table. "I know I messed up, Uncle Aaron. I wanted to tell you. I just didn't know how."

Aaron's gaze went to his other daughter. "Monie, did you have a role in any of this?"

Monie sat back in her chair, her mouth hanging open.

"No," her sister said. "I kept her out of it because... I thought only one of us should get in trouble." Mattsie's cheeks were wet with tears. "I told the police I was fourteen so they wouldn't ask for an ID, and I gave them a made up name—Brandy White. I knew if Tiffany Lynn did anything, her mom would find out and do something awful. I mean, if she could turn her back on one daughter, she could turn her back on the other."

Aaron pursed his lips, looking from his daughter to his niece. "You thought I'd let that happen?"

"No, Uncle Aaron." Tiffany Lynn shook her head. "I knew you wouldn't. But I was scared. I thought... I don't know what I thought. Mom could have turned you against me, or convinced you that I did something awful... I was confused. I needed time. Remy knew my mom would interrogate him and all my friends, so I told him, 'Stay quiet until I

TIFFANY LYNN IS MISSING

contact you, but if Ashley shows up first, threaten to take the story to the press.' That's one thing that would make her back off—bad publicity. Her daughter involved in a murder? That would keep Mom in Orlando."

Jett nodded. "And your letters would help keep her in Florida."

"Plus, sometimes she paid off employees to stay quiet about embarrassing stuff," Tiffany Lynn said. "I've seen her do it. So I told Remy to demand ten thousand dollars—and it worked. She had somebody pay it to him, and he turned around and sent it to me."

"That's how you learned how to hide a $30,000 cash transfer," Jett said. "You watched how Ashley sent the ten thousand to Remy. You knew she would avoid creating an easy trail to follow."

"Yes, ma'am."

"But you can't access that much cash from a wire service without an ID," Jett said. "And using a second source ID might tip off Ashley to where you were if she pulled a credit report. So you could get the $30,000 out of petty cash and to a Western Union, but you couldn't pick it up."

"Uh..." Tiffany Lynn looked away.

Jett glanced at Mattsie. "You?"

"Yeah." She peered at her father. "I took the $30,000 from the petty cash funds, Daddy, and I picked it up for Tiffany Lynn at Western Union. But I knew you'd see it was missing, and that when you did, everything would get found out and you'd help us. We just..." She shrugged. "We needed a little time."

Tiffany Lynn wiped her eyes. "It was just temporary. I couldn't get a job or an apartment without an ID, so we bought one. I just couldn't be Darling Ashley Wells' daughter anymore. I wrote the letters because I wanted to hurt her, and I came out here to start a new life, with my sister and a good family... your family, Uncle Aaron. But everything just kind of went sideways."

"It's, uh..." Aaron cleared his throat. "A lot of times, it's hard to do the right thing. Especially when you're young and don't know the rules yet."

"I was planning on paying you back once I started earning some money." Tiffany Lynn reached into her pocket. "I already have $200 put away." She held out a wad of crumpled bills.

Aaron smiled, pushing her hand away. "You know I'd have paid a lot more than $30,000 to get you back safe, and we got you back safe. I just wish you'd have trusted me to help you."

"We did," she said. "We were coming to see you when... when the accident happened."

The young woman's shoulders slouched.

"My whole life, I had a twin sister. I got to know her for a few weeks and then she was gone. She's dead because of me."

Aaron sat forward, putting a hand on his niece's shoulder. "Tamara died because she went too far. You wanted to stop her from killing someone. That's a big deal. You said the rest was an accident, and I believe you." He put a finger under her chin, lifting her face up and looking into her eyes. "You're a good person. And I'll tell you something else. The

TIFFANY LYNN IS MISSING

kind of person you are depends on what *you* do, not because of whose kid you are."

"What do we do about Tamara?" Mattsie said. "The police still don't know the truth."

"I suppose we…" Aaron cleared his throat again, his voice wavering. "We call the sheriff and tell him what happened. There'll be an official inquiry…"

"You're afraid we'll be in trouble."

"I don't know." He looked at Jett. "You were a lawyer. What do you think?"

"It's okay, Dad." Mattsie squeezed her father's hand. "I can take whatever punishment I deserve. I'm just sorry if I embarrassed you."

Jett pursed her lips, glancing at the girls. "I think… an anonymous call to the sheriff would tie up the loose ends." Sighing, her eyes met Aaron's. "Beyond that, I think a terrible, tragic accident happened, and scared a bunch of well-meaning kids. You can turn yourselves in if you want, but I think you've all been punished plenty. I don't believe Lady Justice has a further interest in what happened up on that mountain trail. It's called an accident for a reason."

DAN ALATORRE

CHAPTER 42

As Jett brushed her teeth, she caught Aaron's reflection as he returned from seeing the girls off to bed. She rinsed the thin ring of foam off her lips and leaned toward the door frame. "How'd it go? Think any of them will actually be able to fall asleep after all that excitement?"

"Yeah." He walked across the master bedroom. "Mattsie's exhausted from all the emotion and stress. She was practically asleep before I left her bedroom. Monie's always been a pretty good sleeper. She'll be out soon."

"What about your niece?" Shutting off the bathroom light, she strolled toward the bed.

"Wherever I've lived, it's always been a second home to Tiffany Lynn. She'll be fine." He untucked his shirt and stared at the bed, his shoulders slouching. "I can't believe how tired I am. I've negotiated deals worth hundreds of millions of dollars and I've never been as exhausted as I am right now."

"Long day, huh?" Jett went to Aaron, wrapping her arms around him. "And what happens next, Mr. Wells?"

"I'll be spending a lot more time in Florida trying to clean up the mess my sister plunged our company into—starting tomorrow morning. I'd like you to come, too, so we can talk about a show for you. I was serious about what I said—about creating an investigative reporting series and having you head up the news division."

Jett sat on the mattress, taking Aaron's hand and pulling him down beside her. He flopped onto his back, closing his eyes and letting out a long, slow breath.

"You know," Aaron said. "I really owe you a lot. You opened my eyes about my sister, you stuck with this thing to figure out what happened to my niece... Without you coming on board, it all goes a very different way. I'm not sure how I can ever repay you."

"We'll think of something." She snuggled up next to him, leaning on one elbow. "I like the idea of my own investigative show. That's always been my dream. Rico might be able to help get a news division up and running. He did it for Martin, who just let him go."

"He's hired. See if he can start tomorrow morning." Aaron lifted his head from the mattress. "And when would you want to start work on your new investigative show?"

TIFFANY LYNN IS MISSING

Jett smiled. "We already started. We've been working on it for over a week now." Leaning over, she brushed her lips across his, cooing softly. "How am I doing?"

Aaron gazed into her eyes. "I think you're great."

"Hmm. Are we still talking about my work?"

"Maybe." He raised his head to kiss her, letting his lips linger on hers. "How about you sign your contract so it's official?"

"I'll sign it in the morning, after I have a chance to read it thoroughly." She kissed him again. "But I'm very excited about what comes next."

* * * * *

The red-eye flight delivered Aaron and Jett to Miami at a little after eight-thirty in the morning. By nine, their taxi had dropped them at a high rise on Brickell Avenue, at the law offices of Fineman and Burgess.

"This way, please." The firm's receptionist walked in front of them, down a long hallway made of hardwood flooring overlaid with Persian rug-style runners.

Jett held Aaron's arm. "What's with all the secrecy? Why can't I know what this meeting is for?"

"It's a surprise. Trust me, would you?" He patted his briefcase. "Did you sign your contract yet?"

"No. I ended up being busy last night—didn't quite get a chance to read it. I did look at it on the plane, though. I had a question about the clause that says you're offering a ten percent equity interest in

Wells Television Properties USA. I'm not sure it's much of a kicker to own ten percent of a small Orlando TV station that just lost its only major star and is embroiled in scandal."

He lifted her hand from the crook of his elbow but held onto it, walking hand in hand with her through the corridor. "I'm expecting your newfound internet fame to raise the value of the company. You took down the crooked Darling Ashley Wells *and* solved the case of her missing daughter. That's a big boost to whoever signs you, and I want that to be me. Would fifty percent be a better number?"

Jett cringed. "To be honest, I'm not sure. My last network TV show wasn't pulling much in the way of ratings."

"Then I guess you're just gonna have to trust me for a little bit, okay? I'm good at this stuff."

"But how—"

He smiled. "Everything's about to be explained."

"Okay, but when?"

"Here we are." The receptionist stopped by a set of wooden double doors, putting her hand on the knob. "Please, go right in. They're waiting for you."

"Thank you." Aaron turned to Jett. "Ready?"

"For what?"

"You'll see." Aaron stepped through the conference room door.

At the table were several people in business suits, and two familiar faces—Martin Brennan and Mr. Parker Nesmith.

Jett's stomach lurched.

TIFFANY LYNN IS MISSING

What are they doing here?

Aaron waved, walking to an empty chair. "What's up, Marty? Parker?"

"Aaron Wells." Martin snorted. "I should've known when a secretive Cayman Islands corporation was buying our company that the stench of the Wells family would be involved. And Jessica Thacker. It's the good the bad and the ugly—minus the good."

Aaron put his briefcase on the table and sat down, Jett sitting next to him.

What is this? What's he doing?

Opening the case, Aaron took out a file folder. "Marty, if by ugly you are referring to my sister the felon, then... we agree, because even a blind man couldn't dispute the beauty of Ms. Thacker." He beamed at Jett. "Ashley's on her way out—she can't run a network from prison. But Miami 5 got bought by me, not her."

Jett shifted on her seat, heat rising to her cheeks at Aaron's compliments.

As the two power players of Miami 5 began to speak, Collier Bristol walked in. "Sorry, I'm late, everyone."

Aaron swept his hand over the table. "You all know my attorney, Collier Bristol. He's been working behind the scenes on my behalf over the last week or so to negotiate the exceedingly sweet deal you gentlemen closed yesterday—on behalf of Wells TV Properties USA."

Collie opened his briefcase, handing files out to all the attendees.

Martin snorted. "You mean Cayman TV Properties. Do you have so many crooked enterprises that you can't remember their names?"

Aaron smiled.

"These documents," Collie said, "will show Cayman TV Properties as a wholly-owned subsidiary of Wells TV Properties USA, a Colorado corporation—and Aaron Wells is its sole owner."

Aaron glanced at his lawyer. "So, I had the name correct?"

"Indeed," Collie said.

Jett sat back in amazement.

He bought the station! Am I getting my old job back?

Aaron's lawyer handed a stack of papers to Parker Nesmith and Martin. "These are copies of the purchase documents and the other agreements you both signed yesterday, in case you'd forgotten."

"Congratulations, Wells." Martin sneered. "You bought a TV network—and paid considerably higher than market value."

"I did more than that." Aaron looked at Martin, then to Nesmith. "I locked you both up for five years to work for me."

Jett gripped the arms of her chair.

No! He wants me to work with those two snakes again?

"You locked us up at twice our old salary." Martin chuckled. "I can't say I'm upset."

"Well, hold that thought." Aaron set down his copy of the documents. "You both remember Jett?"

TIFFANY LYNN IS MISSING

He put his hand on hers, smiling. "Oh, but I'm getting ahead of myself."

Jett managed a smile, but not much else.

What is happening? He signed them both to contract extensions? He has to know it will be impossible to work together with them after what they did... right? He has to know that!

Standing, Aaron buttoned his suitcoat and strolled around the table. "Your new employment agreements are for five years at double your old salaries—that's correct. They also have a non-compete clause that keeps you from quitting and going down the street and starting up a new station to compete against me."

"At double my old salary," Martin said, "I'll be happy to work for you for five years, Wells. Our old schedule had us on the golf course by ten most days. My game should really improve now."

Jett squirmed, her heart racing.

They tried to ruin me. Why would you—

"And now..." Aaron clasped his hands together. "Marty, Parker—you're both fired."

Martin recoiled. "What!"

Fighting the urge to bury her head in her hands, Jett remained upright and smiling.

Oh, Aaron, you just gave away a lot of money.

"Fired? That's fine." Parker Nesmith slipped his reading glasses on and flipped through the agreements. "We have a valid, enforceable contract, paying us twenty-five percent over market value for Miami 5, and now you'll have to pay us double our salaries to play golf while we *don't* work for you."

Mr. Nesmith removed his glasses and set them on the table. "Too bad you didn't go to law school, Aaron. You'd have known that's not how things work. The noncompete clause you insisted on says we still get paid if you fire us."

"Yeah." Aaron put his hands in his pockets, shrugging. "Unless there's a morals clause in the contract. Which there is. That you violated."

Jett sat upright.

I can't believe it!

Frowning, Nesmith reached for the stack of papers again. "But we didn't..."

Aaron turned and pointed at Jett. "Your former employee, Ms. Thacker, is a recovering lawyer. Maybe she'd like to handle this one. Jett?"

"A morals clause..." Jett cleared her throat. "It's a provision that gives an owner the unilateral right to terminate a contract and take remedial action if the breaching party engages in misconduct that might negatively impact the company's reputation."

Aaron smiled. "I'm no lawyer, but I think in layman's terms that means you two idiots lied about Jett and you trashed her reputation for no valid reason. That's a violation of that nice, new contract you signed, and since there's a noncompete, you get no payout and you can't work at any TV station in the state of Florida for the next five years."

Martin pounded the table. "But we didn't work for you when we did that!"

Nesmith's jaw dropped. "Martin! Shut up!"

"So," Aaron said, "we agree that you trashed her reputation before you signed the contract—as

TIFFANY LYNN IS MISSING

you just admitted." He sauntered around the table, pointing into the air. "But you haven't actually *ceased* doing it after you signed the contracts yesterday. That puts you in breach. Jett?"

She nodded. "It does."

Aaron shrugged, looking at Martin. "Oopsie."

"I'll—" Martin's face turned red. "I'll sue you, Wells!

"Oh, I hope you do, Martin." Aaron rushed to the table, scowling as he put his hands on the surface and leaned forward. "I'm looking forward to the sworn depositions where we put your tech guy under oath and ask him all about the untrue things you instructed him to say about Jett on the internet. He'll be forced to tell the truth—and destroy your reputation in a very, very public way. Kind of like what you did to Jett, but legal."

"You son of a..." Martin looked at his lawyers, the force going out of his words. "He can't do that... can he?"

The attorneys suddenly looked very busy with the papers in front of them.

"Stop it, Martin." Nesmith put a hand on his colleague's arm.

Aaron grinned. "It's a big lose-lose for you, guys."

"You weasel!" Martin pounded the table again. "You... you snake!"

"Martin, stop it," Nesmith said. "He's right. We still made out very well on the sale of the station, though. Let the rest go."

"I'm not going down without a fight, Wells." Martin slammed his briefcase shut. "You'll hear from my lawyer."

"Bring it," Aaron said. "They say the truth is the best defense, Marty. You know what you did, and other people know what you did. They have a lot more to lose because they don't have millions of dollars behind them."

Martin glared at Jett. "Okay, so we trashed her! So what?" His eyes turned to Aaron. "With the money you paid for the station, I'll still bury you in legal actions. You're a dead man walking, Wells."

Jett looked at Aaron.

"Uh, here's the thing about that." Aaron stroked his chin. "I hate to keep referring to these pesky legally binding agreements you signed—but we also had a reversion clause in the purchase contract. Remember that? Or did the rush to grab all that cash from the Cayman Islands cause you to hurry up and sign the papers without reading the fine print? Because it says if you lie—which you just admitted to doing…"

"What?" Martin shouted. "I did no such thing!"

Aaron laughed. "You kinda did. And I think a court of law might agree that the statement 'we trashed her' *might* qualify as an admission, since we all know the statements you put out weren't true." He held up a copy of the agreement. "And *if* you lie—which you did, *while* under contract—which you are, *then* the purchase price of the station reverts to half of what I paid." Aaron lowered the contract, smiling

TIFFANY LYNN IS MISSING

at his adversaries. "So, you didn't get twenty-five percent above market for Miami 5, you got about twenty-five percent below market. Which is less than the mortgage you're carrying on the station, according to your most recent public filings. You fellows might need to cut back a bit on the golfing while you look for new jobs—not in TV—and figure out how you're going to repay me over fifty million dollars." He tossed the papers into his briefcase and sat down, folding his arms behind his head. "Wanna keep playing? I can go all day."

Parker Nesmith's face turned green. "Martin, you idiot! You've bankrupted us both!"

"It was your idea!" Martin shouted.

Jett leaned back in her chair, stunned.

As the two former power players of Miami 5 attempted to strangle each other at the table, Aaron turned to Collie. "I'm going to take Jett out for some Cuban coffee and a *pastelita*. You got this, right?"

Collier nodded. "Piece of cake, Aaron."

"Okay." He faced Jett. "On the way, let's see if we can find a pen and get your contract signed."

She stood, smiling. "Now I really need to read this thing thoroughly! I had no idea you were so sneaky."

"I'm not sneaky, I'm appreciative." He got to his feet and followed her to the conference room door. "Maybe I should explain. Your share of the network should be worth over twenty-five million dollars as soon as your signature is on that piece of paper."

She gasped.

"But it's all worth zero without a talented star on board. See?"

Jett peered at him over her shoulder. "So you need me?"

"Yes, I do. A lot." He reached out and took her hand. "I think I've needed you for quite a while. For years, and probably longer. I just didn't realize it."

A knot formed in her stomach again—and this time, she didn't mind.

Aaron was putting all her dreams on a silver platter, and he had the power to make them come true—but only because he decided *she* was capable and competent.

That's how he lured all those talented people to work at his resort. I get it now.

In the hallway, Aaron slipped his arm around hers as they walked. "We should make an announcement about you joining the team. Maybe something simultaneously broadcasted to your massive social media following, followed by a barrage of old media interviews—TV, radio… The value of the networks will skyrocket the minute word gets out."

"Twenty-five million dollars." Jett rubbed her abdomen. "A week ago, I was broke."

"That's just for starters. Then it would go up. What do you think?"

Stopping at the elevator, Jett pressed the call button and turned to Aaron. "I think we should announce our agreement tomorrow morning."

"Tomorrow?" he said. "Why not today?"

TIFFANY LYNN IS MISSING

"Because twenty-five million dollars is a lot of money, so I'll need an iron-clad contract. We need to go back to my apartment and engage in some very intense negotiations before I finalize my deal."

"Intense, huh?"

"Very intense." Jett smiled, pulling him close for a kiss. "Now, let's get downstairs and hail a cab. I want to begin preliminary actions right away."

THE END

Jett Thacker will return in
Killer In The Dark
Jett Thacker, book 2
Order it now!

Note to Readers
If you have the time, I would deeply appreciate a review on Amazon or Goodreads. I learn a great deal from them, and I'm always grateful for any encouragement. Reviews are a very big deal and help authors like me to sell a few more books. Every review matters, even if it's only a few words.

Thanks,
Dan Alatorre

DAN ALATORRE

ABOUT THE AUTHOR

International bestselling author Dan Alatorre has published more than 40 titles and has been translated into over a dozen languages. His ability to surprise readers and make them laugh, cry, or hang onto the edge of their seats, has been enjoyed all around the world.

Dan's success is widespread and varied. In addition to being a bestselling author, he achieved President's Circle with two different Fortune 500 companies, and mentors grade school children through his Young Authors Club. Dan resides in the Tampa, Florida, area with his wife and daughter.

Join Dan's exclusive Reader's Club today at DanAlatorre.com and find out about new releases and special offers!

DAN ALATORRE

OTHER THRILLERS BY DAN ALATORRE

Killer In The Dark, *Jett Thacker book 2*

The Gamma Sequence, *a medical thriller*
Rogue Elements, *The Gamma Sequence Book 2*
Terminal Sequence, *The Gamma Sequence Book 3*
The Keepers, *The Gamma Sequence Book 4*
Dark Hour, *The Gamma Sequence Book 5*

Double Blind, *an intense murder mystery*
Primary Target, *Double Blind Book 2*
Third Degree, *Double Blind Book 3*

A Place Of Shadows, *a paranormal thriller*
The Navigators, *a time travel thriller*